Bowen McCurdy   Kaitlyn Musto

SPECTER INSPECTORS ™

Series Designer
Michelle Ankley

Collection Designer
Chelsea Roberts

Assistant Editor
Kenzie Rzonca

Editor
Sophie Philips-Roberts

Senior Editor
Shannon Watters

SPECTER INSPECTORS, August 2022. Published by BOOM! Box, a division of Boom
Entertainment, Inc. Specter Inspectors is ™ & © 2022 Bowen McCurdy and Kaitlyn Musto.
Originally published in single magazine form as SPECTER INSPECTORS No. 1-5. ™ & ©
2021 Bowen McCurdy and Kaitlyn Musto. All rights reserved. BOOM! Box™ and the
BOOM! Box logo are trademarks of Boom Entertainment, Inc., registered in various
countries and categories. All characters, events, and institutions depicted herein
are fictional. Any similarity between any of the names, characters, persons,
events, and/or institutions in this publication to actual names, characters,
and persons, whether living or dead, events, and/or institutions is
unintended and purely coincidental. BOOM! Box does not read or
accept unsolicited submissions of ideas, stories, or artwork.

BOOM! Studios, 5670 Wilshire Boulevard, Suite 400, Los Angeles,
CA 90036-5679. Printed in China. Second Printing.

ISBN: 978-1-68415-740-2, eISBN: 978-1-64668-318-5

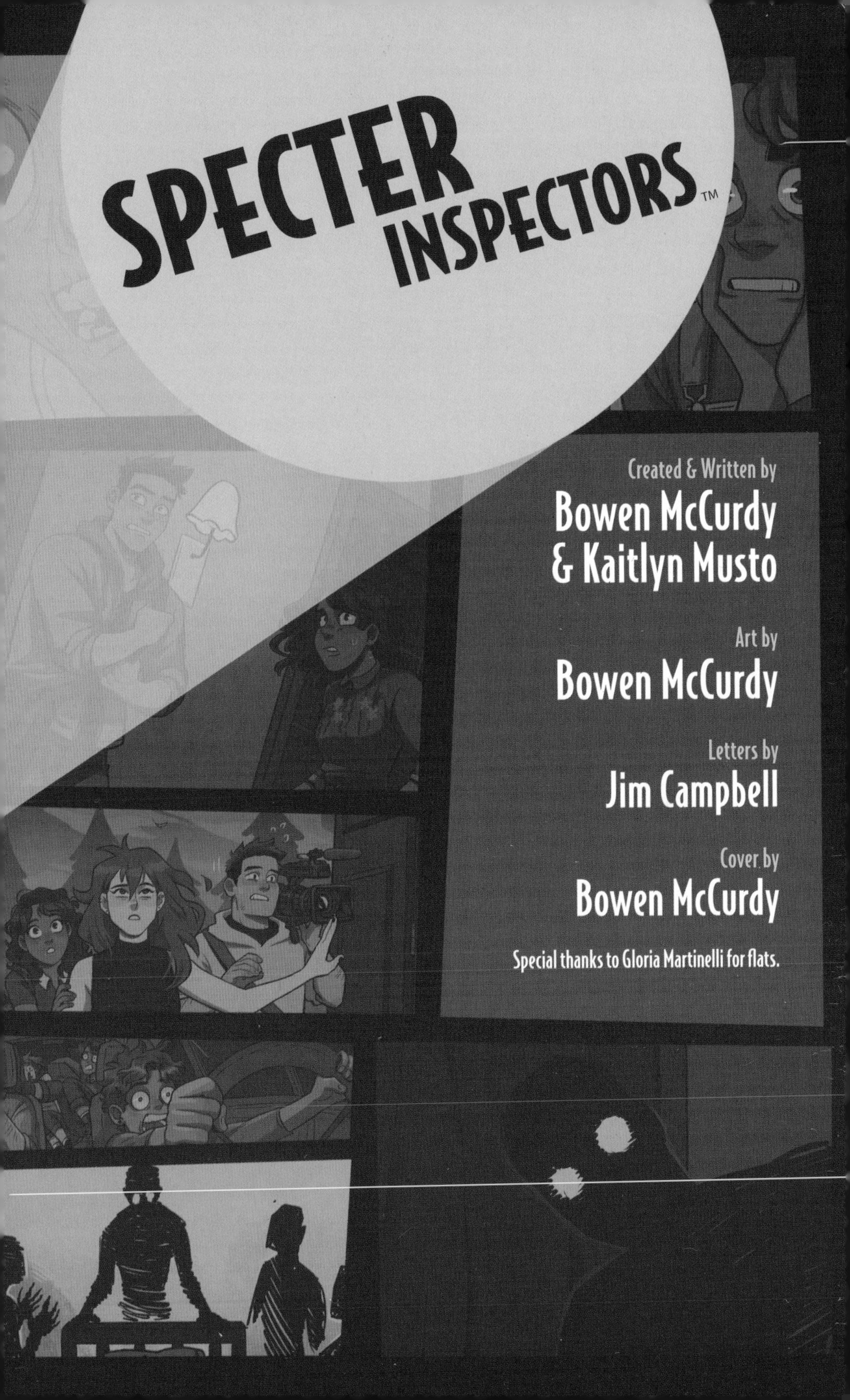

SPECTER INSPECTORS™

Created & Written by
Bowen McCurdy & Kaitlyn Musto

Art by
Bowen McCurdy

Letters by
Jim Campbell

Cover by
Bowen McCurdy

Special thanks to Gloria Martinelli for flats.

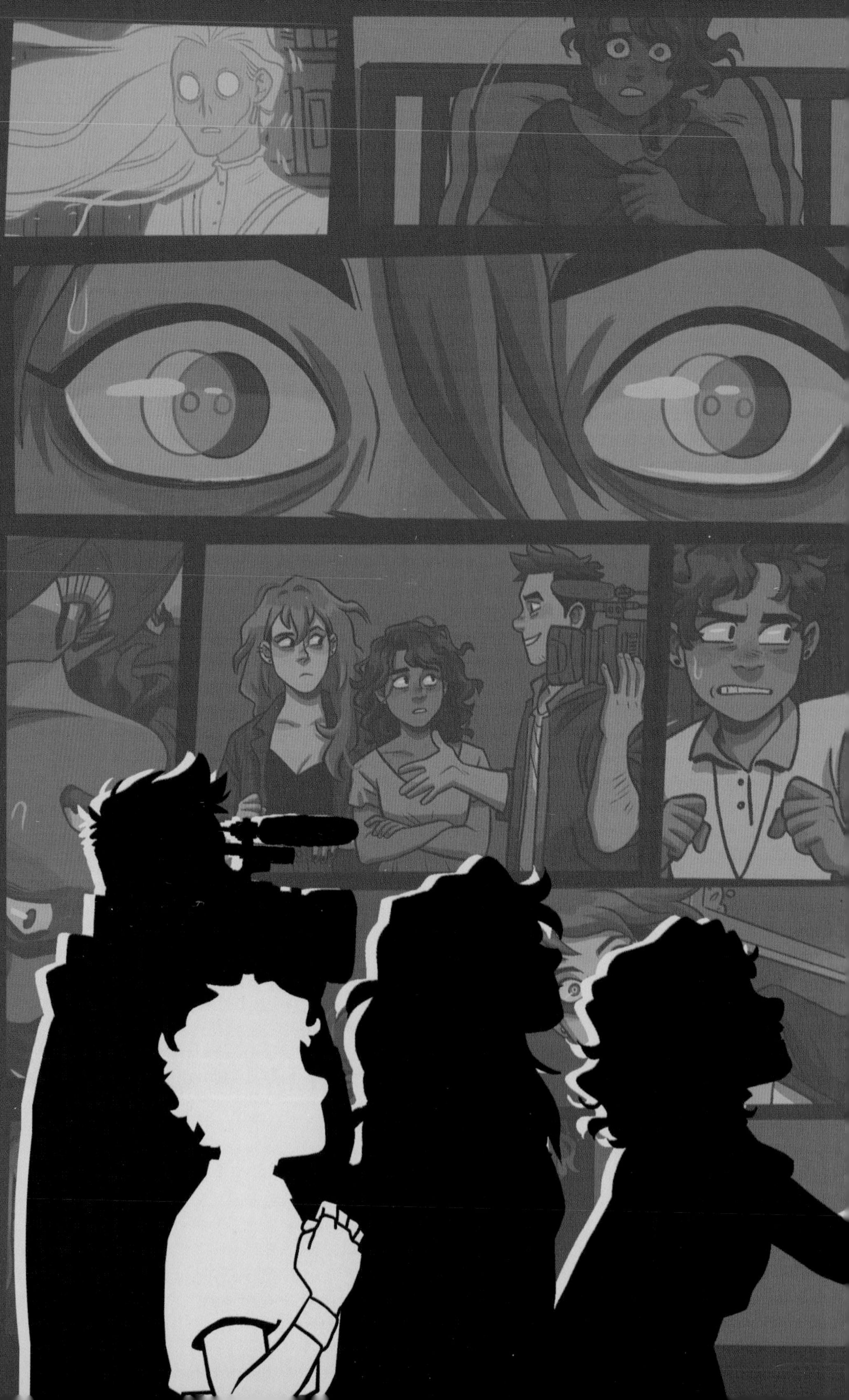

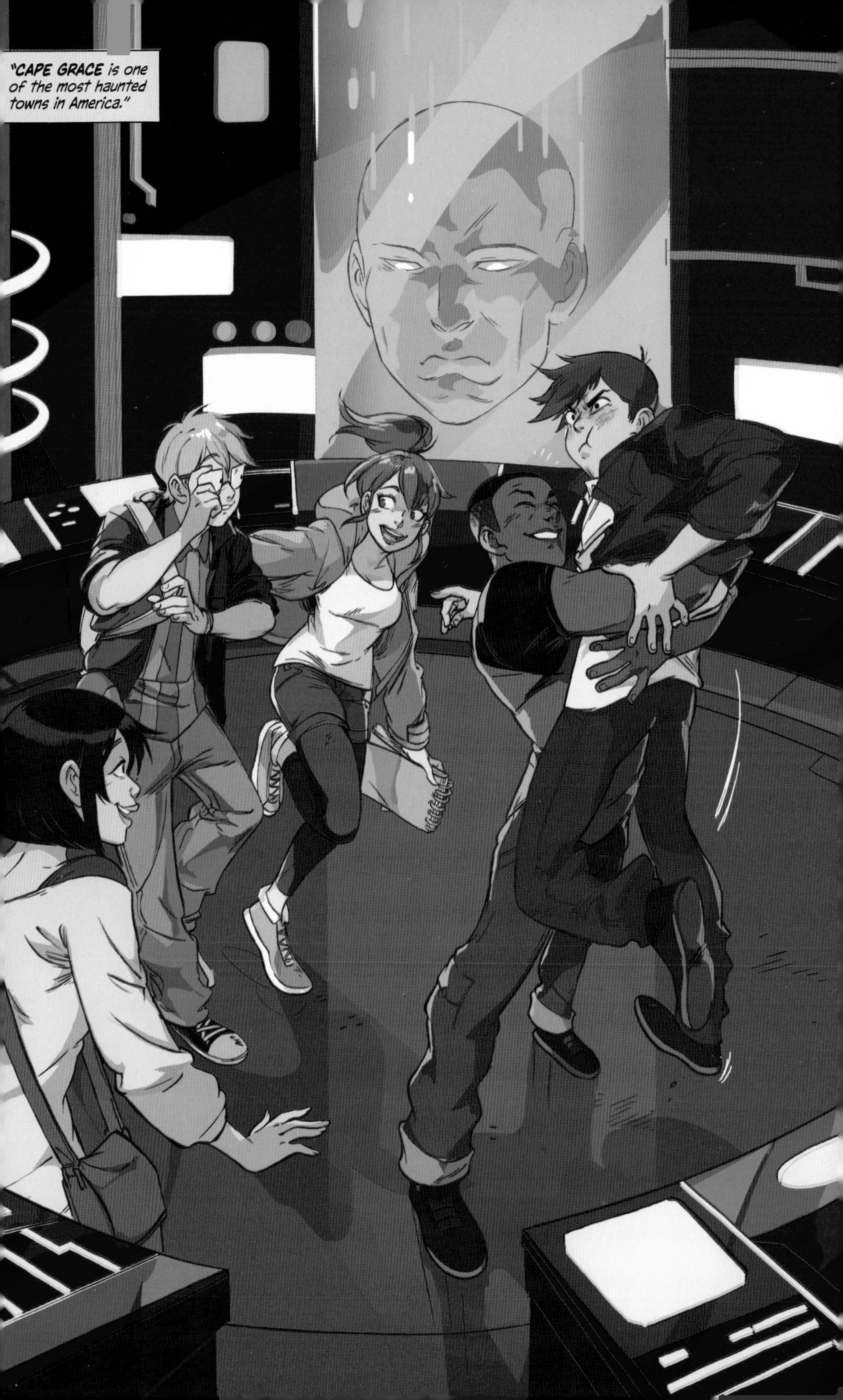
"CAPE GRACE is one of the most haunted towns in America."

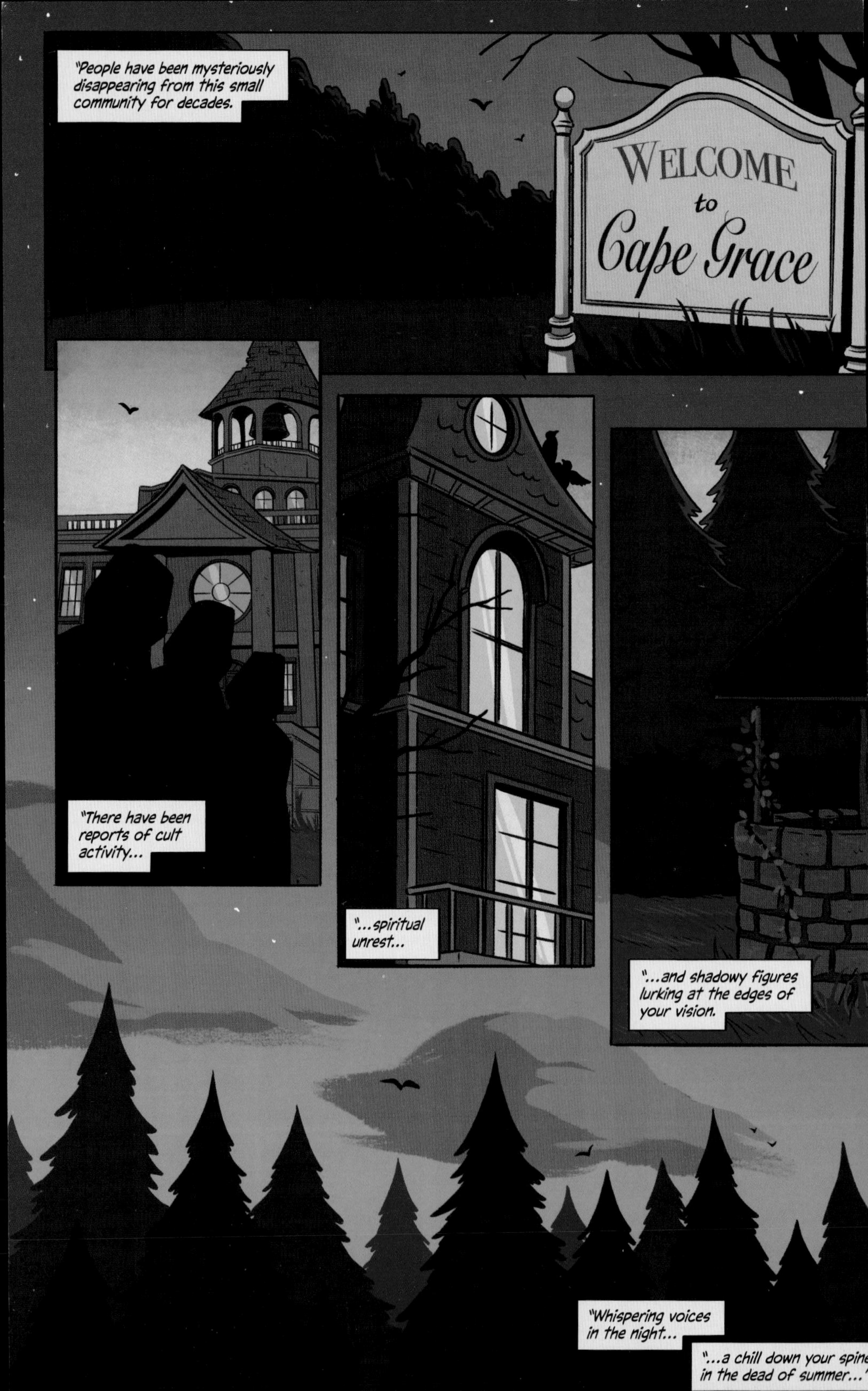
"People have been mysteriously disappearing from this small community for decades.
WELCOME to Cape Grace
"There have been reports of cult activity...
"...spiritual unrest...
"...and shadowy figures lurking at the edges of your vision.
"Whispering voices in the night...
"...a chill down your spine in the dead of summer...

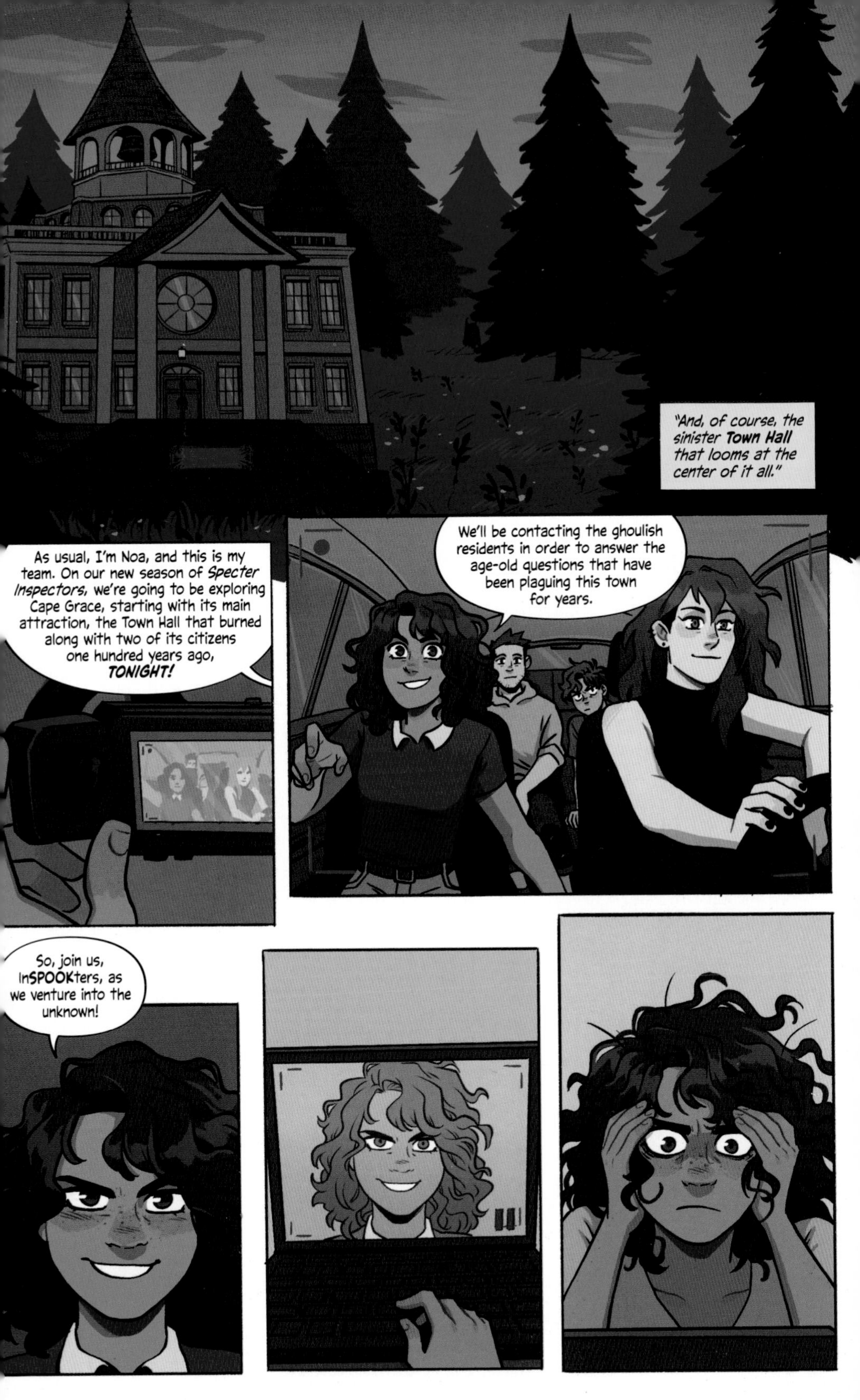
"And, of course, the sinister **Town Hall** that looms at the center of it all."
As usual, I'm Noa, and this is my team. On our new season of *Specter Inspectors,* we're going to be exploring Cape Grace, starting with its main attraction, the Town Hall that burned along with two of its citizens one hundred years ago, ***TONIGHT!***
We'll be contacting the ghoulish residents in order to answer the age-old questions that have been plaguing this town for years.
So, join us, In**SPOOK**ters, as we venture into the unknown!

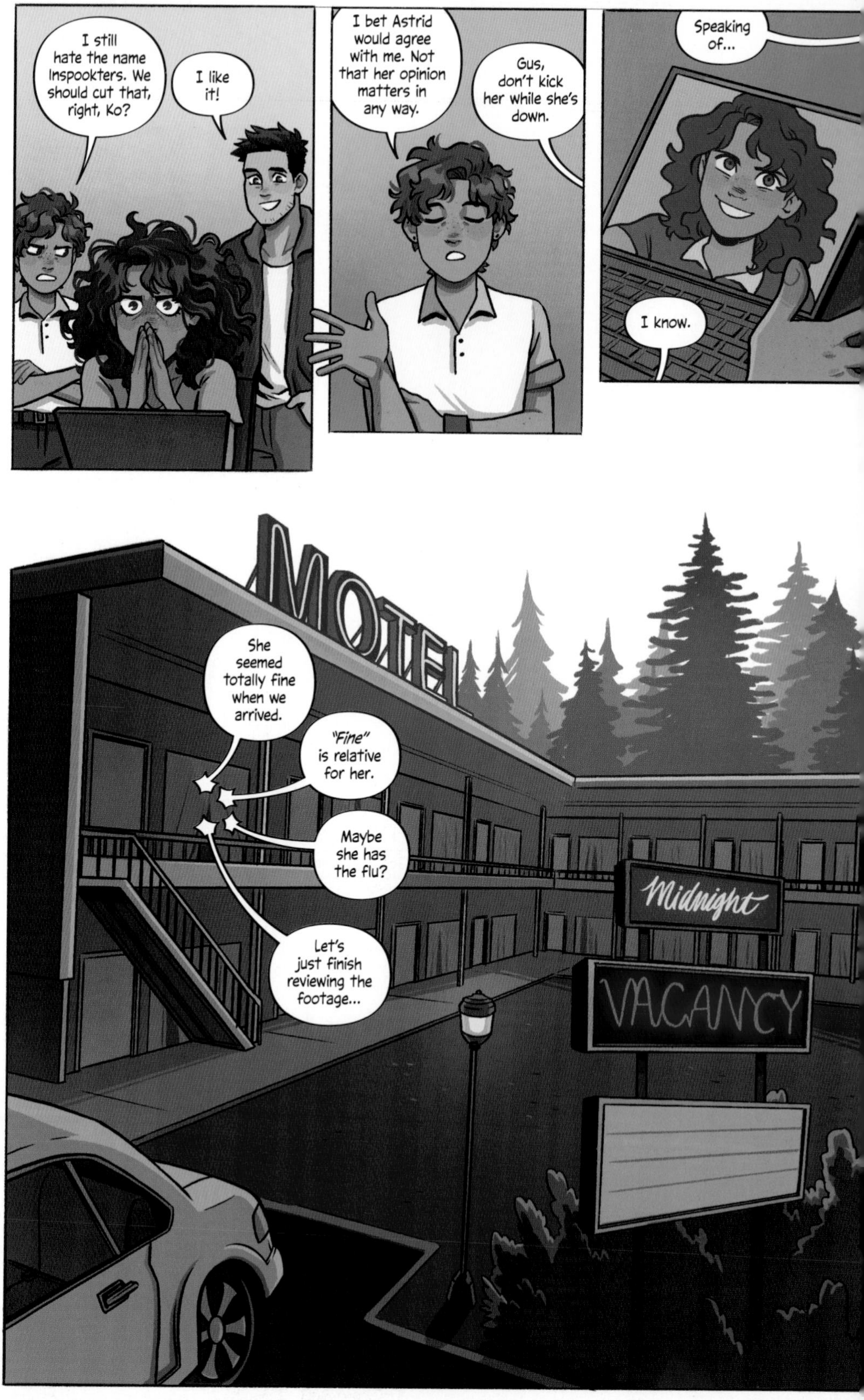
I still hate the name Inspookters. We should cut that, right, Ko?
I like it!
I bet Astrid would agree with me. Not that her opinion matters in any way.
Gus, don't kick her while she's down.
Speaking of...
I know.
MOTEL
She seemed totally fine when we arrived.
"Fine" is relative for her.
Maybe she has the flu?
Let's just finish reviewing the footage...
Midnight
VACANCY

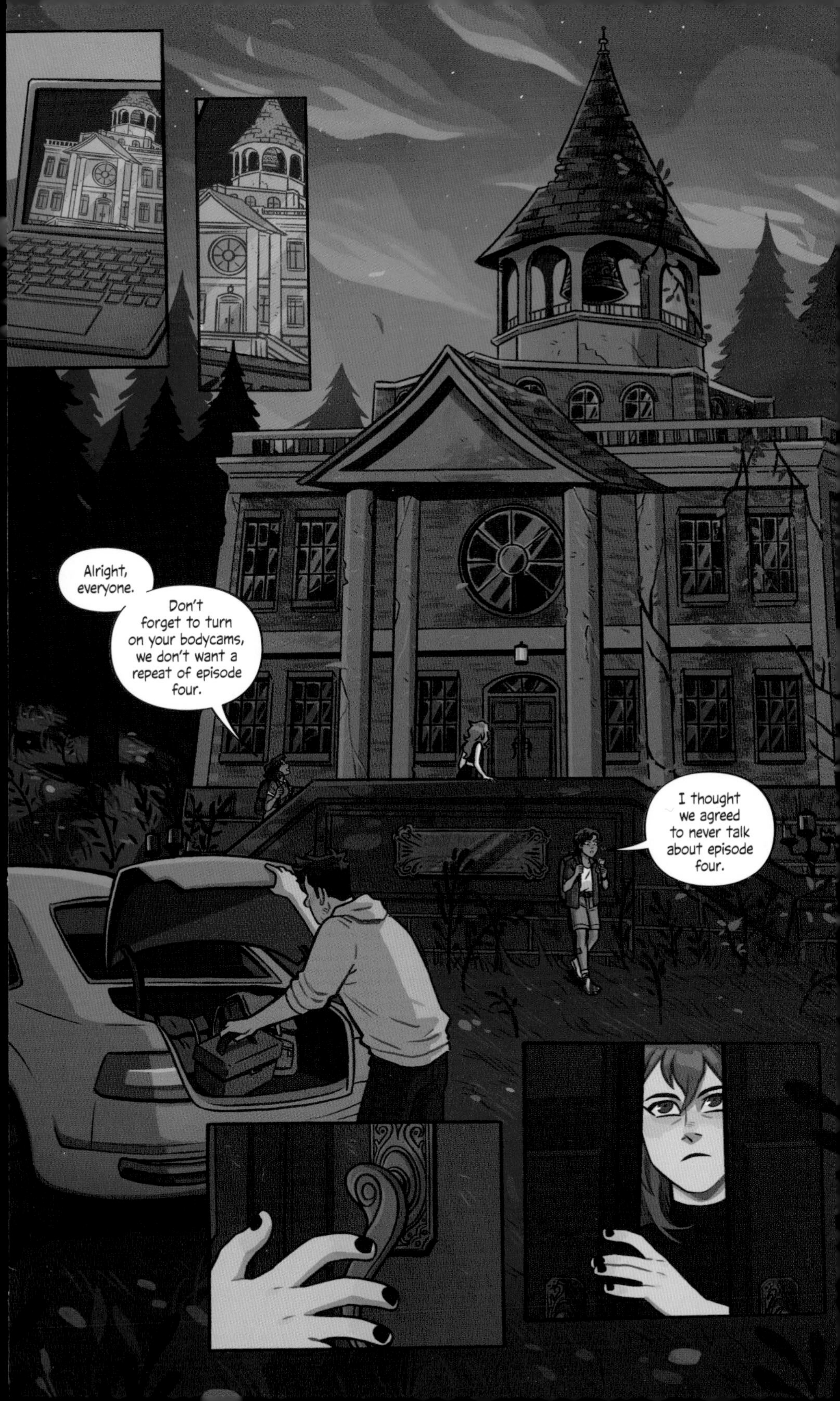

Alright, everyone.
Don't forget to turn on your bodycams, we don't want a repeat of episode four.
I thought we agreed to never talk about episode four.

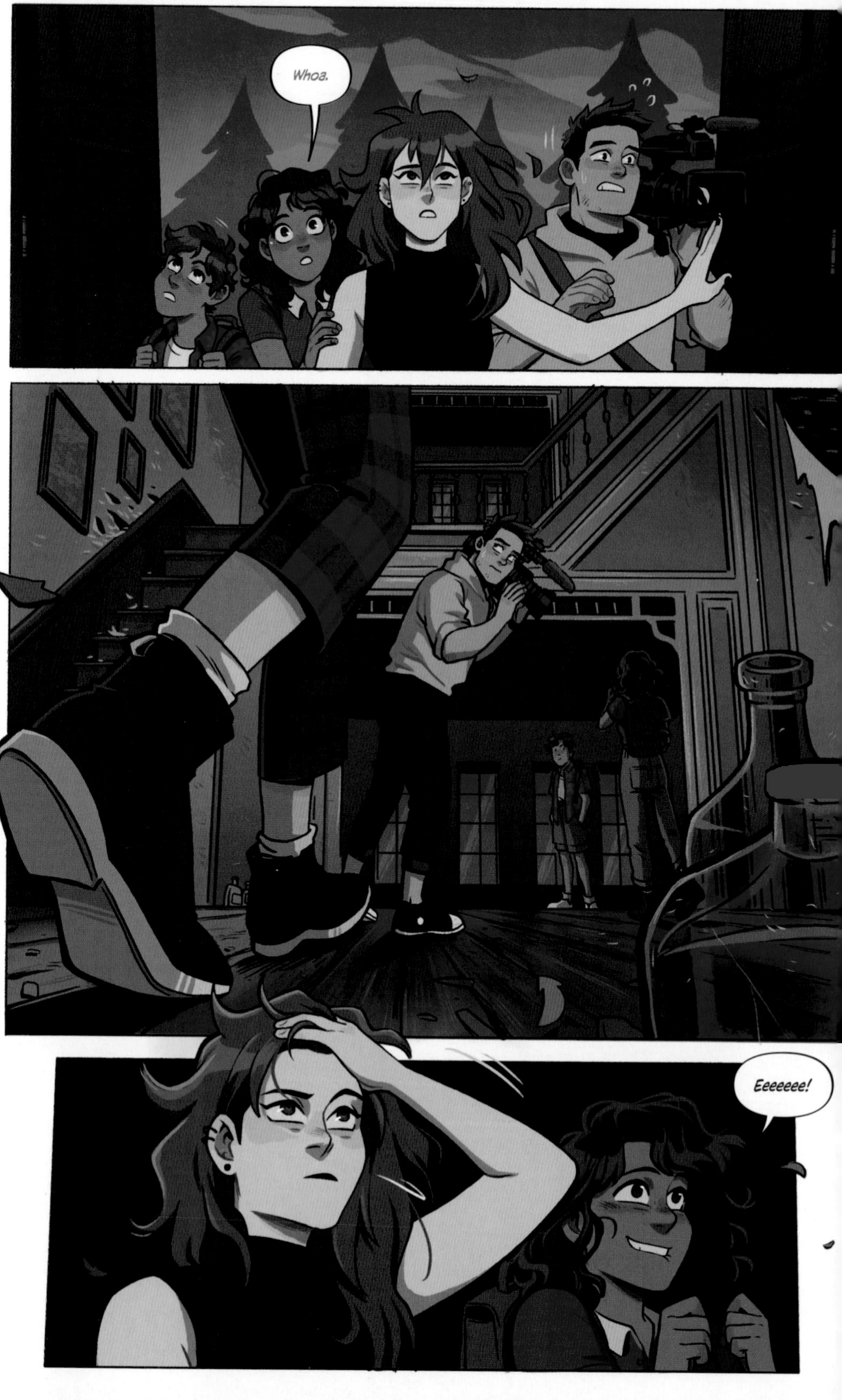
Whoa.
Eeeeeee!

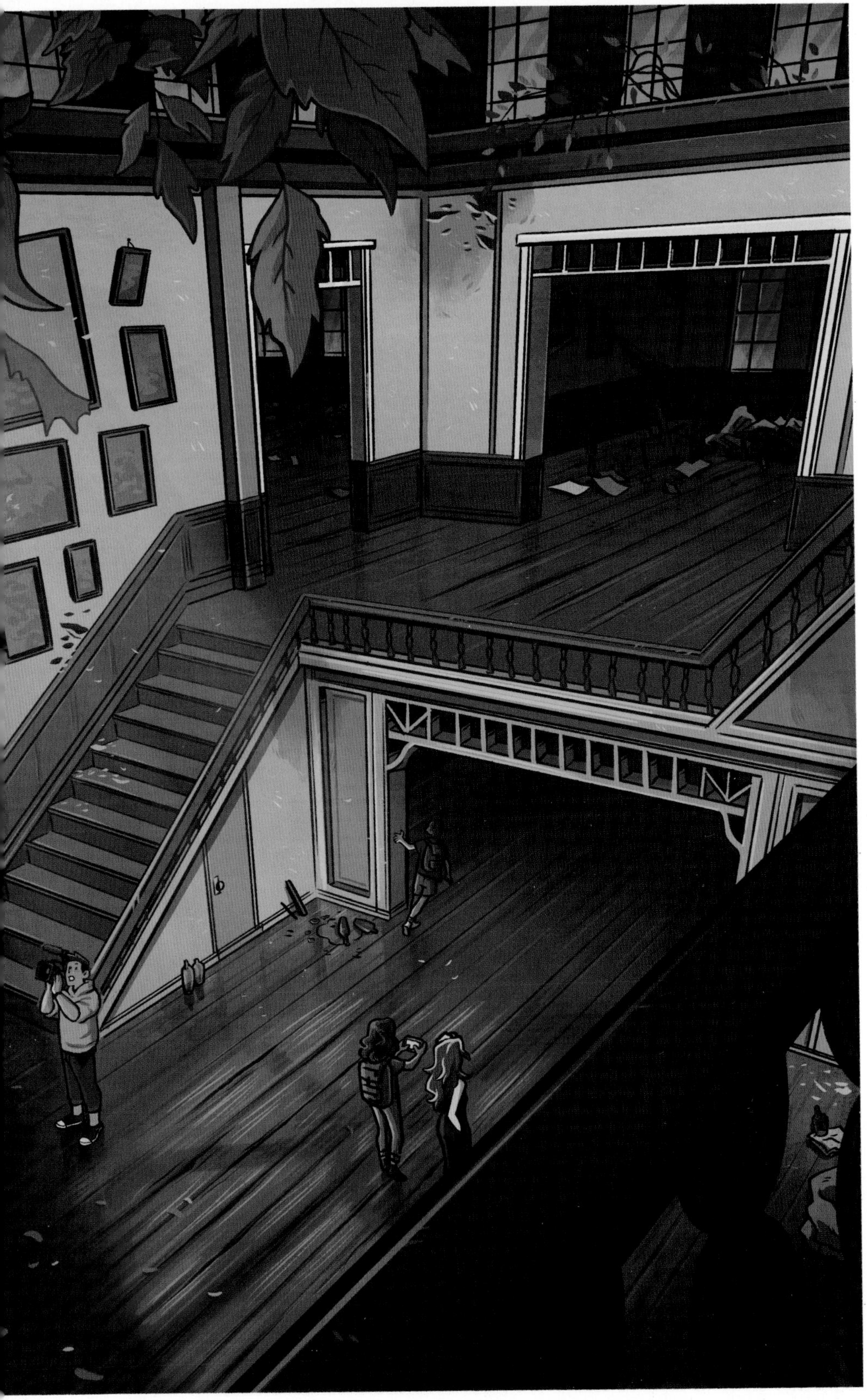

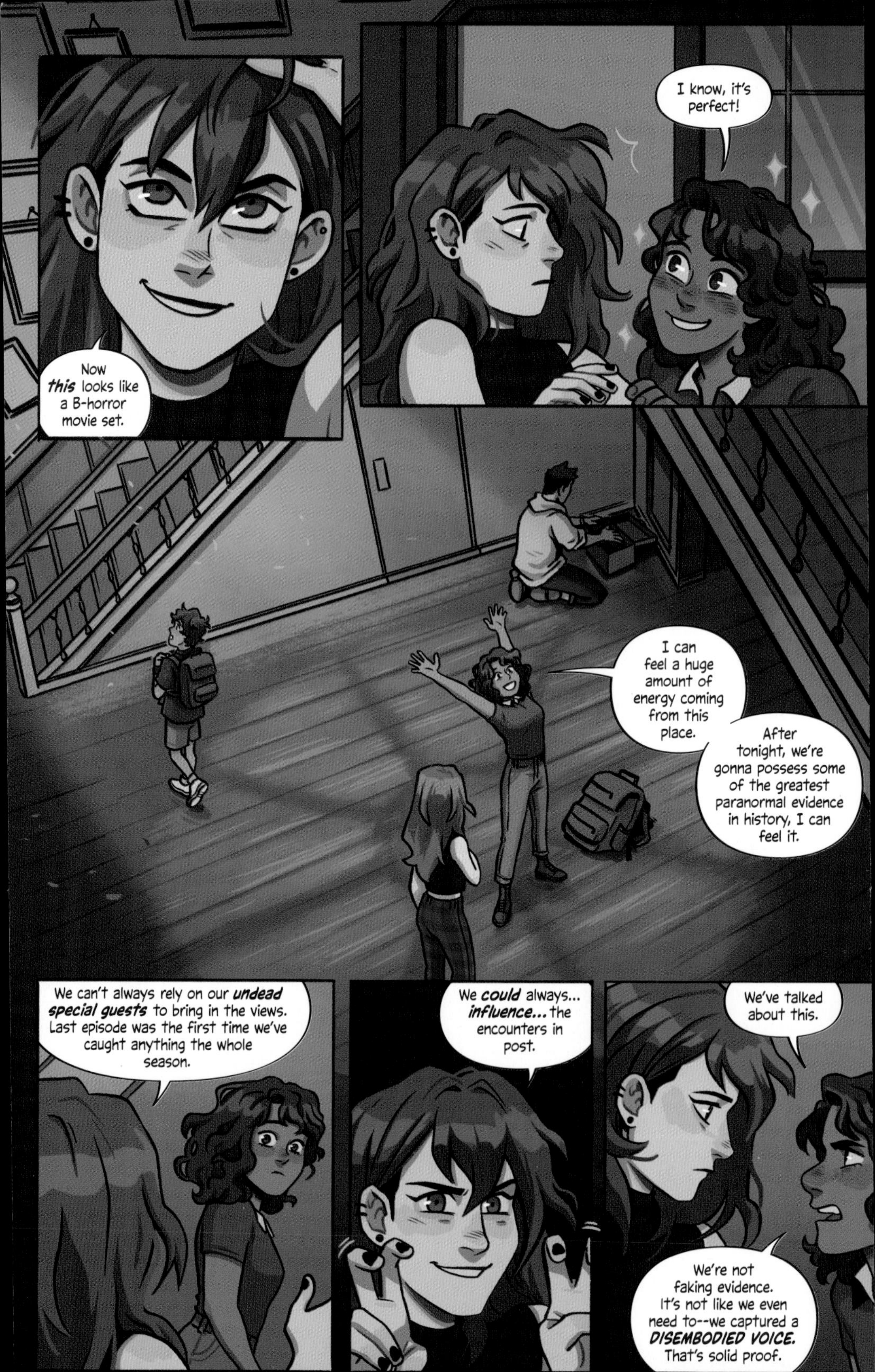
Now *this* looks like a B-horror movie set.
I know, it's perfect!
I can feel a huge amount of energy coming from this place.
After tonight, we're gonna possess some of the greatest paranormal evidence in history, I can feel it.
We can't always rely on our *undead special guests* to bring in the views. Last episode was the first time we've caught anything the whole season.
We *could* always... *influence...* the encounters in post.
We've talked about this.
We're not faking evidence. It's not like we even need to--we captured a ***DISEMBODIED VOICE.*** That's solid proof.

Ko, buddy, what's your stance on this?

Hey, don't look at me, I'm just the camera guy. Leave me out of your ghost drama.

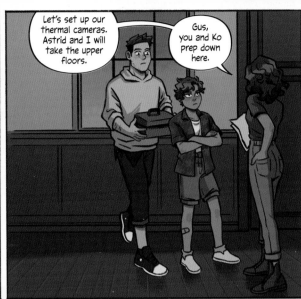

Let's set up our thermal cameras. Astrid and I will take the upper floors.

Gus, you and Ko prep down here.

You're gonna leave me with this oversized cry-baby so you can go off and flirt?

I do not *flirt!* I take my job very *seriously.* I am a professional.

Hey, babe, ready to go?

Mm

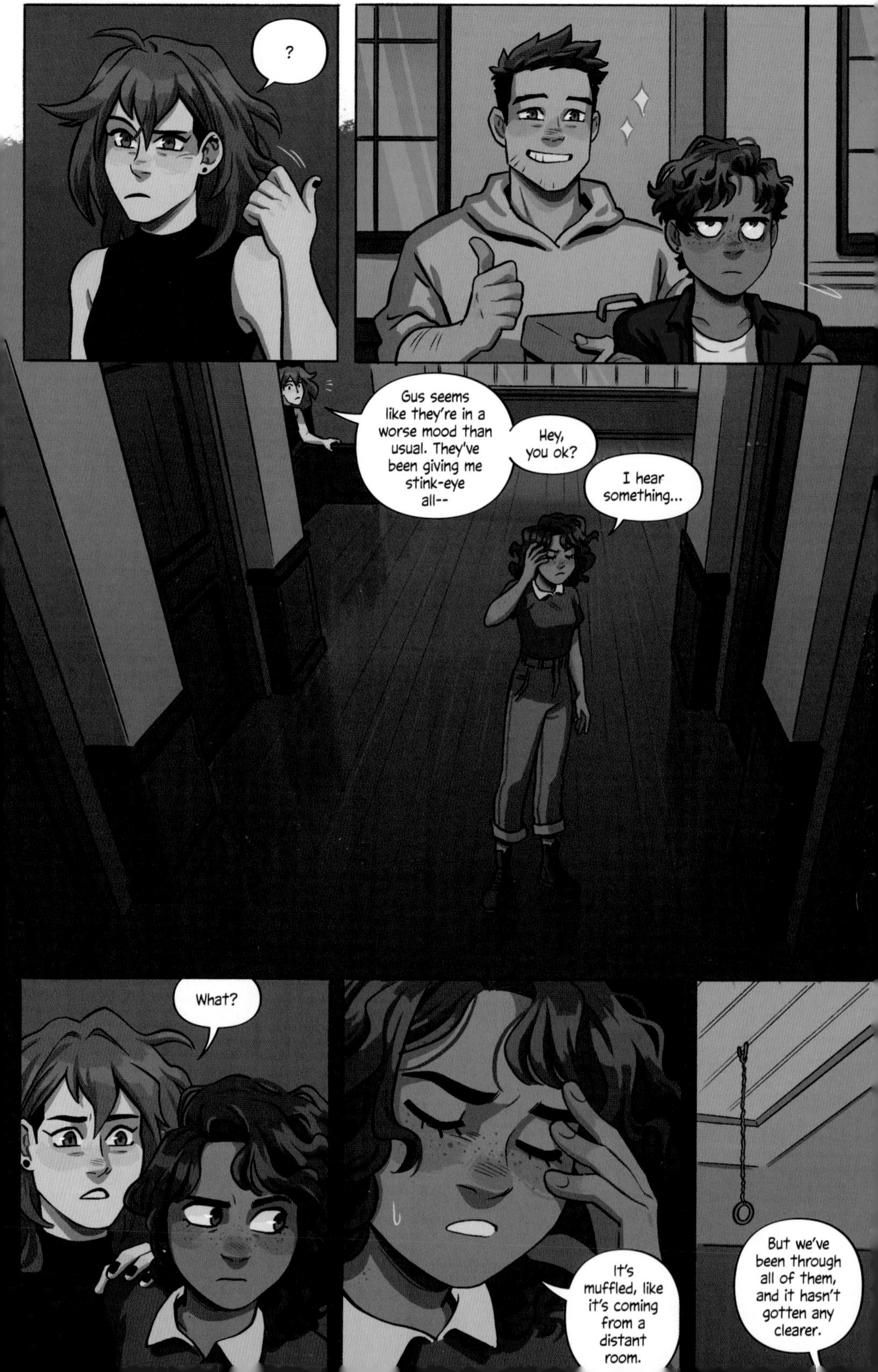
?
Gus seems like they're in a worse mood than usual. They've been giving me stink-eye all--
Hey, you ok?
I hear something...
What?
It's muffled, like it's coming from a distant room.
But we've been through all of them, and it hasn't gotten any clearer.

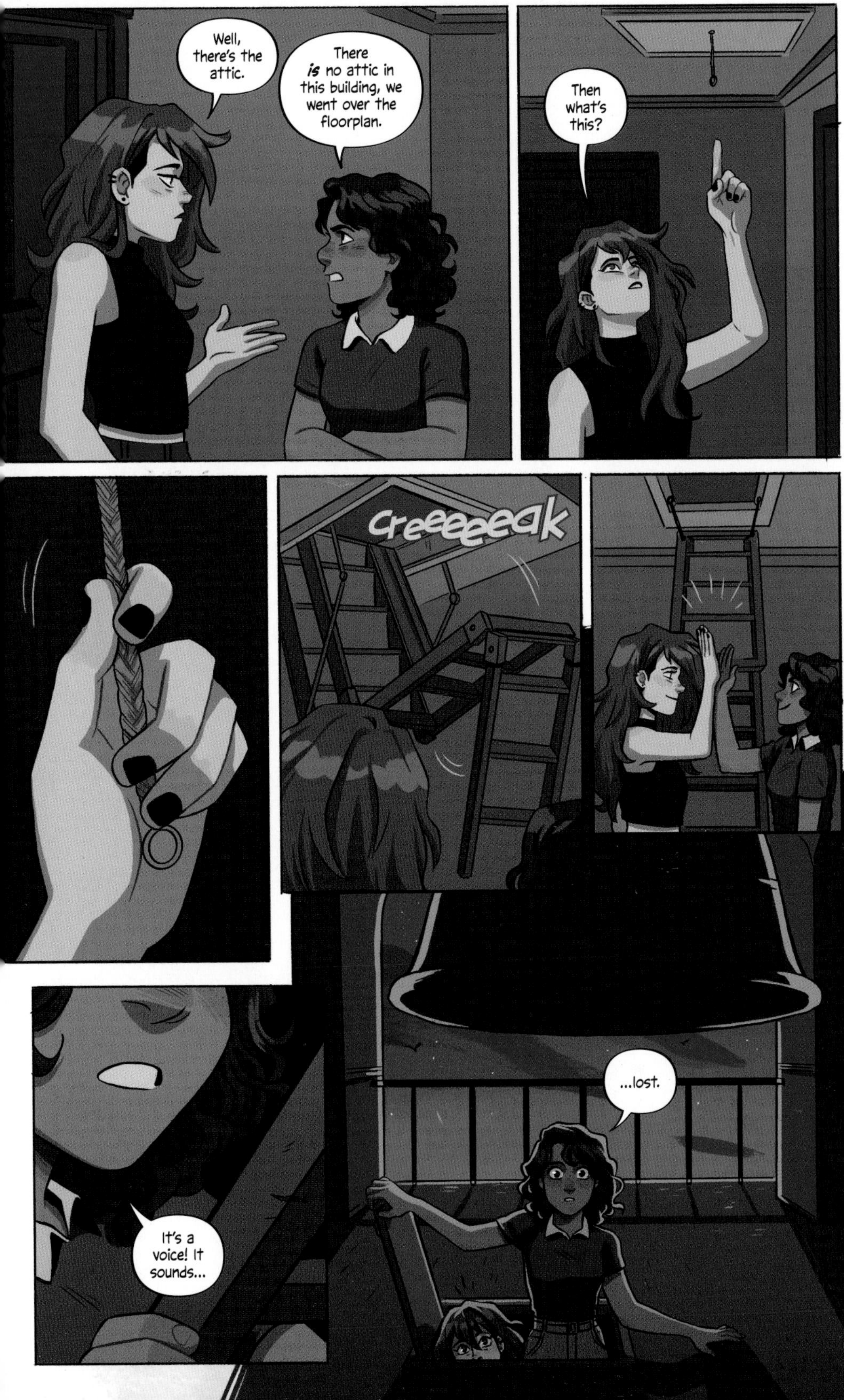
Well, there's the attic.
There *is* no attic in this building, we went over the floorplan.
Then what's this?
Creeeeeeak
It's a voice! It sounds...
...lost.

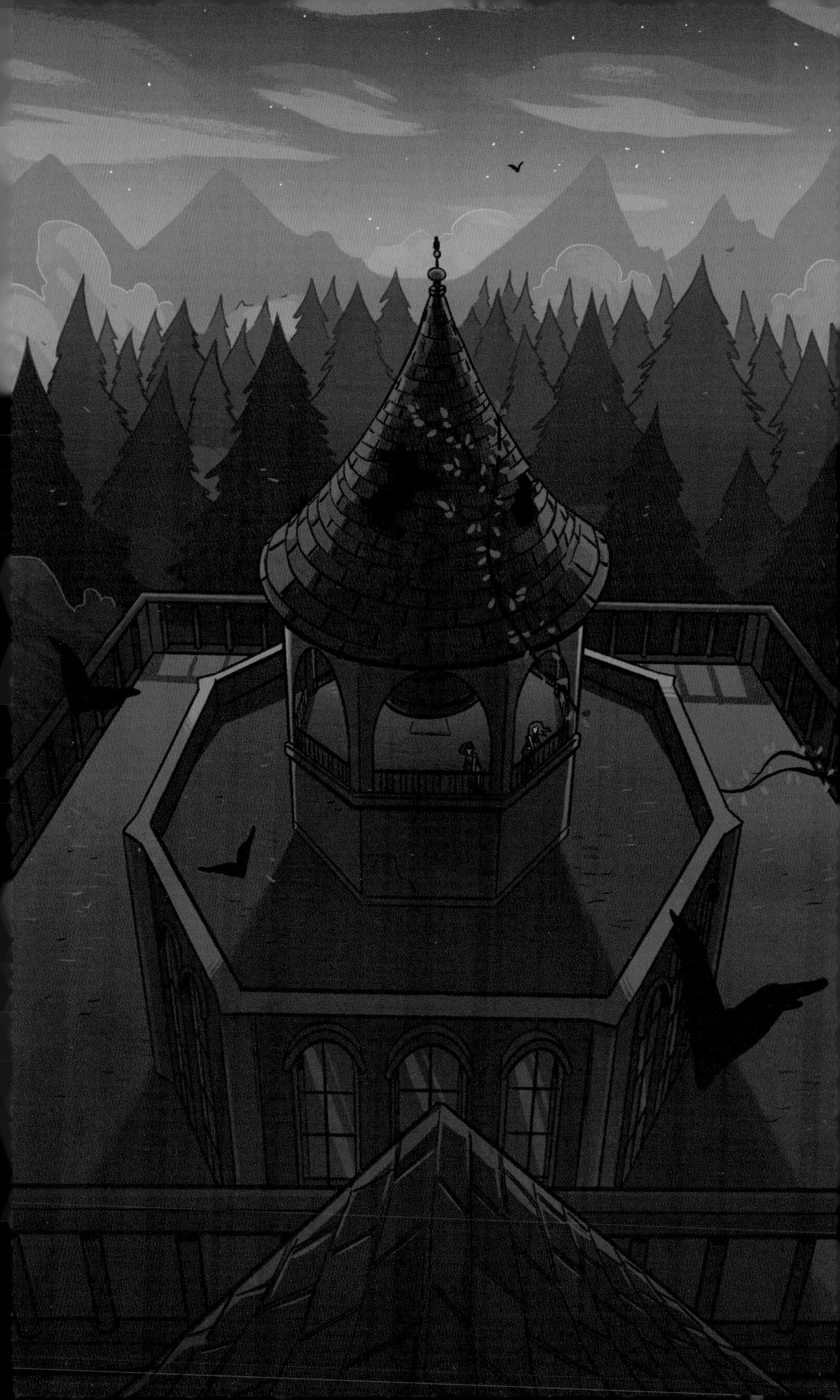

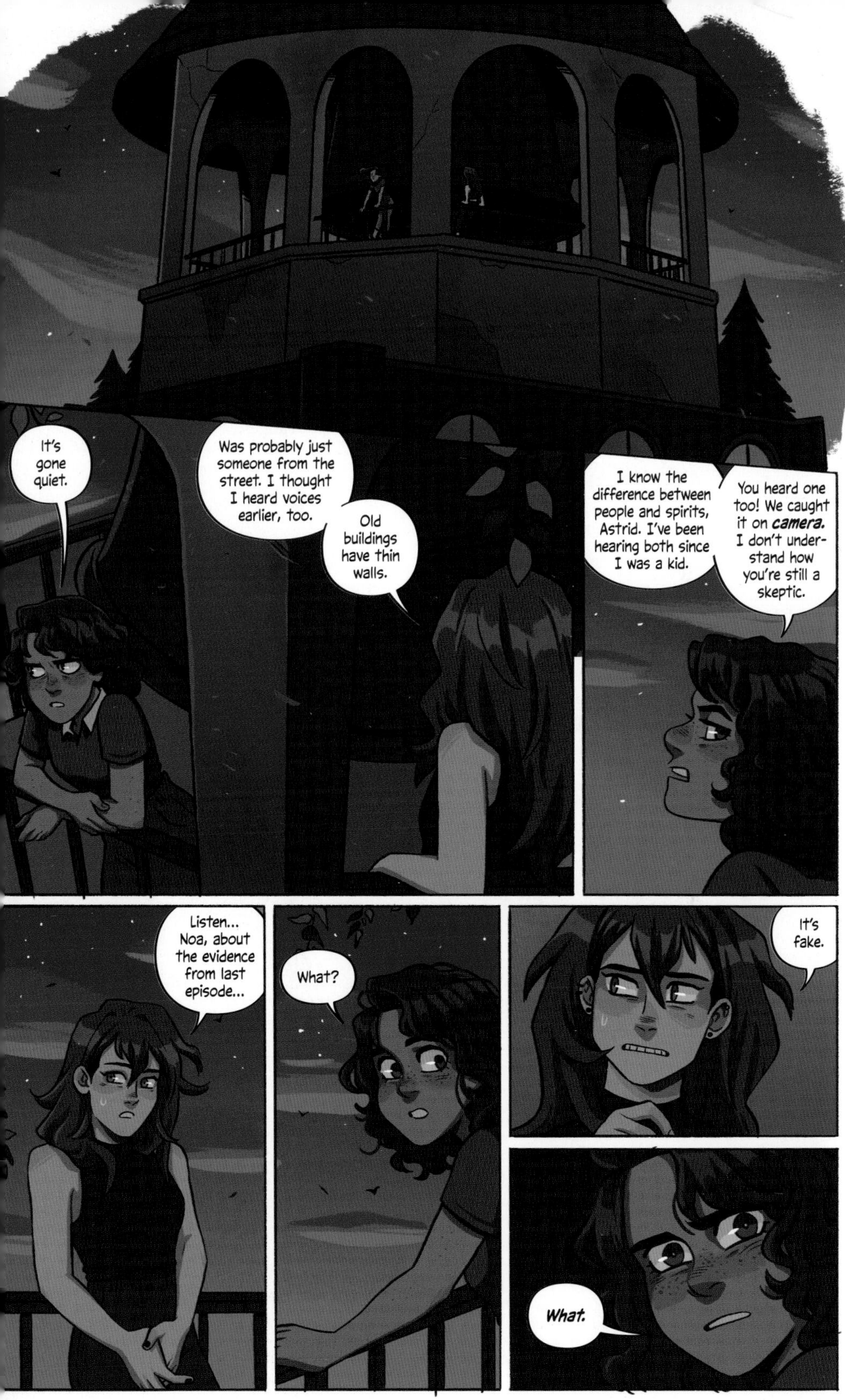
It's gone quiet.
Was probably just someone from the street. I thought I heard voices earlier, too.
Old buildings have thin walls.
I know the difference between people and spirits, Astrid. I've been hearing both since I was a kid.
You heard one too! We caught it on *camera.* I don't understand how you're still a skeptic.
Listen... Noa, about the evidence from last episode...
What?
It's fake.
What.

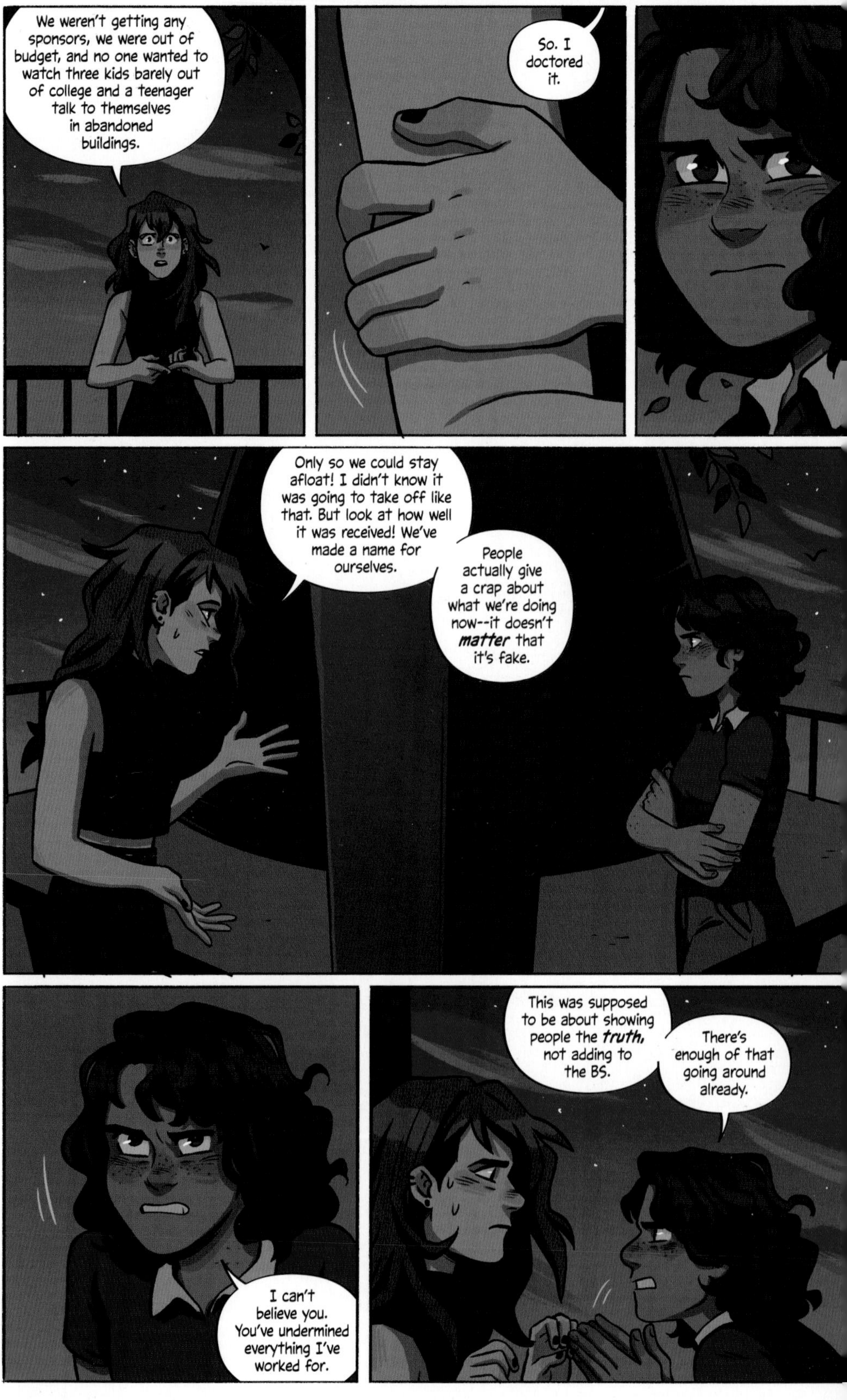
We weren't getting any sponsors, we were out of budget, and no one wanted to watch three kids barely out of college and a teenager talk to themselves in abandoned buildings.
So. I doctored it.
Only so we could stay afloat! I didn't know it was going to take off like that. But look at how well it was received! We've made a name for ourselves.
People actually give a crap about what we're doing now--it doesn't *matter* that it's fake.
I can't believe you. You've undermined everything I've worked for.
This was supposed to be about showing people the *truth,* not adding to the BS.
There's enough of that going around already.

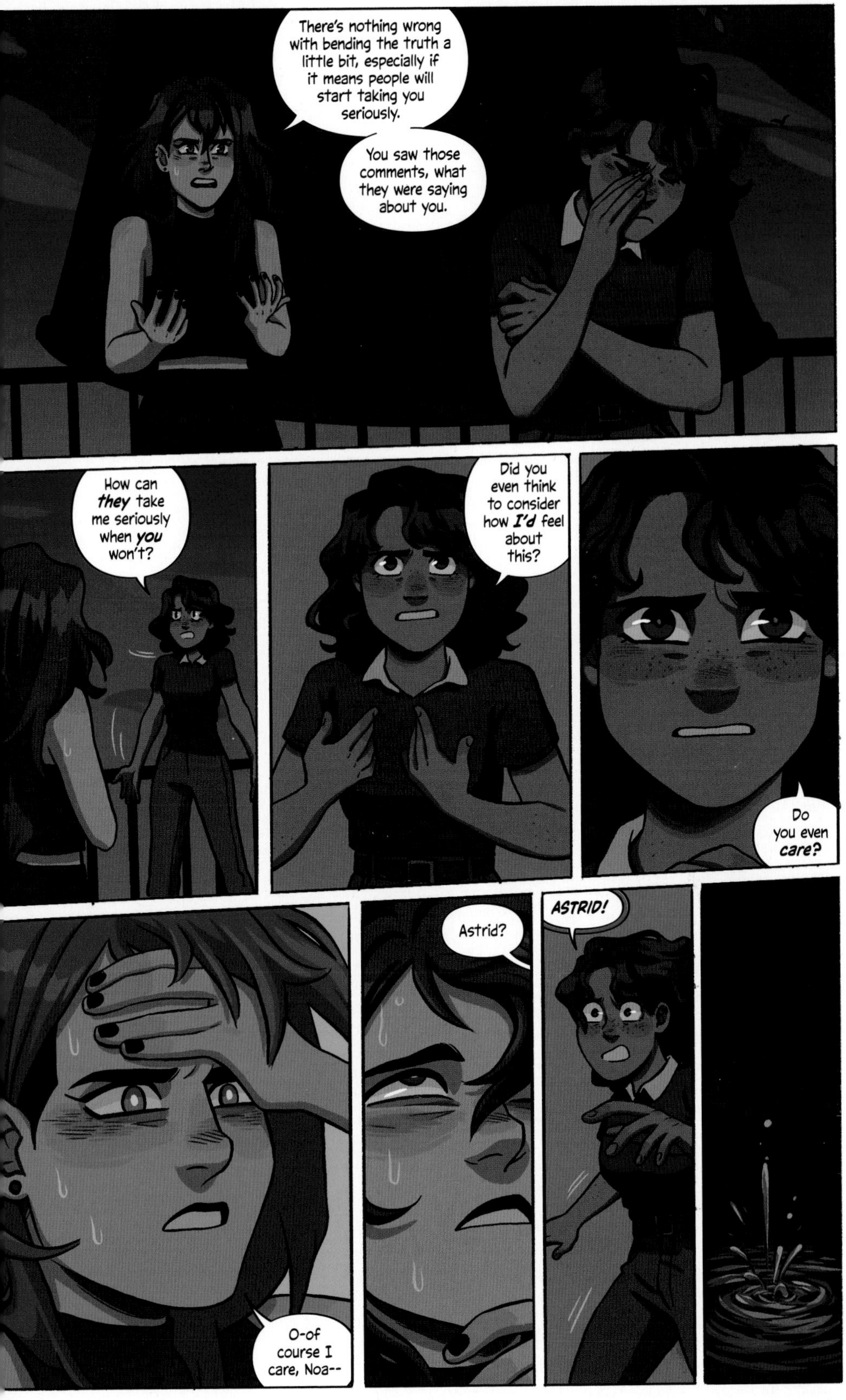
There's nothing wrong with bending the truth a little bit, especially if it means people will start taking you seriously.
You saw those comments, what they were saying about you.
How can *they* take me seriously when *you* won't?
Did you even think to consider how *I'd* feel about this?
Do you even *care?*
O-of course I care, Noa--
Astrid?
ASTRID!

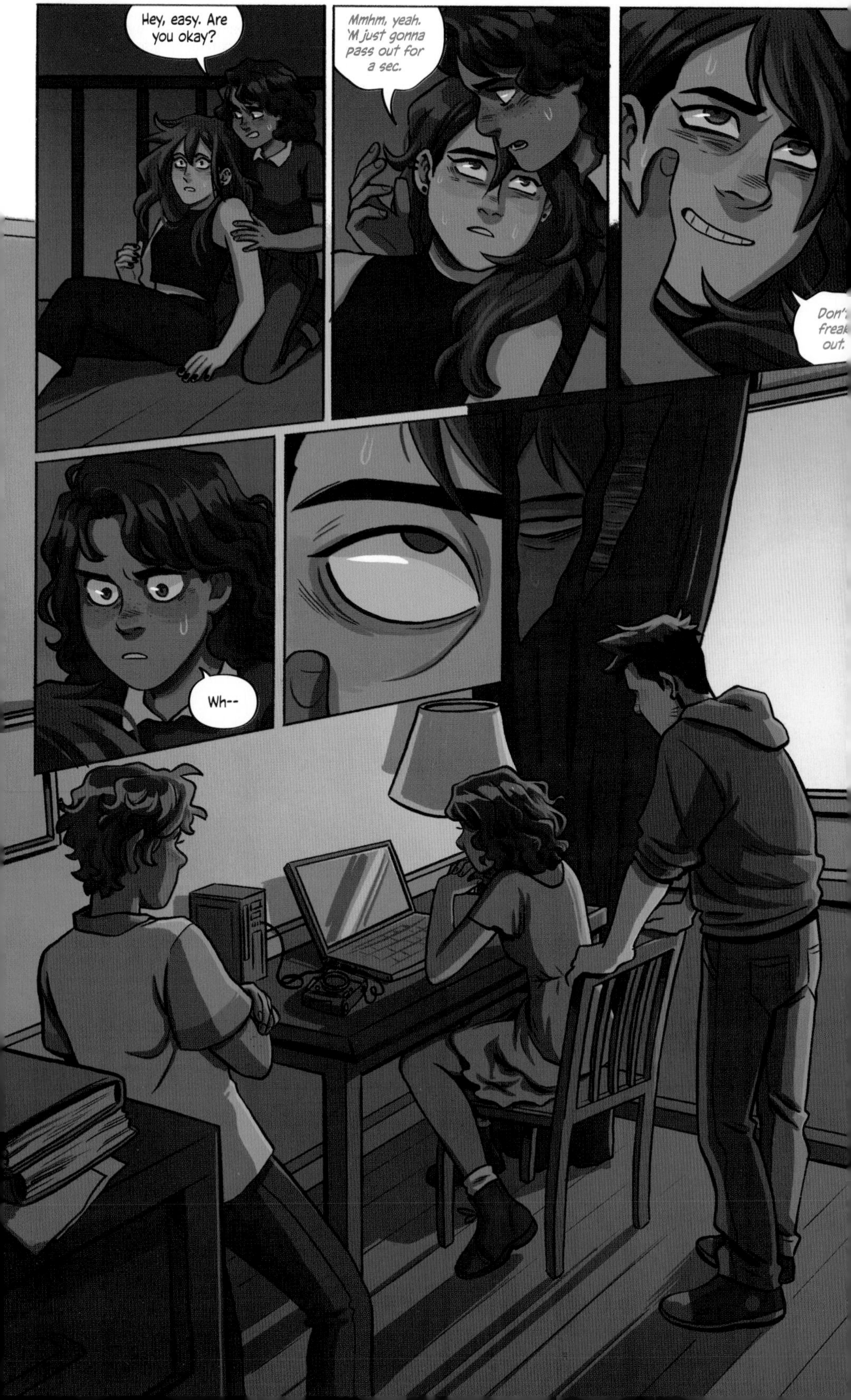
Hey, easy. Are you okay?
Mmhm, yeah. 'M just gonna pass out for a sec.
Don't freak out.
Wh--

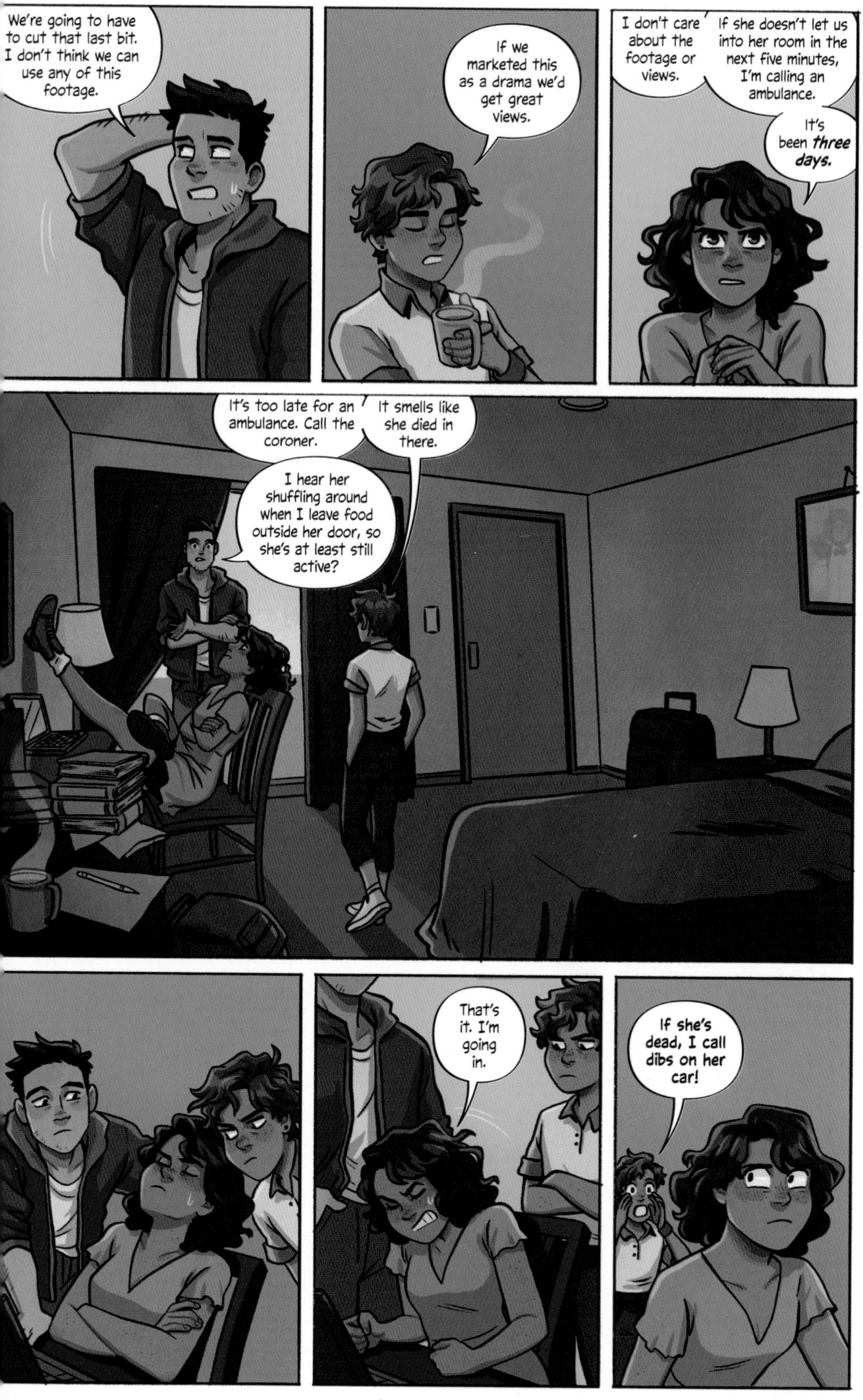
We're going to have to cut that last bit. I don't think we can use any of this footage.
If we marketed this as a drama we'd get great views.
I don't care about the footage or views.
If she doesn't let us into her room in the next five minutes, I'm calling an ambulance.
It's been *three days.*
It's too late for an ambulance. Call the coroner.
It smells like she died in there.
I hear her shuffling around when I leave food outside her door, so she's at least still active?
That's it. I'm going in.
If she's dead, I call dibs on her car!

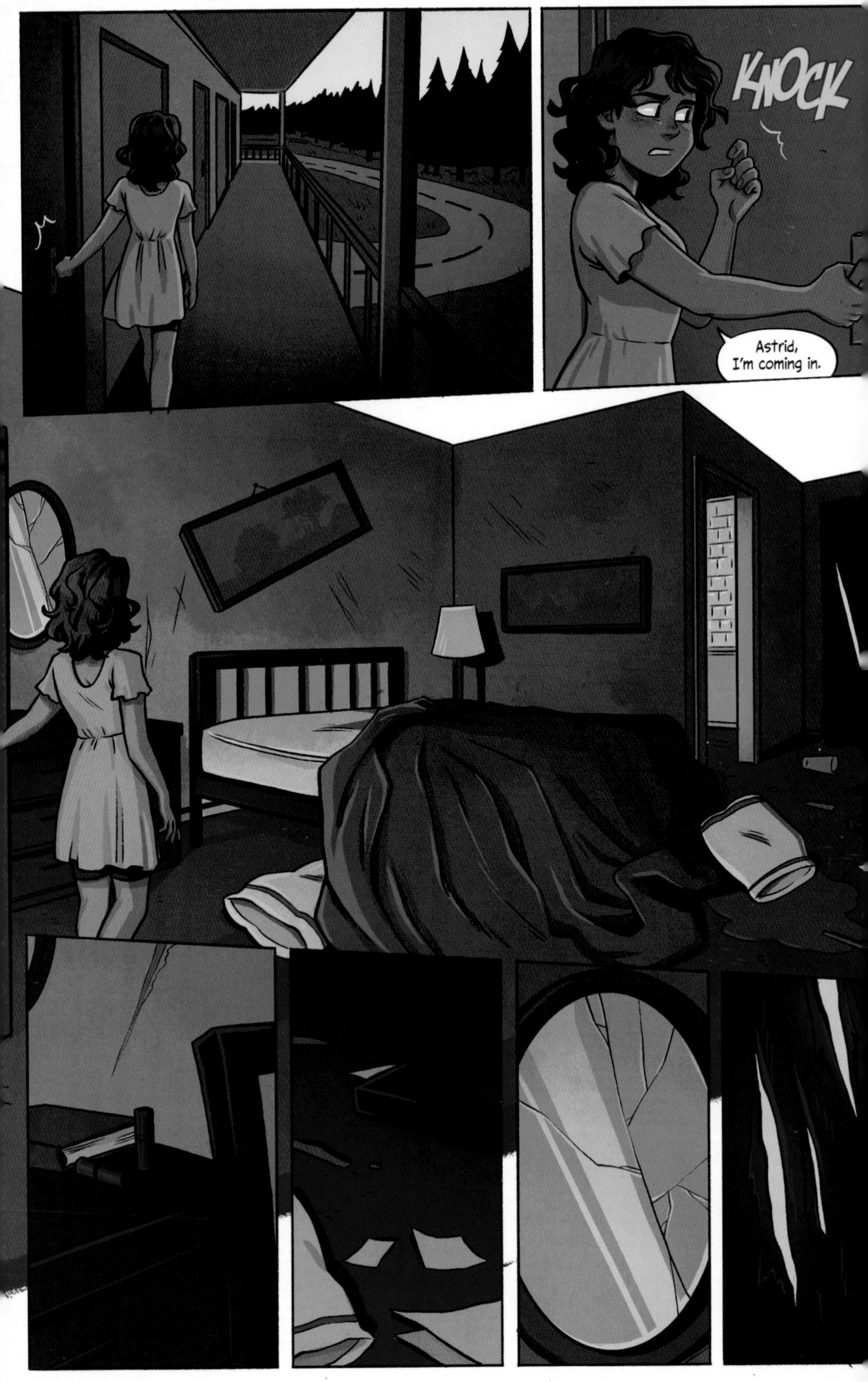
KNOCK
Astrid, I'm coming in.

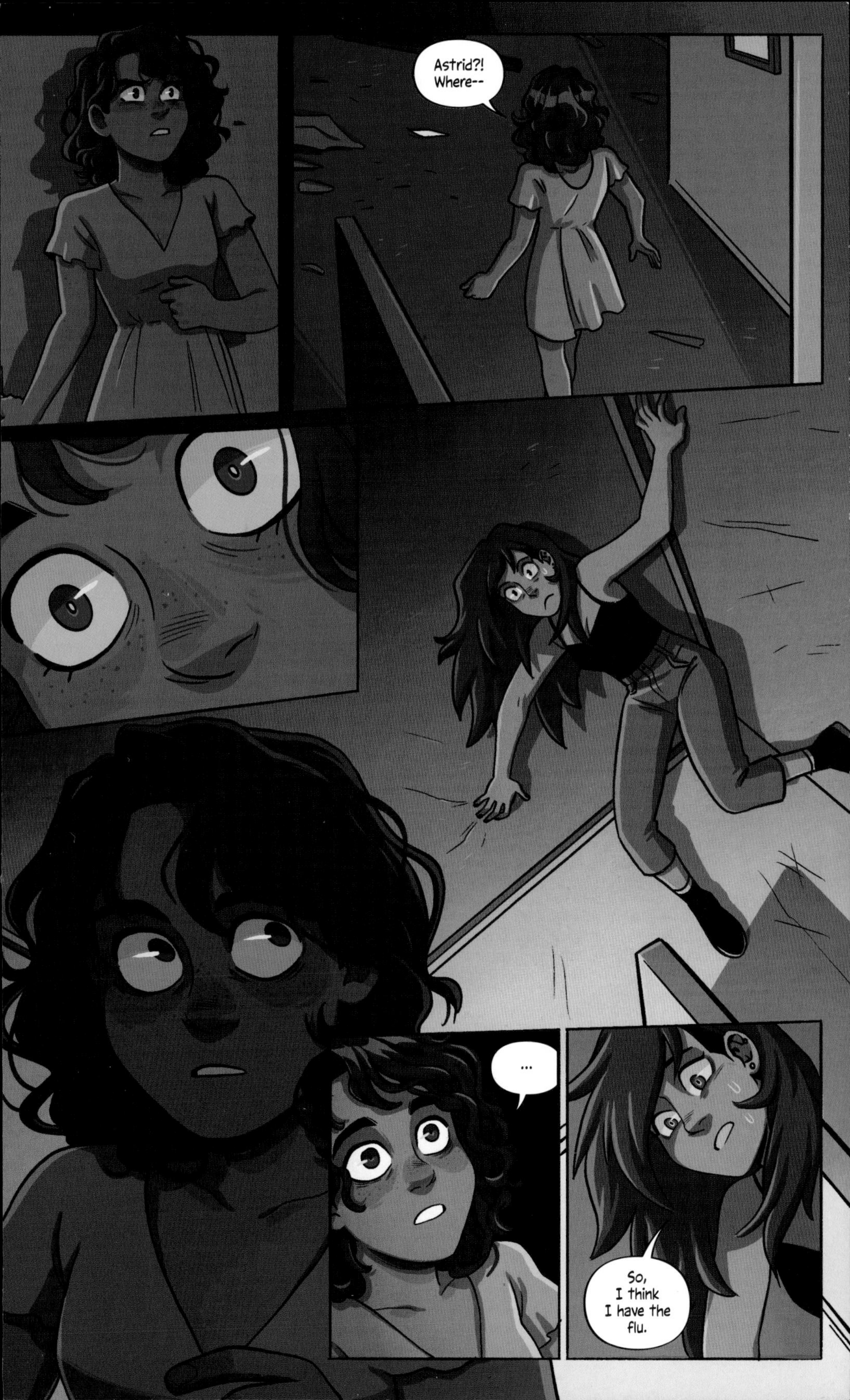
Astrid?! Where--
...
So, I think I have the flu.

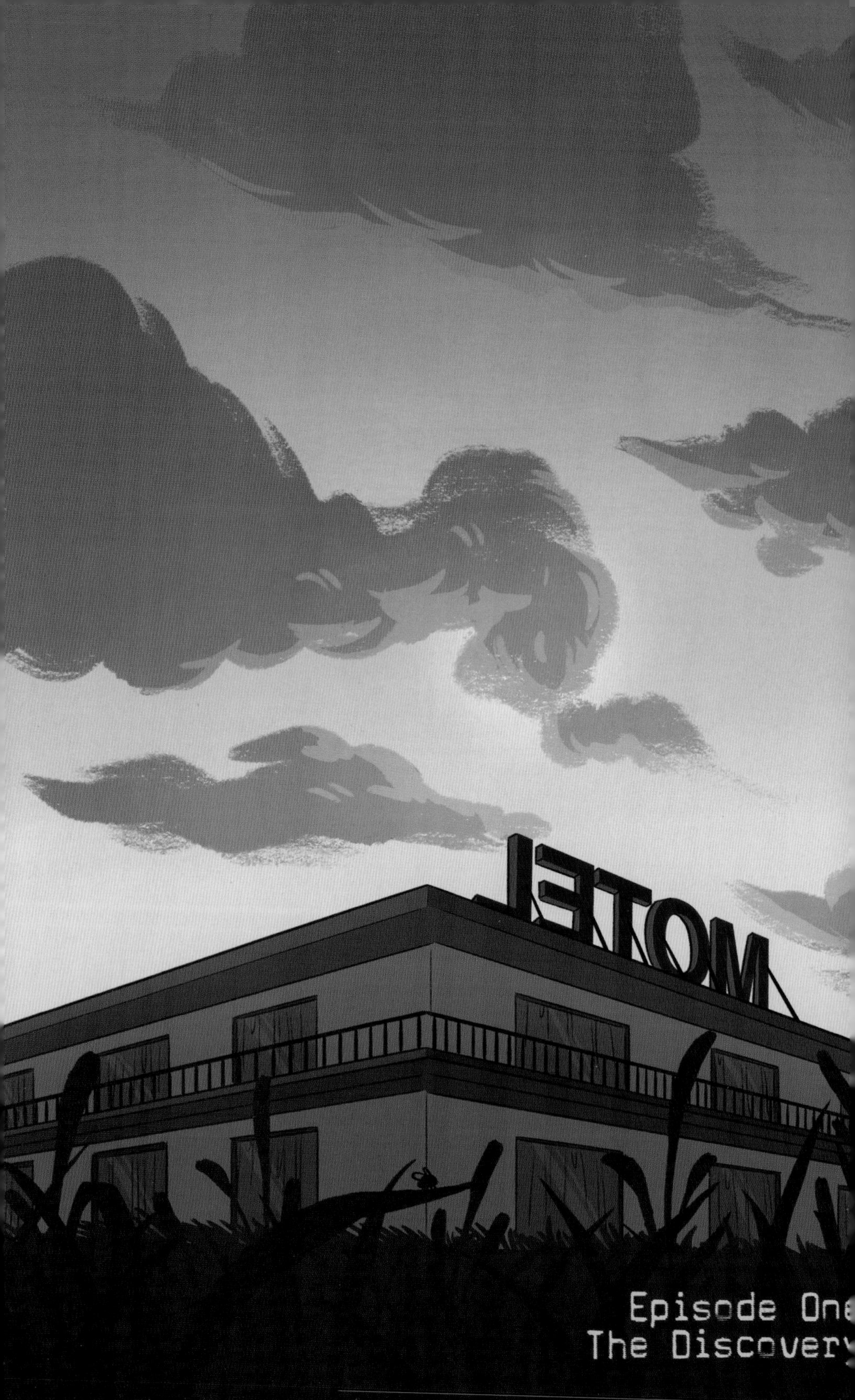
MOTEL

Episode One
The Discovery

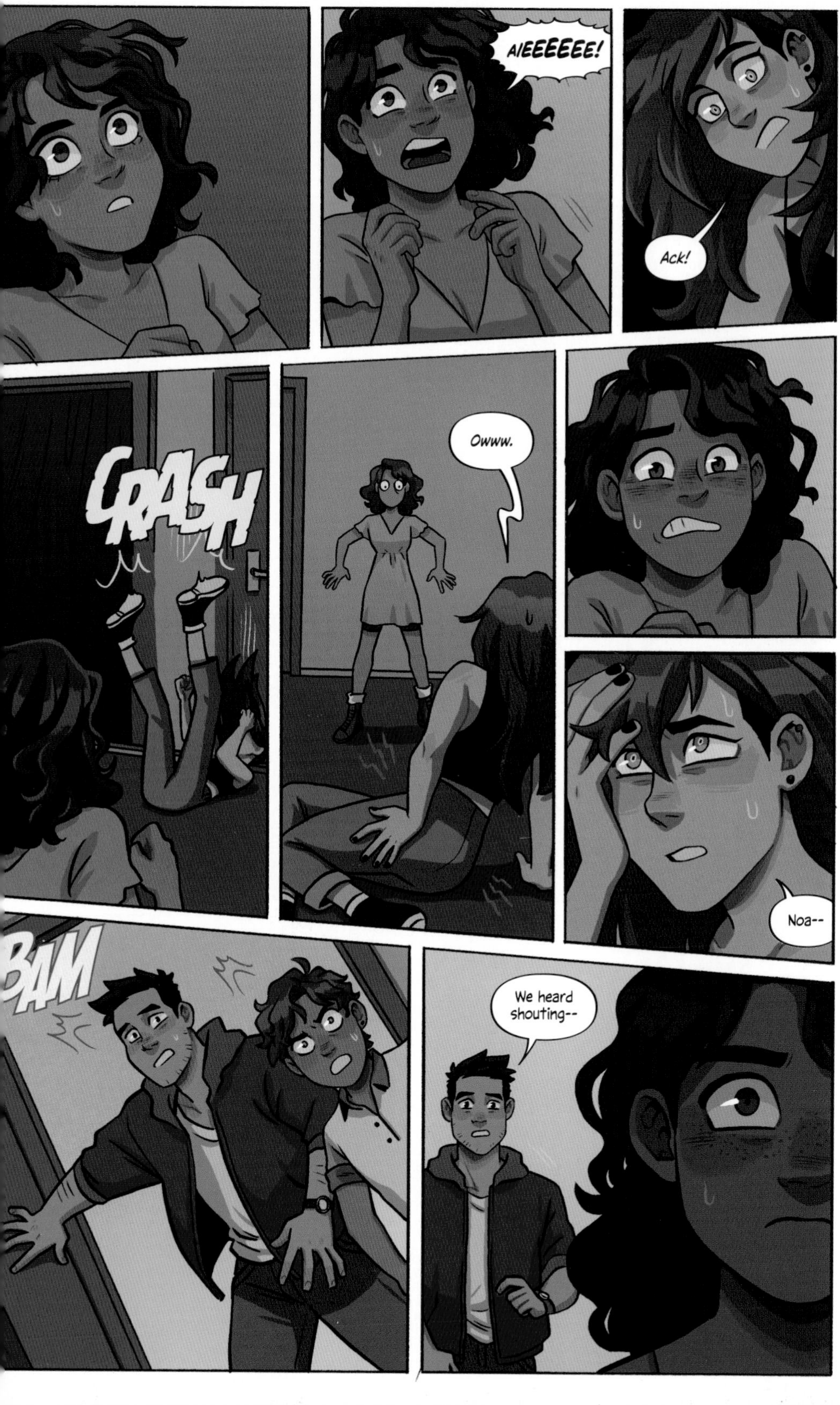
AIEEEEEE!
Ack!
CRASH
Owww.
Noa--
BAM
We heard shouting--

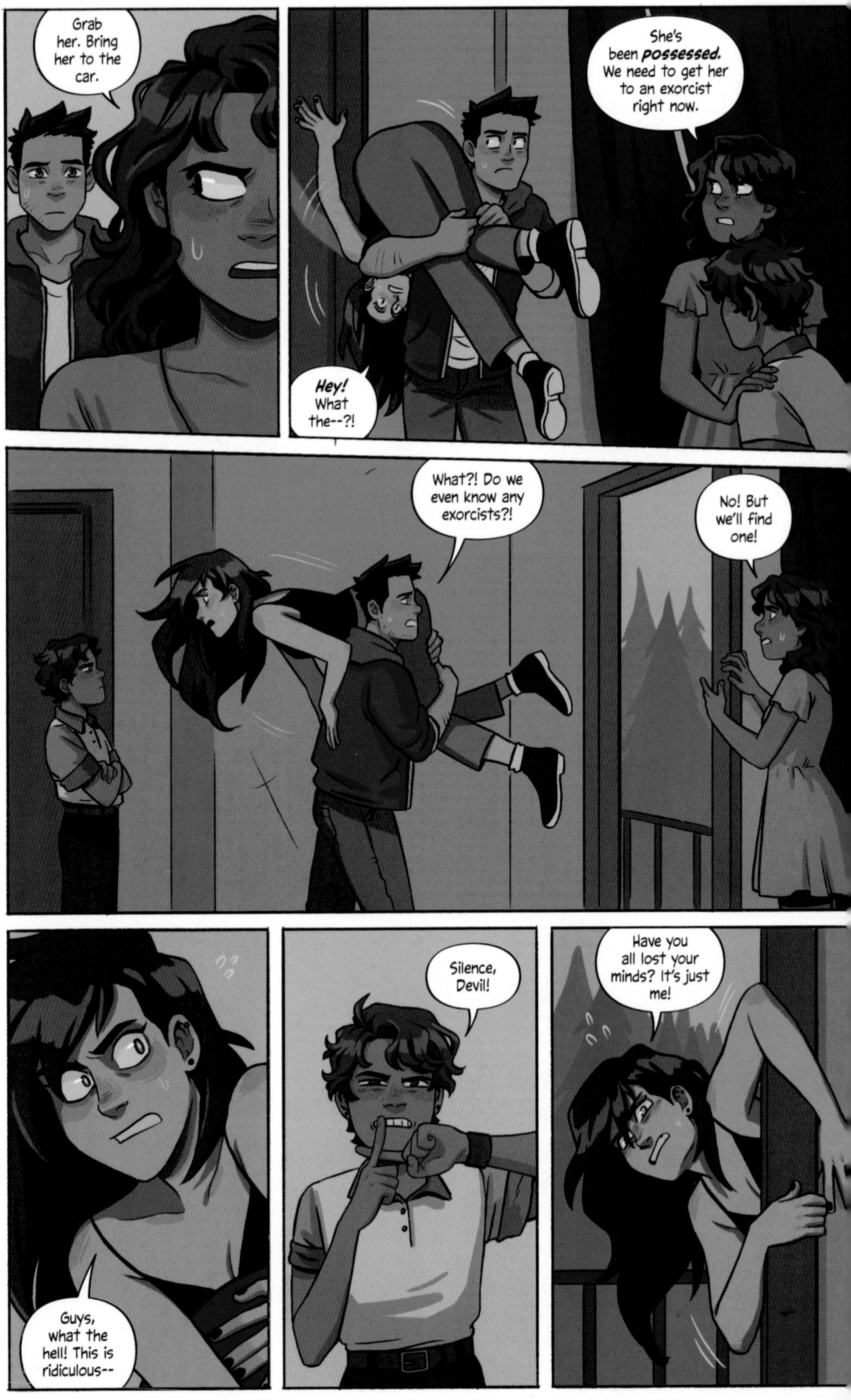
Grab her. Bring her to the car.
She's been ***possessed.*** We need to get her to an exorcist right now.
Hey! What the--?!
What?! Do we even know any exorcists?!
No! But we'll find one!
Guys, what the hell! This is ridiculous--
Silence, Devil!
Have you all lost your minds? It's just me!

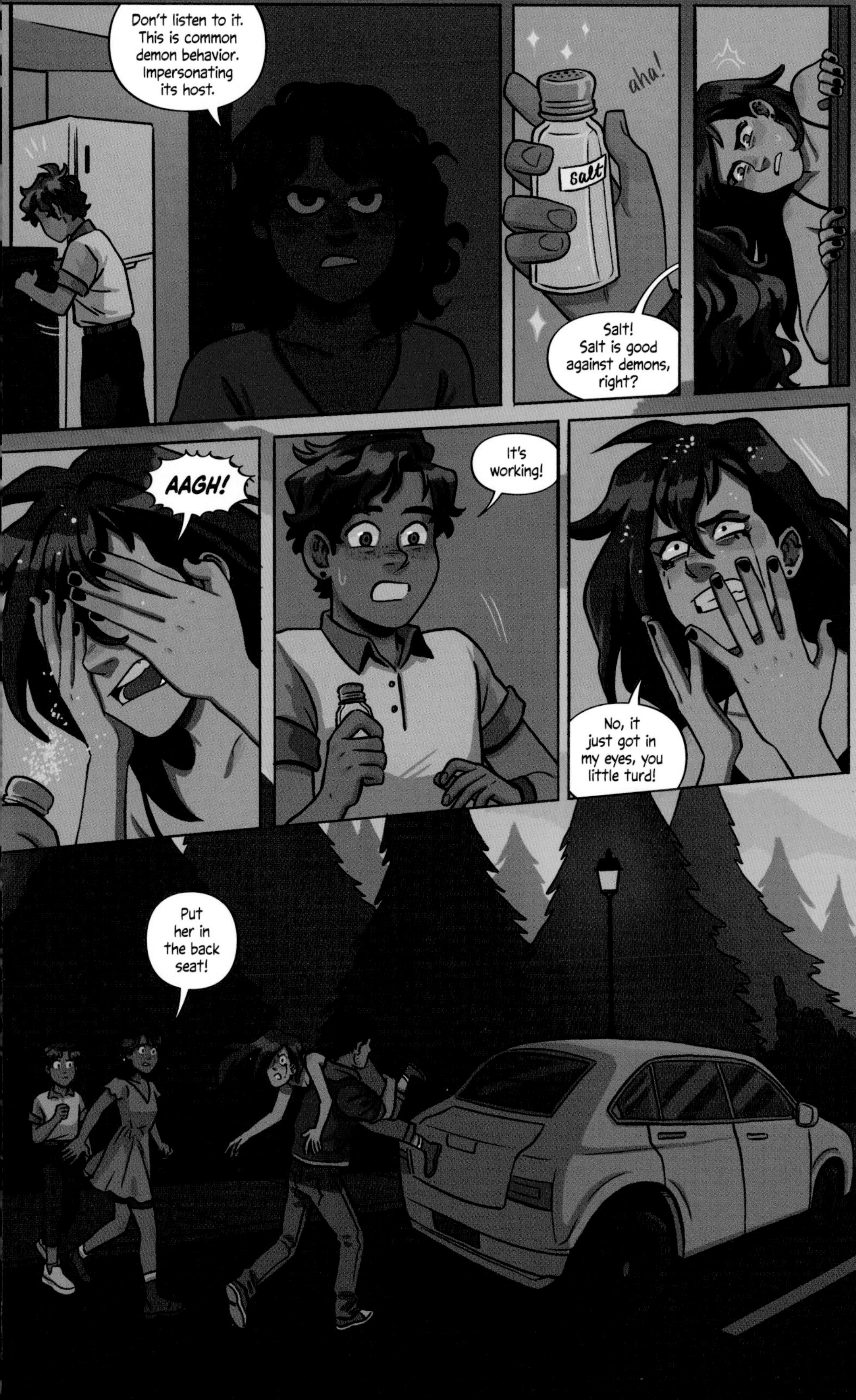
Don't listen to it. This is common demon behavior. Impersonating its host.
aha!
salt
Salt! Salt is good against demons, right?
AAGH!
It's working!
No, it just got in my eyes, you little turd!
Put her in the back seat!

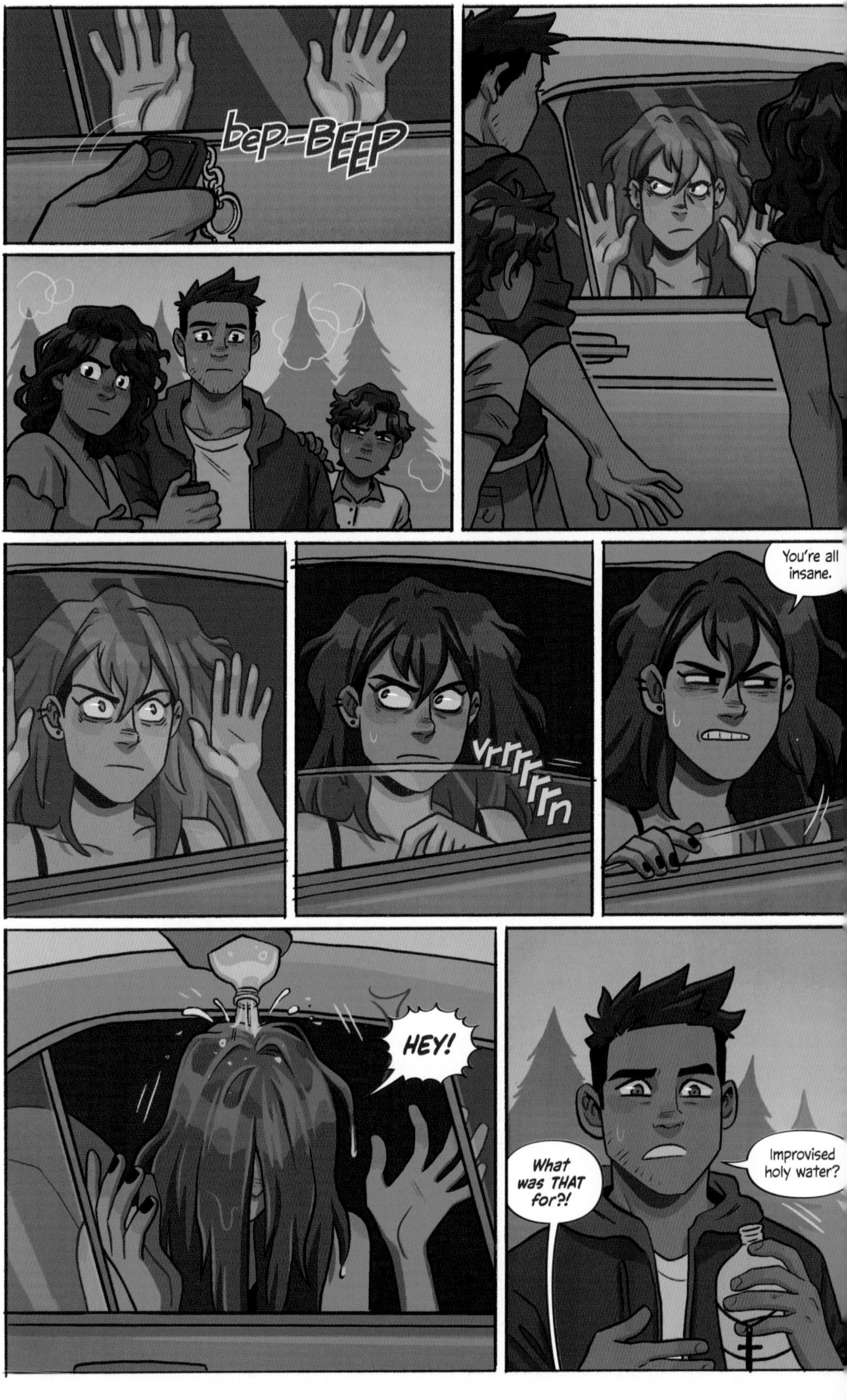

bep-BEEP
vrrrrrrn
You're all insane.
HEY!
What was THAT for?!
Improvised holy water?

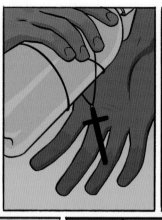

Give me that for a sec.

:gasp:

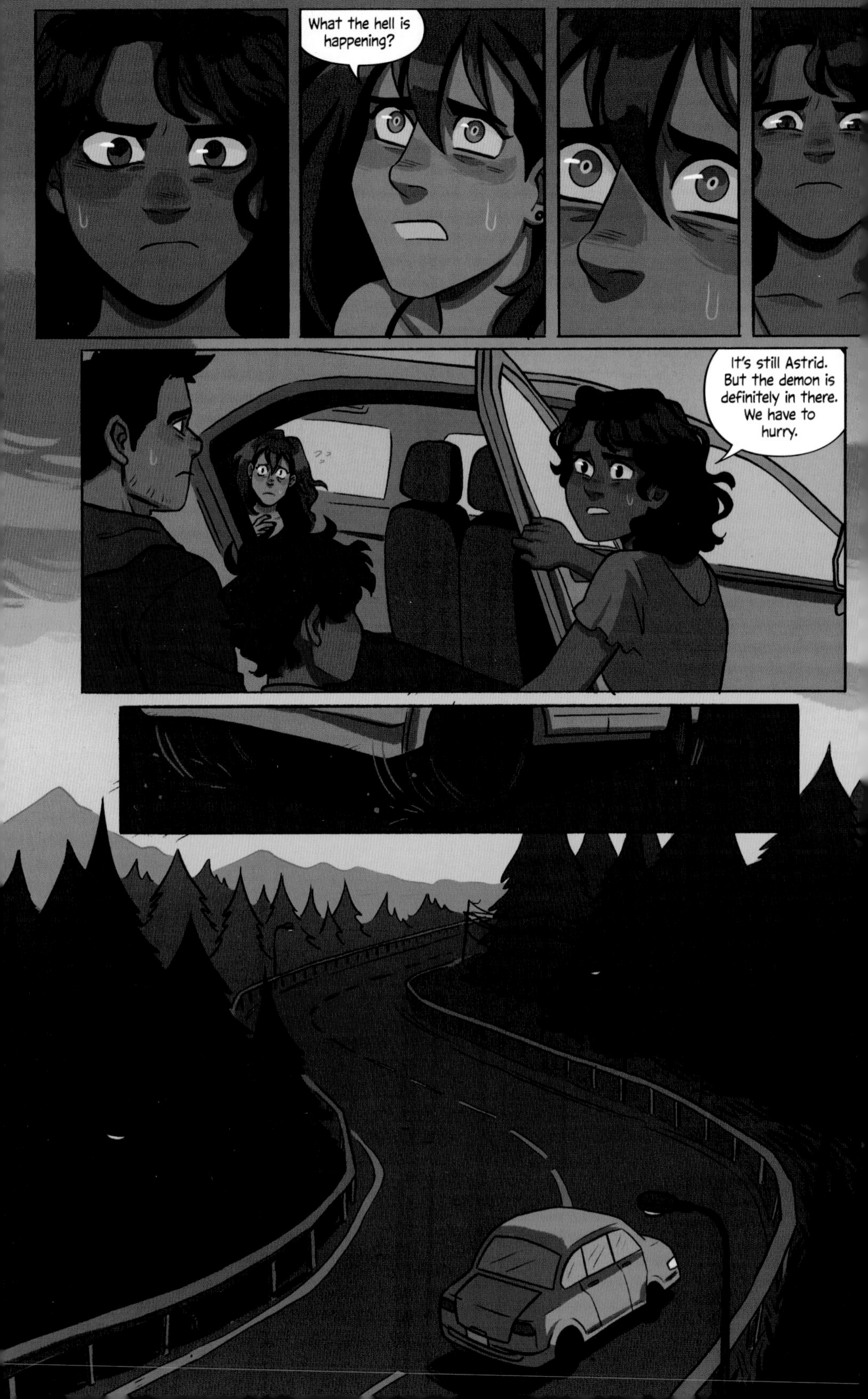
What the hell is happening?
It's still Astrid. But the demon is definitely in there. We have to hurry.

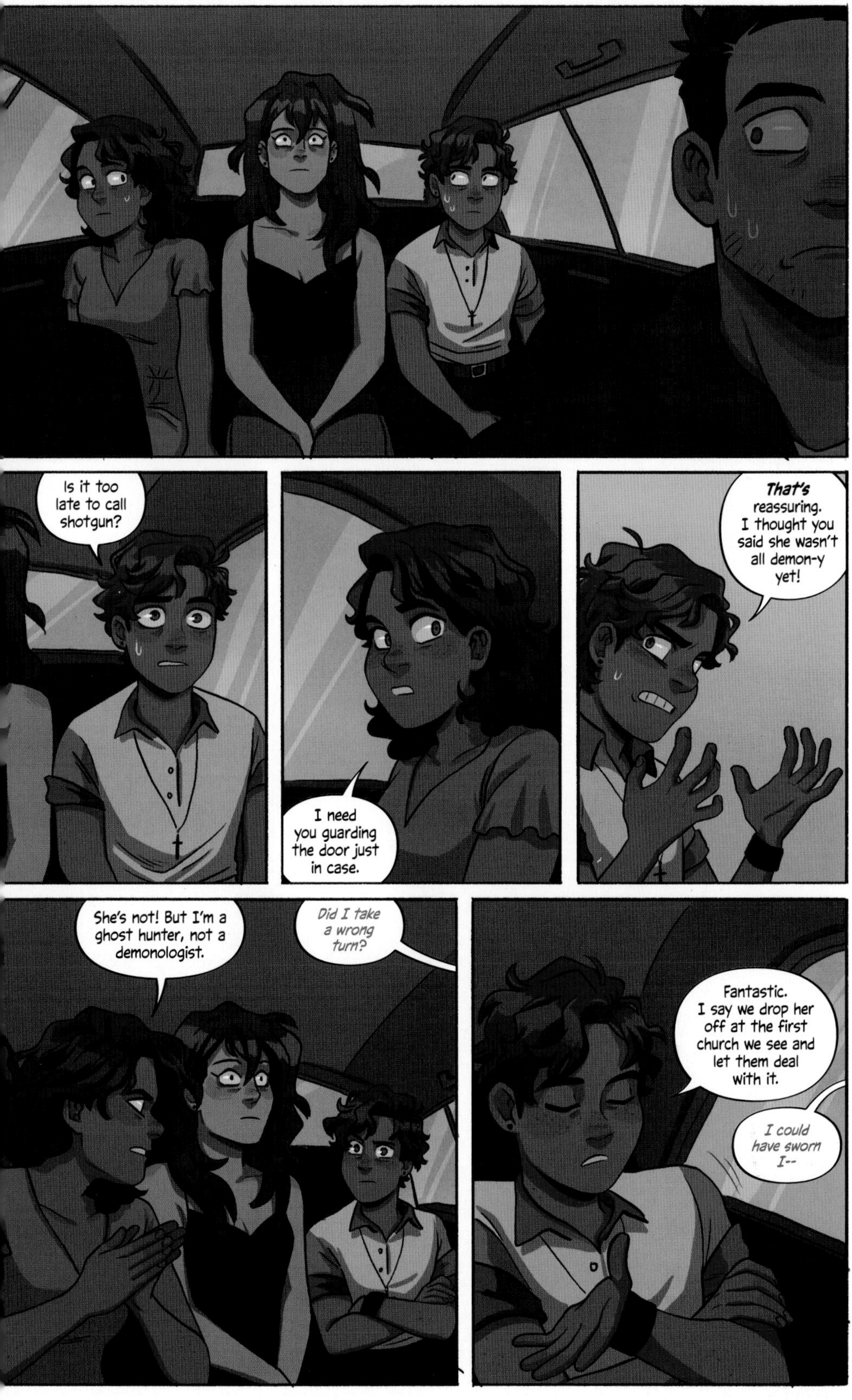
Is it too late to call shotgun?
I need you guarding the door just in case.
That's reassuring. I thought you said she wasn't all demon-y yet!
She's not! But I'm a ghost hunter, not a demonologist.
Did I take a wrong turn?
Fantastic. I say we drop her off at the first church we see and let them deal with it.
I could have sworn I--

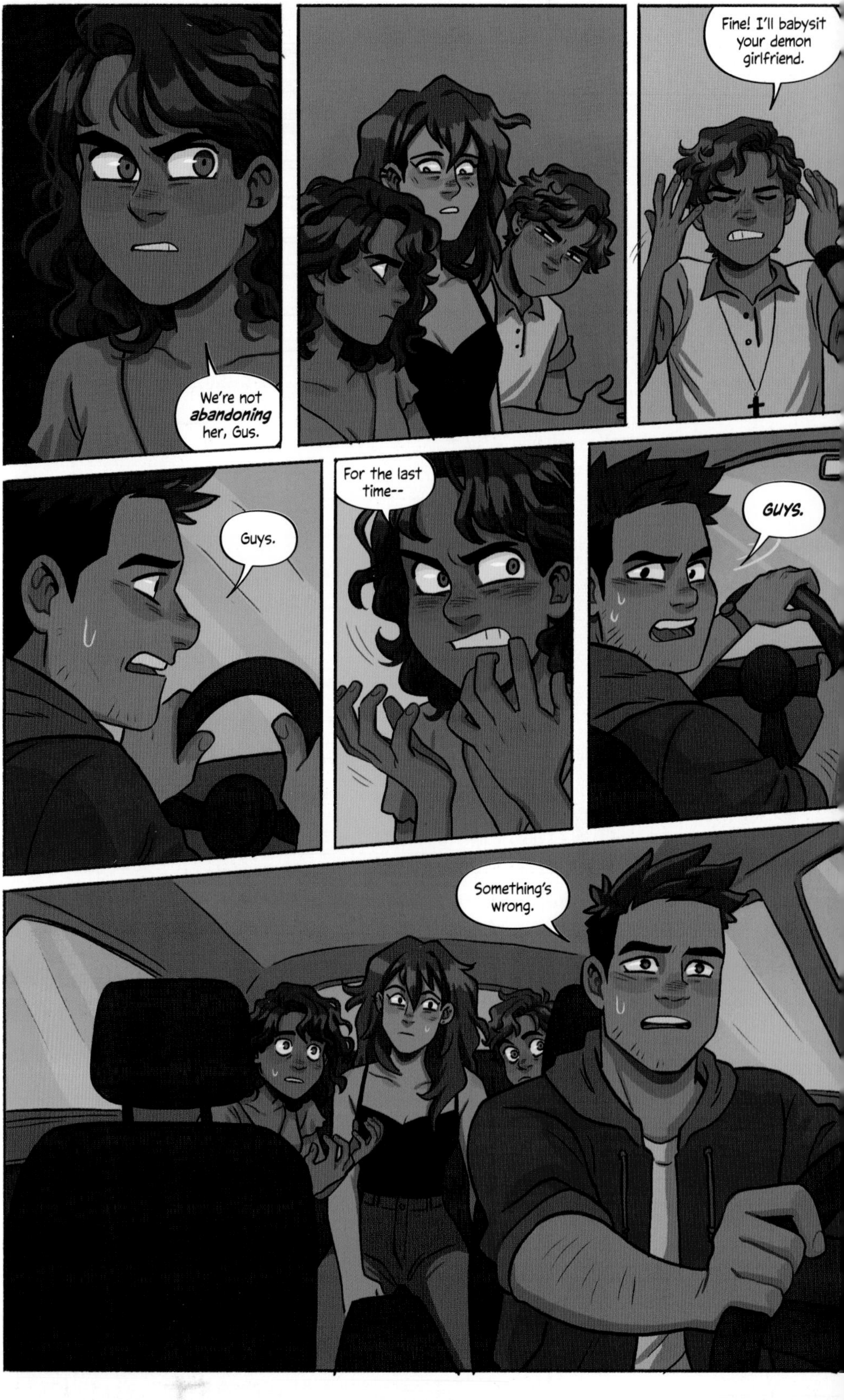
We're not *abandoning* her, Gus.
Fine! I'll babysit your demon girlfriend.
Guys.
For the last time--
GUYS.
Something's wrong.

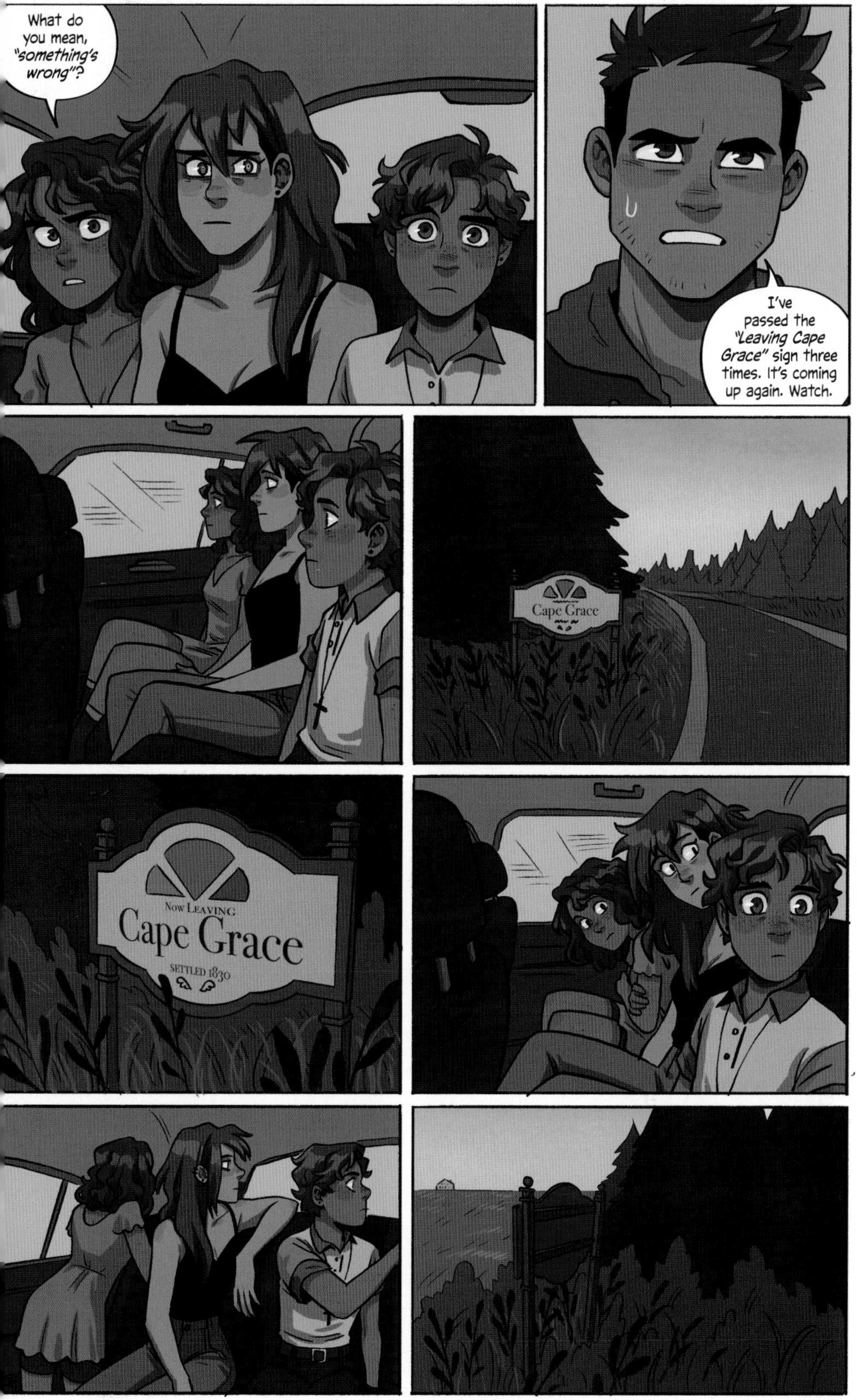

What do you mean, *"something's wrong"*?
I've passed the *"Leaving Cape Grace"* sign three times. It's coming up again. Watch.
Cape Grace
Now Leaving
Cape Grace
Settled 1830

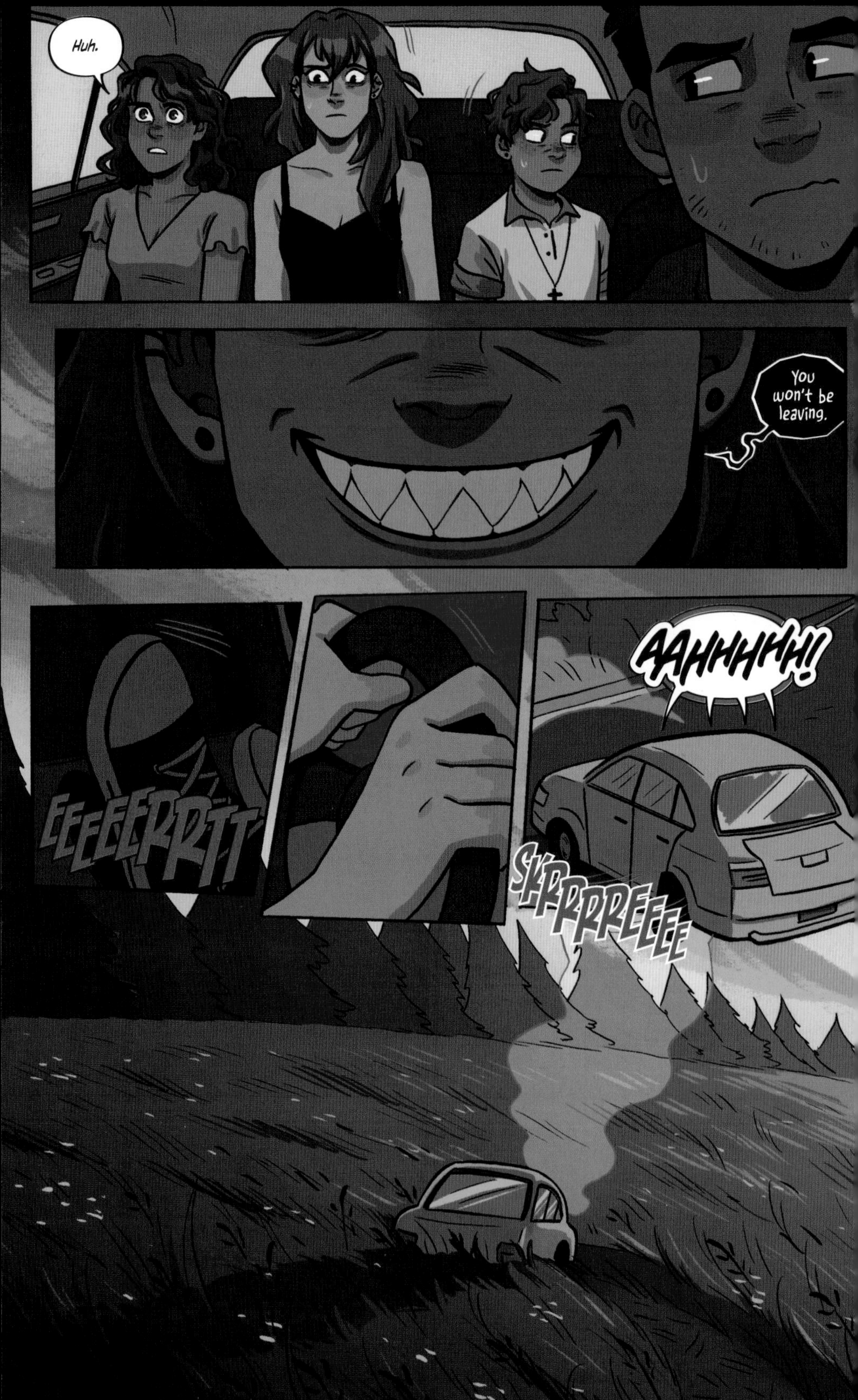
Huh.
You won't be leaving.
EEEEERRTT
AAHHHHH!
SKRRRREEEE

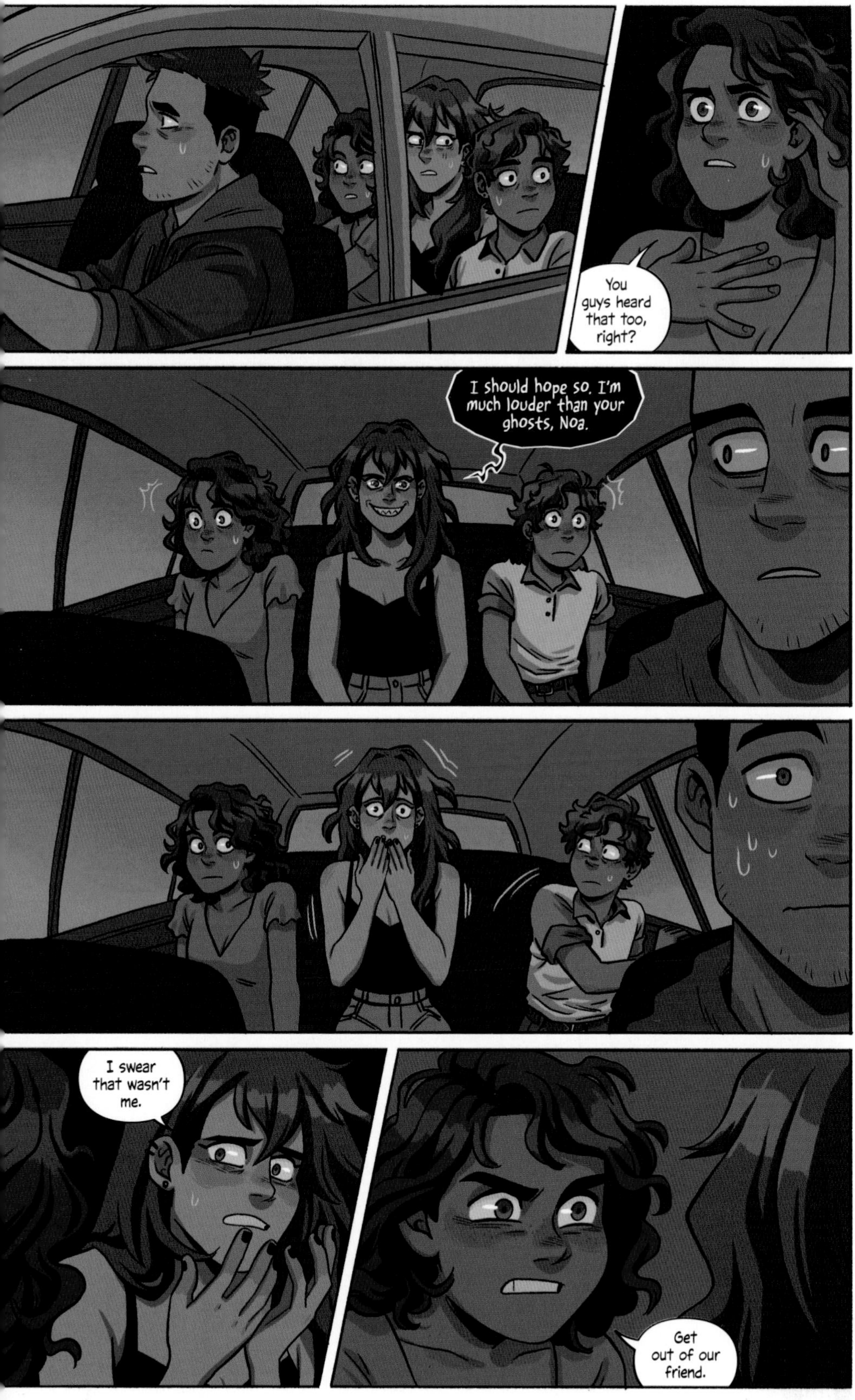
You guys heard that too, right?
I should hope so. I'm much louder than your ghosts, Noa.
I swear that wasn't me.
Get out of our friend.

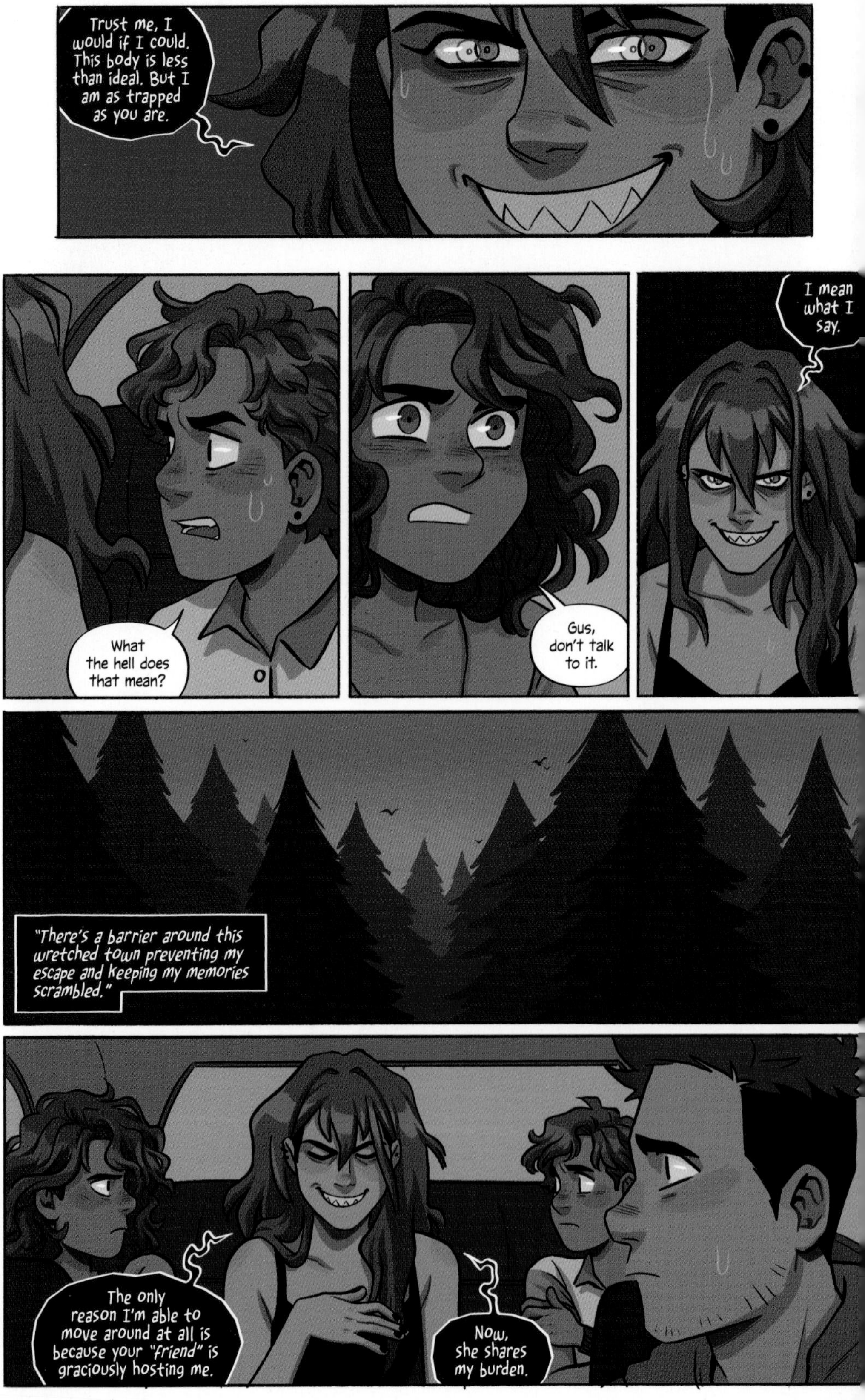
Trust me, I would if I could. This body is less than ideal. But I am as trapped as you are.
What the hell does that mean?
Gus, don't talk to it.
I mean what I say.
"There's a barrier around this wretched town preventing my escape and keeping my memories scrambled."
The only reason I'm able to move around at all is because your "friend" is graciously hosting me.
Now, she shares my burden.

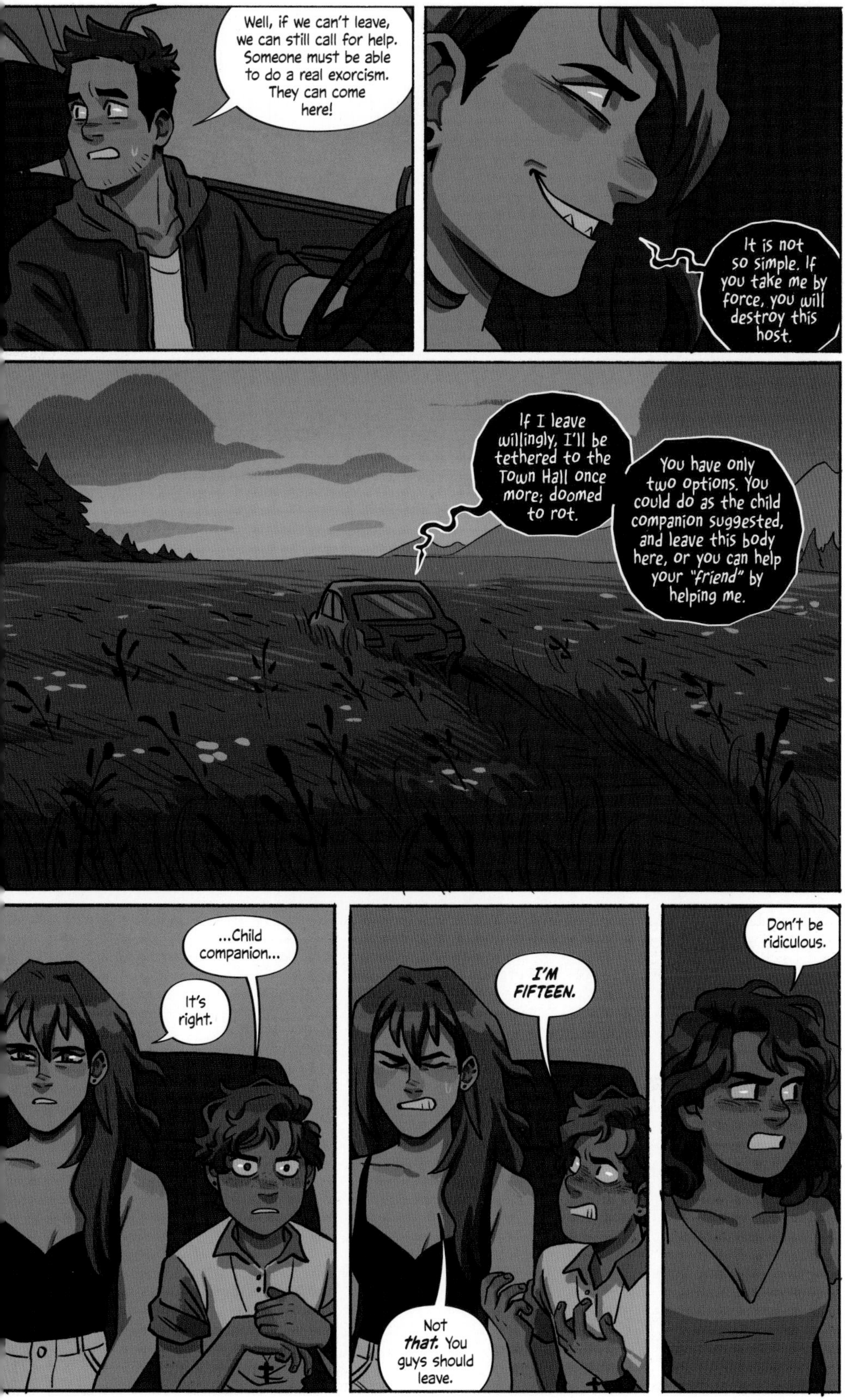
Well, if we can't leave, we can still call for help. Someone must be able to do a real exorcism. They can come here!
It is not so simple. If you take me by force, you will destroy this host.
If I leave willingly, I'll be tethered to the Town Hall once more; doomed to rot.
You have only two options. You could do as the child companion suggested, and leave this body here, or you can help your "friend" by helping me.
...Child companion...
It's right.
I'M FIFTEEN.
Not that. You guys should leave.
Don't be ridiculous.

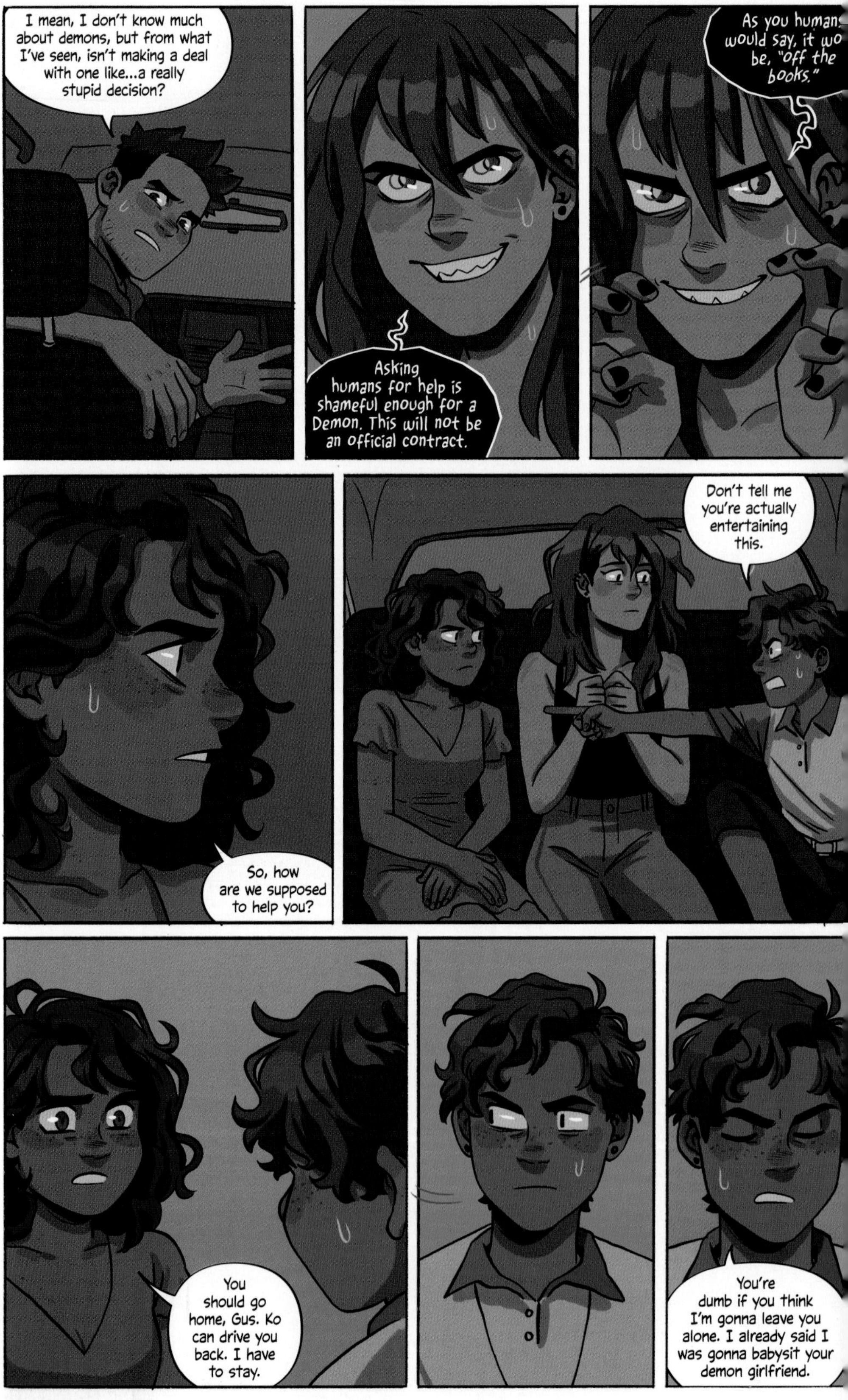
I mean, I don't know much about demons, but from what I've seen, isn't making a deal with one like...a really stupid decision?
Asking humans for help is shameful enough for a Demon. This will not be an official contract.
As you humans would say, it wo be, "off the books."
So, how are we supposed to help you?
Don't tell me you're actually entertaining this.
You should go home, Gus. Ko can drive you back. I have to stay.
You're dumb if you think I'm gonna leave you alone. I already said I was gonna babysit your demon girlfriend.

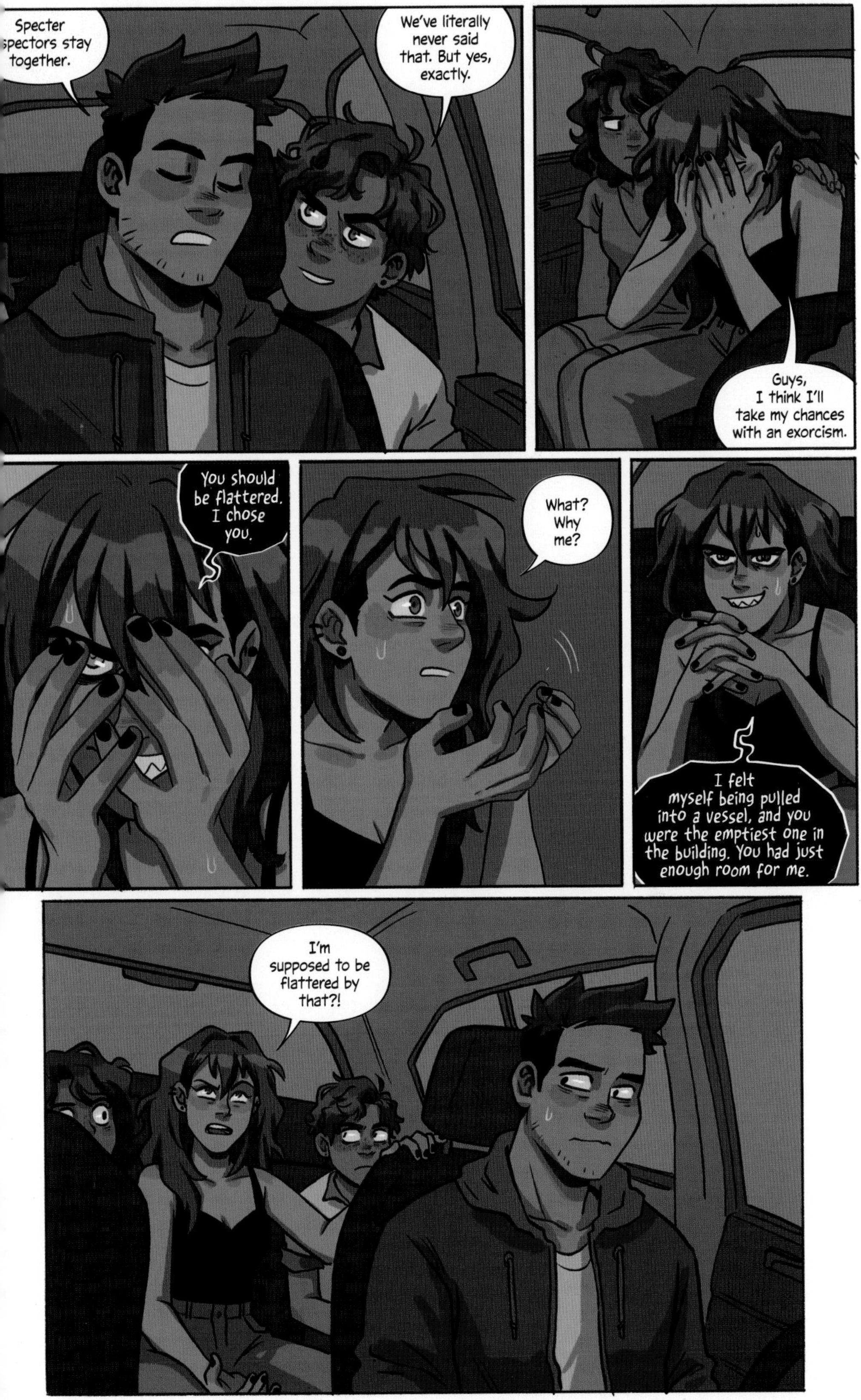

Specter spectors stay together.
We've literally never said that. But yes, exactly.
Guys, I think I'll take my chances with an exorcism.
You should be flattered. I chose you.
What? Why me?
I felt myself being pulled into a vessel, and you were the emptiest one in the building. You had just enough room for me.
I'm supposed to be flattered by that?!

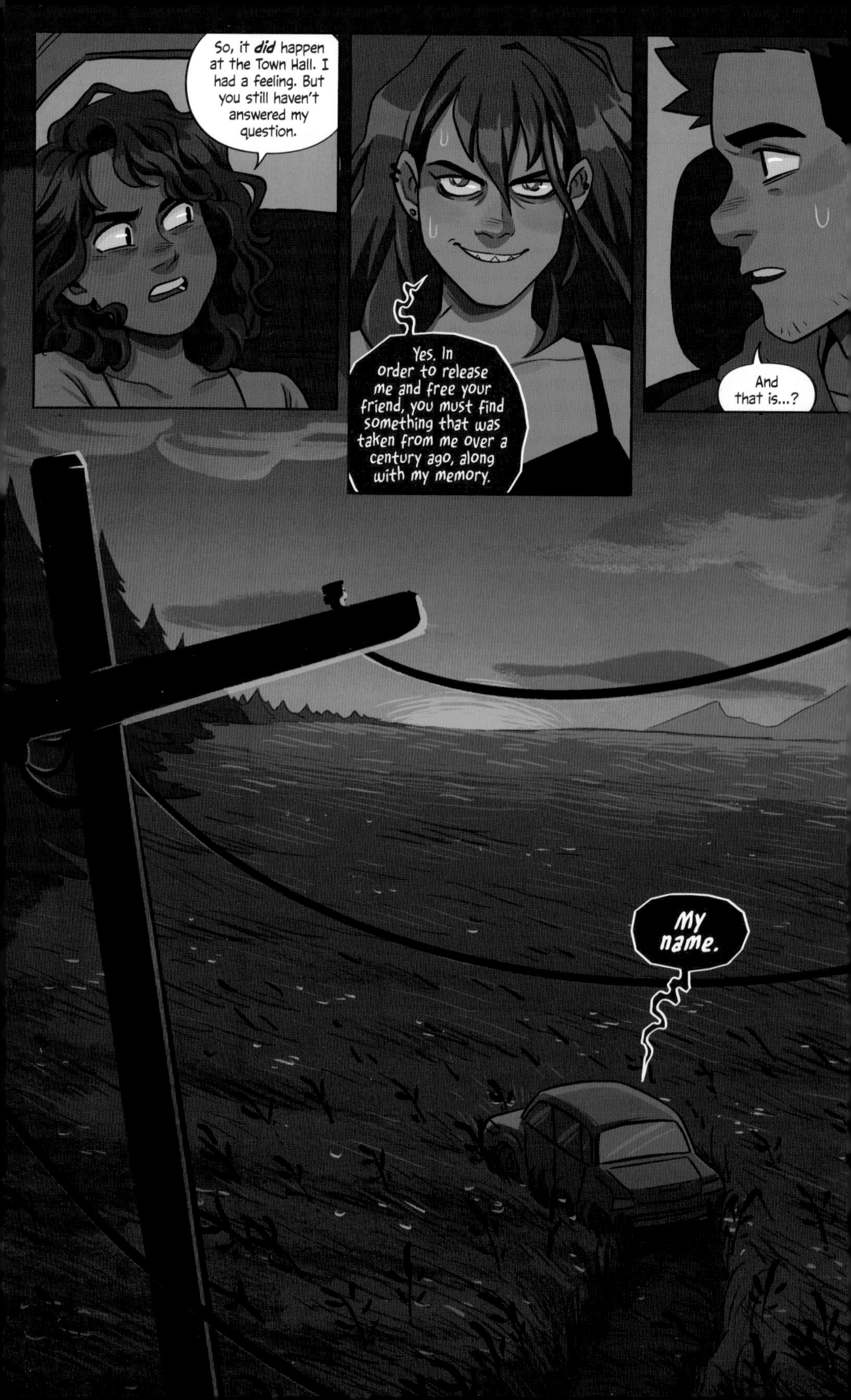
So, it did happen at the Town Hall. I had a feeling. But you still haven't answered my question.
Yes. In order to release me and free your friend, you must find something that was taken from me over a century ago, along with my memory.
And that is...?
My name.

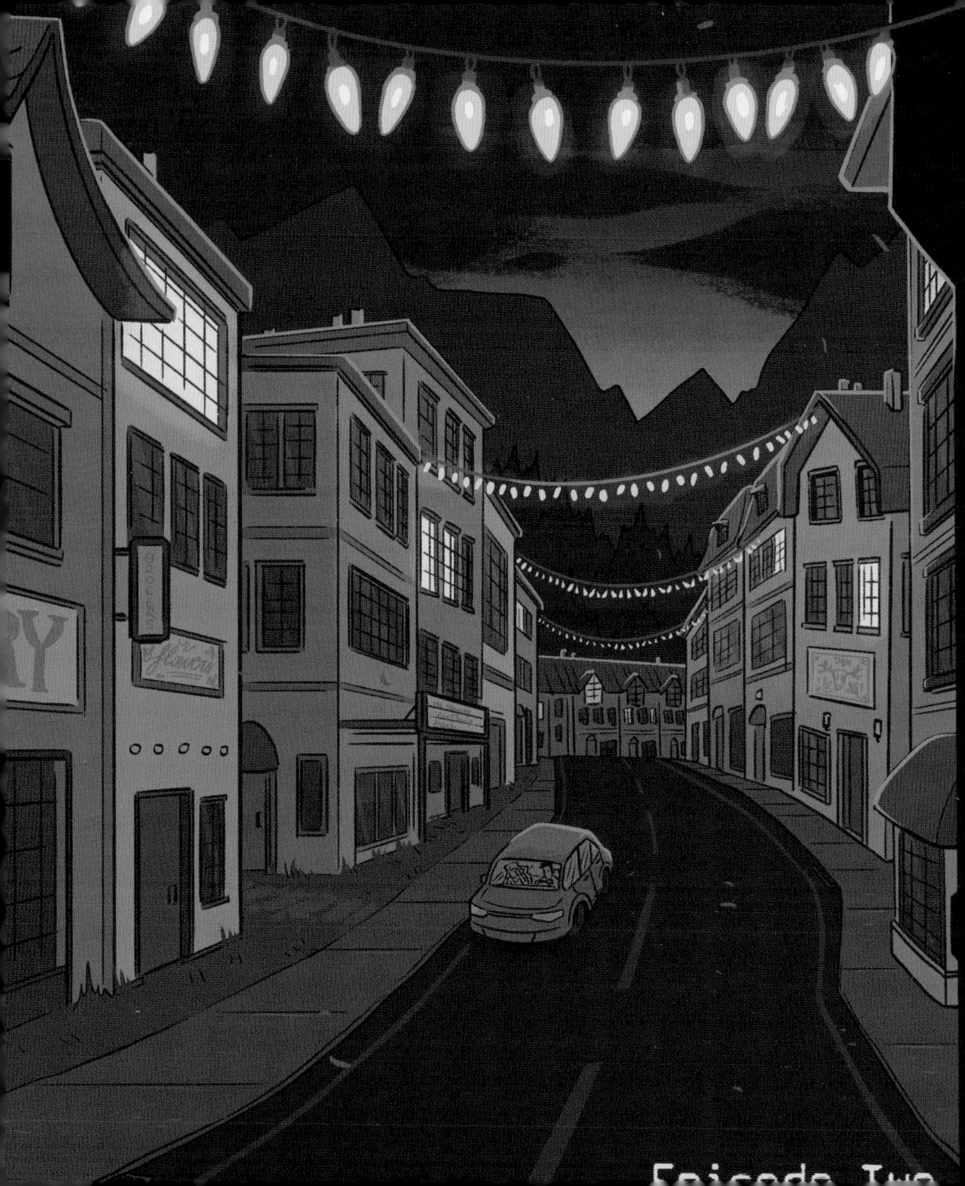

Episode Two

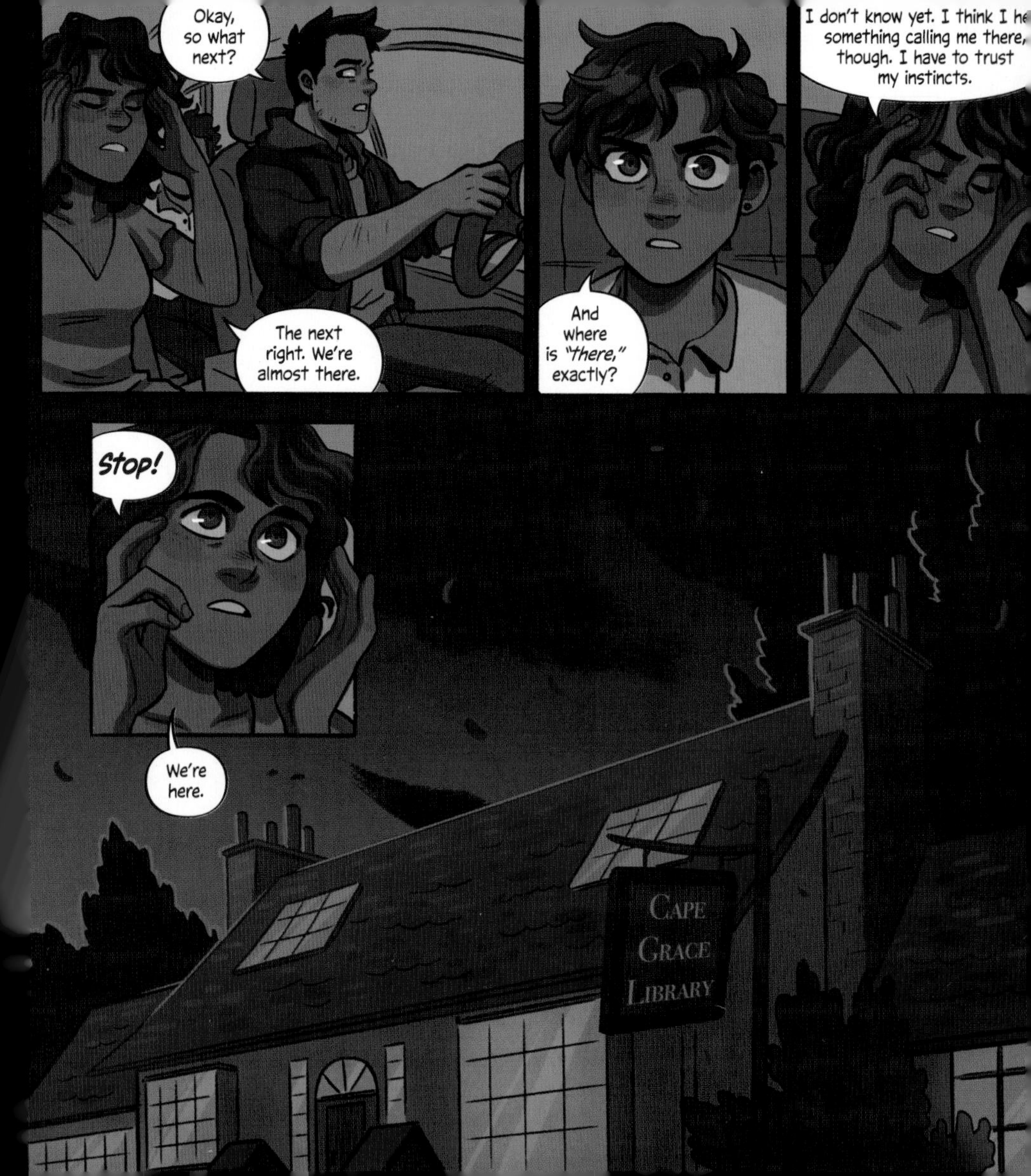
Okay, so what next?
The next right. We're almost there.
And where is "there," exactly?
I don't know yet. I think I he something calling me there, though. I have to trust my instincts.
Stop!
We're here.
CAPE GRACE LIBRARY

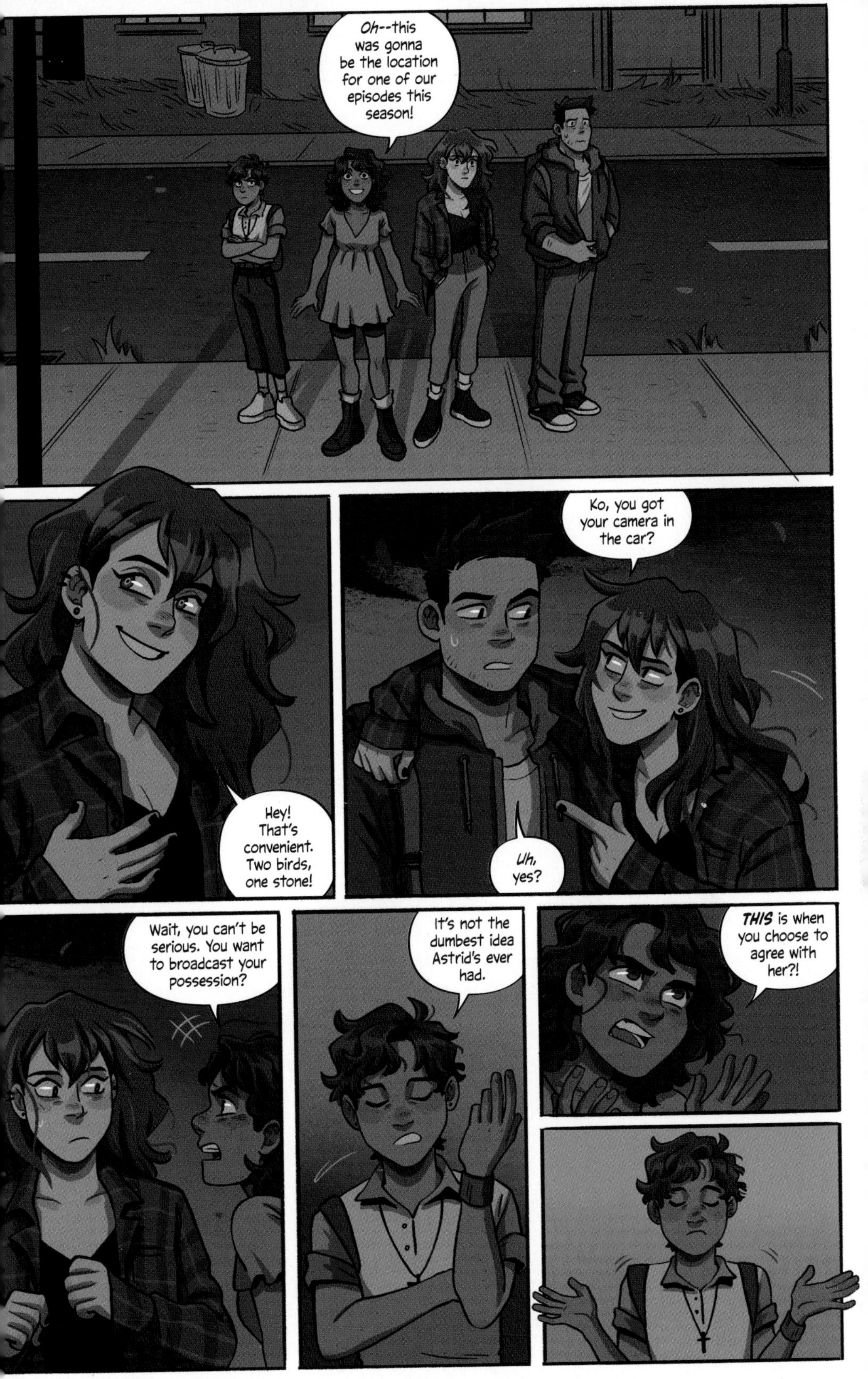

Oh--this was gonna be the location for one of our episodes this season!
Hey! That's convenient. Two birds, one stone!
Ko, you got your camera in the car?
Uh, yes?
Wait, you can't be serious. You want to broadcast your possession?
It's not the dumbest idea Astrid's ever had.
THIS is when you choose to agree with her?!

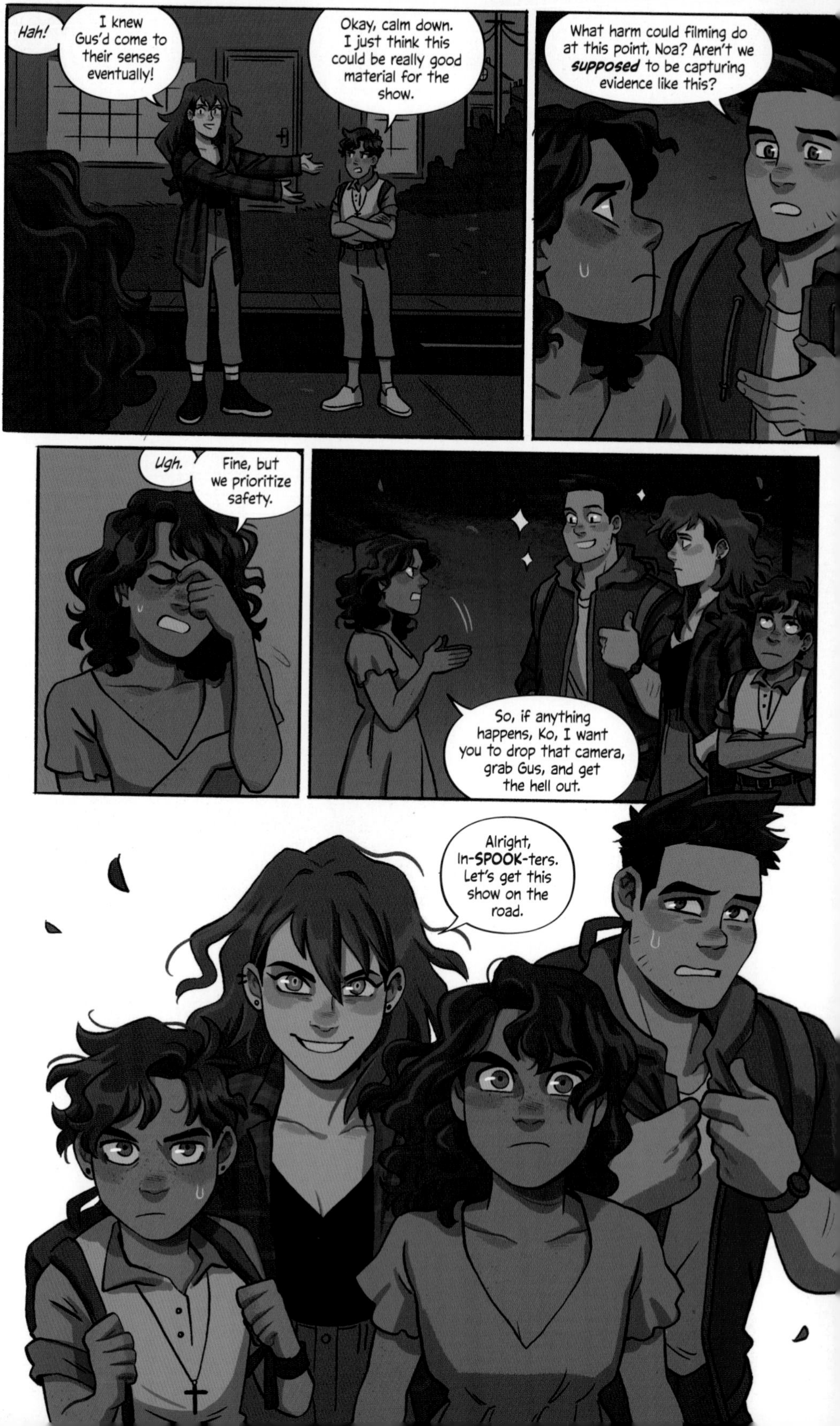
Hah!
I knew Gus'd come to their senses eventually!
Okay, calm down. I just think this could be really good material for the show.
What harm could filming do at this point, Noa? Aren't we **supposed** to be capturing evidence like this?
Ugh.
Fine, but we prioritize safety.
So, if anything happens, Ko, I want you to drop that camera, grab Gus, and get the hell out.
Alright, In-**SPOOK**-ters. Let's get this show on the road.

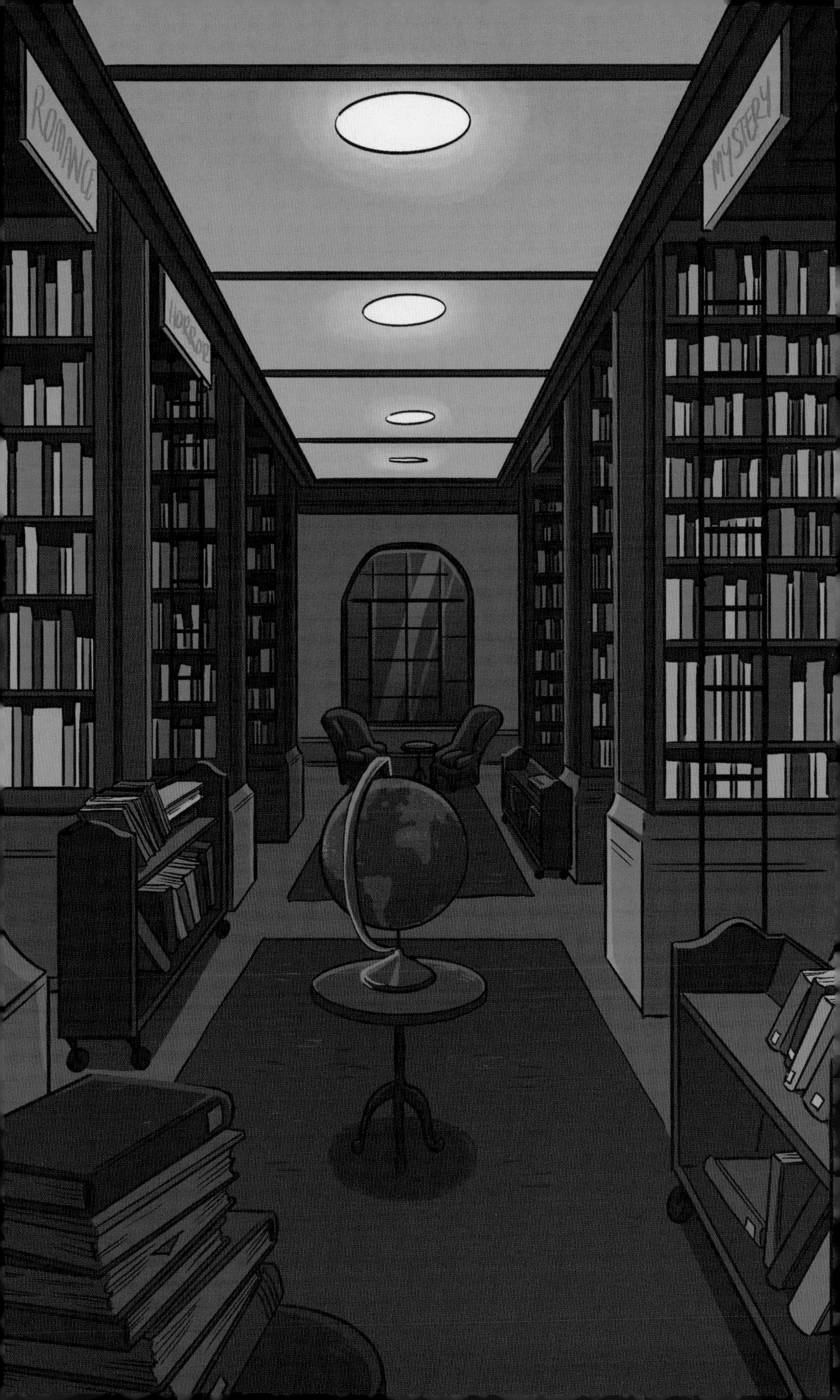
ROMANCE
HORROR
MYSTERY

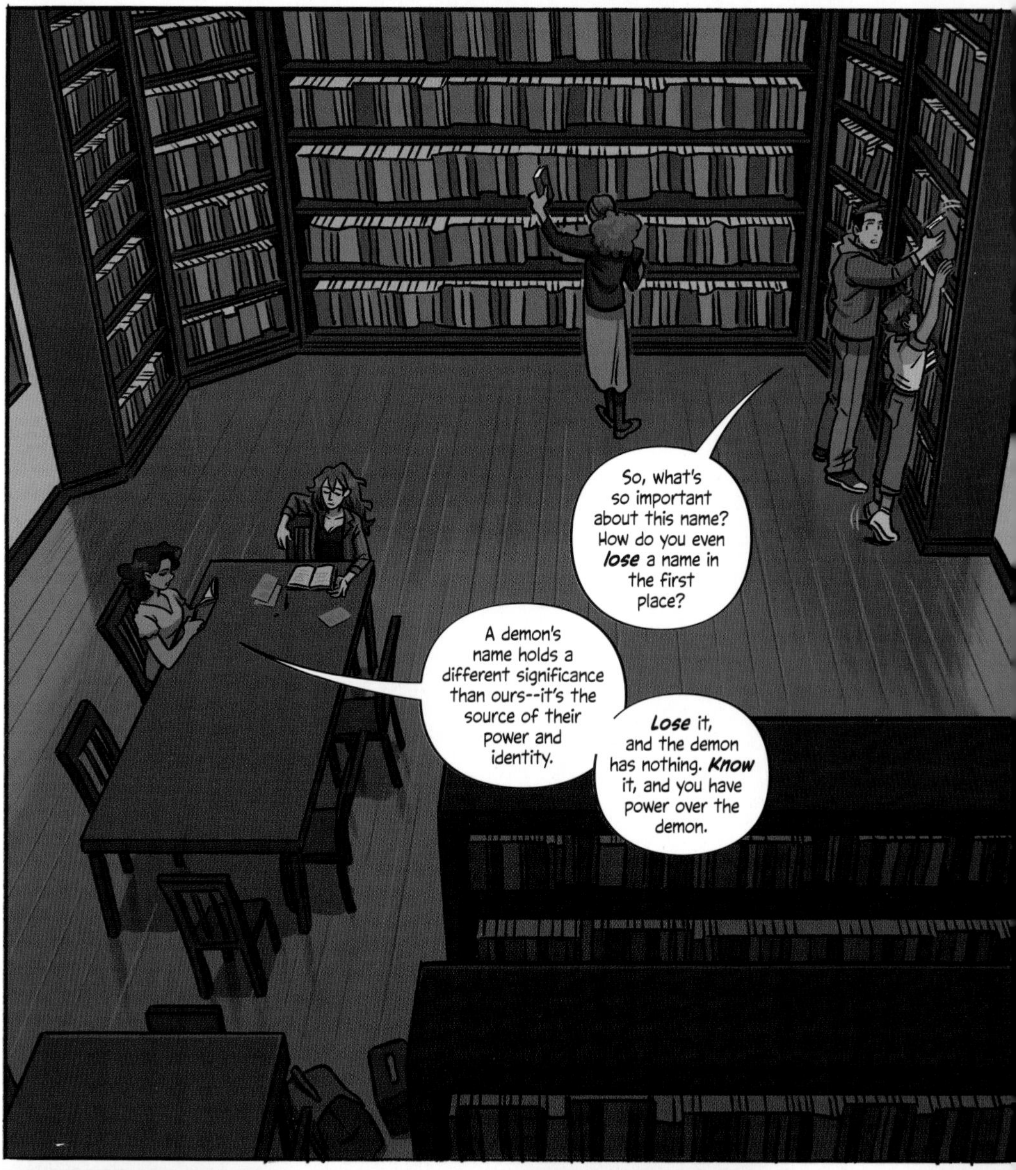
So, what's so important about this name? How do you even *lose* a name in the first place?
A demon's name holds a different significance than ours--it's the source of their power and identity.
Lose it, and the demon has nothing. *Know* it, and you have power over the demon.

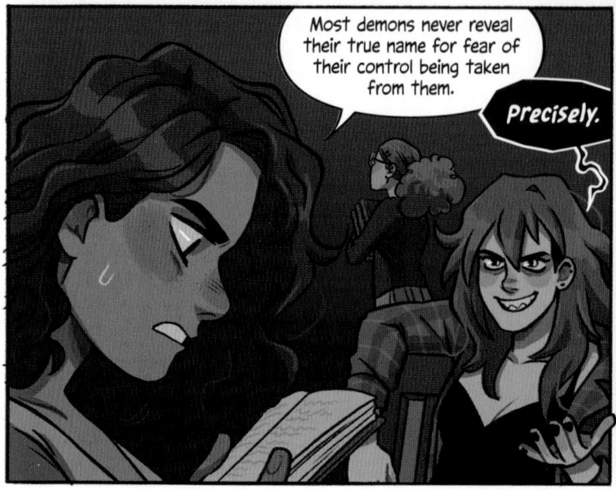
Most demons never reveal their true name for fear of their control being taken from them.
Precisely.

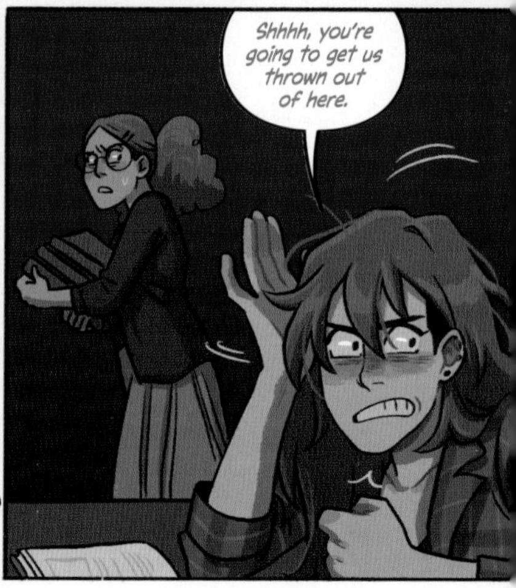
Shhhh, you're going to get us thrown out of here.

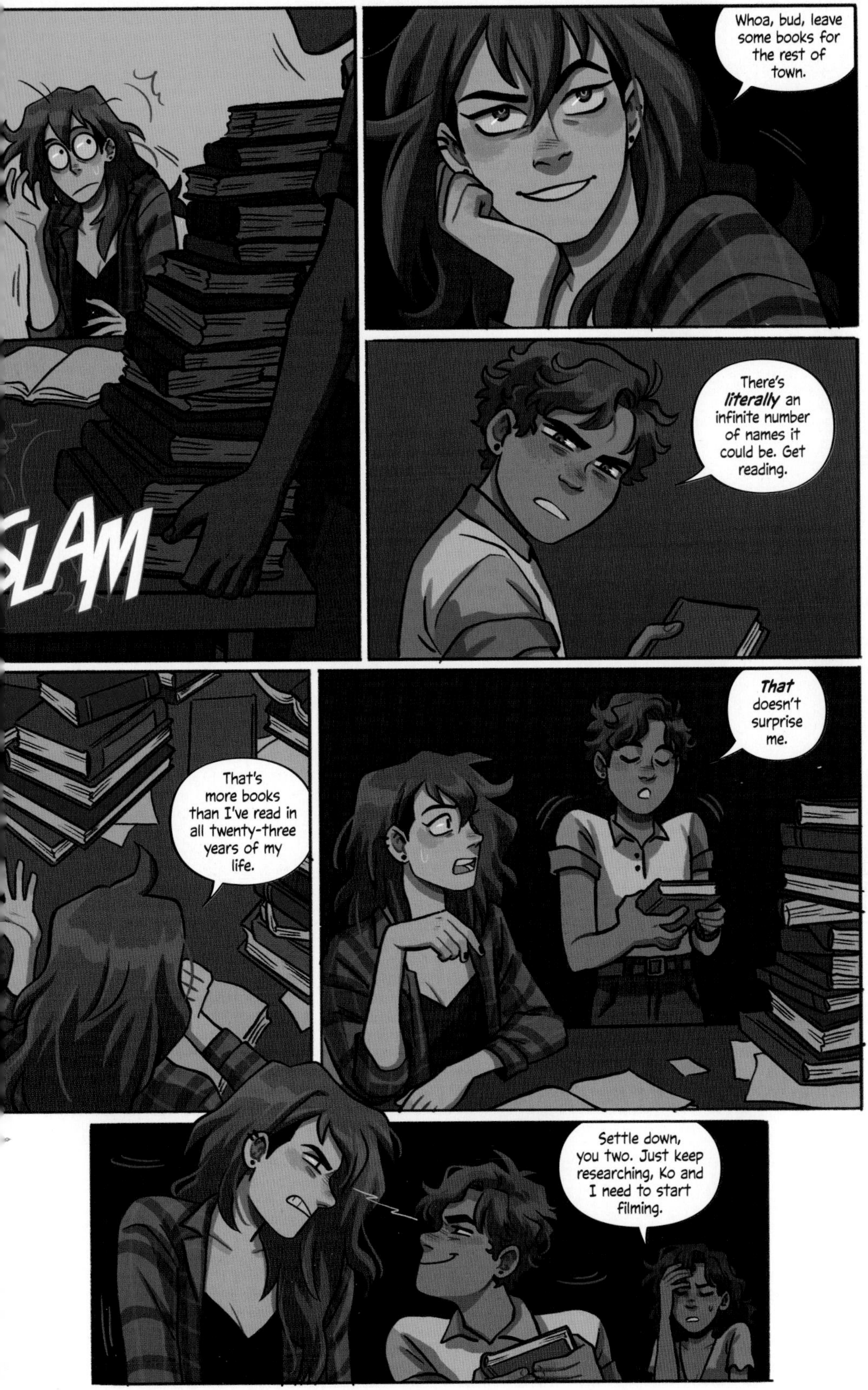

SLAM
Whoa, bud, leave some books for the rest of town.
There's *literally* an infinite number of names it could be. Get reading.
That's more books than I've read in all twenty-three years of my life.
That doesn't surprise me.
Settle down, you two. Just keep researching, Ko and I need to start filming.

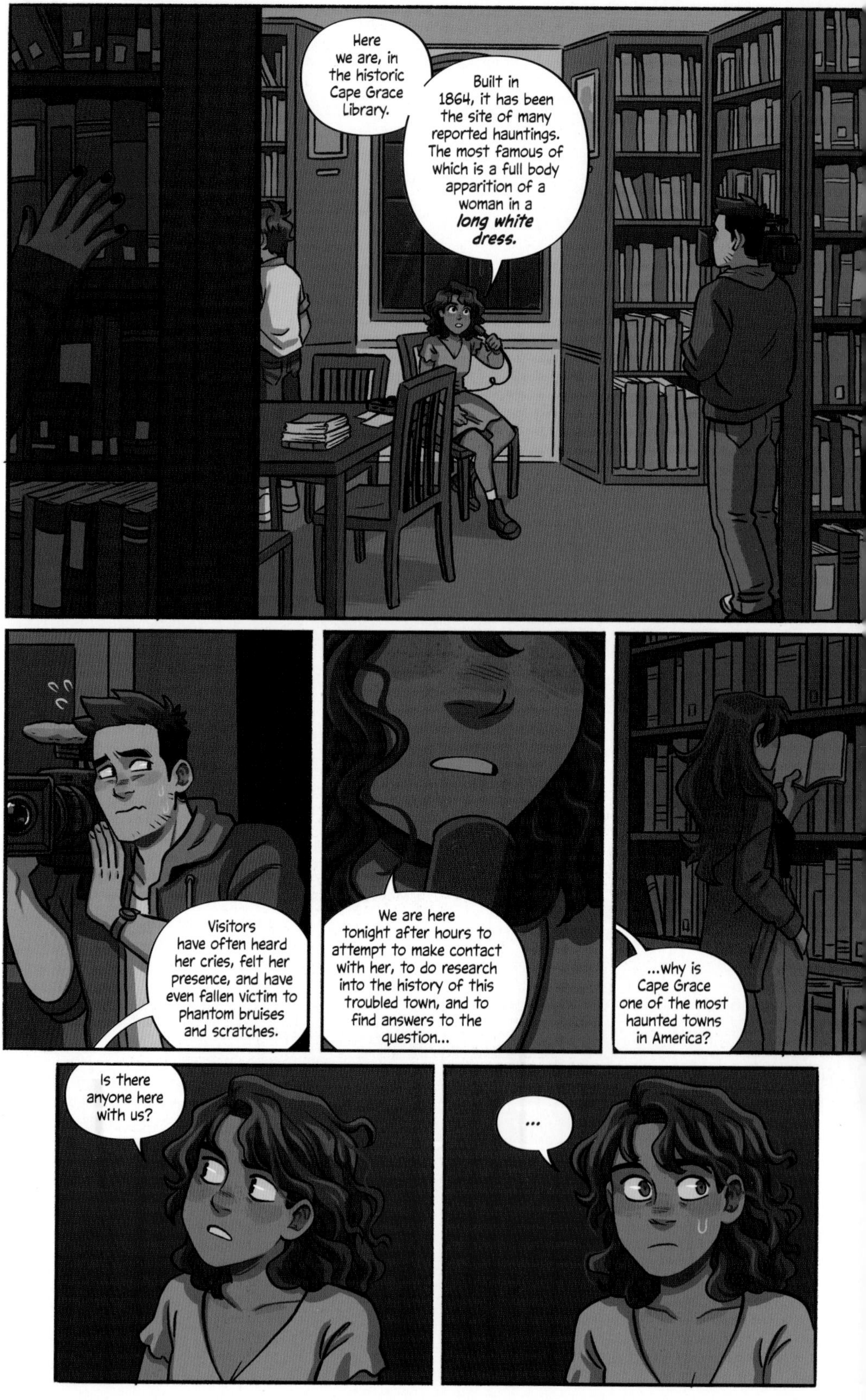
Here we are, in the historic Cape Grace Library.
Built in 1864, it has been the site of many reported hauntings. The most famous of which is a full body apparition of a woman in a ***long white dress.***
Visitors have often heard her cries, felt her presence, and have even fallen victim to phantom bruises and scratches.
We are here tonight after hours to attempt to make contact with her, to do research into the history of this troubled town, and to find answers to the question...
...why is Cape Grace one of the most haunted towns in America?
Is there anyone here with us?
...

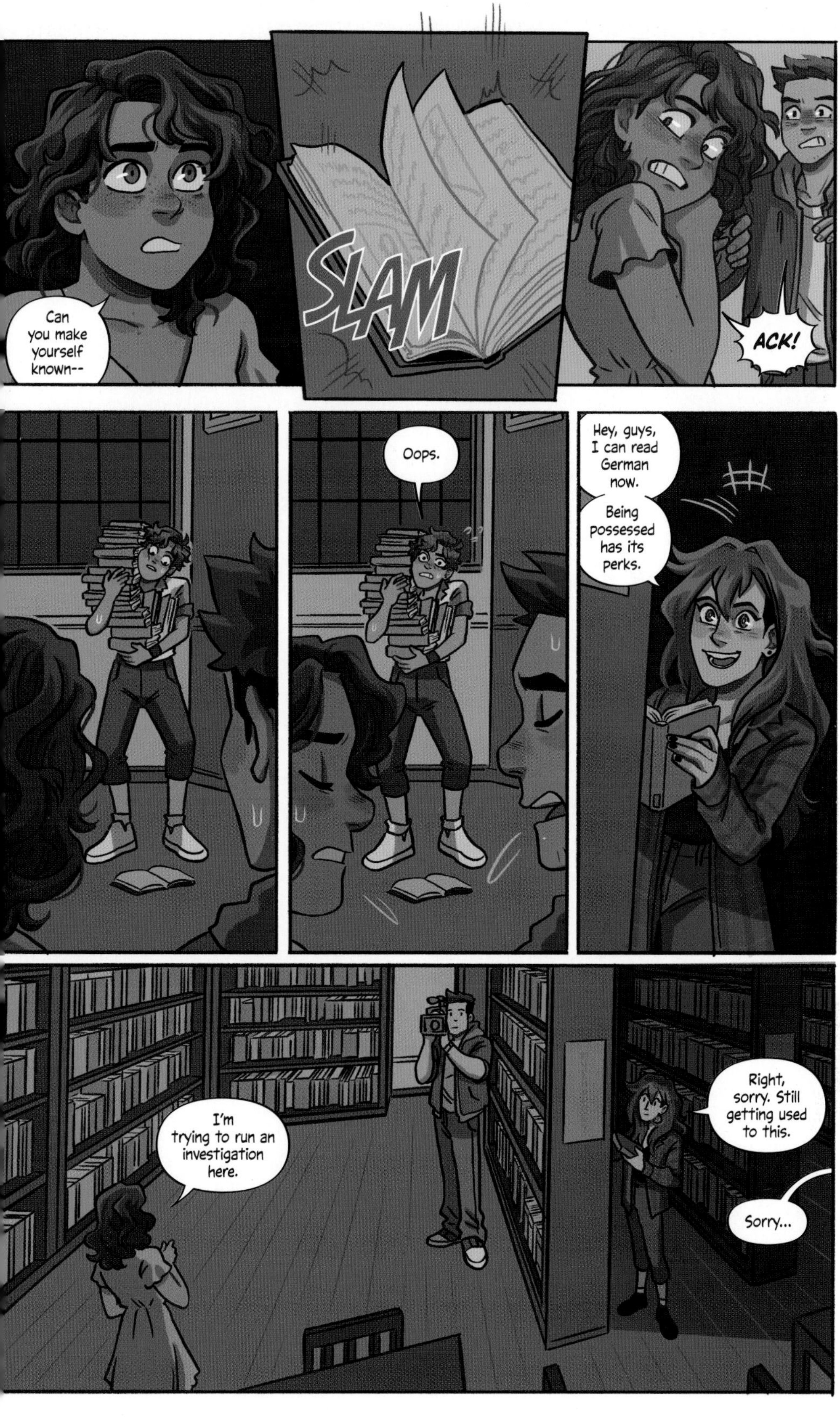
Can you make yourself known--
SLAM
ACK!
Oops.
Hey, guys, I can read German now.
Being possessed has its perks.
I'm trying to run an investigation here.
Right, sorry. Still getting used to this.
Sorry...

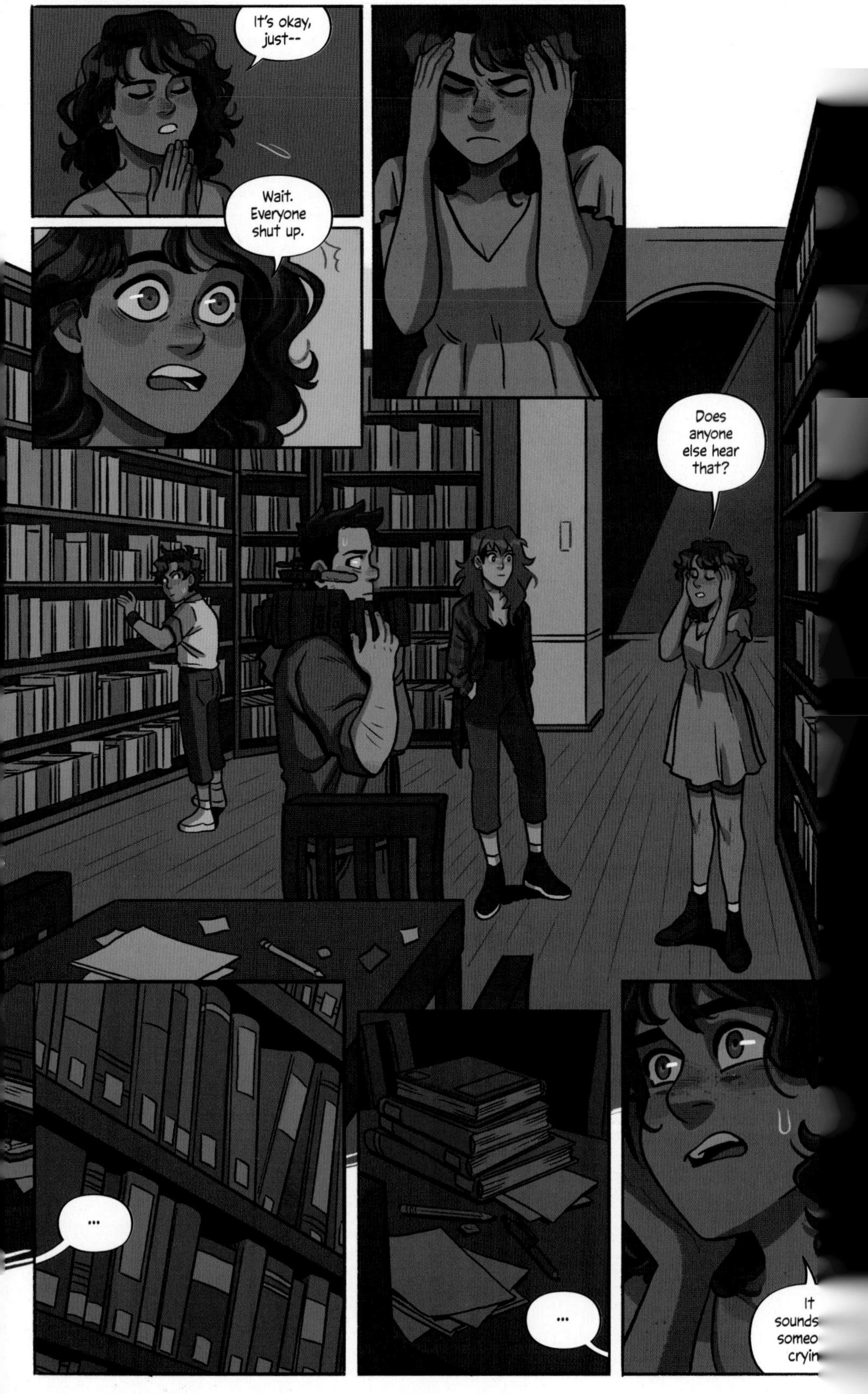
It's okay, just--
Wait. Everyone shut up.
Does anyone else hear that?
...
...
It sounds someo cryin

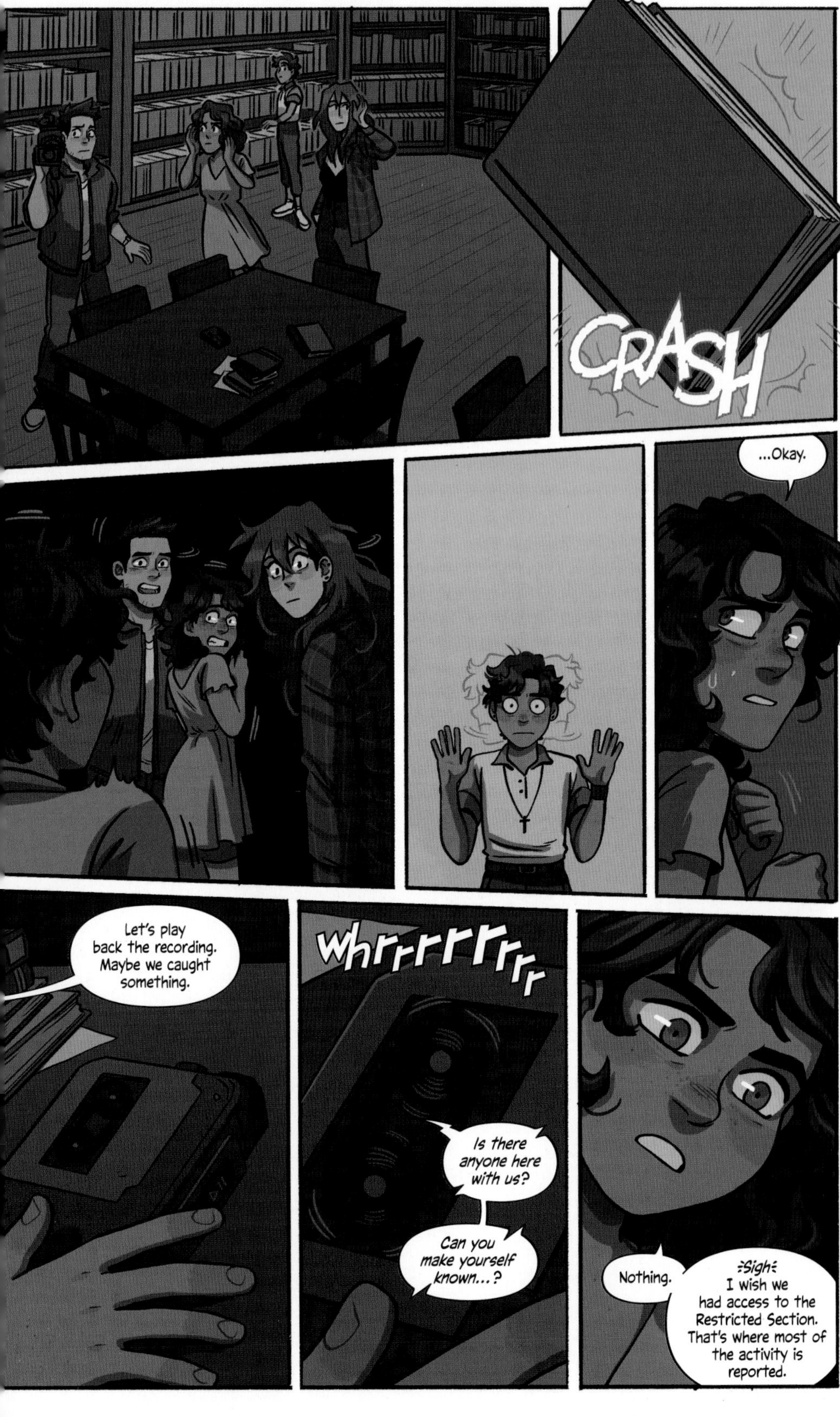
CRASH
...Okay.
Let's play back the recording. Maybe we caught something.
Whrrrrrrrr
Is there anyone here with us?
Can you make yourself known...?
Nothing.
Sigh
I wish we had access to the Restricted Section. That's where most of the activity is reported.

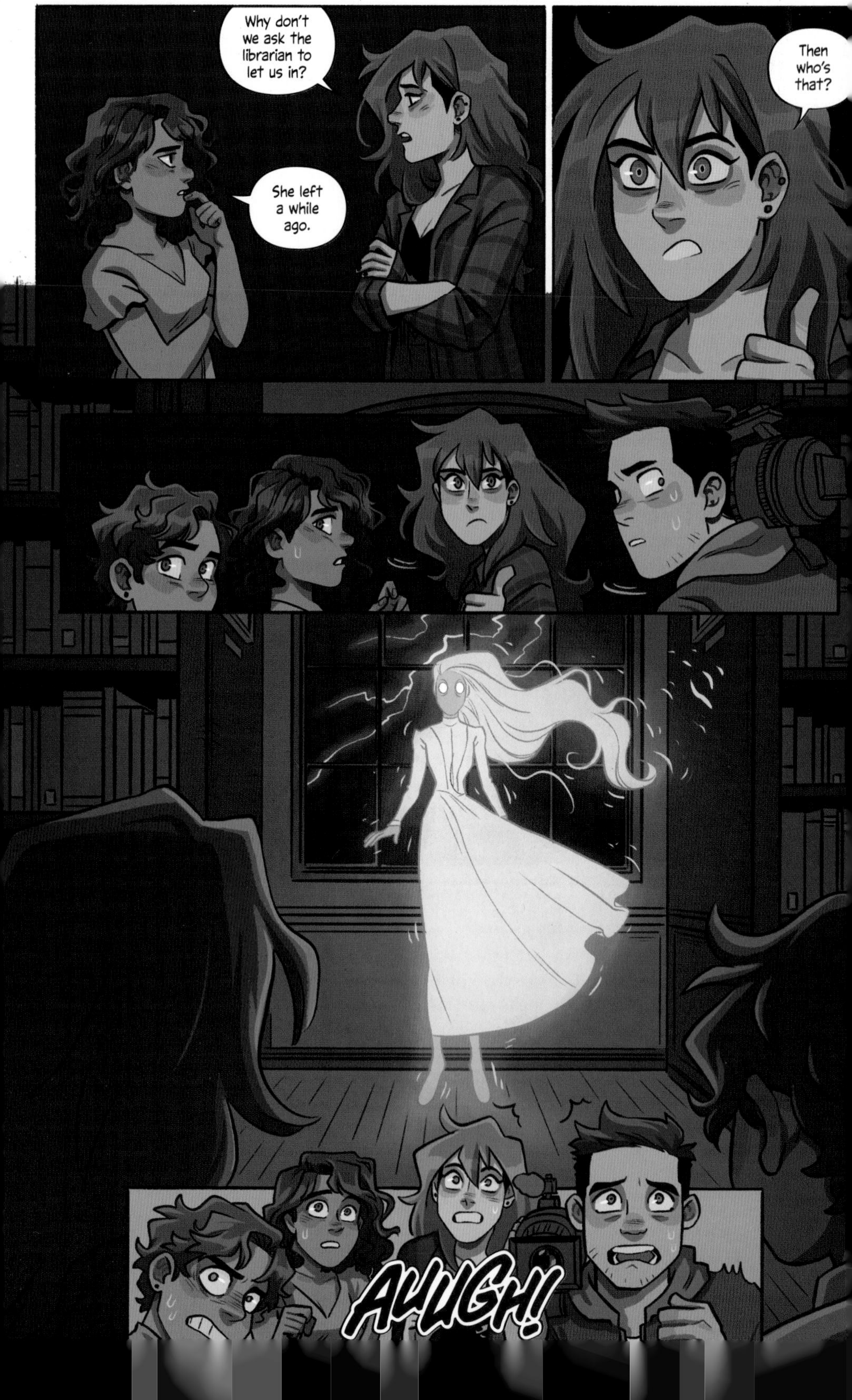

Why don't we ask the librarian to let us in?
She left a while ago.
Then who's that?
AUUGH!

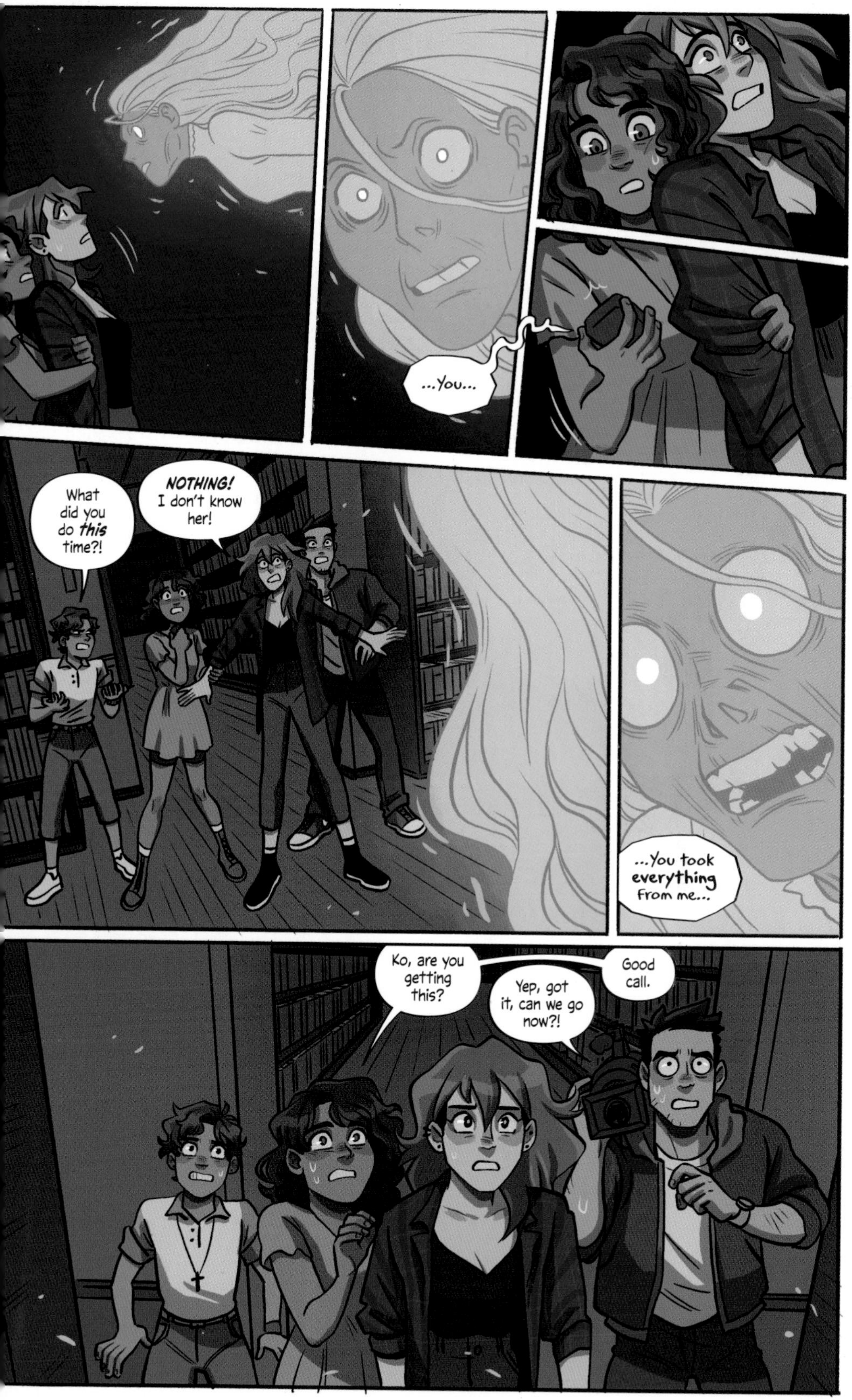
...You...
What did you do *this* time?!
NOTHING! I don't know her!
...You took **everything** from me...
Ko, are you getting this?
Yep, got it, can we go now?!
Good call.

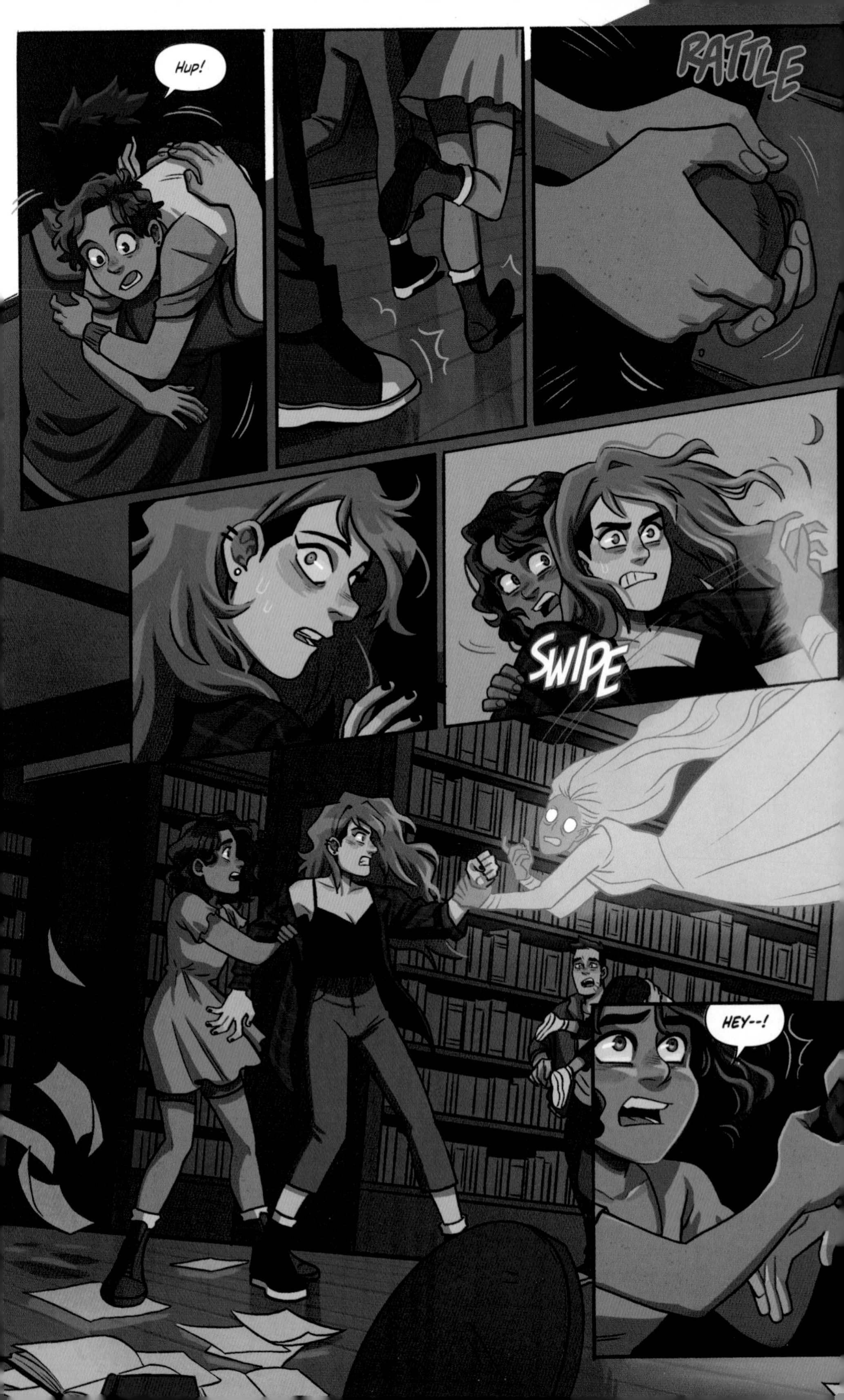
Hup!
RATTLE
SWIPE
HEY--!

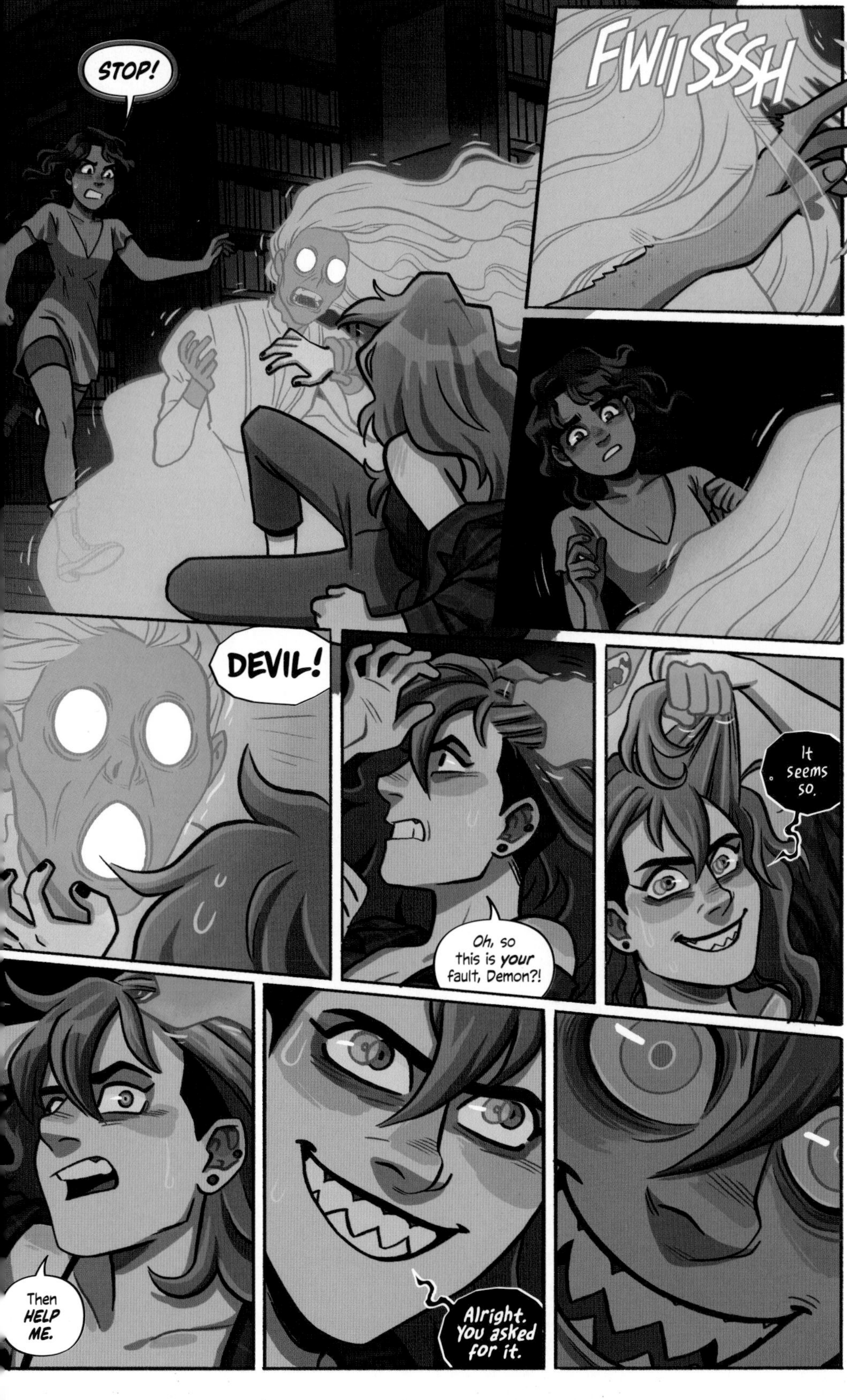
STOP!
FWIISSSH
DEVIL!
Oh, so this is *your* fault, Demon?!
It seems so.
Then **HELP ME.**
Alright. You asked for it.

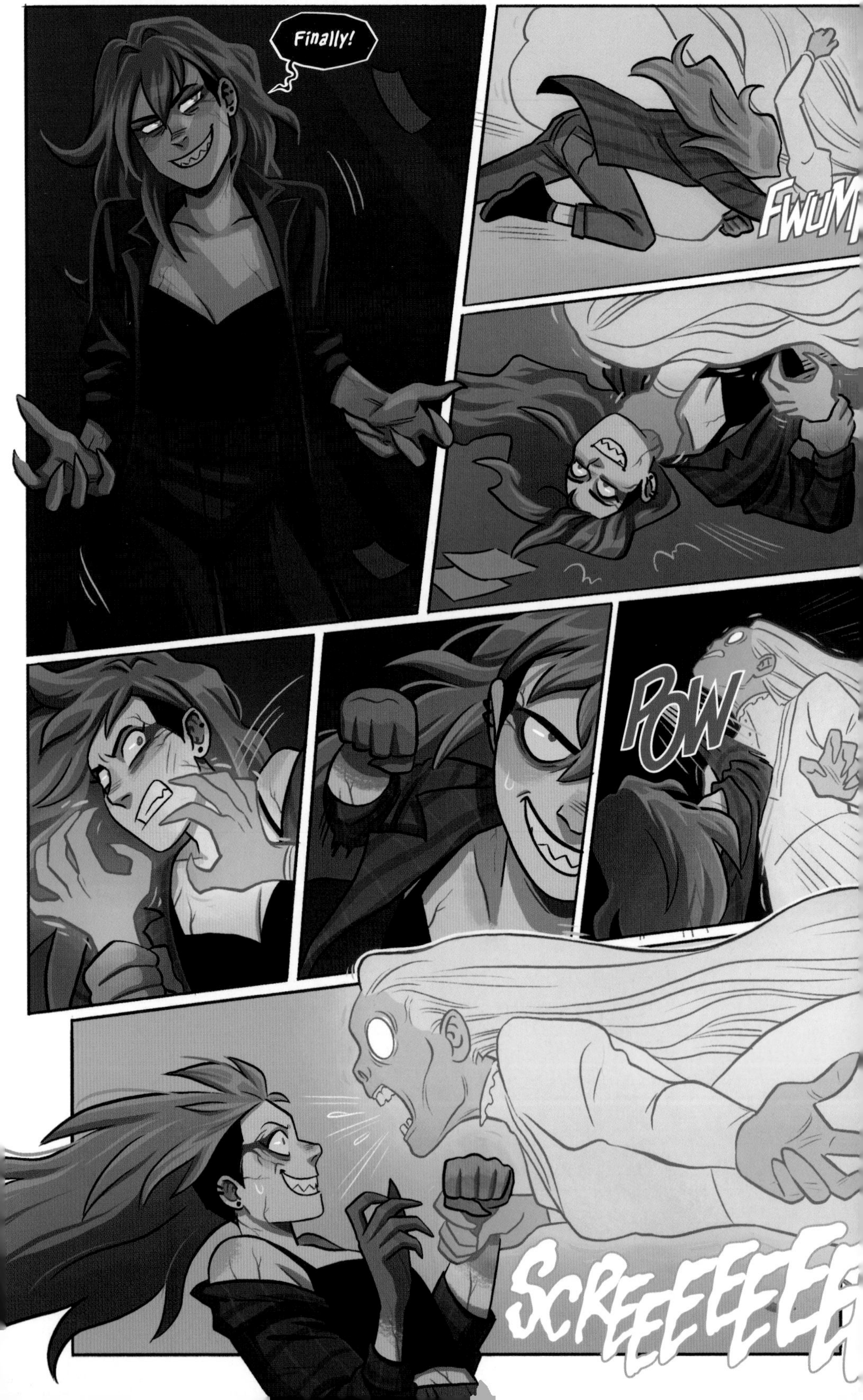
Finally!
FWUMP
POW
SCREEEEEEEE

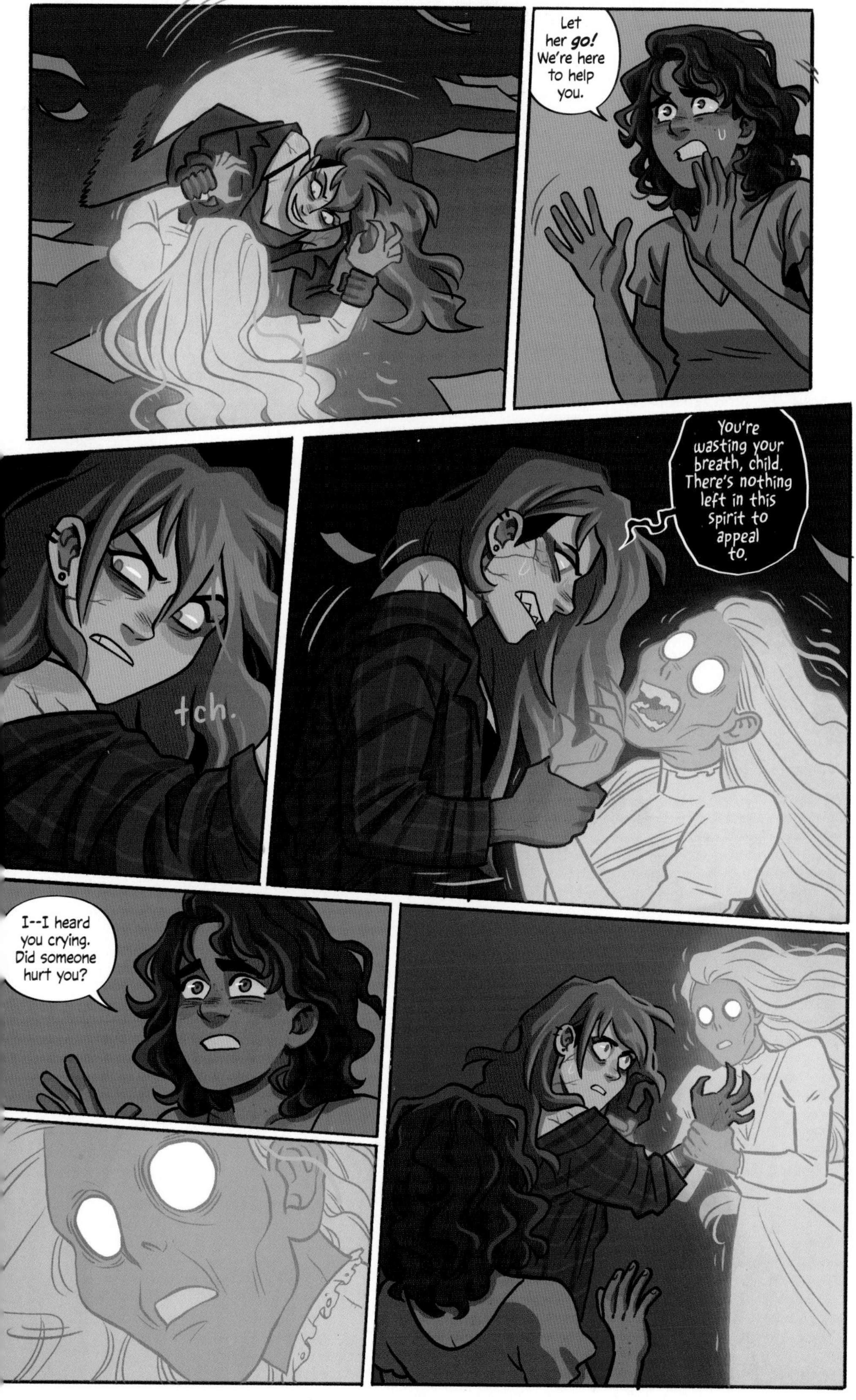
Let her go! We're here to help you.
tch.
You're wasting your breath, child. There's nothing left in this spirit to appeal to.
I--I heard you crying. Did someone hurt you?

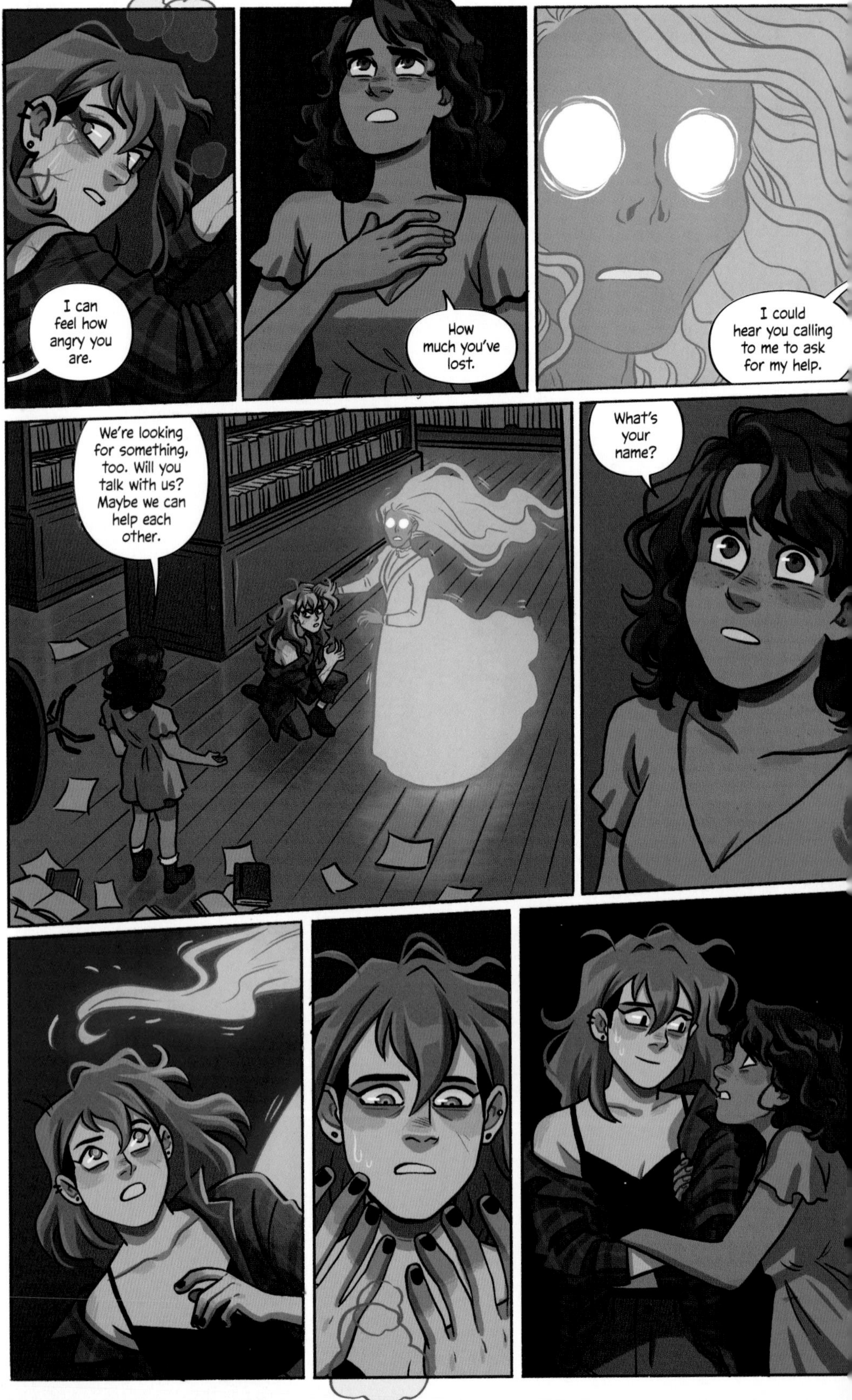
I can feel how angry you are.
How much you've lost.
I could hear you calling to me to ask for my help.
We're looking for something, too. Will you talk with us? Maybe we can help each other.
What's your name?

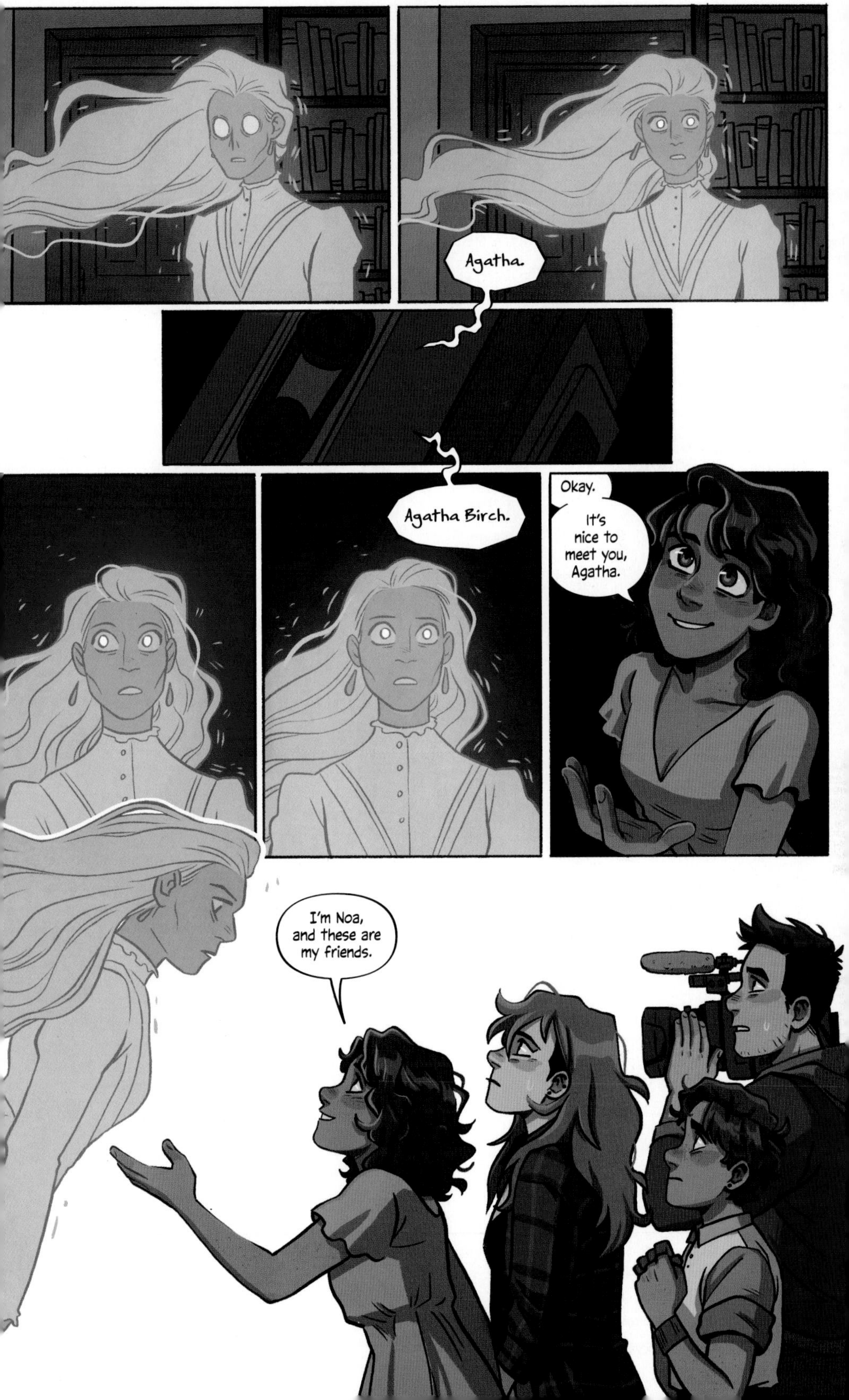
Agatha.
Agatha Birch.
Okay.
It's nice to meet you, Agatha.
I'm Noa, and these are my friends.

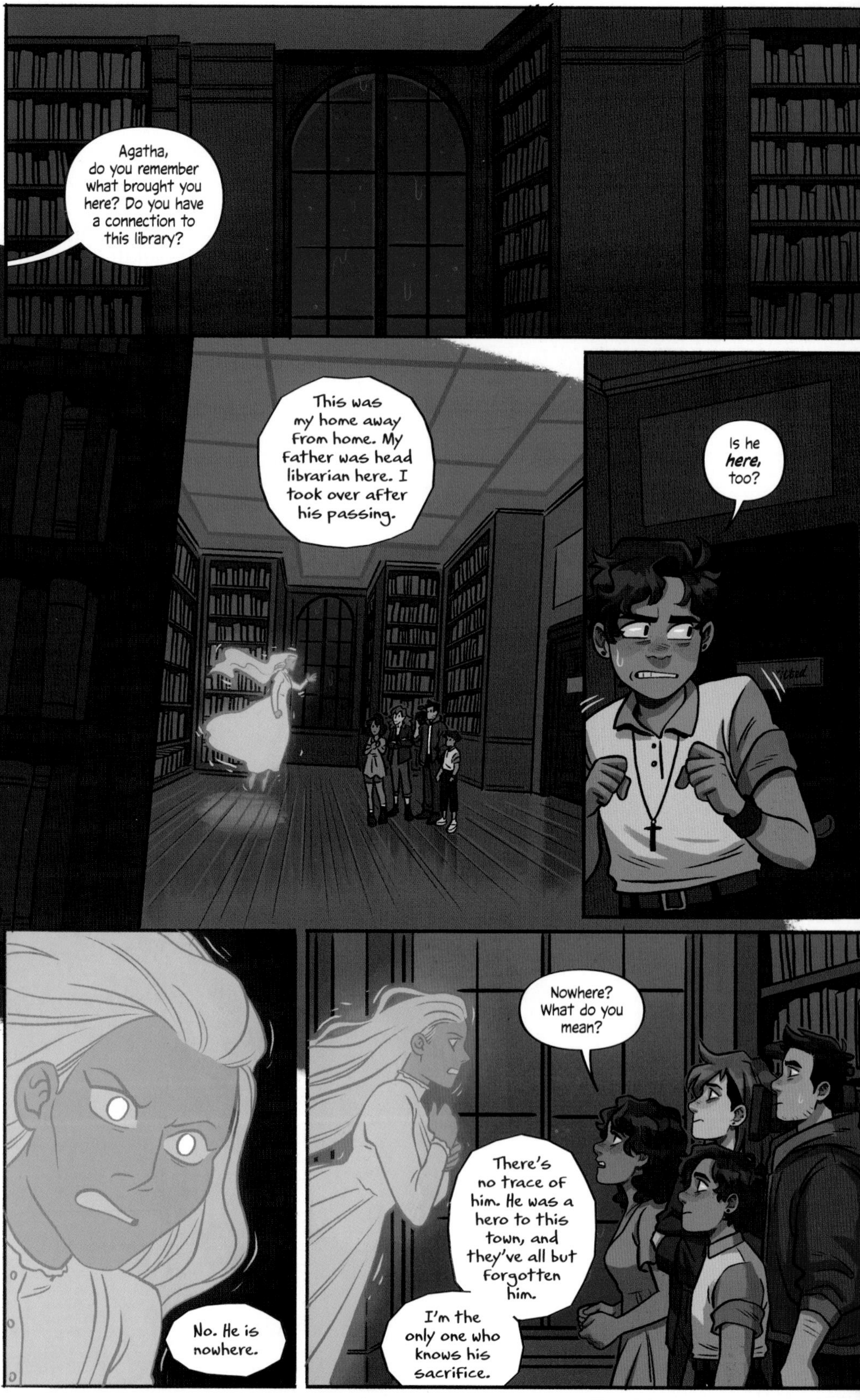

Agatha, do you remember what brought you here? Do you have a connection to this library?
This was my home away from home. My father was head librarian here. I took over after his passing.
Is he *here,* too?
No. He is nowhere.
Nowhere? What do you mean?
There's no trace of him. He was a hero to this town, and they've all but forgotten him.
I'm the only one who knows his sacrifice.

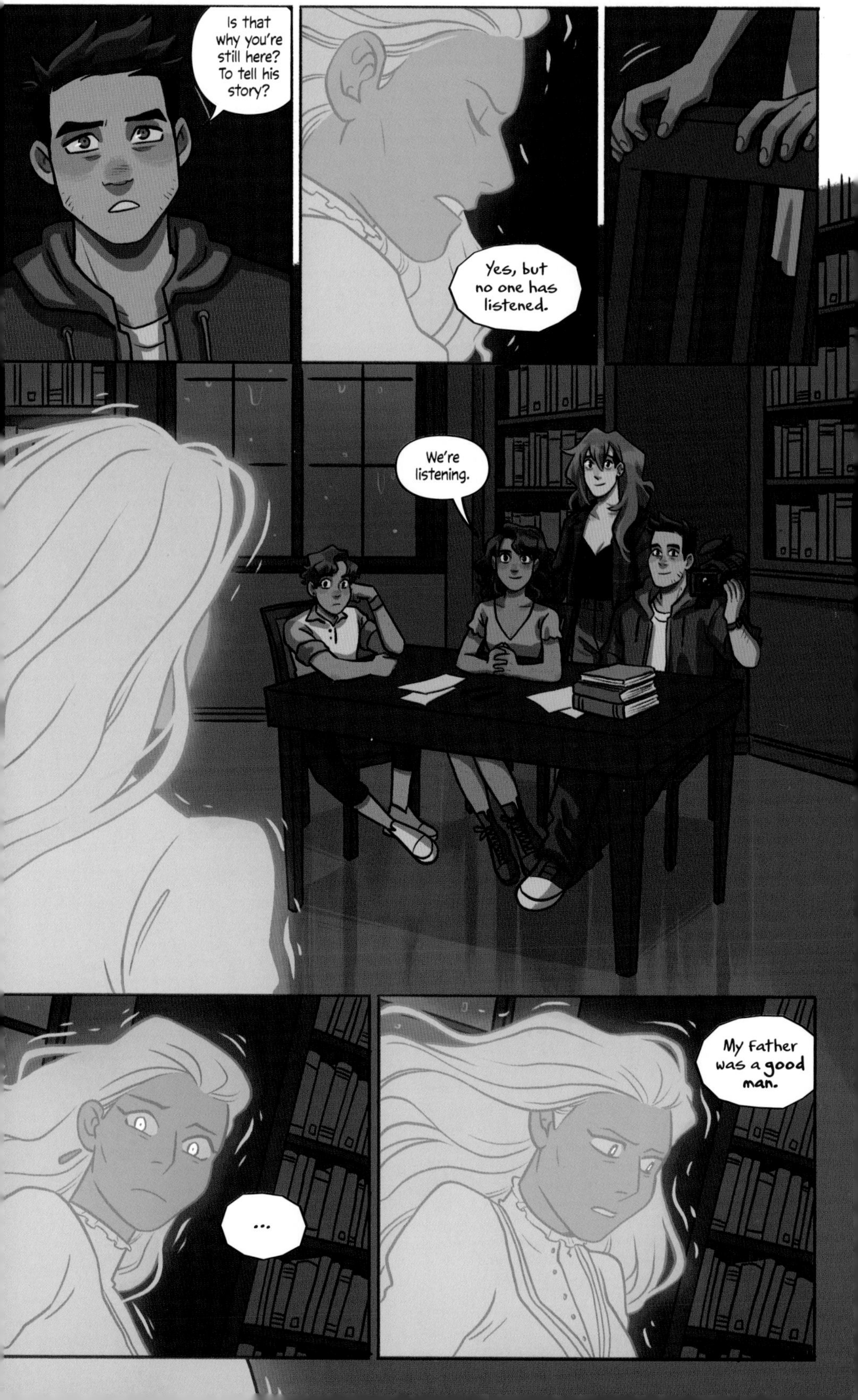

Is that why you're still here? To tell his story?
Yes, but no one has listened.
We're listening.
...
My Father was a good man.

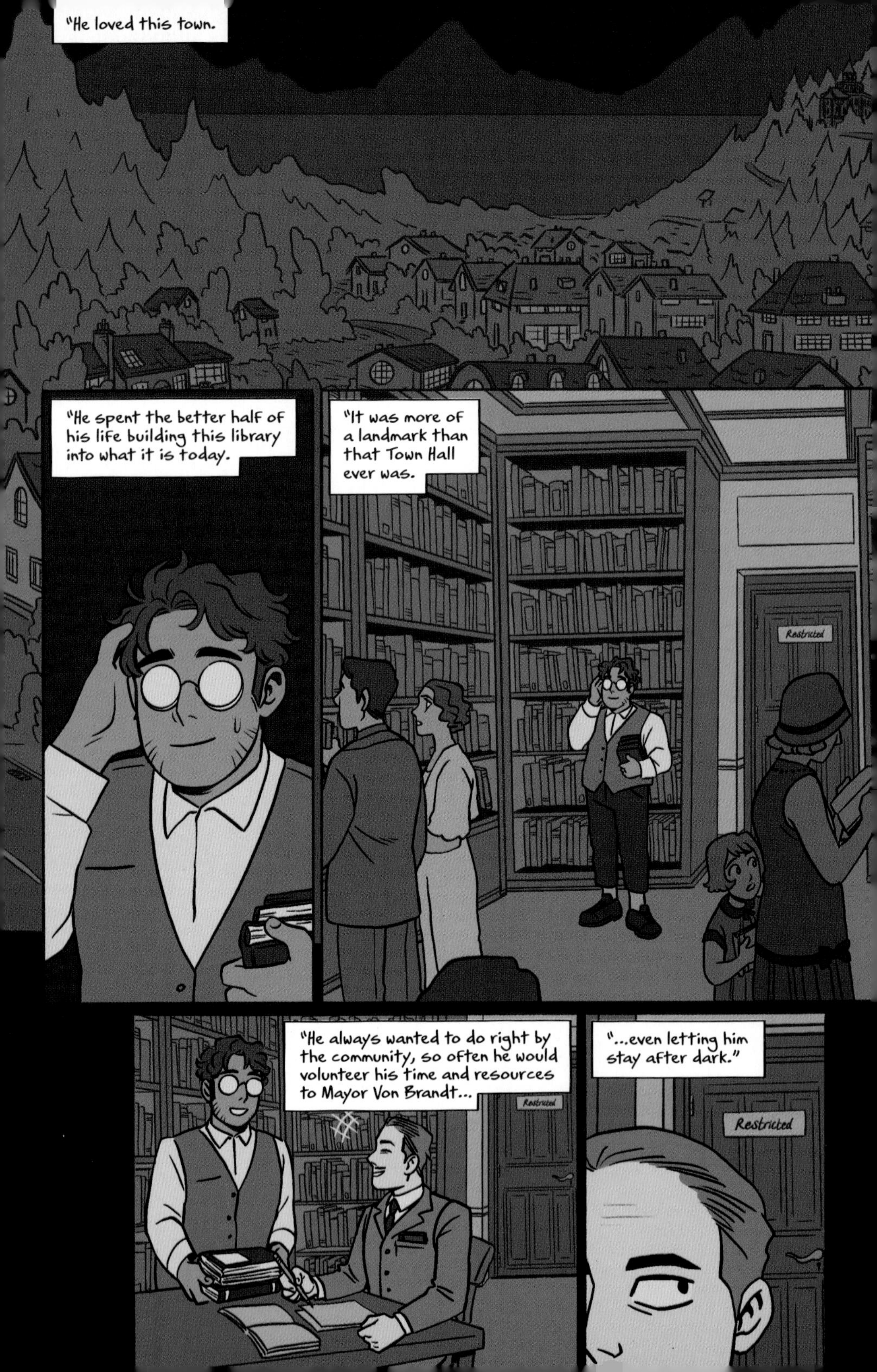
"He loved this town.
"He spent the better half of his life building this library into what it is today.
"It was more of a landmark than that Town Hall ever was.
Restricted
"He always wanted to do right by the community, so often he would volunteer his time and resources to Mayor Von Brandt...
Restricted
"...even letting him stay after dark."
Restricted

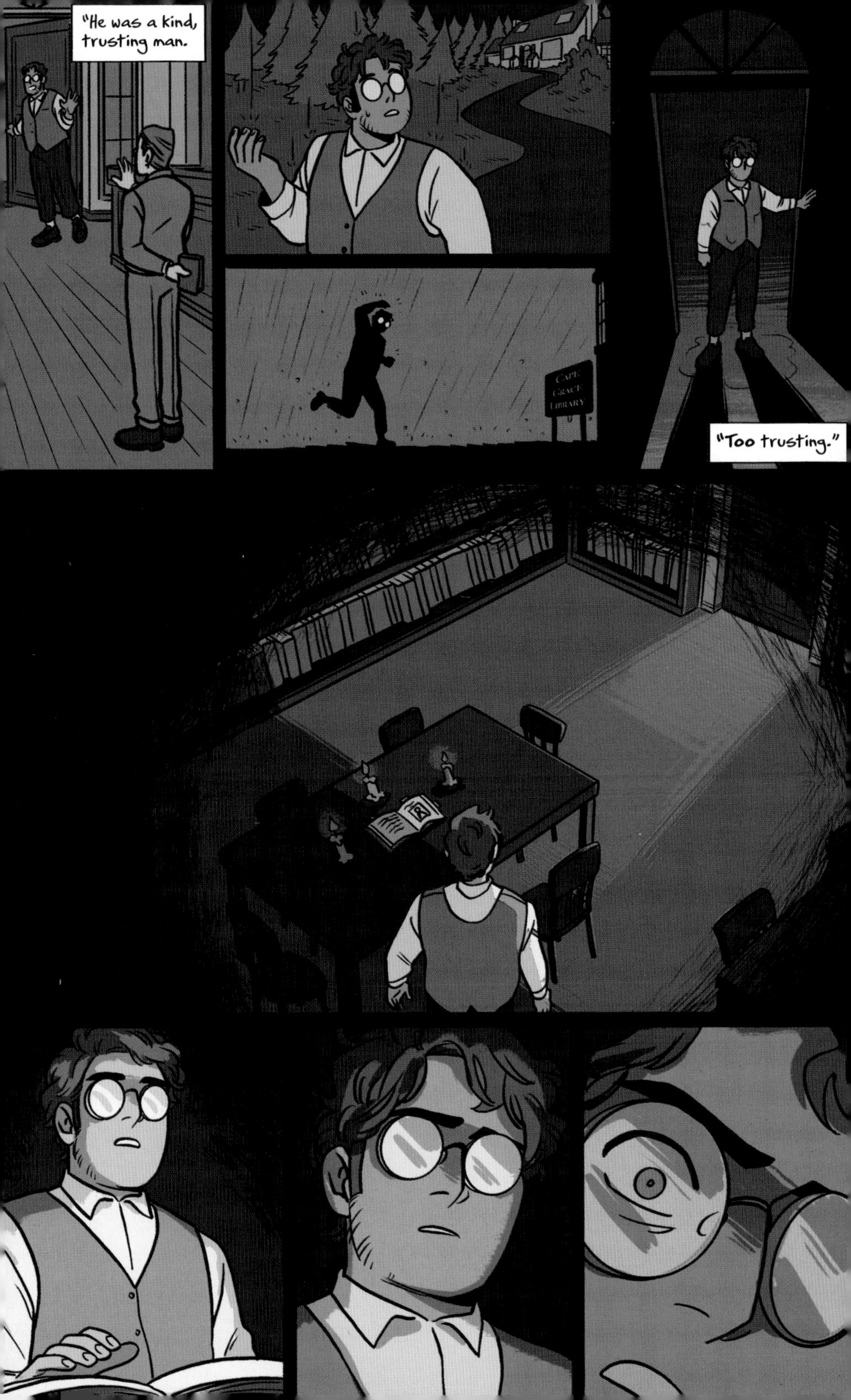
"He was a kind, trusting man.
CAPE GRACE LIBRARY
"Too trusting."

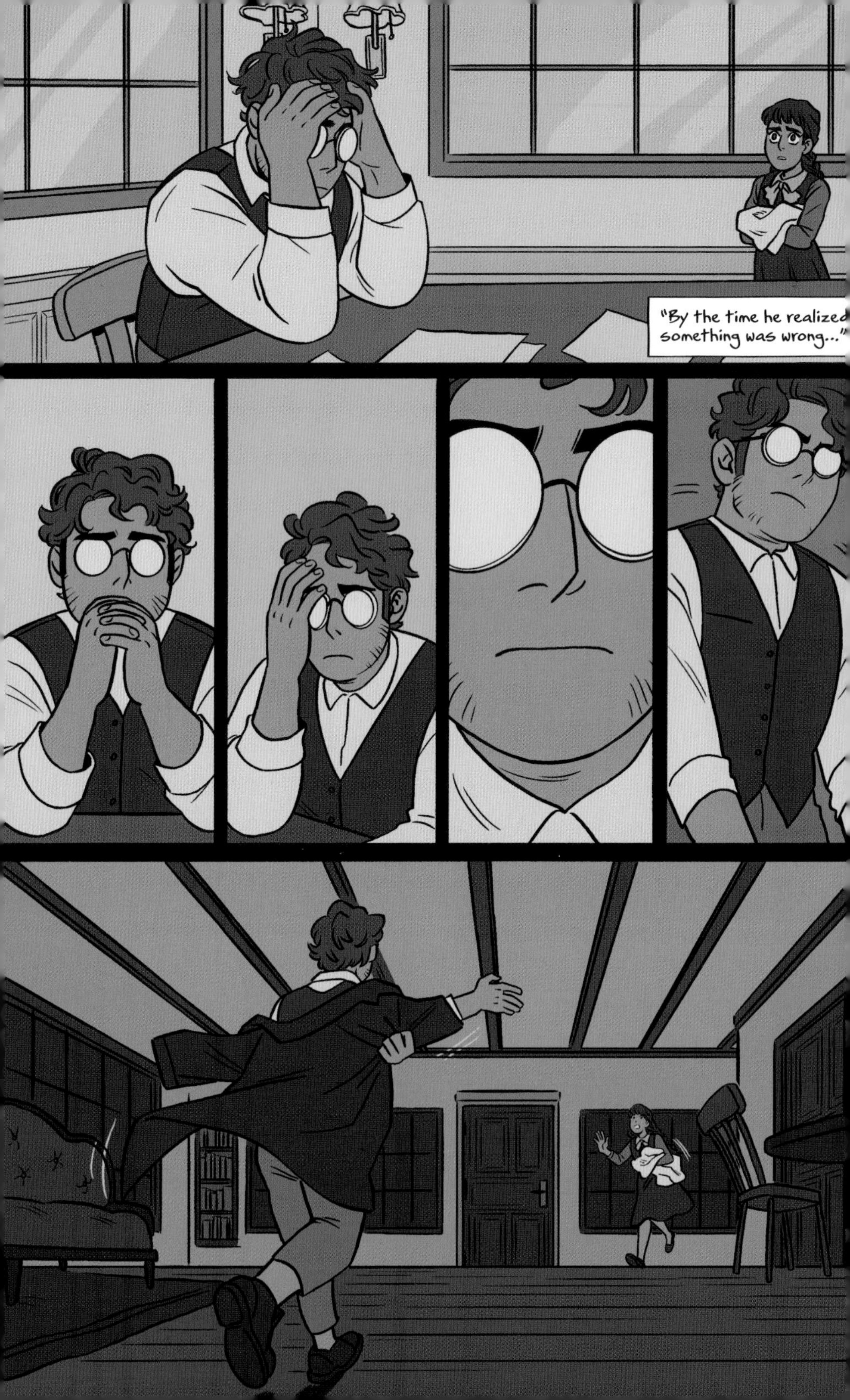
"By the time he realized something was wrong..."

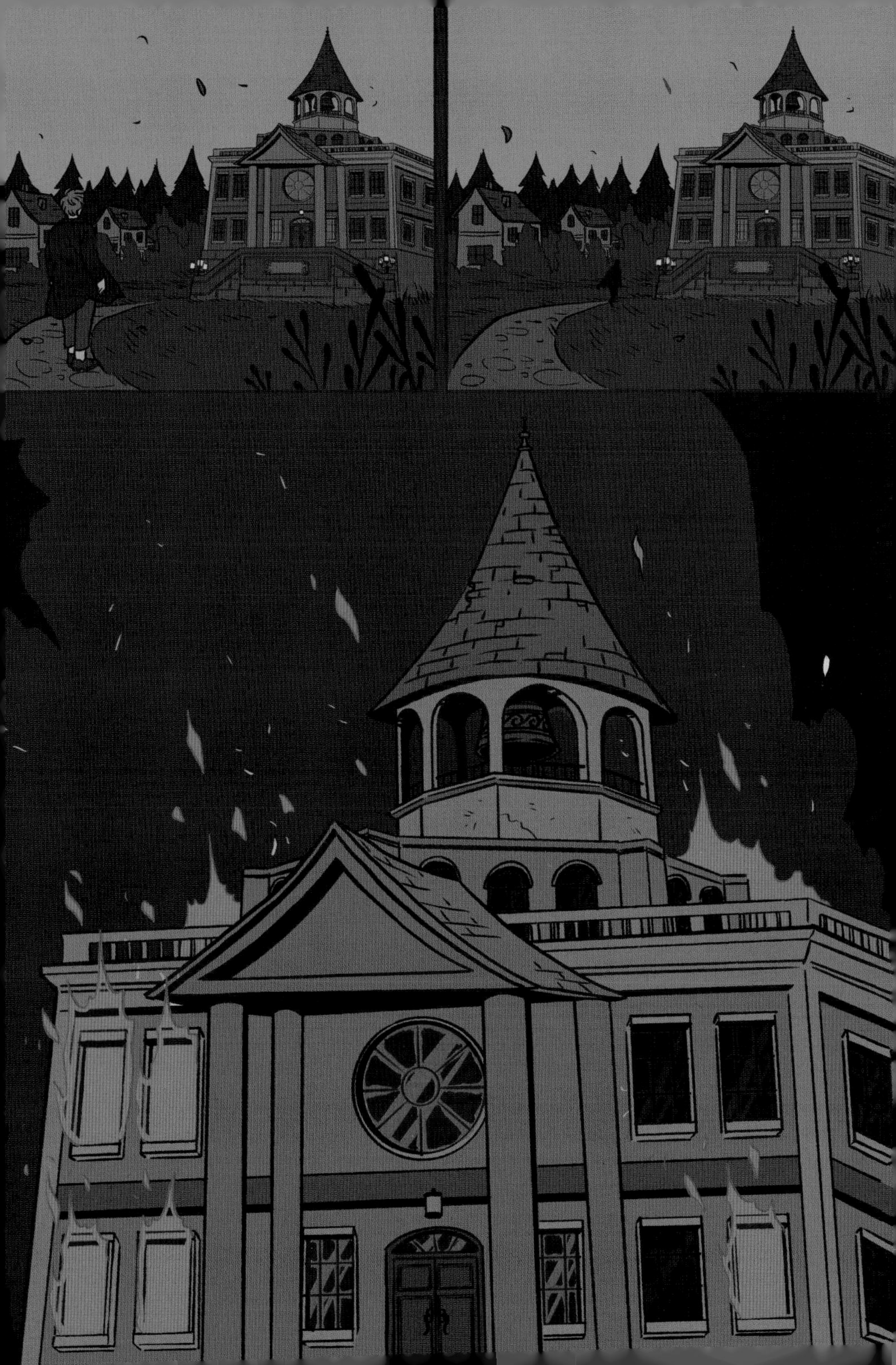

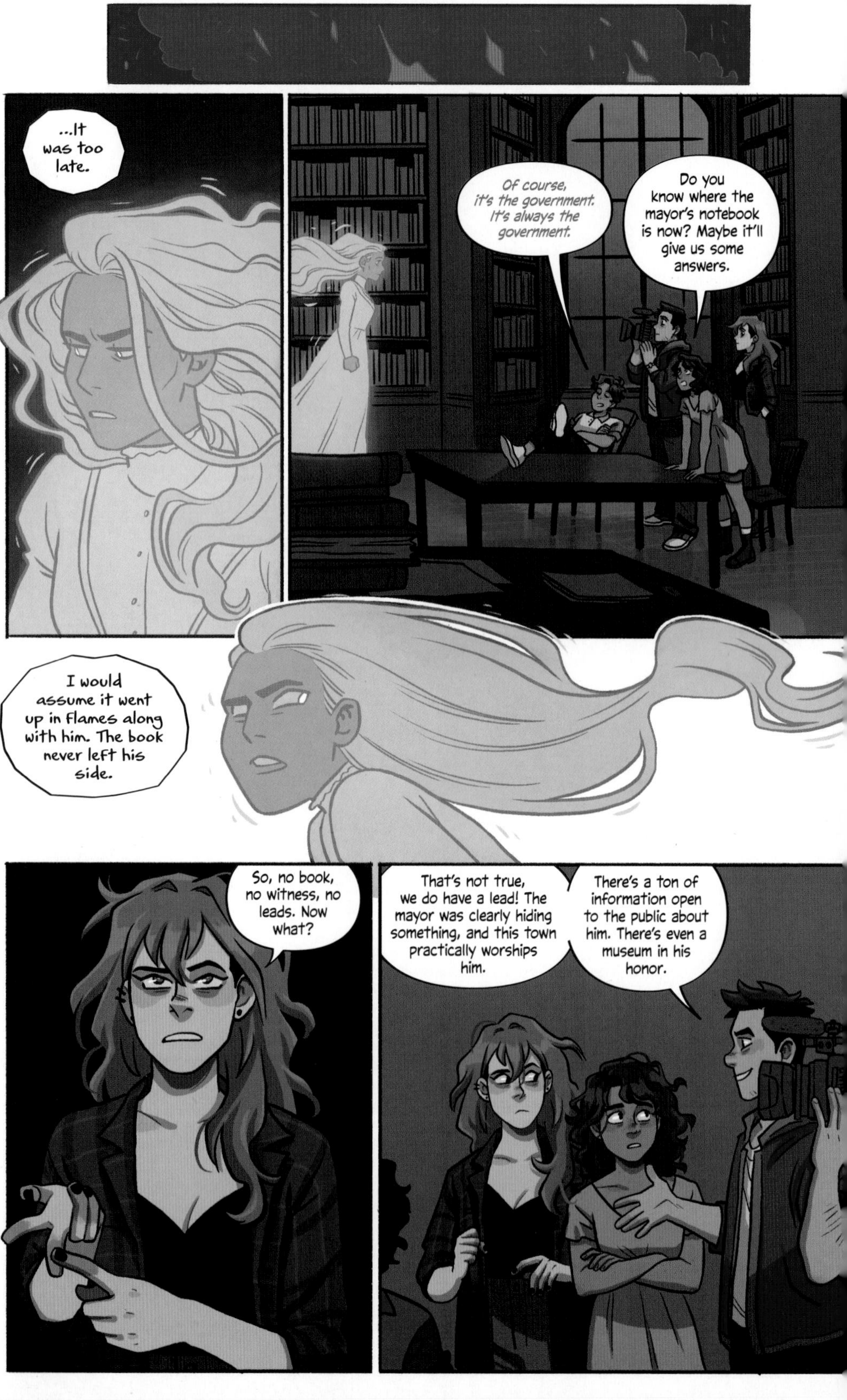
...It was too late.
Of course, it's the government. It's always the government.
Do you know where the mayor's notebook is now? Maybe it'll give us some answers.
I would assume it went up in flames along with him. The book never left his side.
So, no book, no witness, no leads. Now what?
That's not true, we do have a lead! The mayor was clearly hiding something, and this town practically worships him.
There's a ton of information open to the public about him. There's even a museum in his honor.

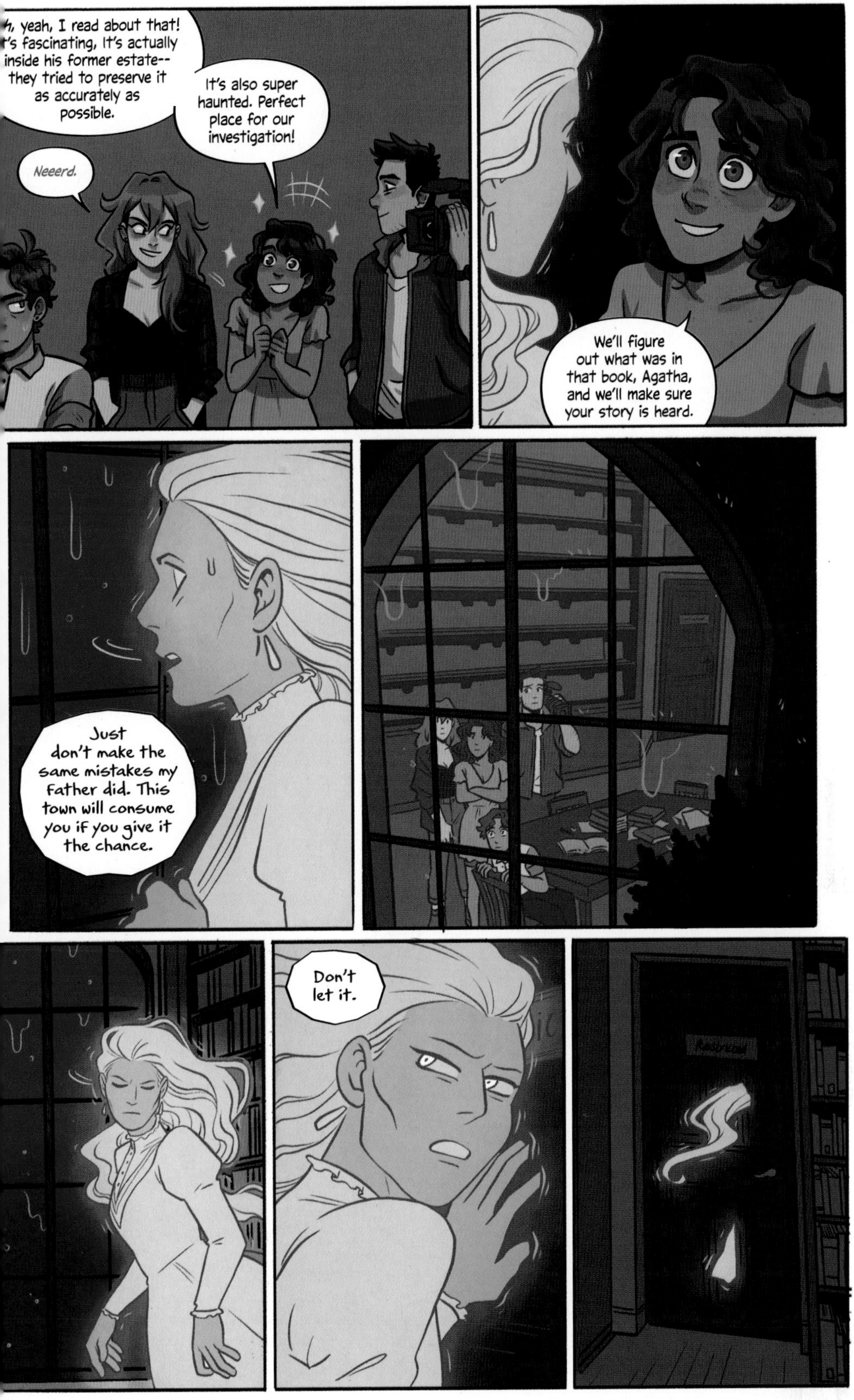
h, yeah, I read about that! t's fascinating, It's actually inside his former estate--they tried to preserve it as accurately as possible.
It's also super haunted. Perfect place for our investigation!
Neeerd.
We'll figure out what was in that book, Agatha, and we'll make sure your story is heard.
Just don't make the same mistakes my father did. This town will consume you if you give it the chance.
Don't let it.

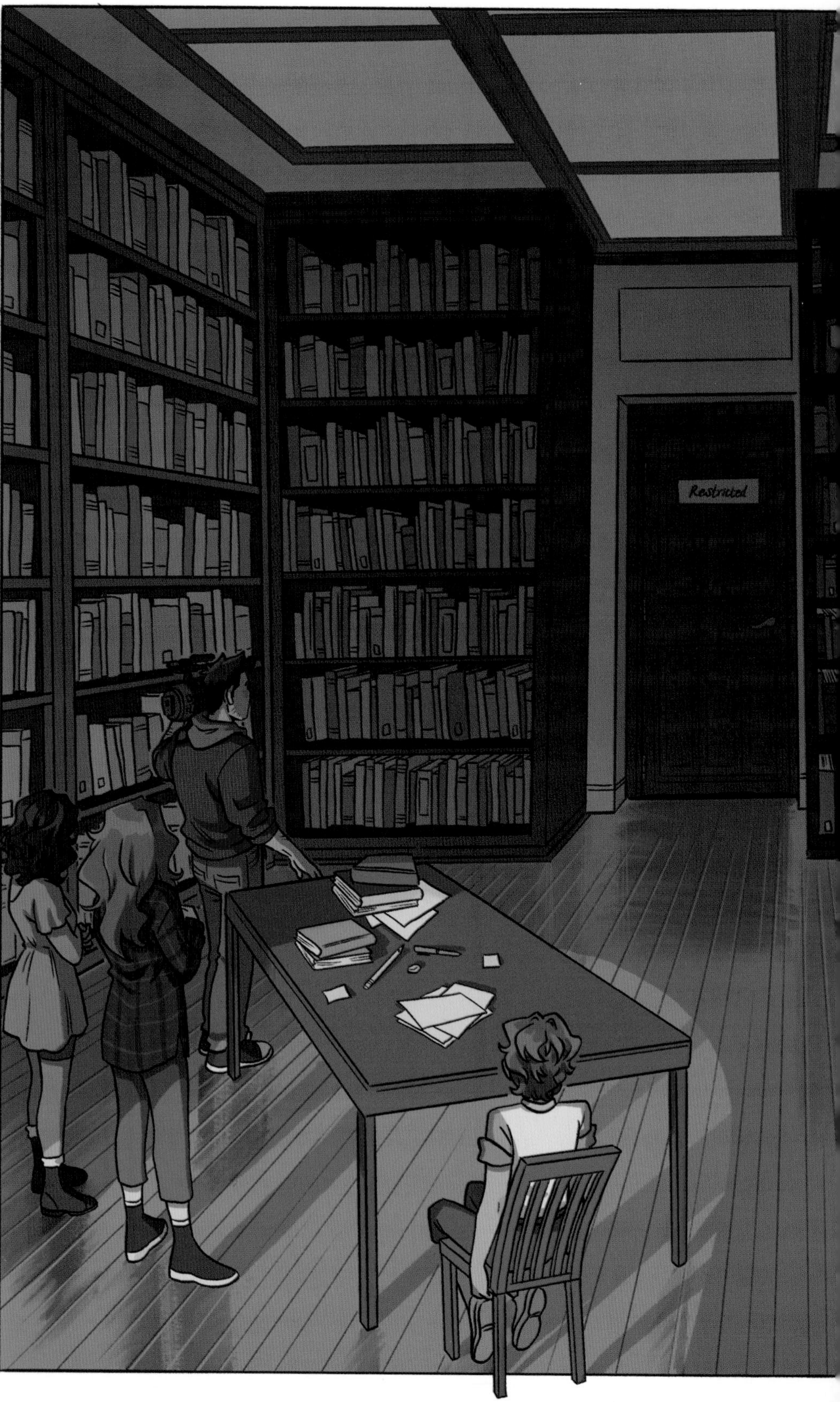

Restricted

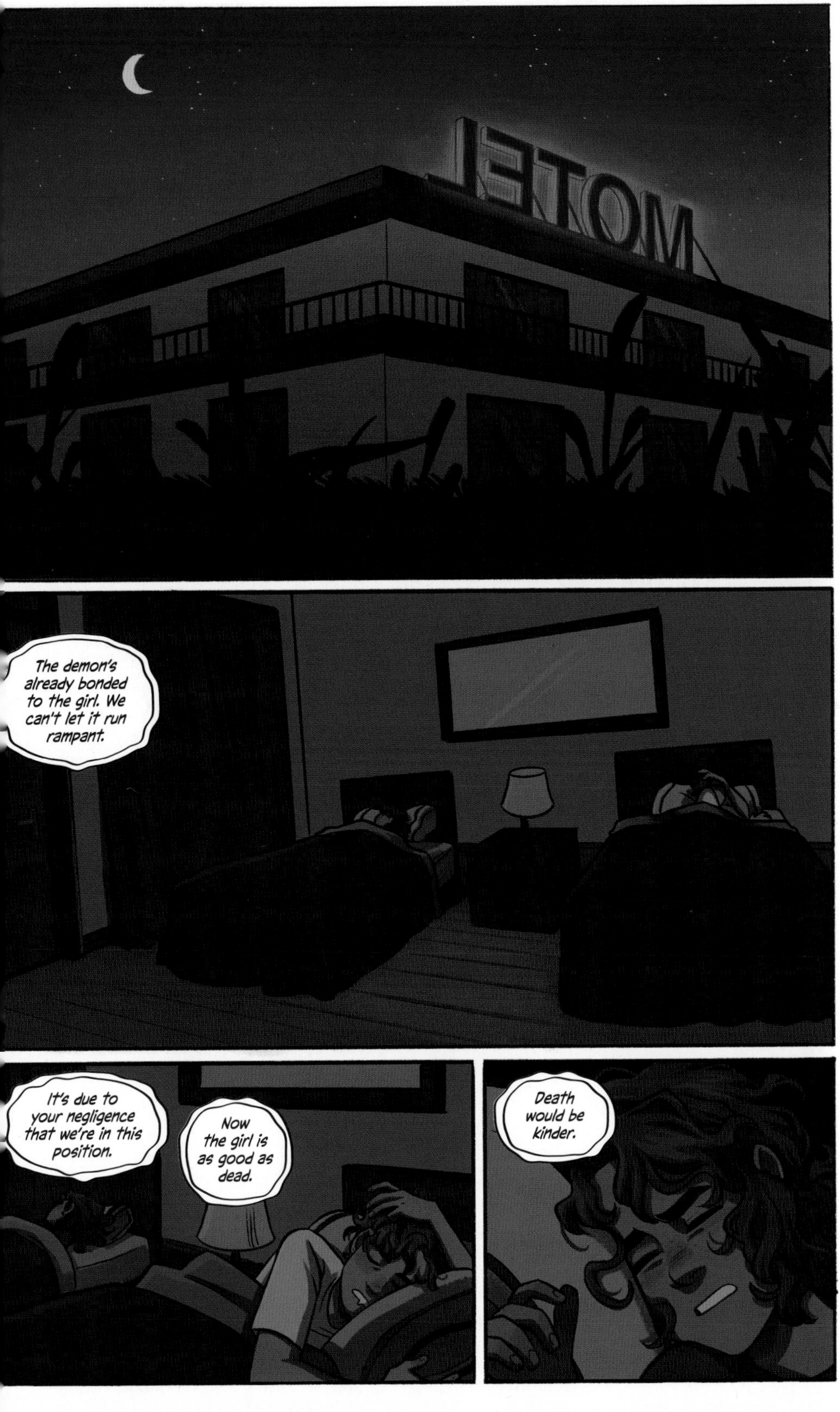

The demon's already bonded to the girl. We can't let it run rampant.
It's due to your negligence that we're in this position.
Now the girl is as good as dead.
Death would be kinder.

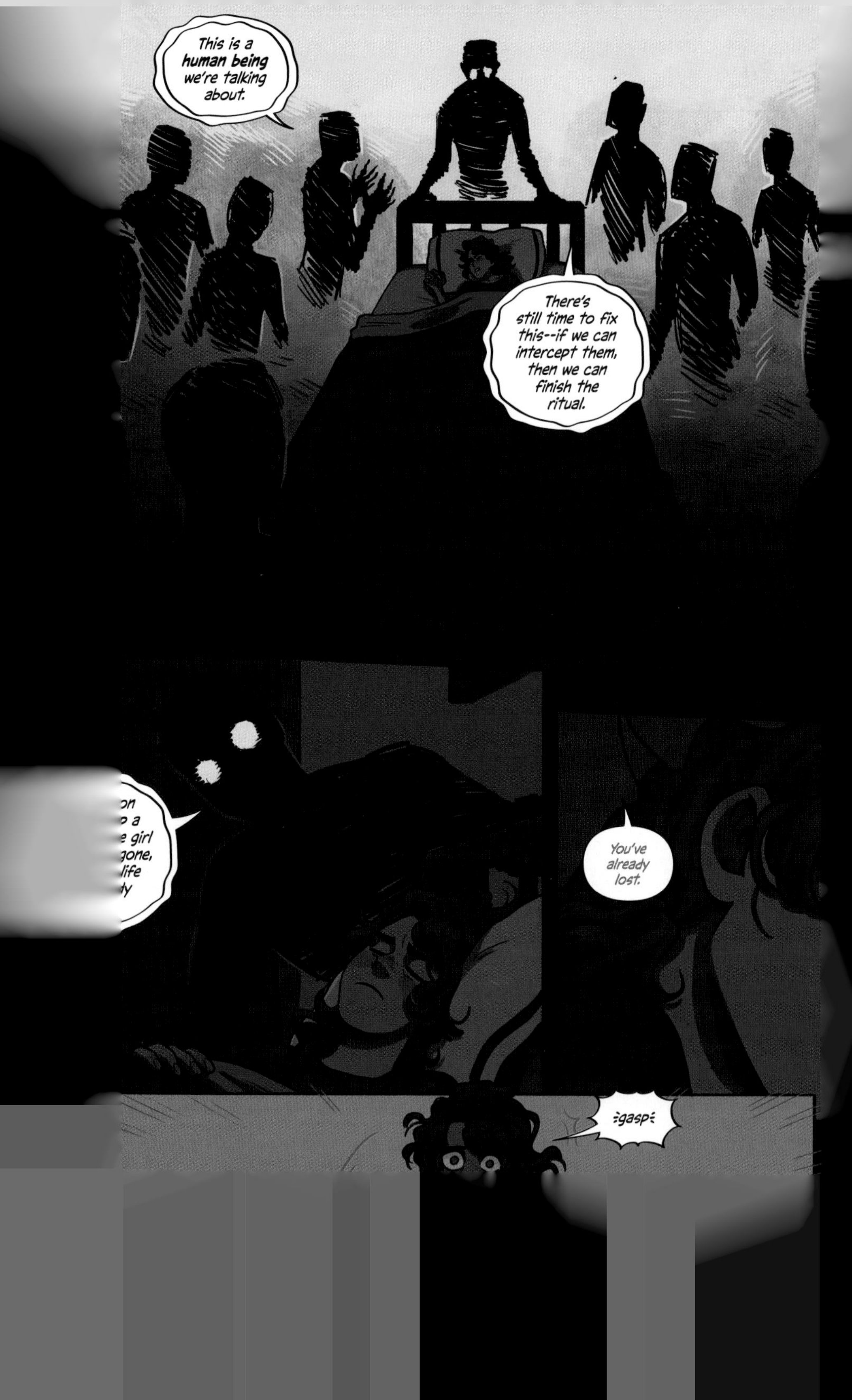
This is a **human being** we're talking about.
There's still time to fix this--if we can intercept them, then we can finish the ritual.
You've already lost.
gasp

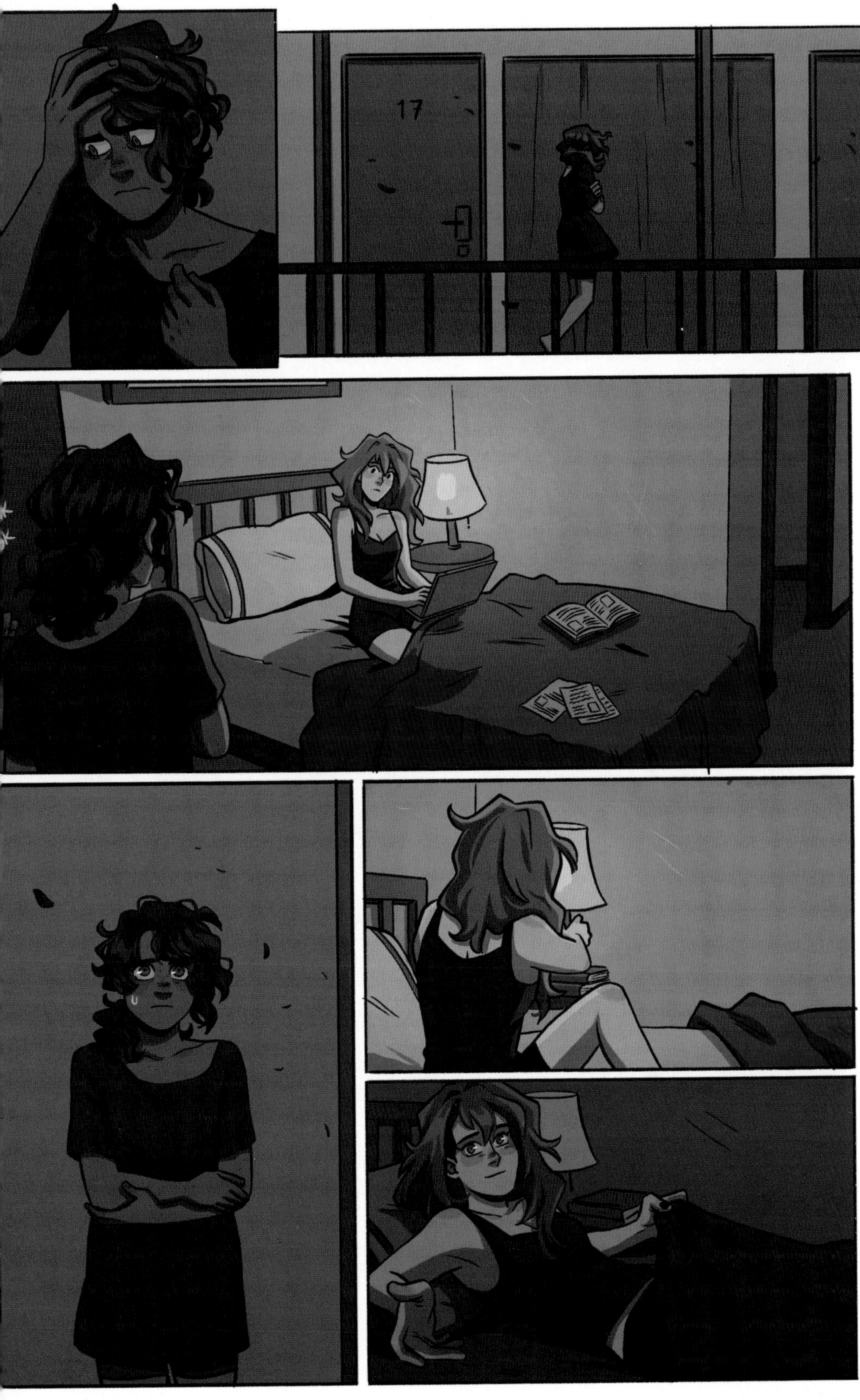
17

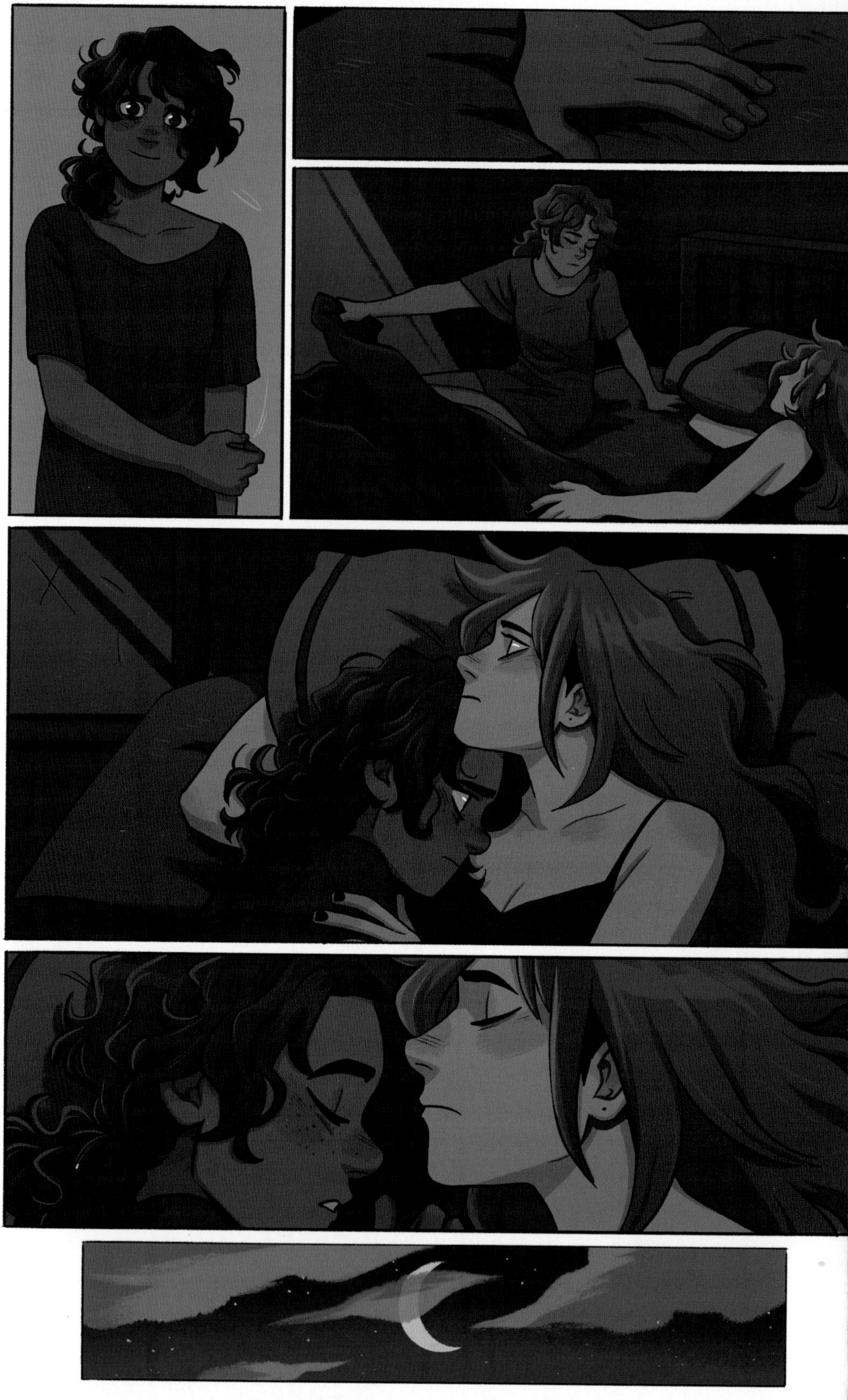

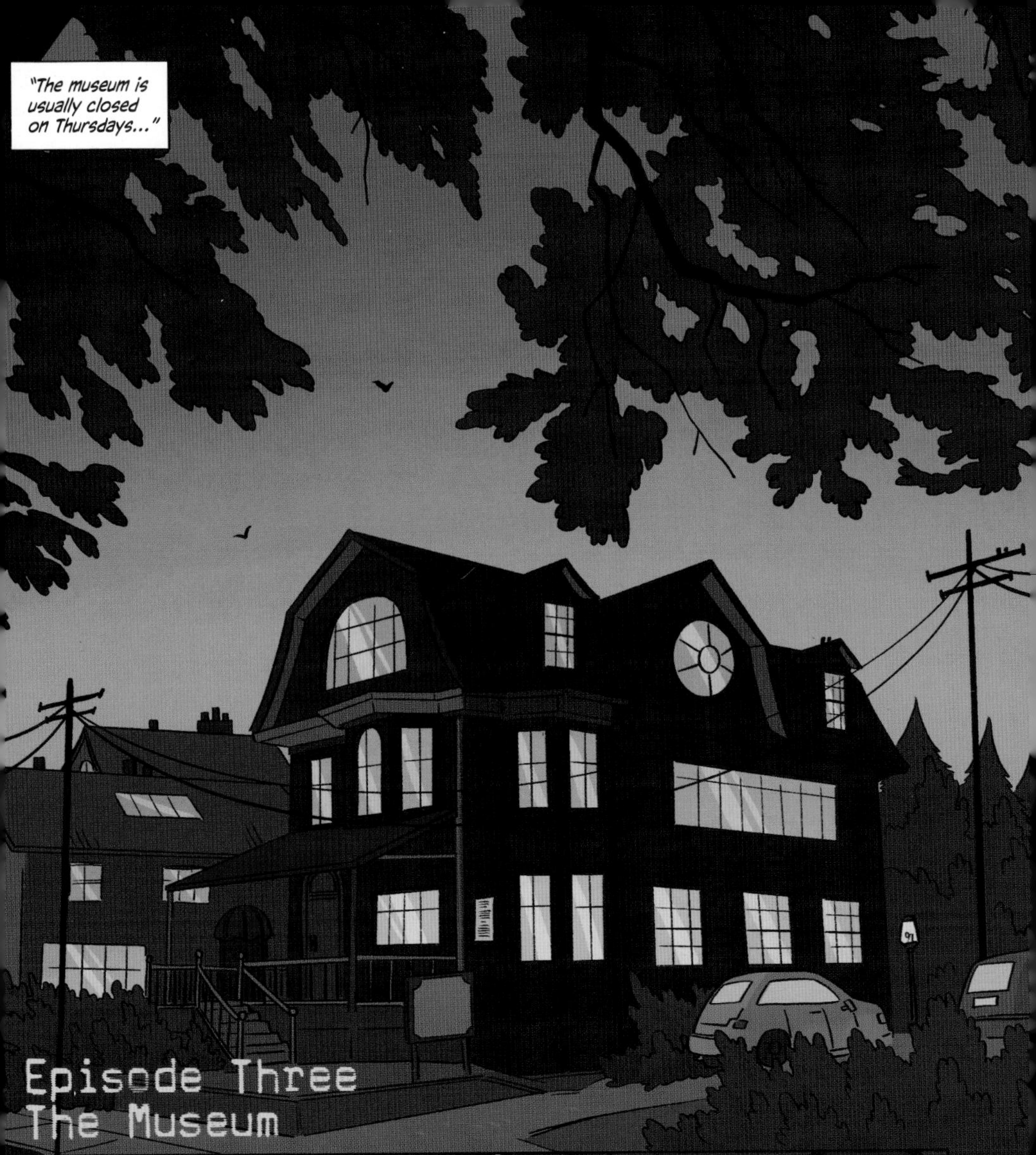
"The museum is usually closed on Thursdays..."
Episode Three
The Museum

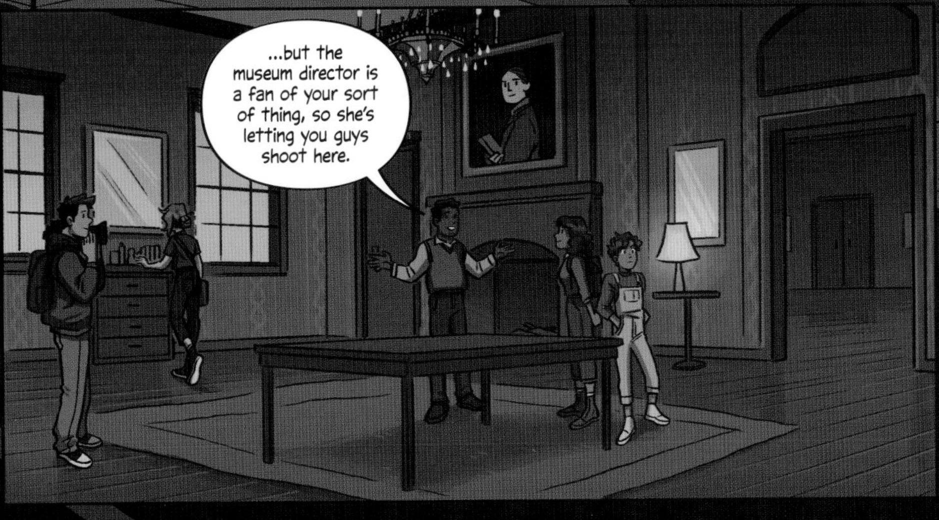
...but the museum director is a fan of your sort of thing, so she's letting you guys shoot here.

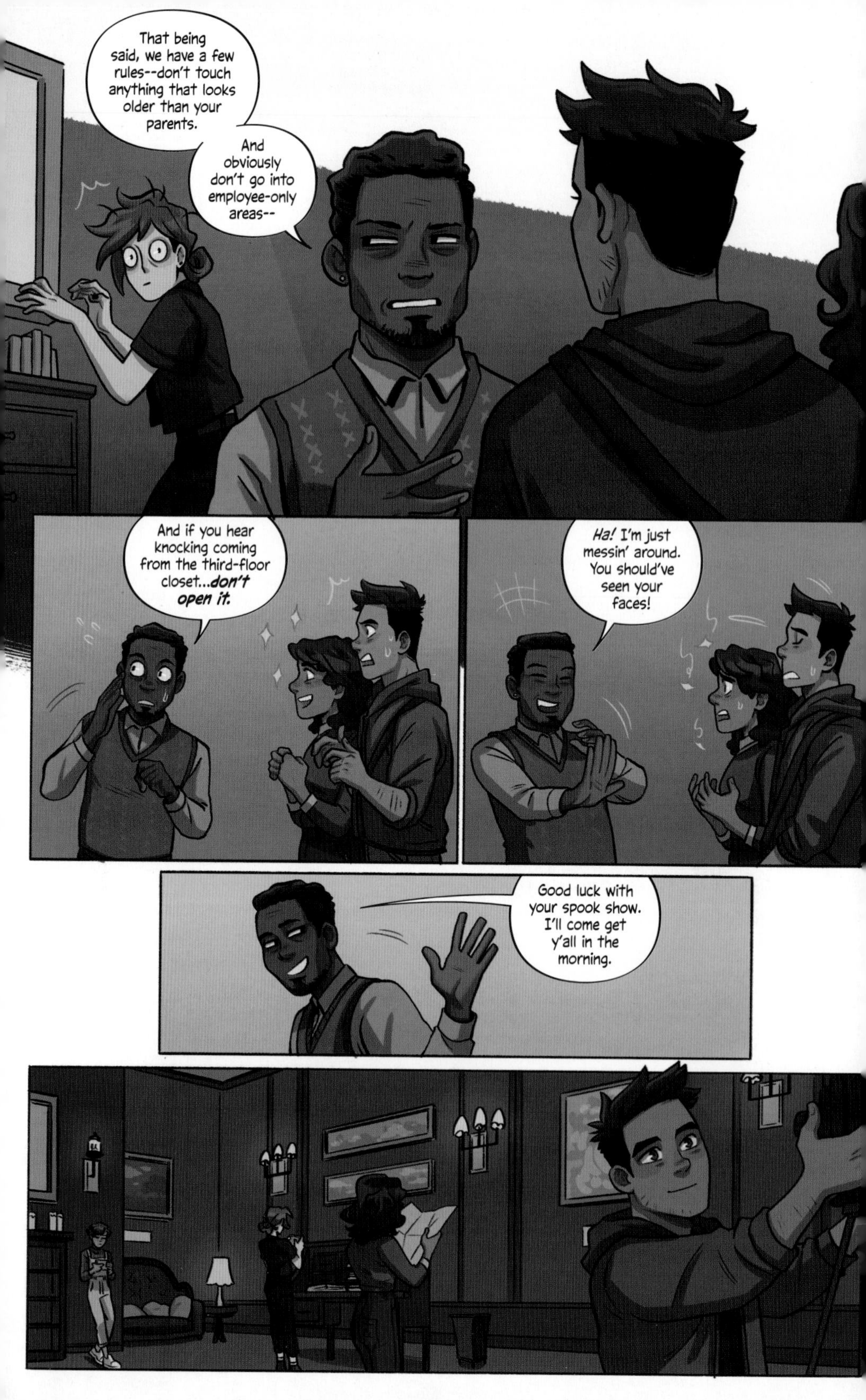
That being said, we have a few rules--don't touch anything that looks older than your parents.
And obviously don't go into employee-only areas--
And if you hear knocking coming from the third-floor closet...*don't open it.*
Ha! I'm just messin' around. You should've seen your faces!
Good luck with your spook show. I'll come get y'all in the morning.

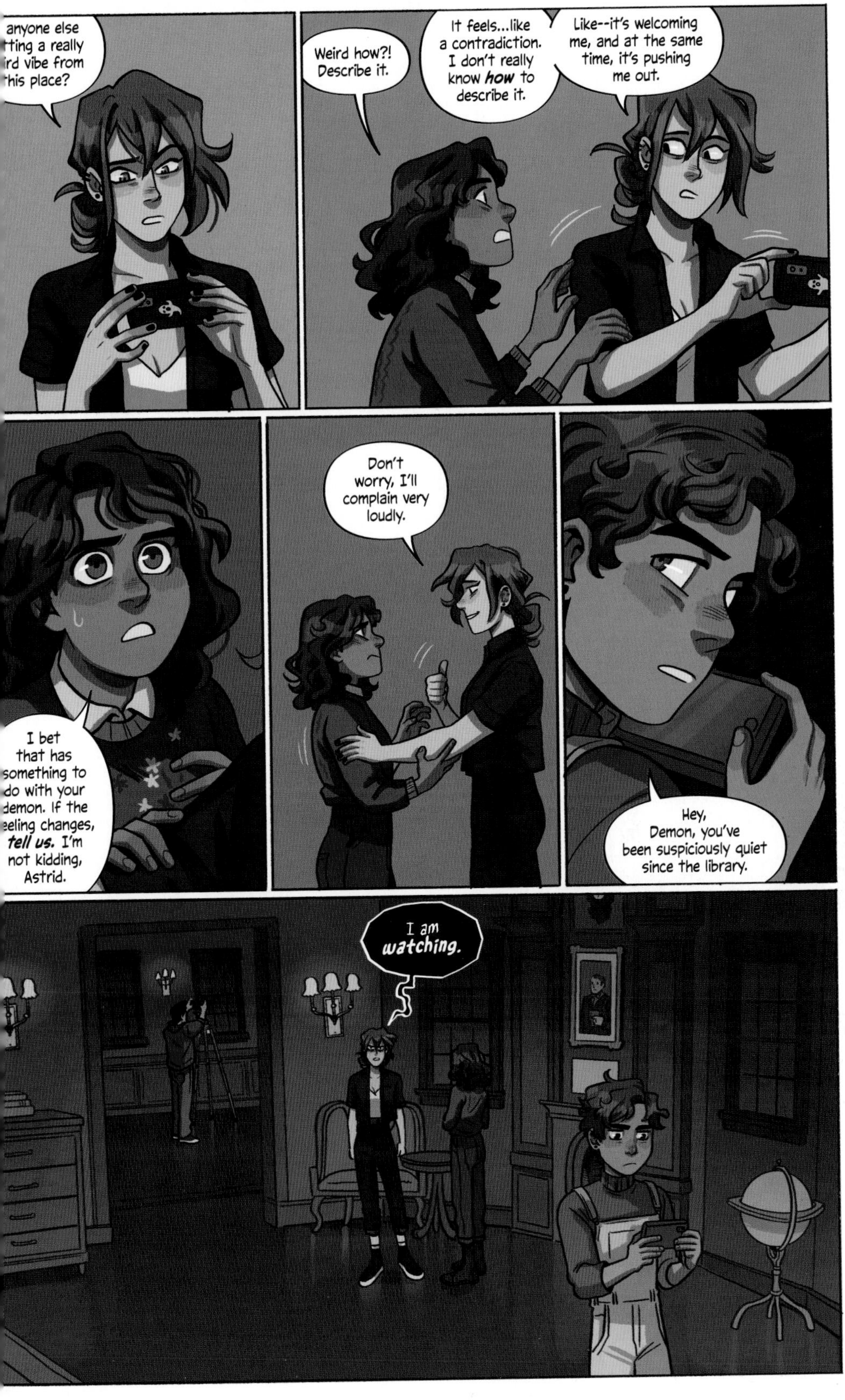
anyone else
tting a really
ird vibe from
this place?
Weird how?! Describe it.
It feels...like a contradiction. I don't really know **how** to describe it.
Like--it's welcoming me, and at the same time, it's pushing me out.
I bet that has something to do with your demon. If the eeling changes, **tell us.** I'm not kidding, Astrid.
Don't worry, I'll complain very loudly.
Hey, Demon, you've been suspiciously quiet since the library.
I am **watching.**

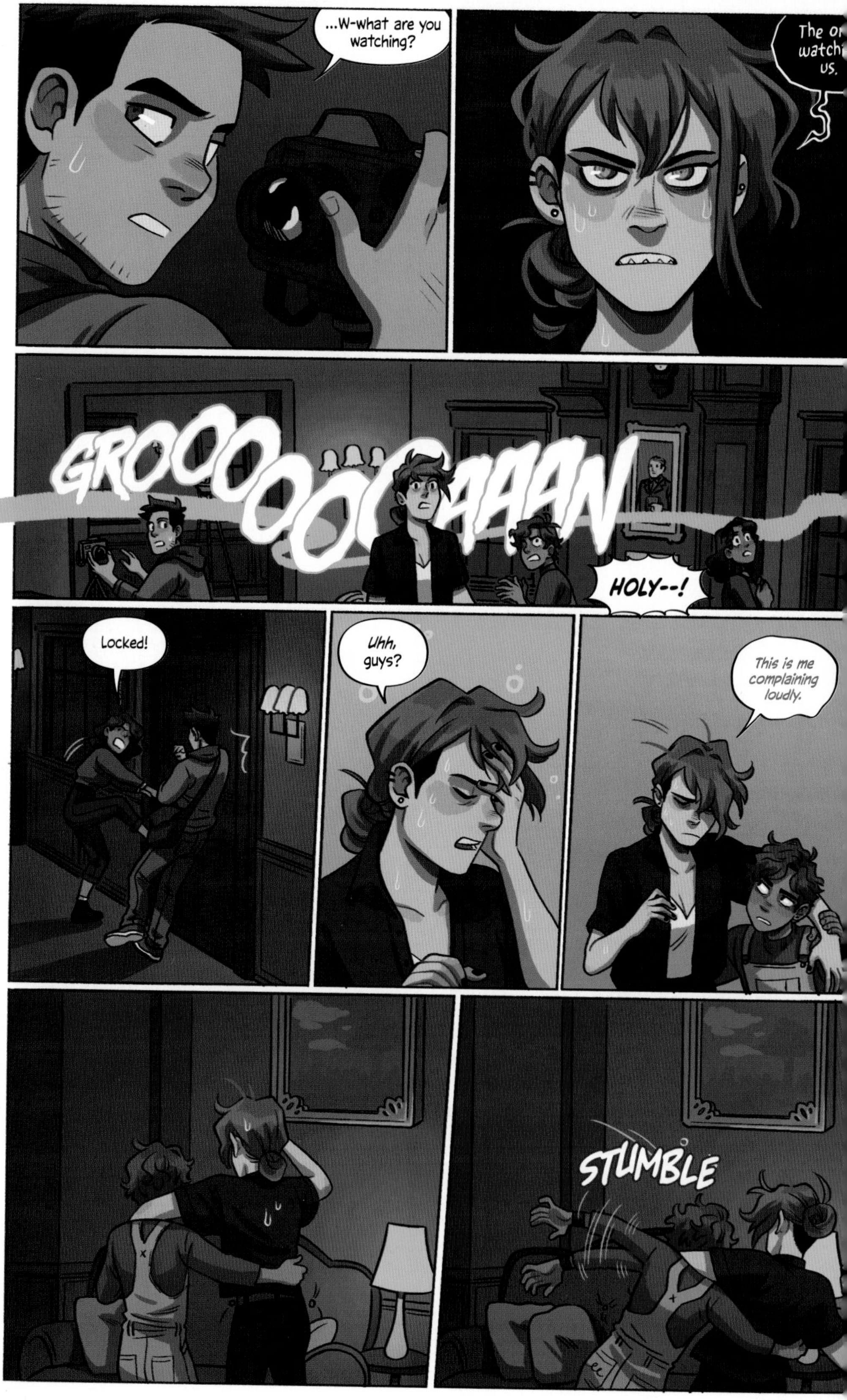
...W-what are you watching?
The o
watch
us.
GROOOOOOOAAAN
HOLY--!
Locked!
Uhh, guys?
This is me complaining loudly.
STUMBLE

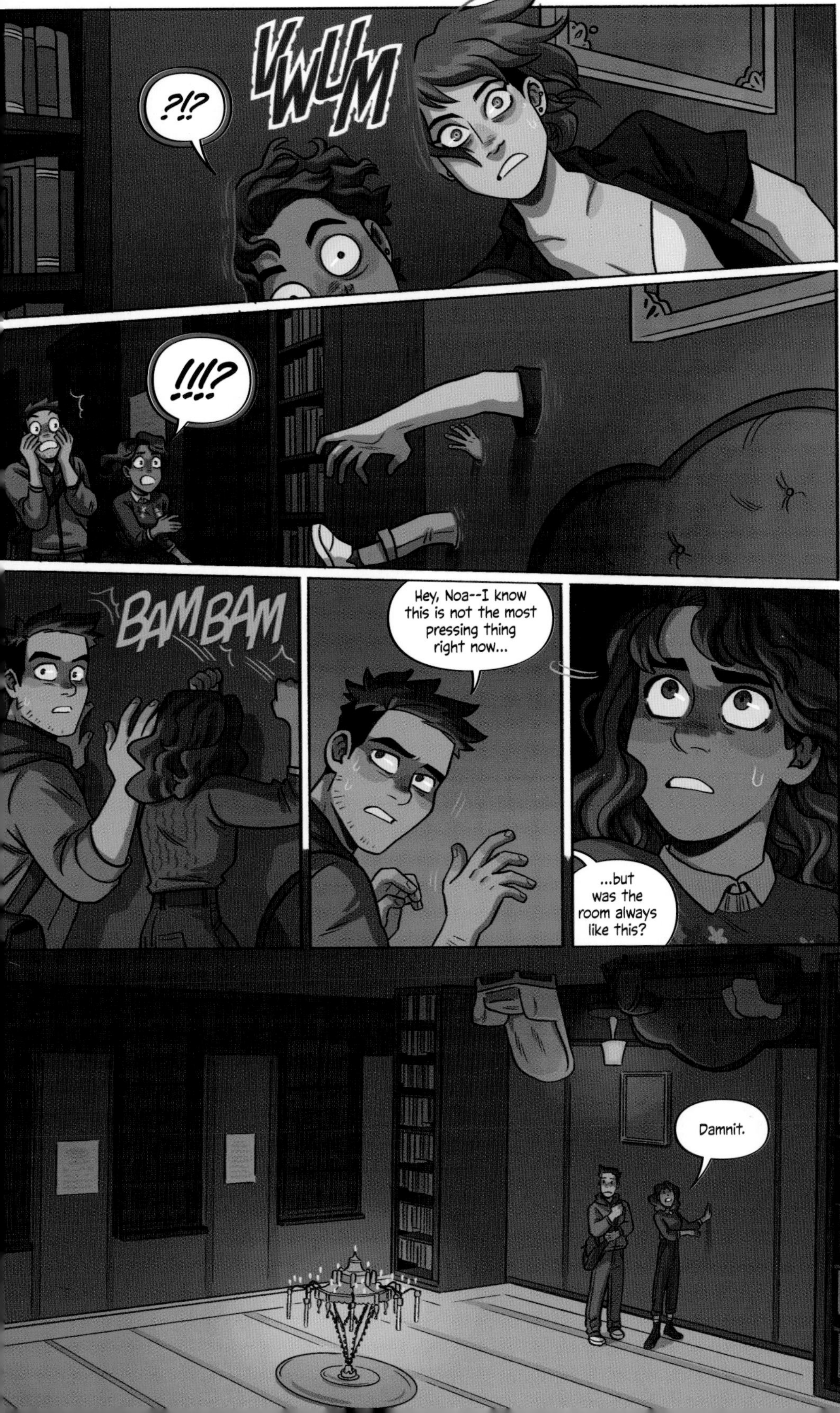
?!?
VWUM
!!!?
BAM BAM
Hey, Noa--I know this is not the most pressing thing right now...
...but was the room always like this?
Damnit.

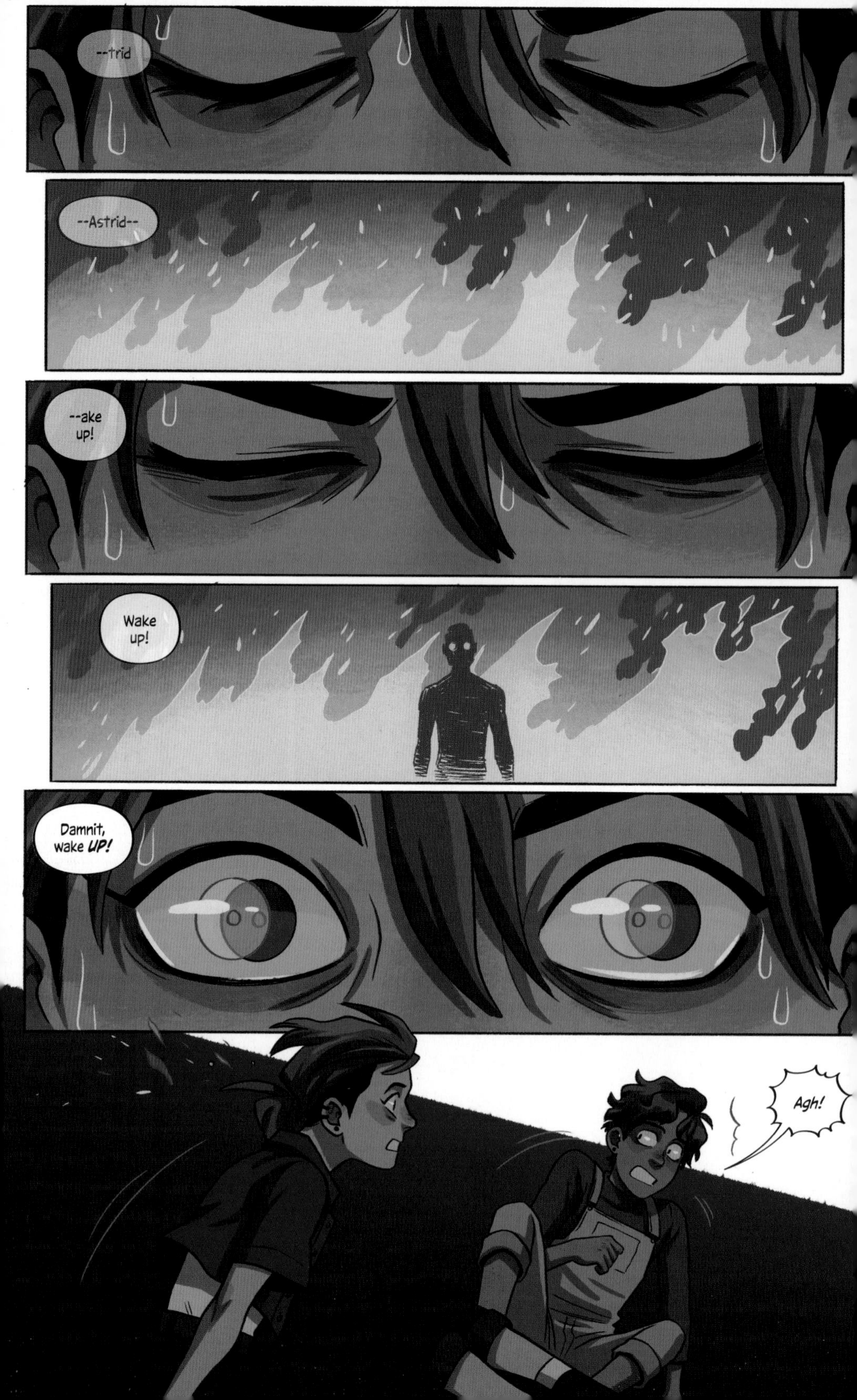

--trid
--Astrid--
--ake up!
Wake up!
Damnit, wake UP!
Agh!

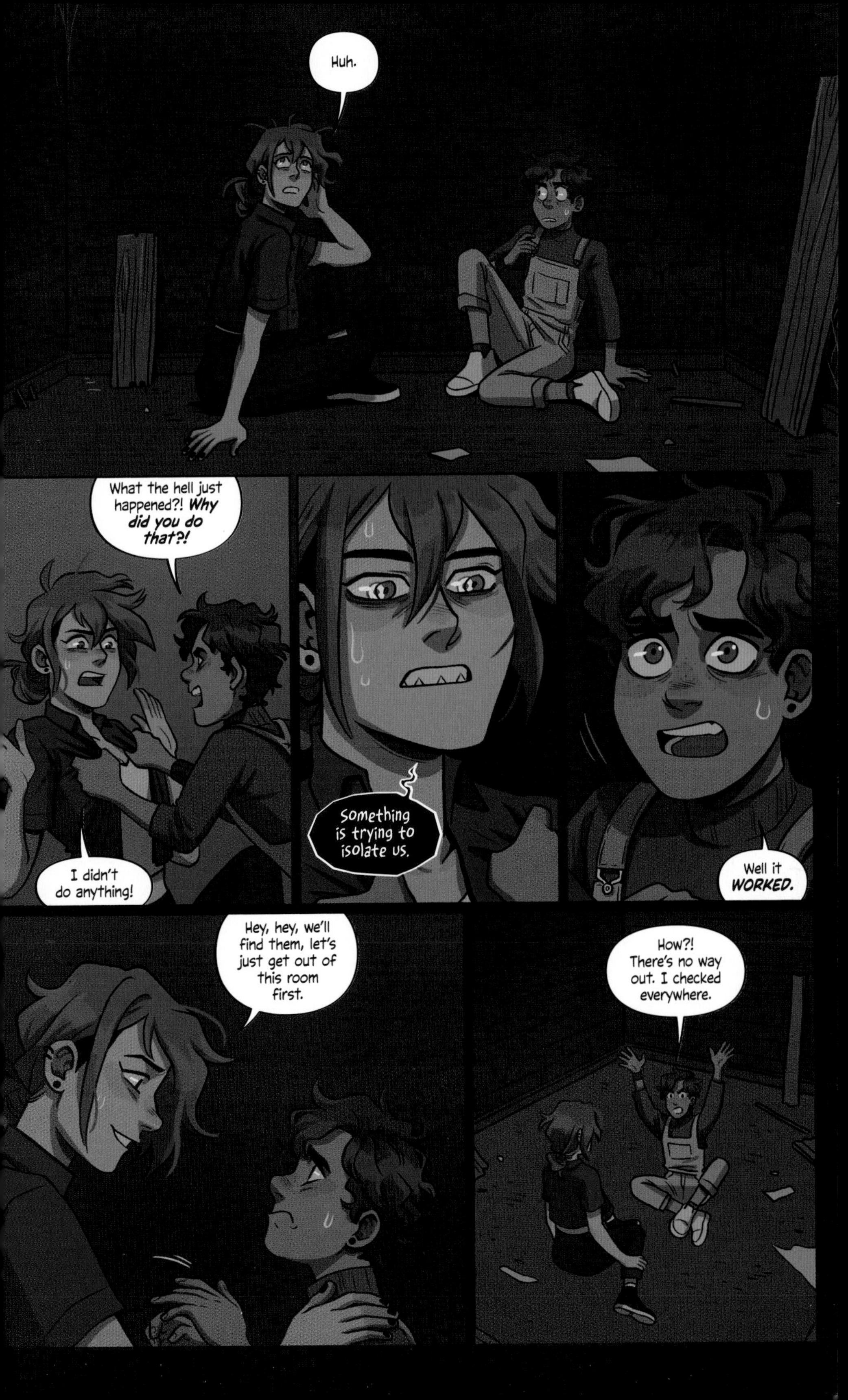
Huh.
What the hell just happened?! *Why did you do that?!*
I didn't do anything!
Something is trying to isolate us.
Well it **WORKED.**
Hey, hey, we'll find them, let's just get out of this room first.
How?! There's no way out. I checked everywhere.

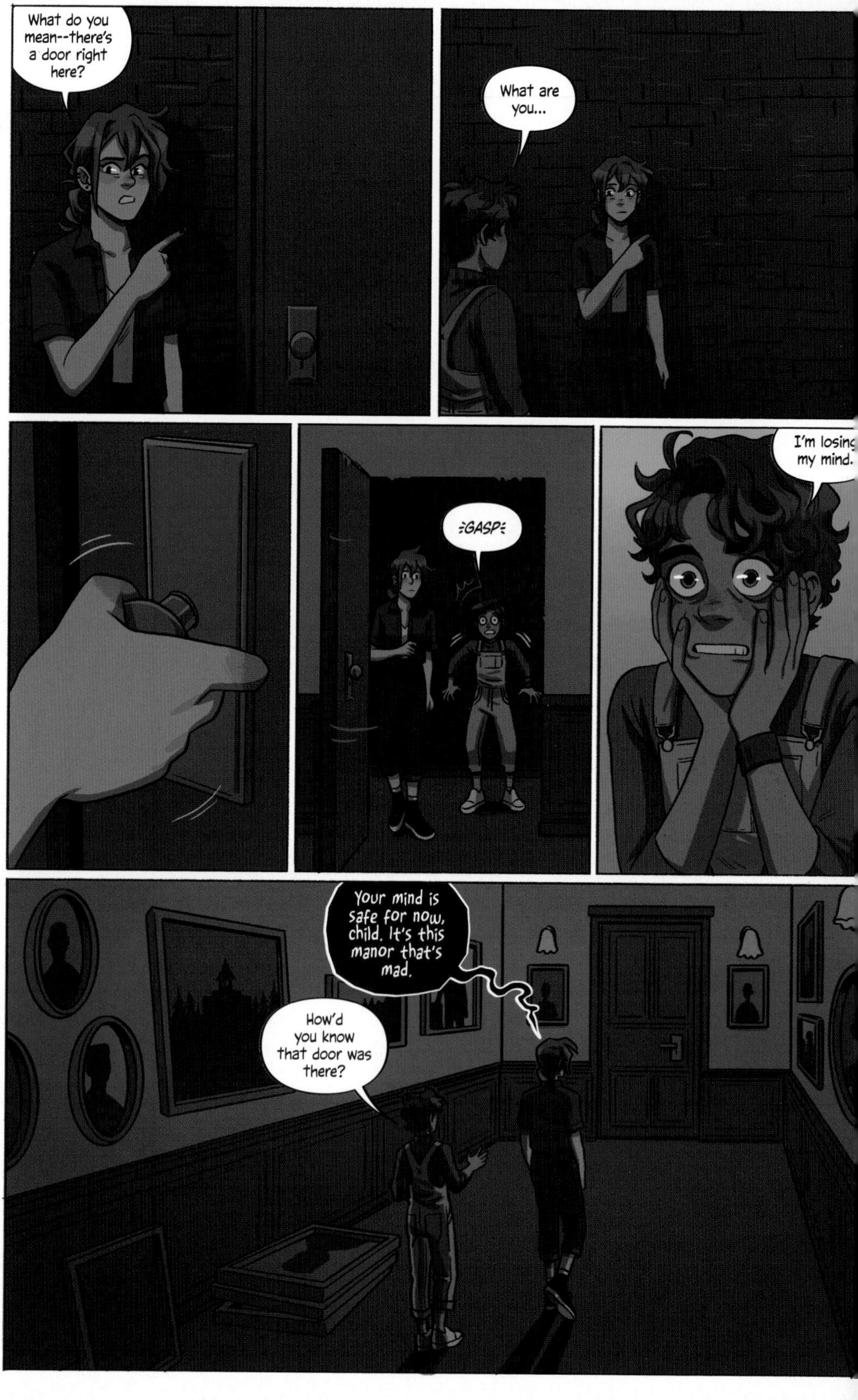
What do you mean--there's a door right here?
What are you...
=GASP=
I'm losing my mind.
Your mind is safe for now, child. It's this manor that's mad.
How'd you know that door was there?

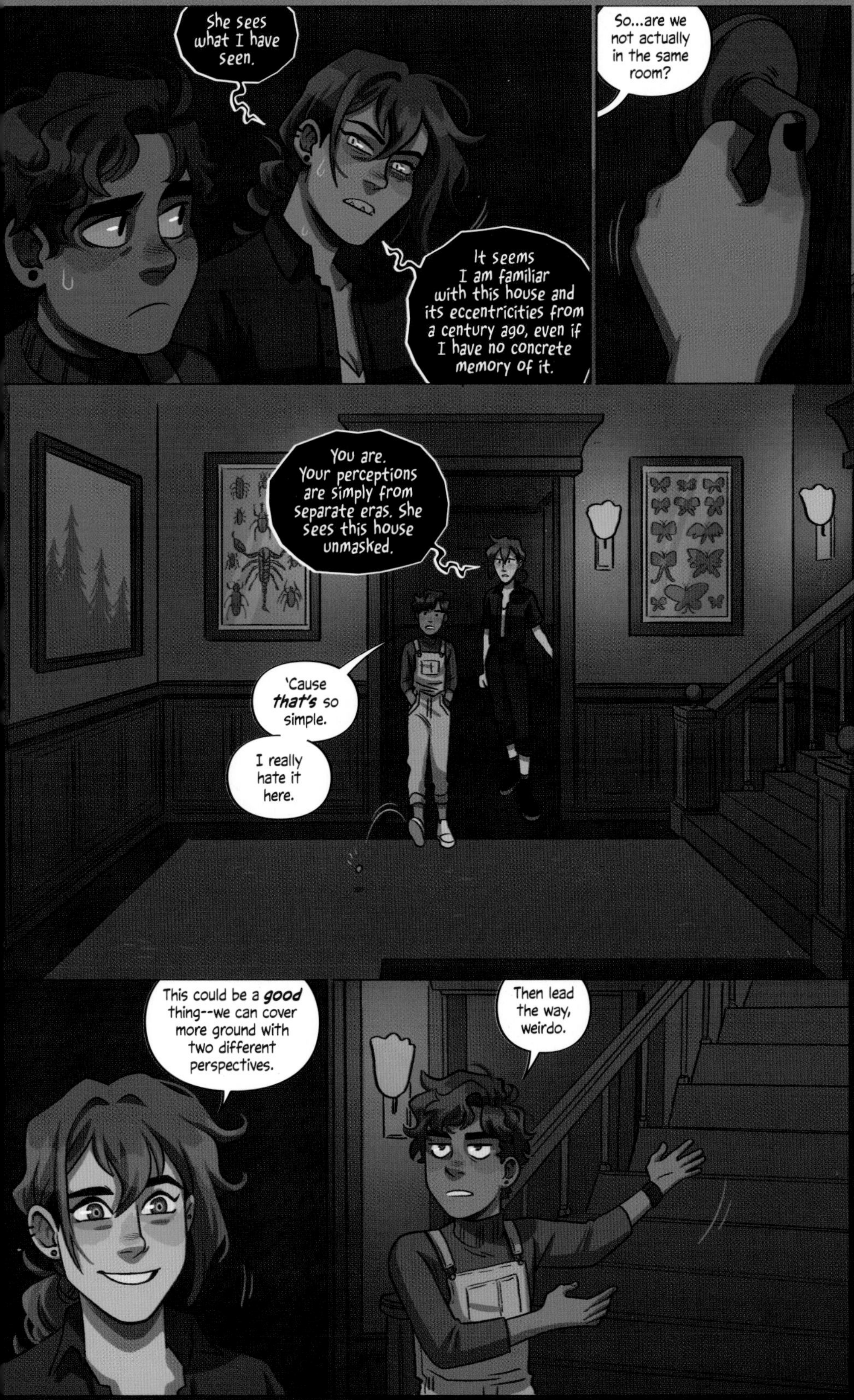

She sees what I have seen.
It seems I am familiar with this house and its eccentricities from a century ago, even if I have no concrete memory of it.
So...are we not actually in the same room?
You are. Your perceptions are simply from separate eras. She sees this house unmasked.
'Cause *that's* so simple.
I really hate it here.
This could be a *good* thing--we can cover more ground with two different perspectives.
Then lead the way, weirdo.

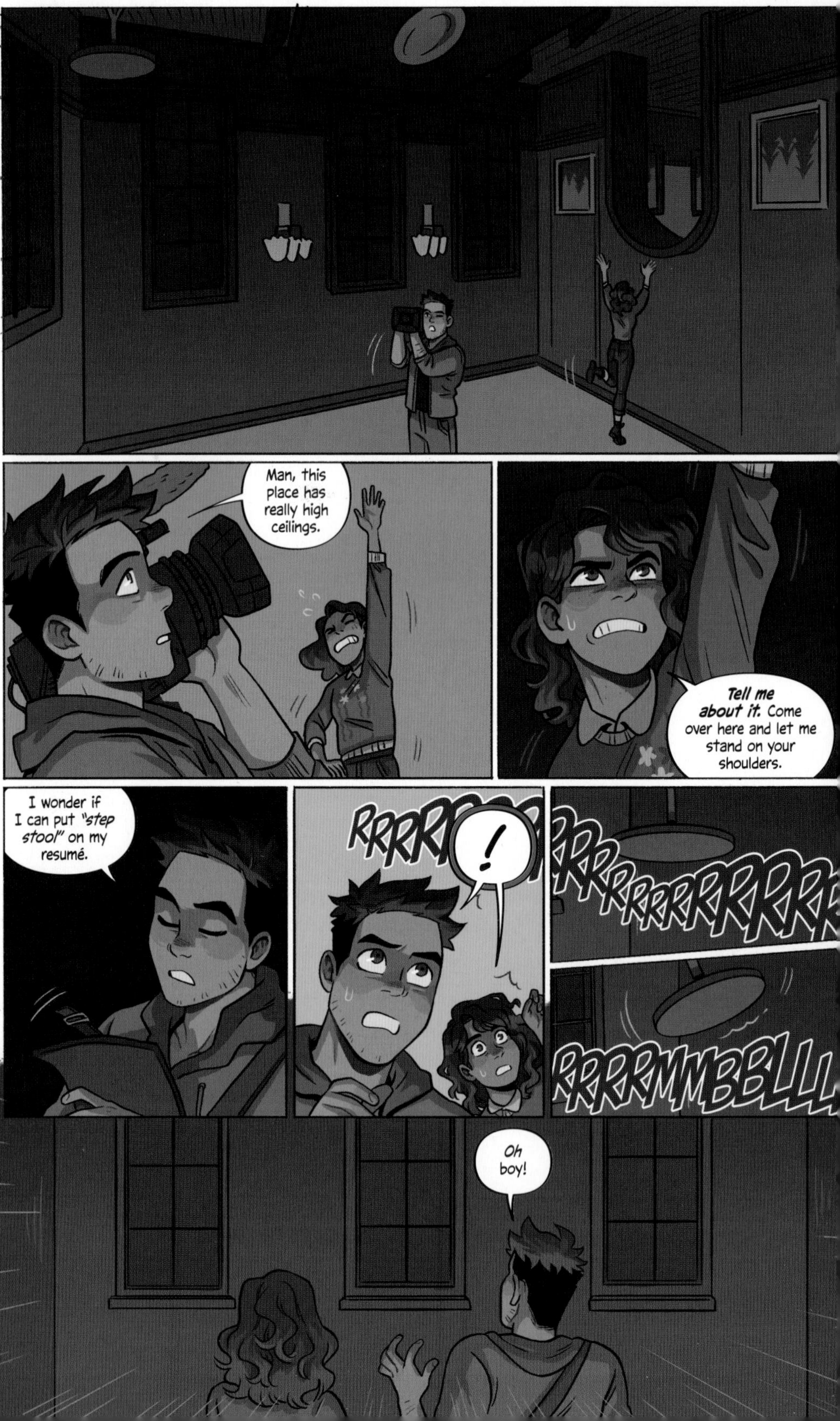
Man, this place has really high ceilings.
Tell me about it. Come over here and let me stand on your shoulders.
I wonder if I can put *"step stool"* on my resumé.
RRRRRRRRRRRRRRRRRRRRRRR
!
RRRRMMBBLLL
Oh boy!

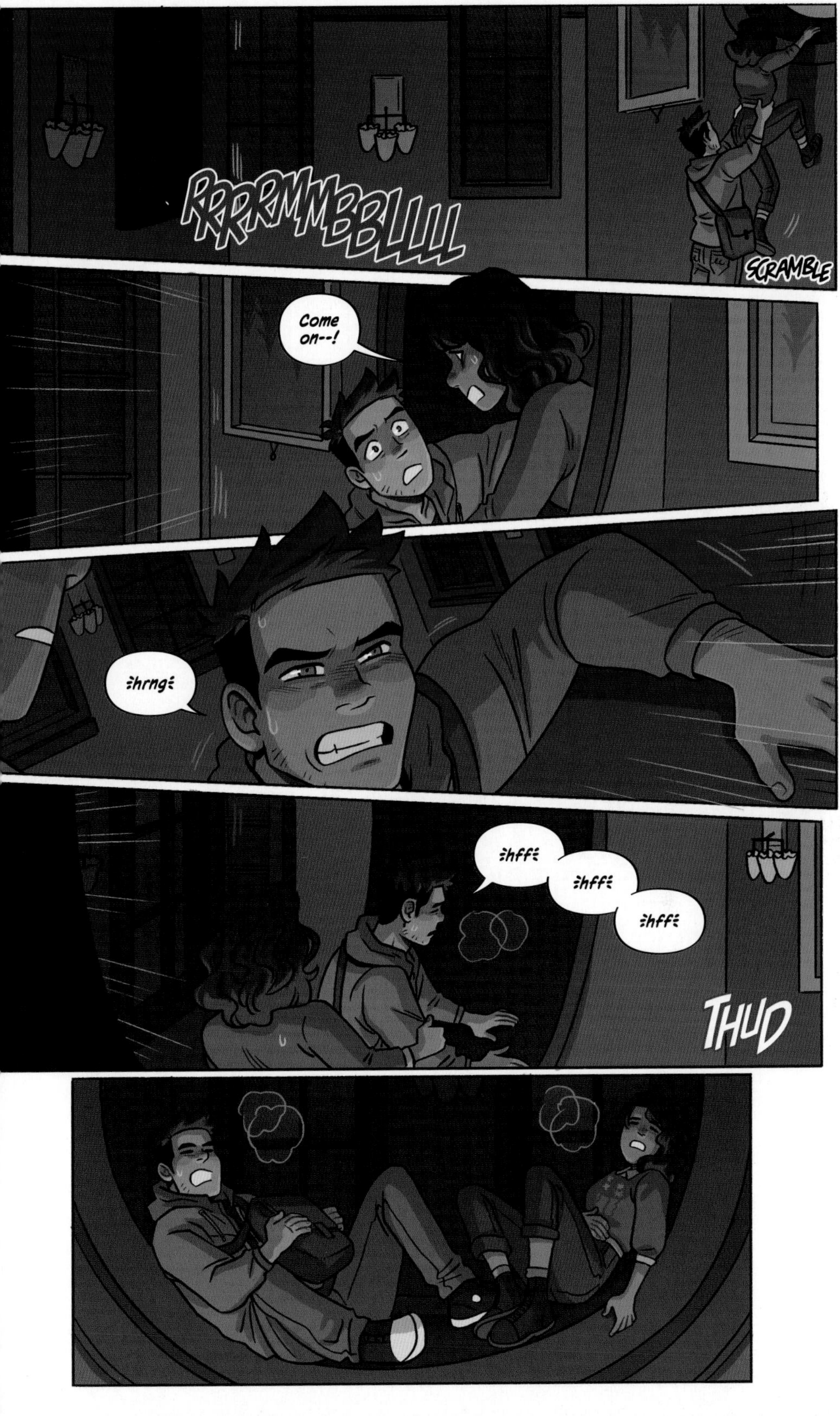
RRRRMMBBLLLL
SCRAMBLE
Come on--!
hrng
hff
hff
hff
THUD

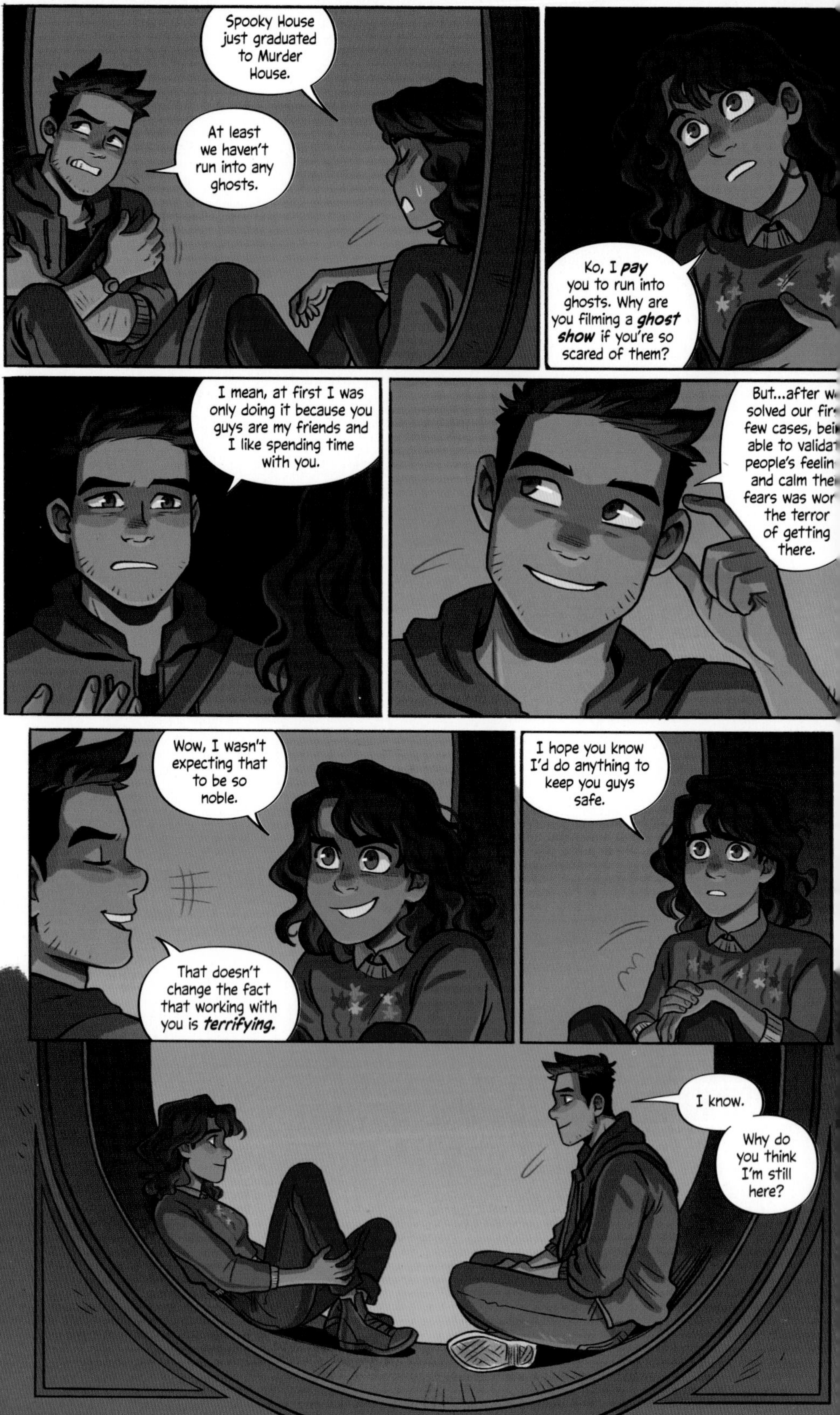

Spooky House just graduated to Murder House.
At least we haven't run into any ghosts.
Ko, I *pay* you to run into ghosts. Why are you filming a ***ghost show*** if you're so scared of them?
I mean, at first I was only doing it because you guys are my friends and I like spending time with you.
But...after w solved our fir few cases, bei able to valida people's feelin and calm the fears was wor the terror of getting there.
Wow, I wasn't expecting that to be so noble.
That doesn't change the fact that working with you is ***terrifying.***
I hope you know I'd do anything to keep you guys safe.
I know.
Why do you think I'm still here?

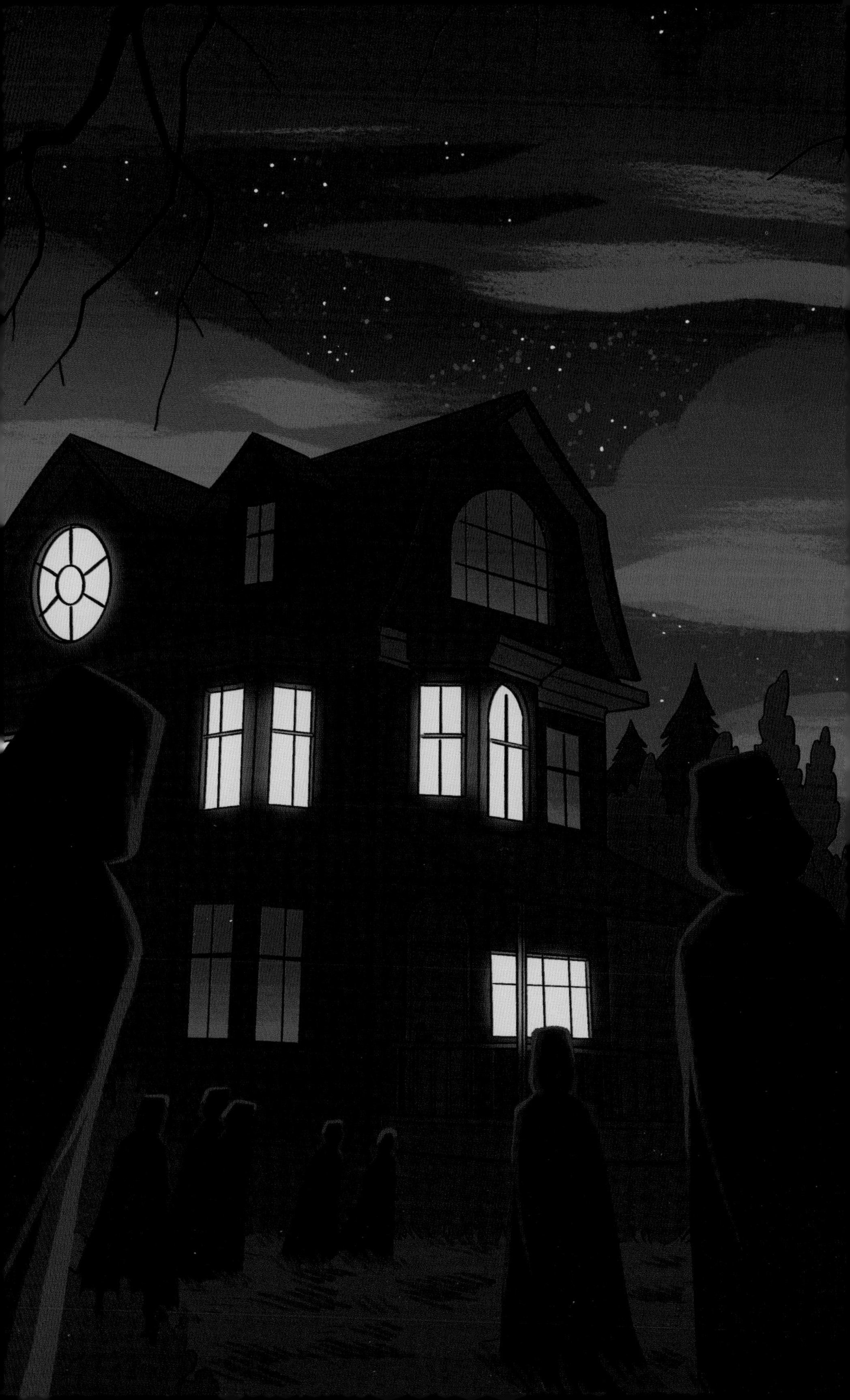

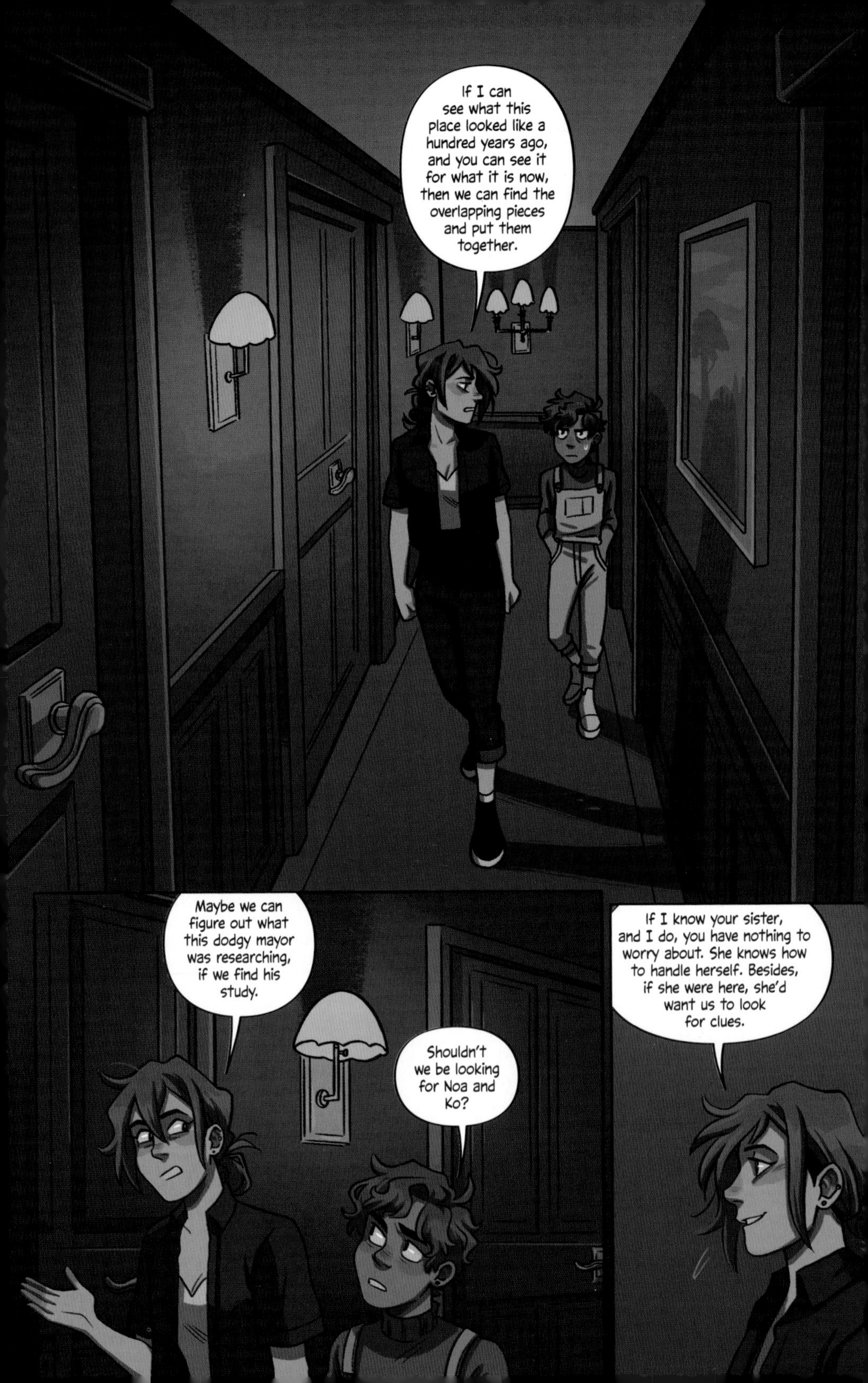
If I can see what this place looked like a hundred years ago, and you can see it for what it is now, then we can find the overlapping pieces and put them together.
Maybe we can figure out what this dodgy mayor was researching, if we find his study.
Shouldn't we be looking for Noa and Ko?
If I know your sister, and I do, you have nothing to worry about. She knows how to handle herself. Besides, if she were here, she'd want us to look for clues.

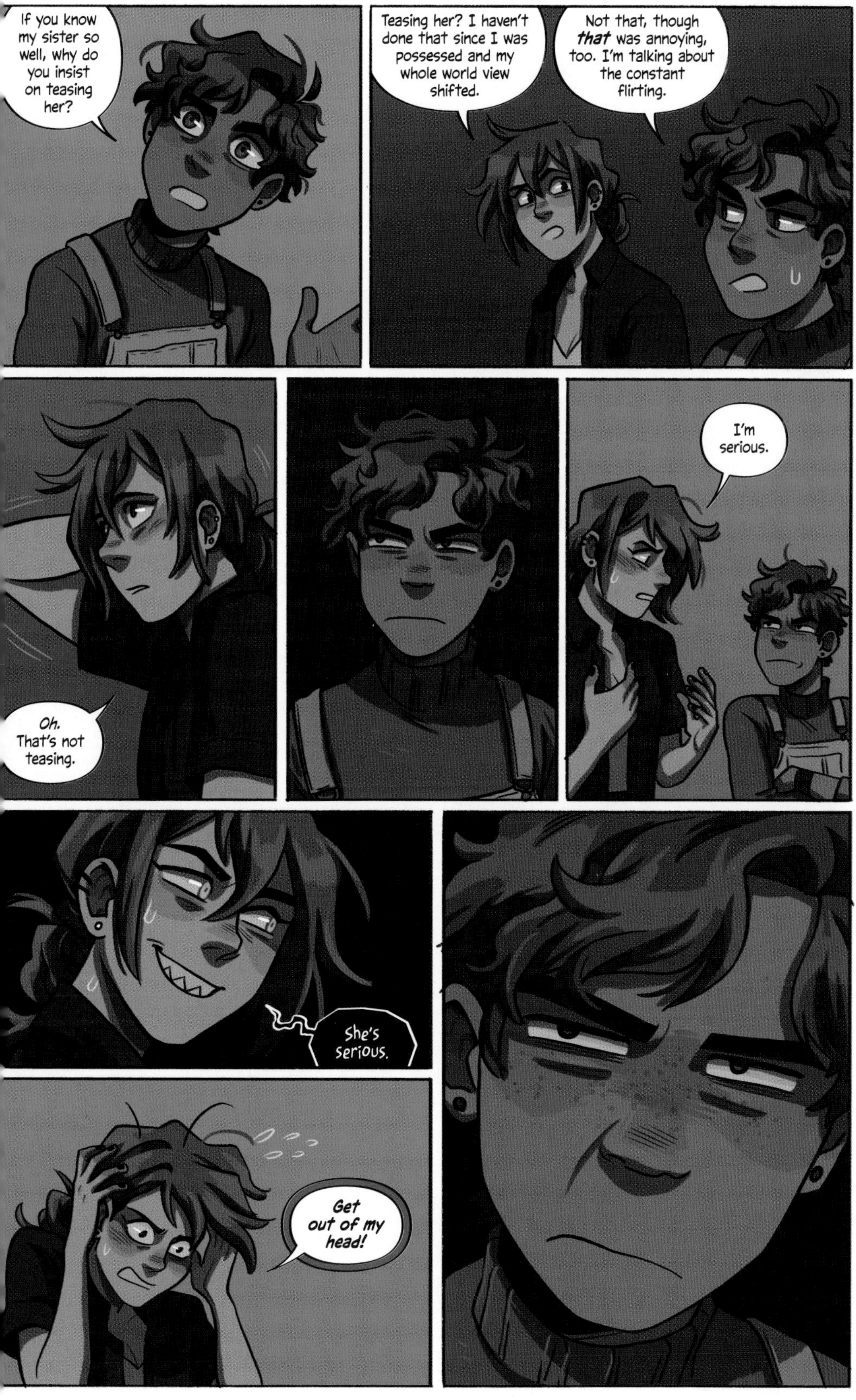
If you know my sister so well, why do you insist on teasing her?
Teasing her? I haven't done that since I was possessed and my whole world view shifted.
Not that, though *that* was annoying, too. I'm talking about the constant flirting.
Oh. That's not teasing.
I'm serious.
She's serious.
Get out of my head!

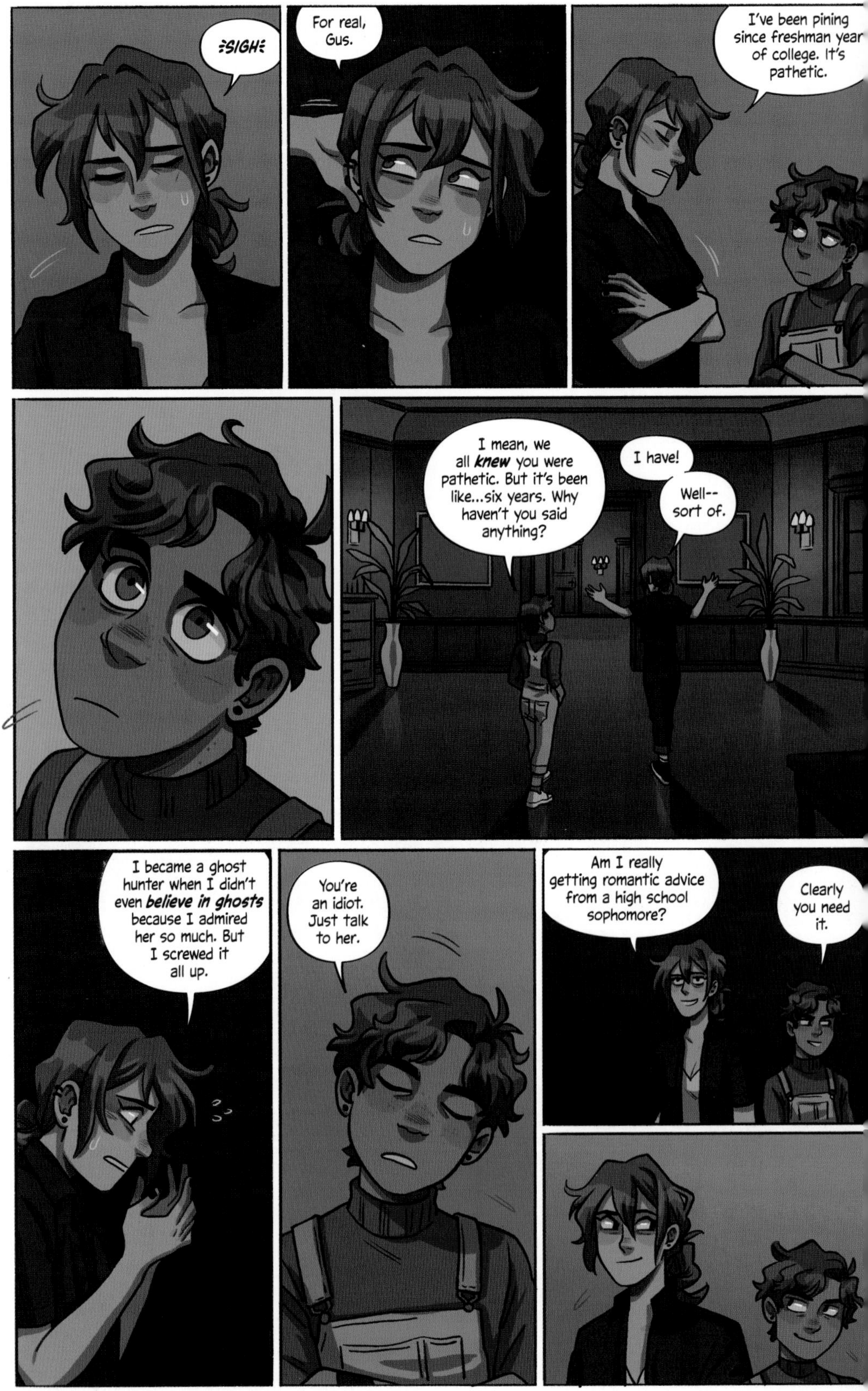
SIGH
For real, Gus.
I've been pining since freshman year of college. It's pathetic.
I mean, we all *knew* you were pathetic. But it's been like...six years. Why haven't you said anything?
I have!
Well-- sort of.
I became a ghost hunter when I didn't even *believe in ghosts* because I admired her so much. But I screwed it all up.
You're an idiot. Just talk to her.
Am I really getting romantic advice from a high school sophomore?
Clearly you need it.

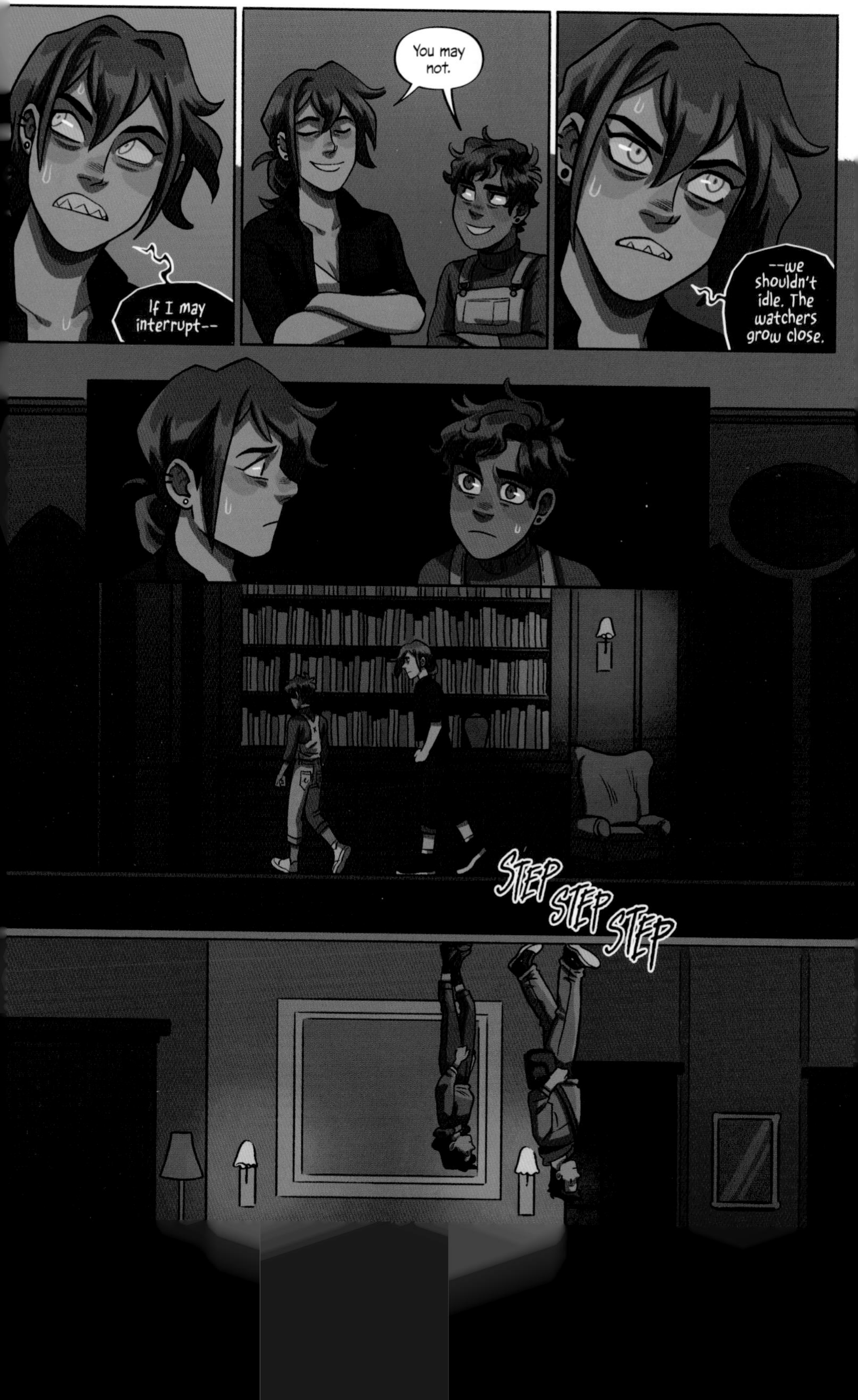
If I may interrupt--
You may not.
--we shouldn't idle. The watchers grow close.
STEP STEP STEP

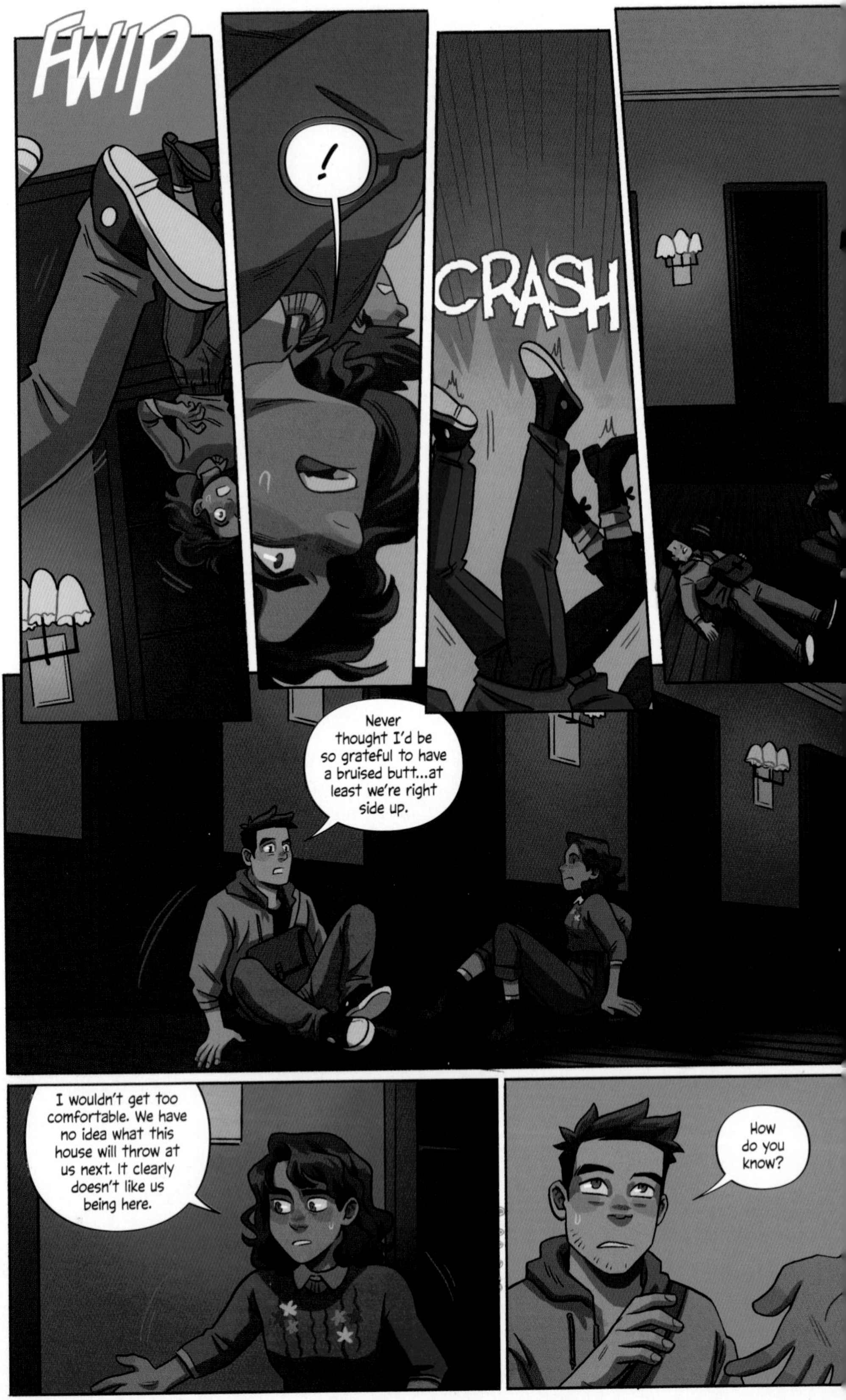
FWIP
!
CRASH
Never thought I'd be so grateful to have a bruised butt...at least we're right side up.
I wouldn't get too comfortable. We have no idea what this house will throw at us next. It clearly doesn't like us being here.
How do you know?

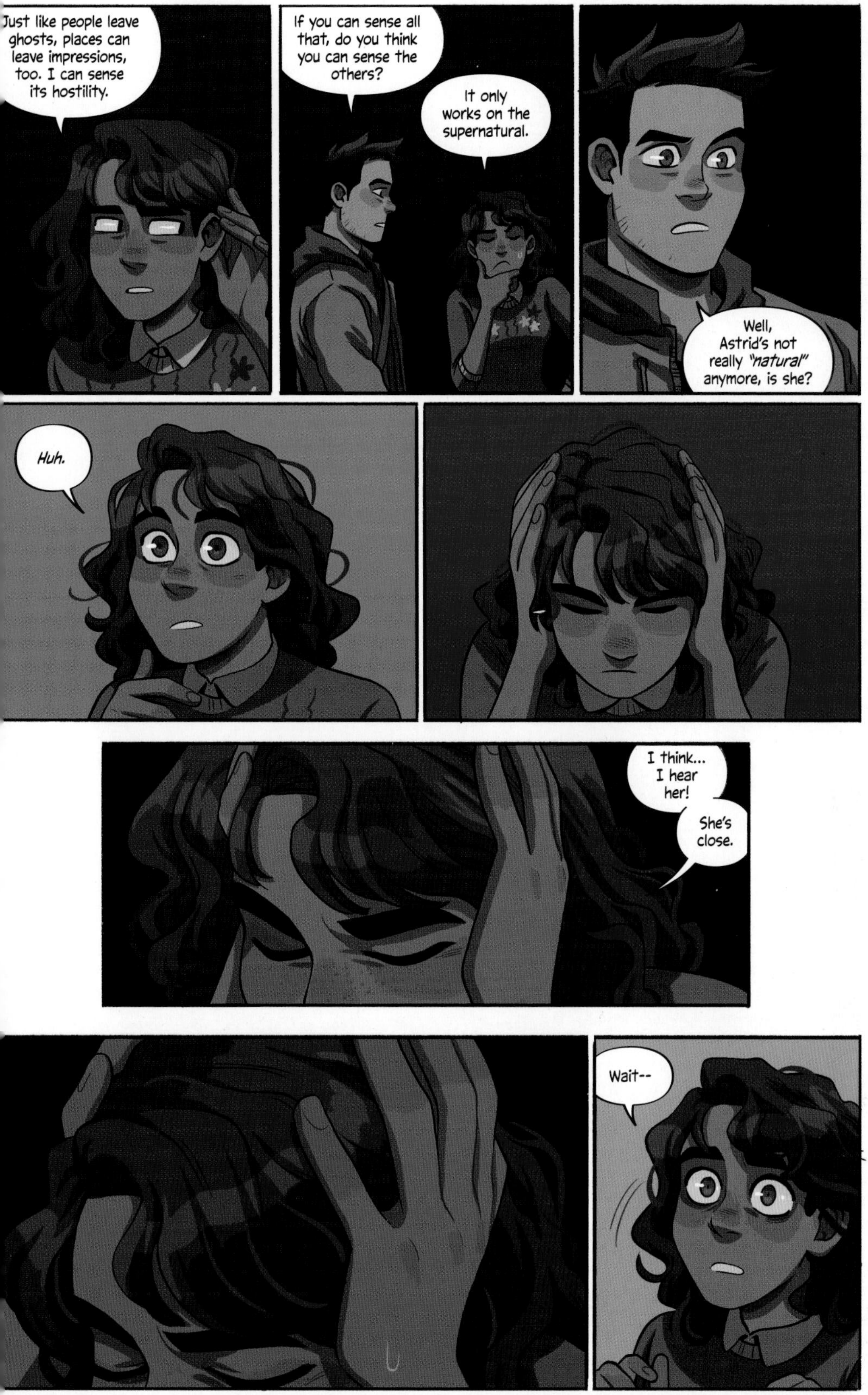
Just like people leave ghosts, places can leave impressions, too. I can sense its hostility.
If you can sense all that, do you think you can sense the others?
It only works on the supernatural.
Well, Astrid's not really "natural" anymore, is she?
Huh.
I think... I hear her!
She's close.
Wait--

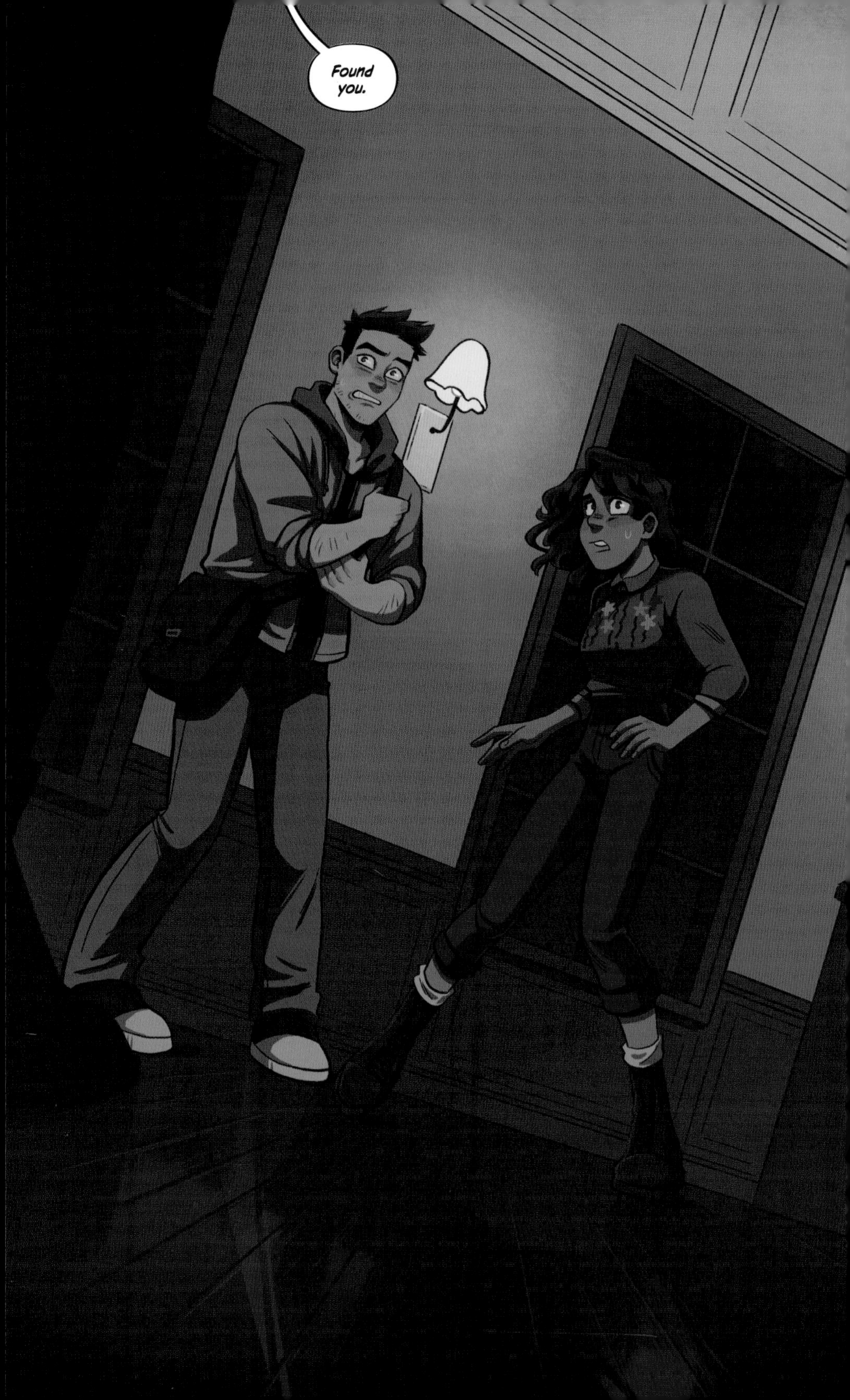
Found you.

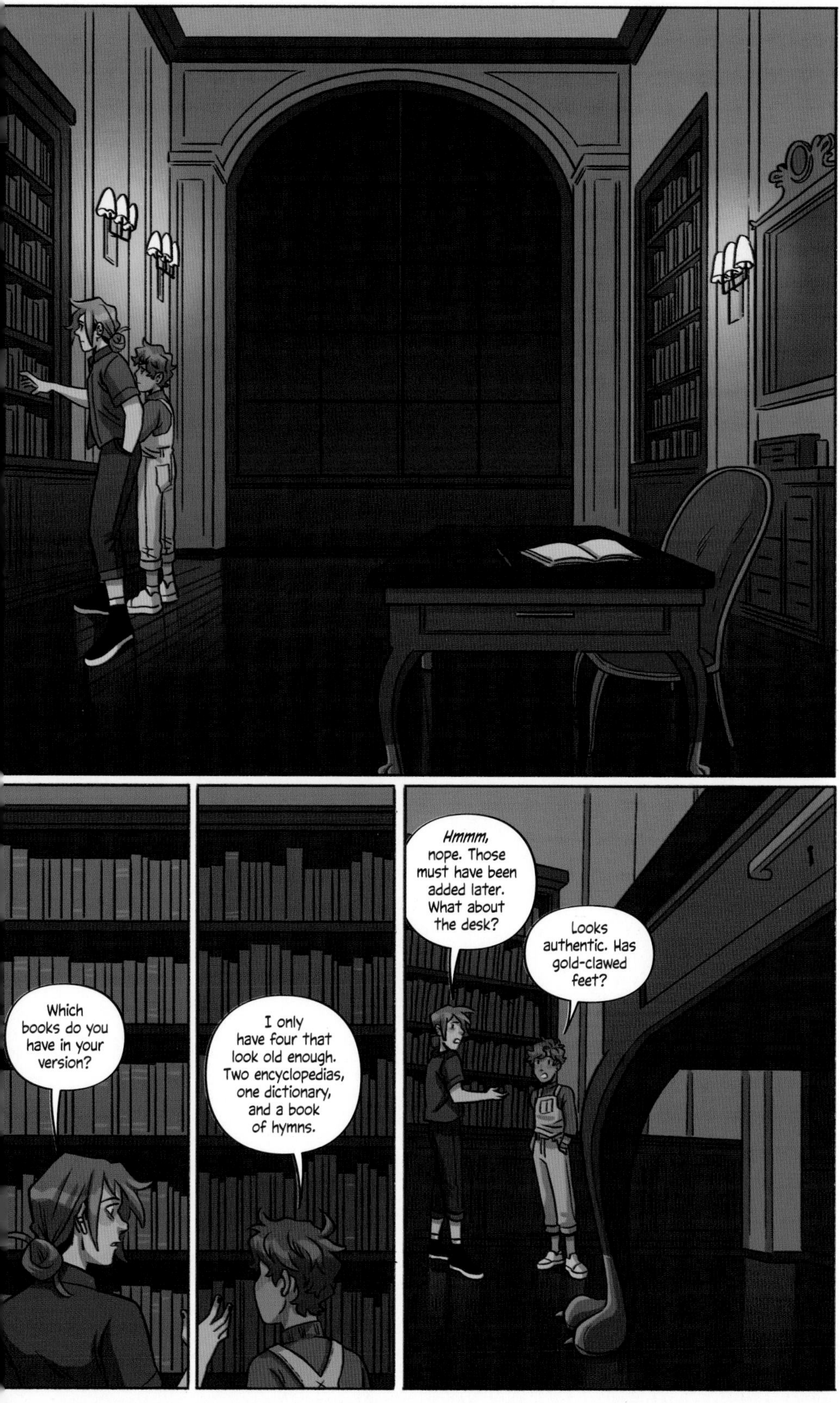
Which books do you have in your version?
I only have four that look old enough. Two encyclopedias, one dictionary, and a book of hymns.
Hmmm, nope. Those must have been added later. What about the desk?
Looks authentic. Has gold-clawed feet?

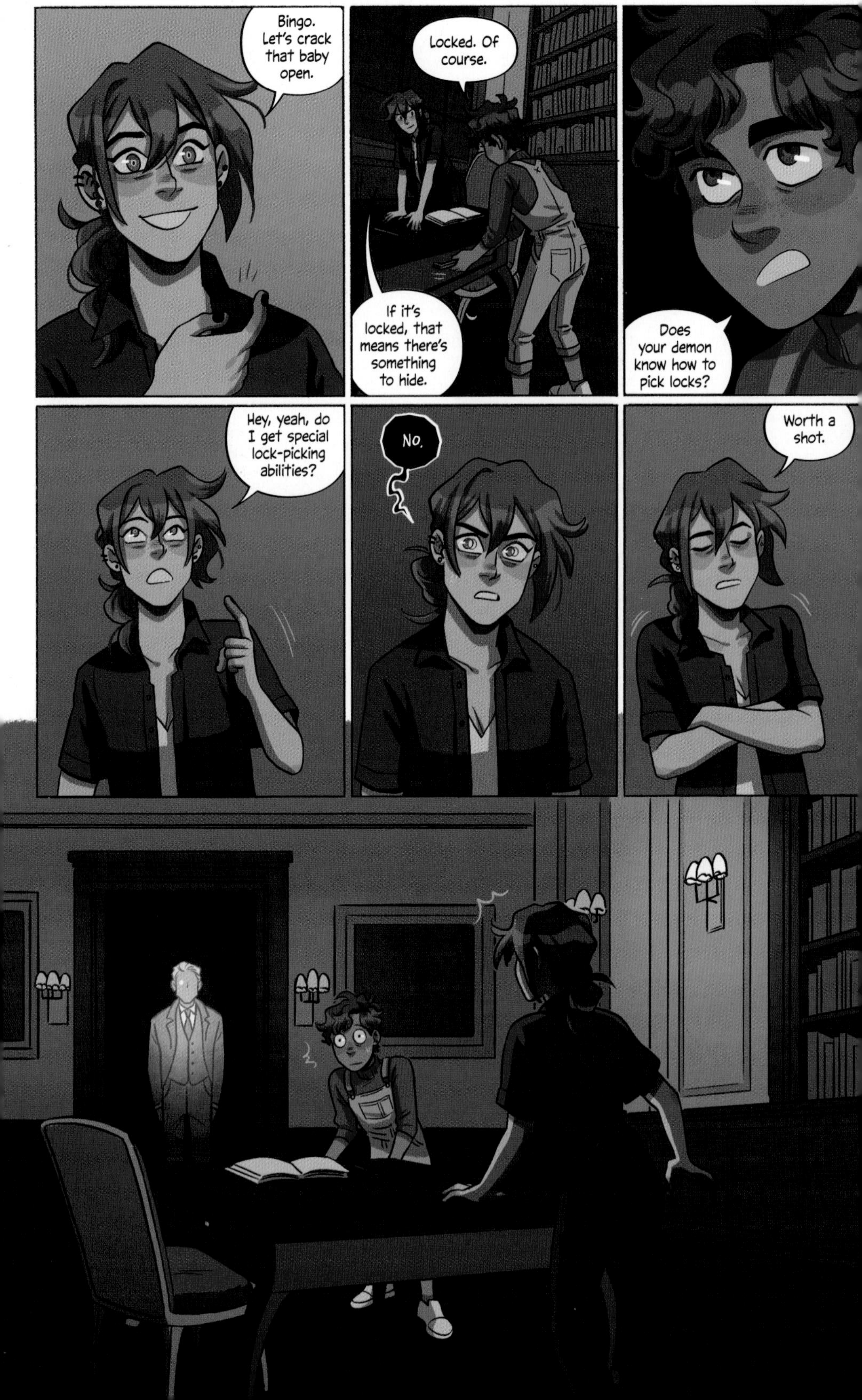
Bingo. Let's crack that baby open.
Locked. Of course.
If it's locked, that means there's something to hide.
Does your demon know how to pick locks?
Hey, yeah, do I get special lock-picking abilities?
No.
Worth a shot.

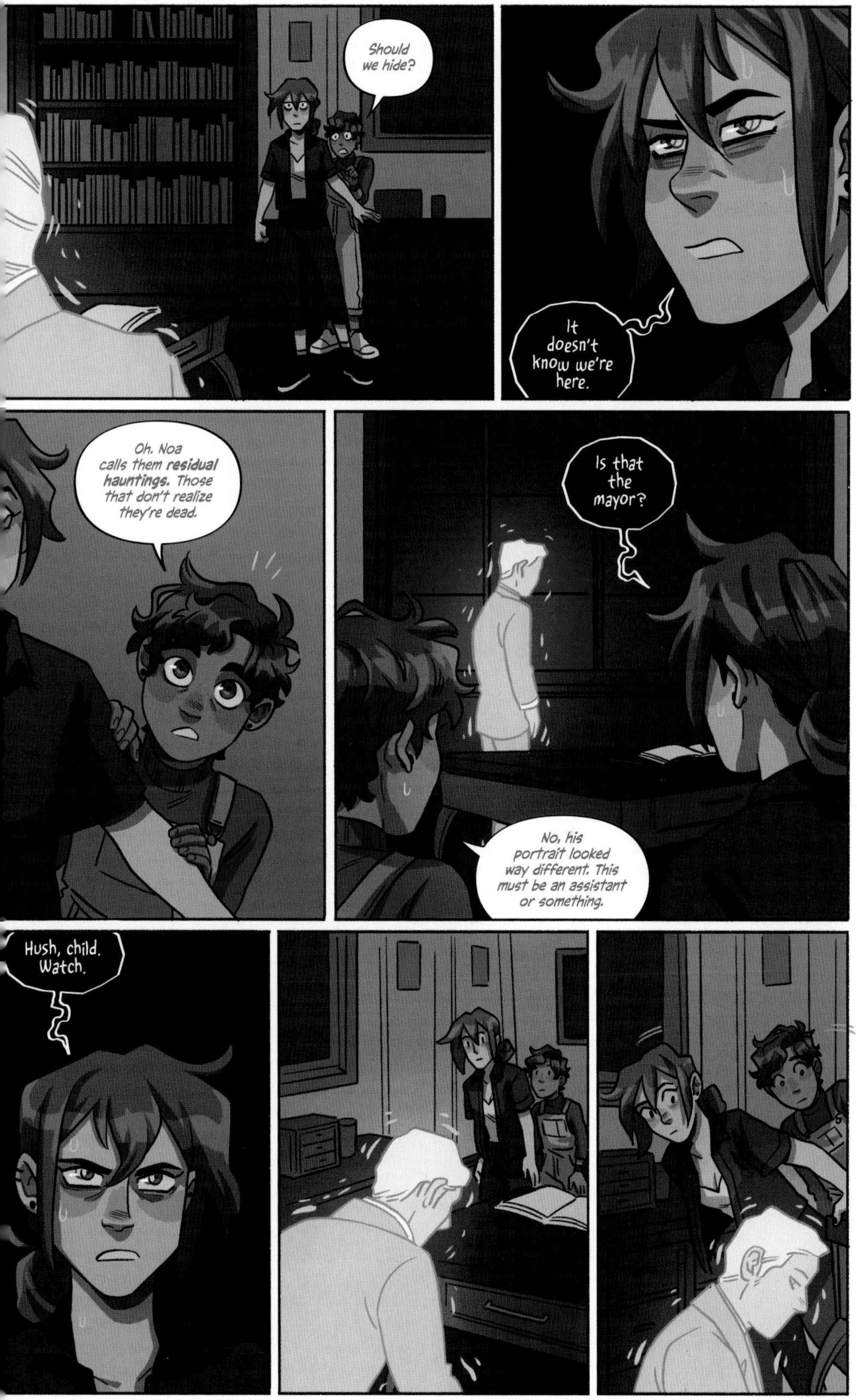
Should we hide?
It doesn't know we're here.
Oh. Noa calls them **residual hauntings.** Those that don't realize they're dead.
Is that the mayor?
No, his portrait looked way different. This must be an assistant or something.
Hush, child. Watch.

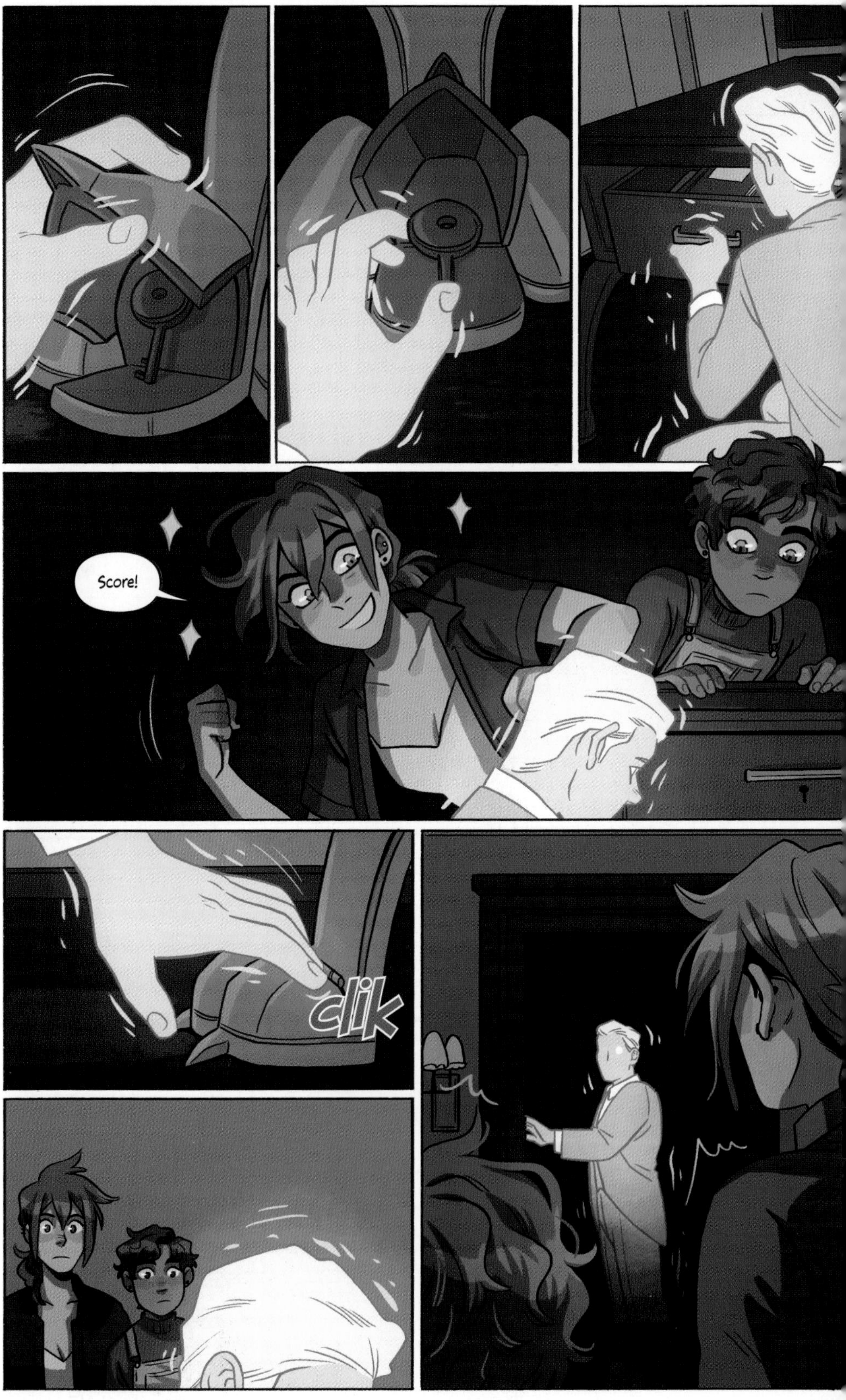
Score!
clik

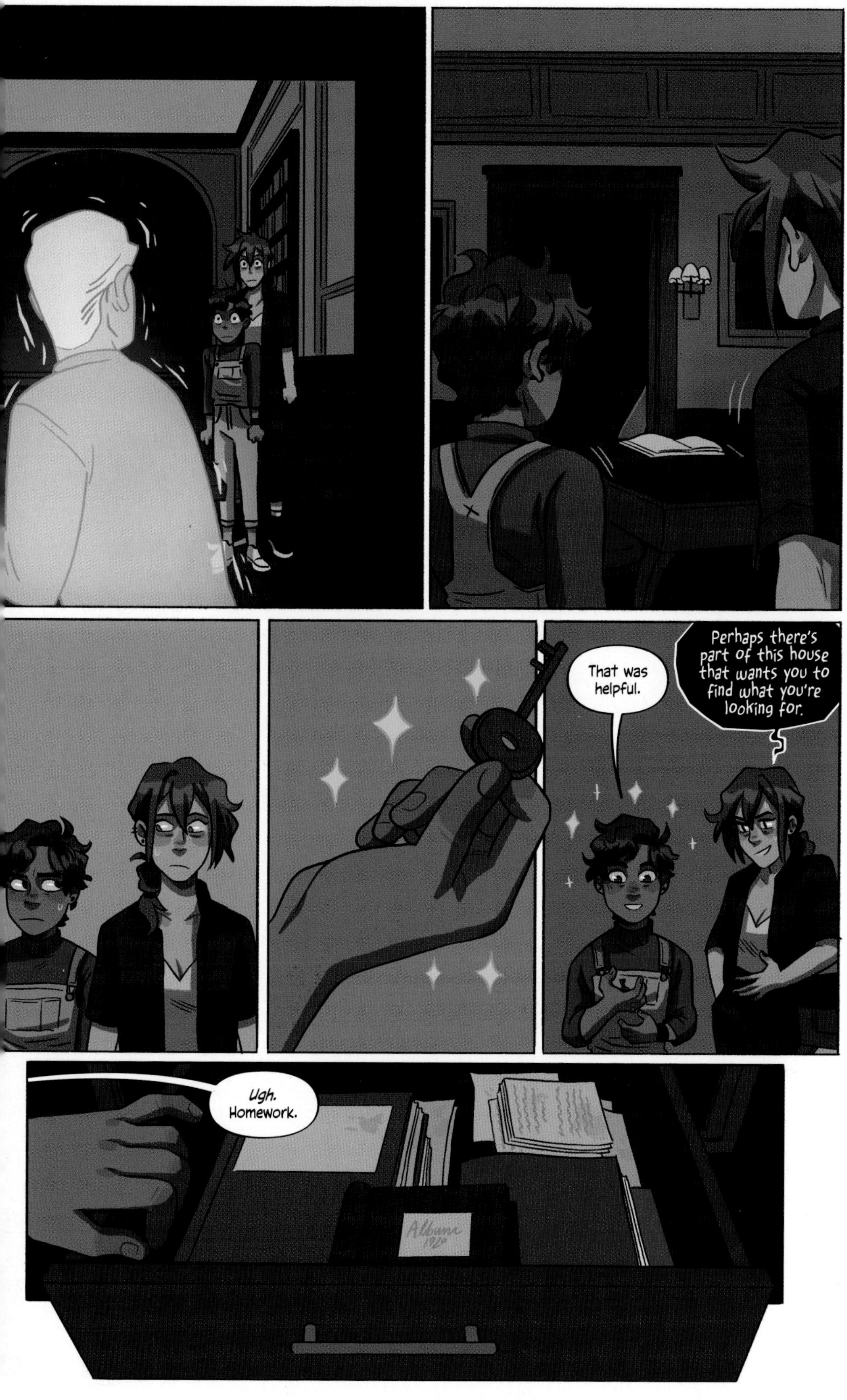
That was helpful.
Perhaps there's part of this house that wants you to find what you're looking for.
Ugh. Homework.
Album 1920

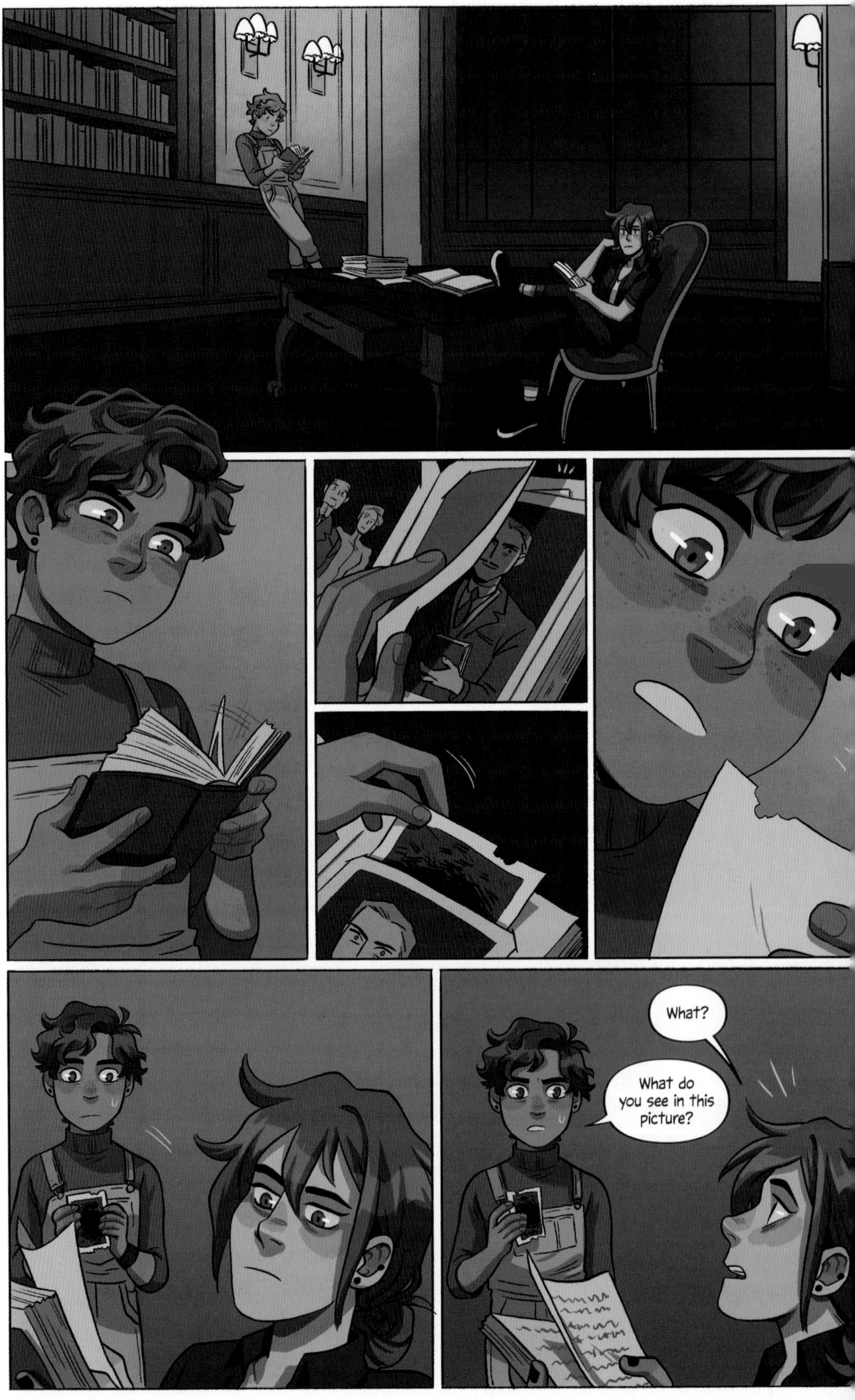
What?
What do you see in this picture?

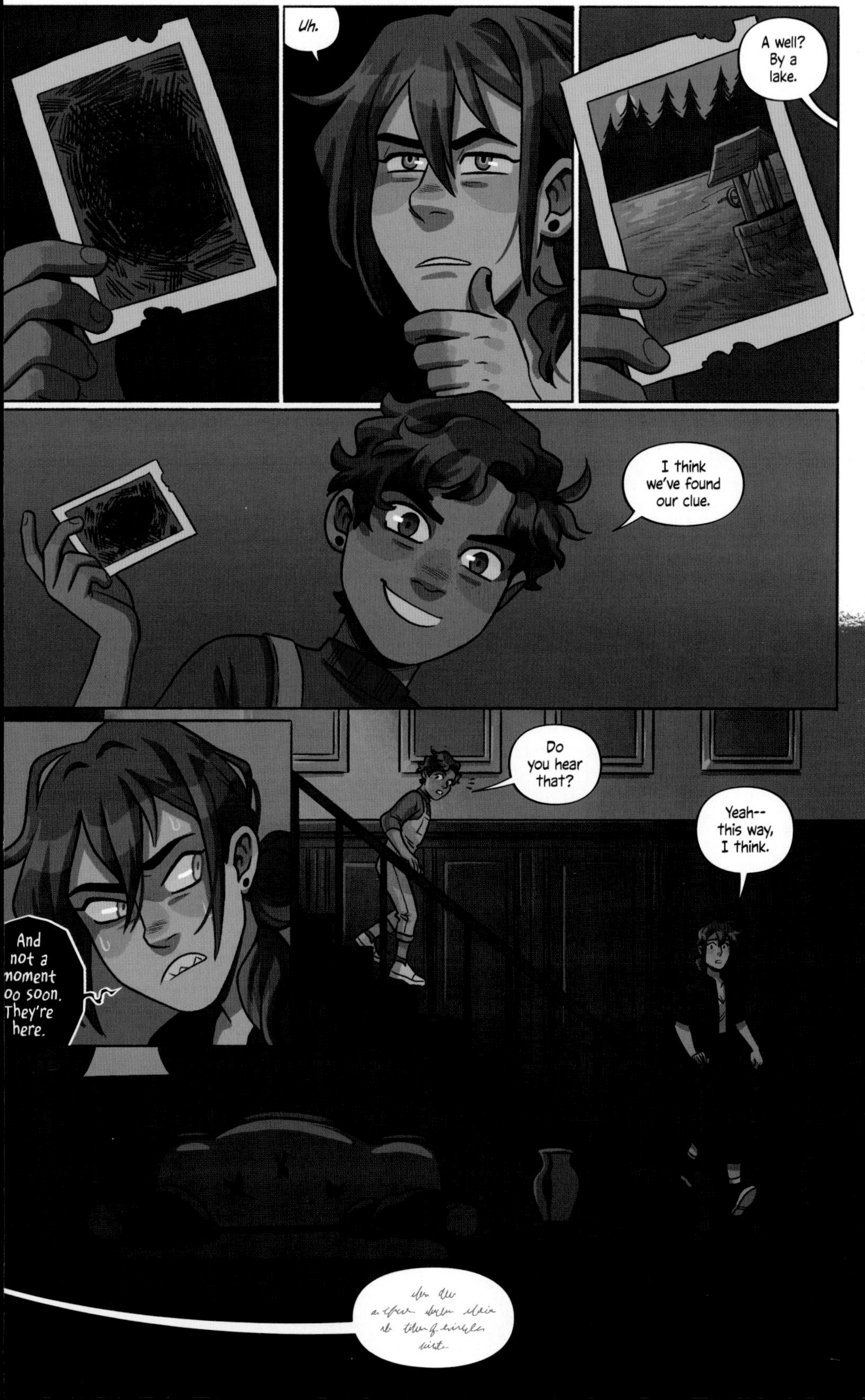

Uh.
A well? By a lake.
I think we've found our clue.
Do you hear that?
Yeah-- this way, I think.
And not a noment oo soon. They're here.

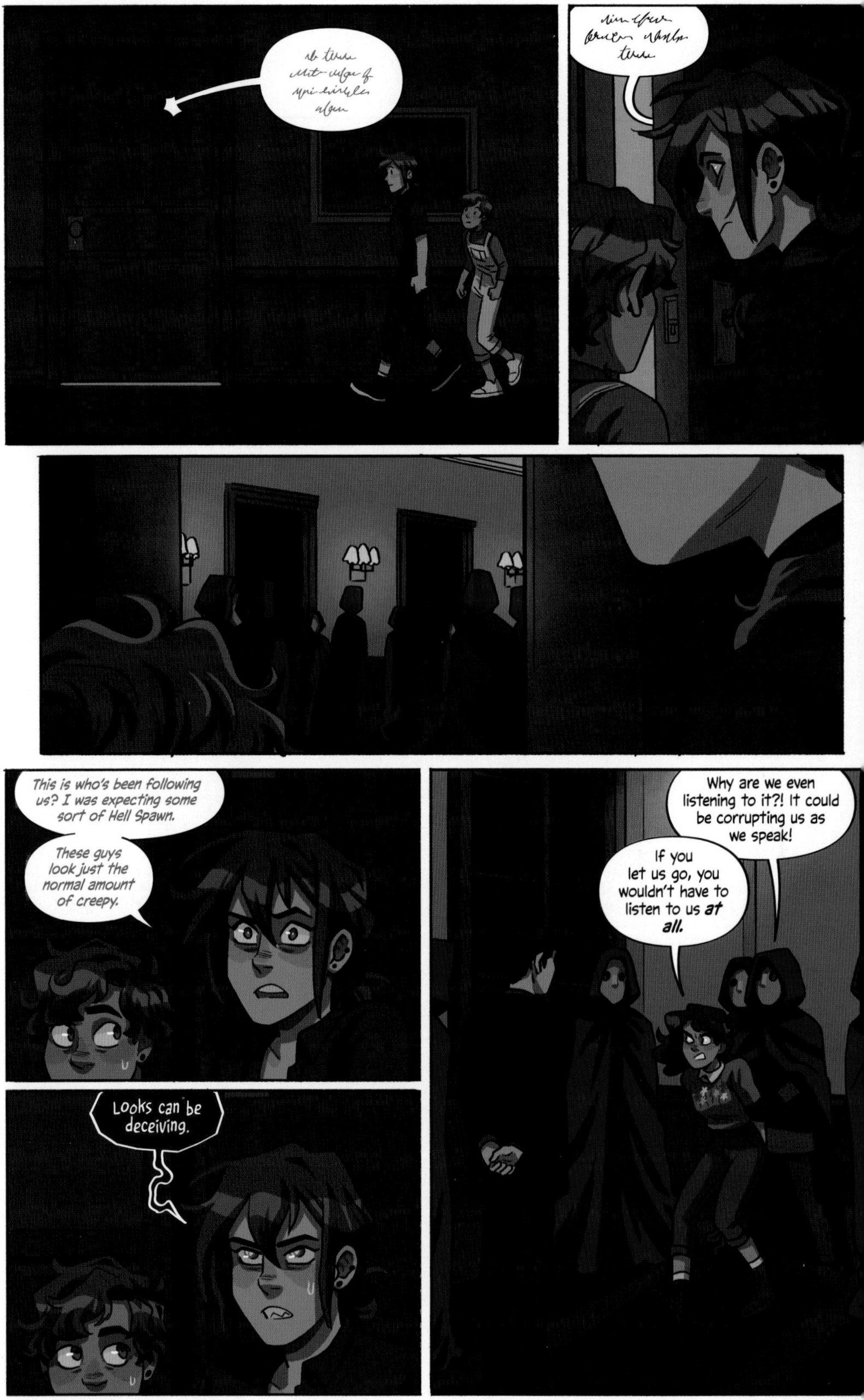
This is who's been following us? I was expecting some sort of Hell Spawn.
These guys look just the normal amount of creepy.
Looks can be deceiving.
Why are we even listening to it?! It could be corrupting us as we speak!
If you let us go, you wouldn't have to listen to us ***at all.***

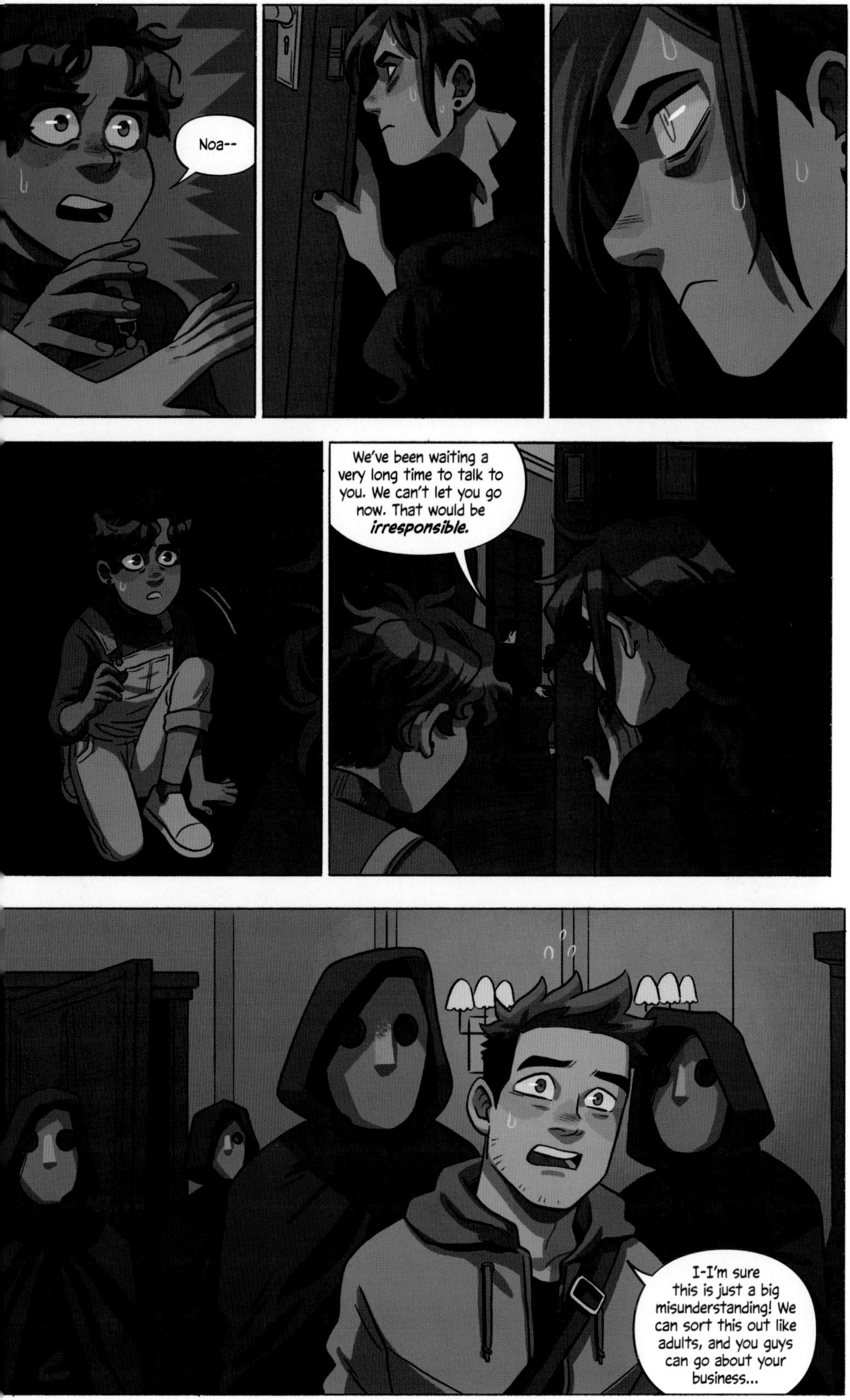
Noa--
We've been waiting a very long time to talk to you. We can't let you go now. That would be *irresponsible.*
I-I'm sure this is just a big misunderstanding! We can sort this out like adults, and you guys can go about your business...

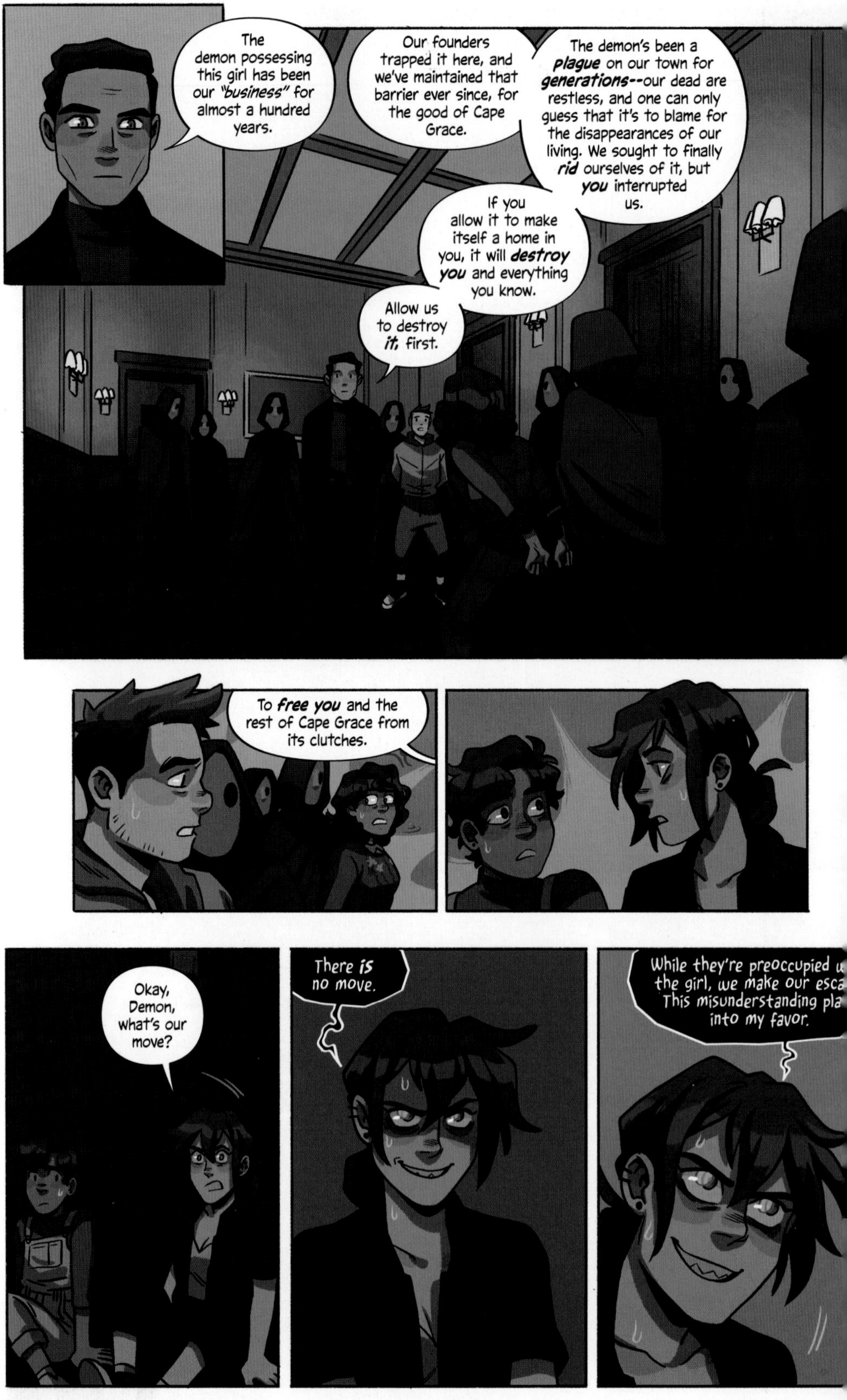

The demon possessing this girl has been our "business" for almost a hundred years.
Our founders trapped it here, and we've maintained that barrier ever since, for the good of Cape Grace.
The demon's been a plague on our town for generations--our dead are restless, and one can only guess that it's to blame for the disappearances of our living. We sought to finally rid ourselves of it, but you interrupted us.
If you allow it to make itself a home in you, it will destroy you and everything you know.
Allow us to destroy it, first.
To free you and the rest of Cape Grace from its clutches.
Okay, Demon, what's our move?
There is no move.
While they're preoccupied
the girl, we make our esca
This misunderstanding pla
into my favor.

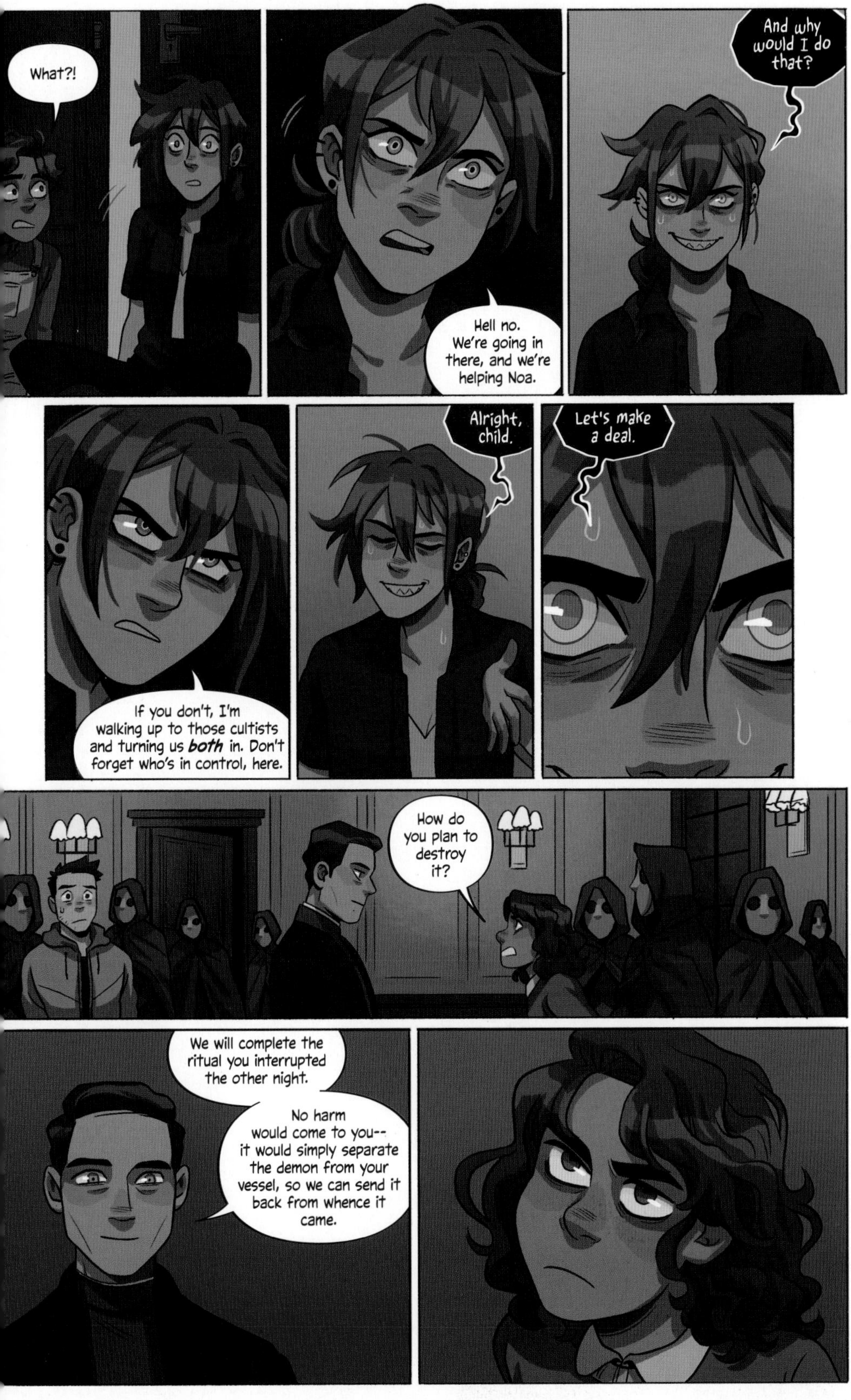
What?!
Hell no. We're going in there, and we're helping Noa.
And why would I do that?
If you don't, I'm walking up to those cultists and turning us **both** in. Don't forget who's in control, here.
Alright, child.
Let's make a deal.
How do you plan to destroy it?
We will complete the ritual you interrupted the other night.
No harm would come to you--it would simply separate the demon from your vessel, so we can send it back from whence it came.

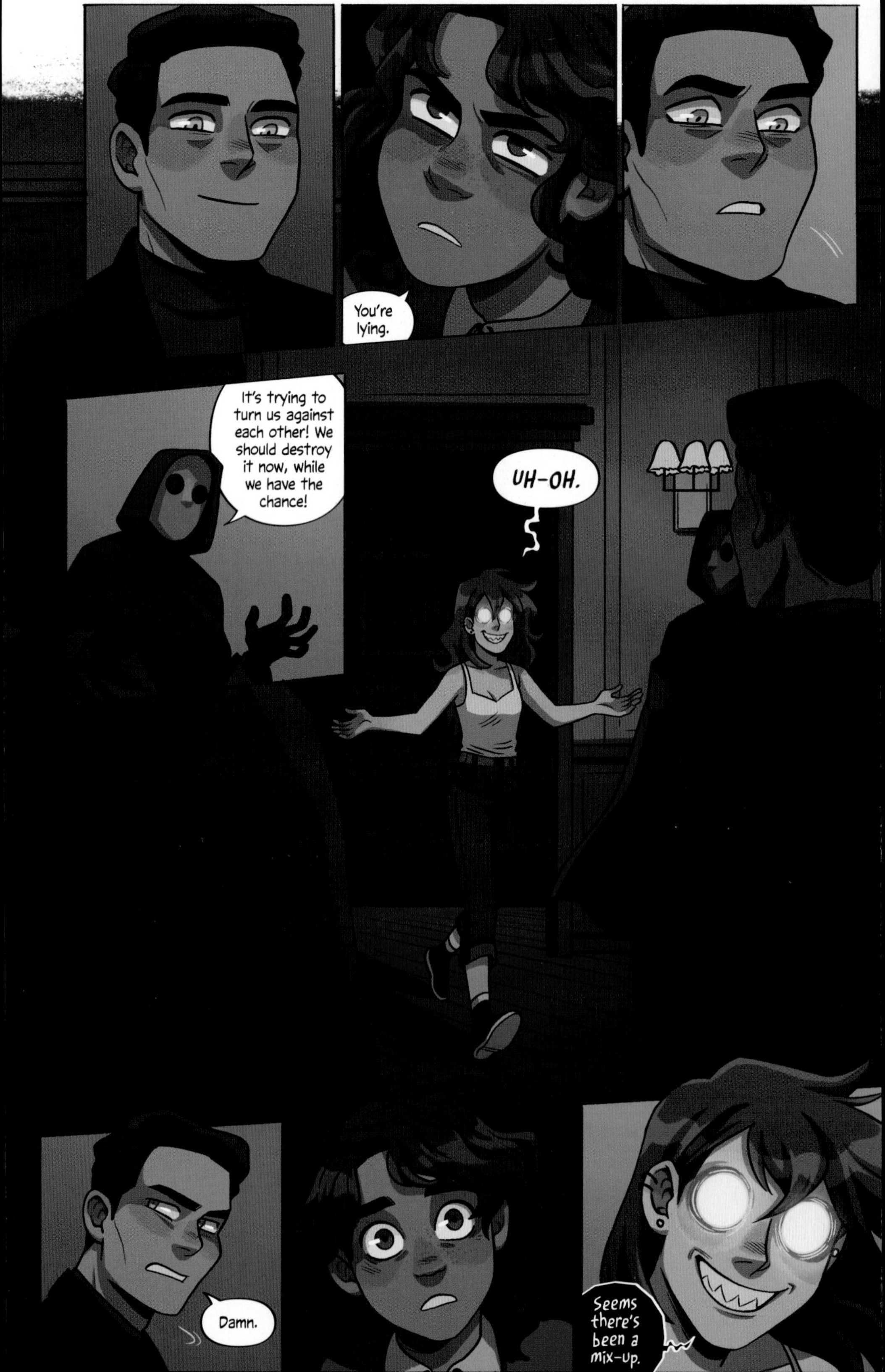
You're lying.
It's trying to turn us against each other! We should destroy it now, while we have the chance!
UH-OH.
Damn.
Seems there's been a mix-up.

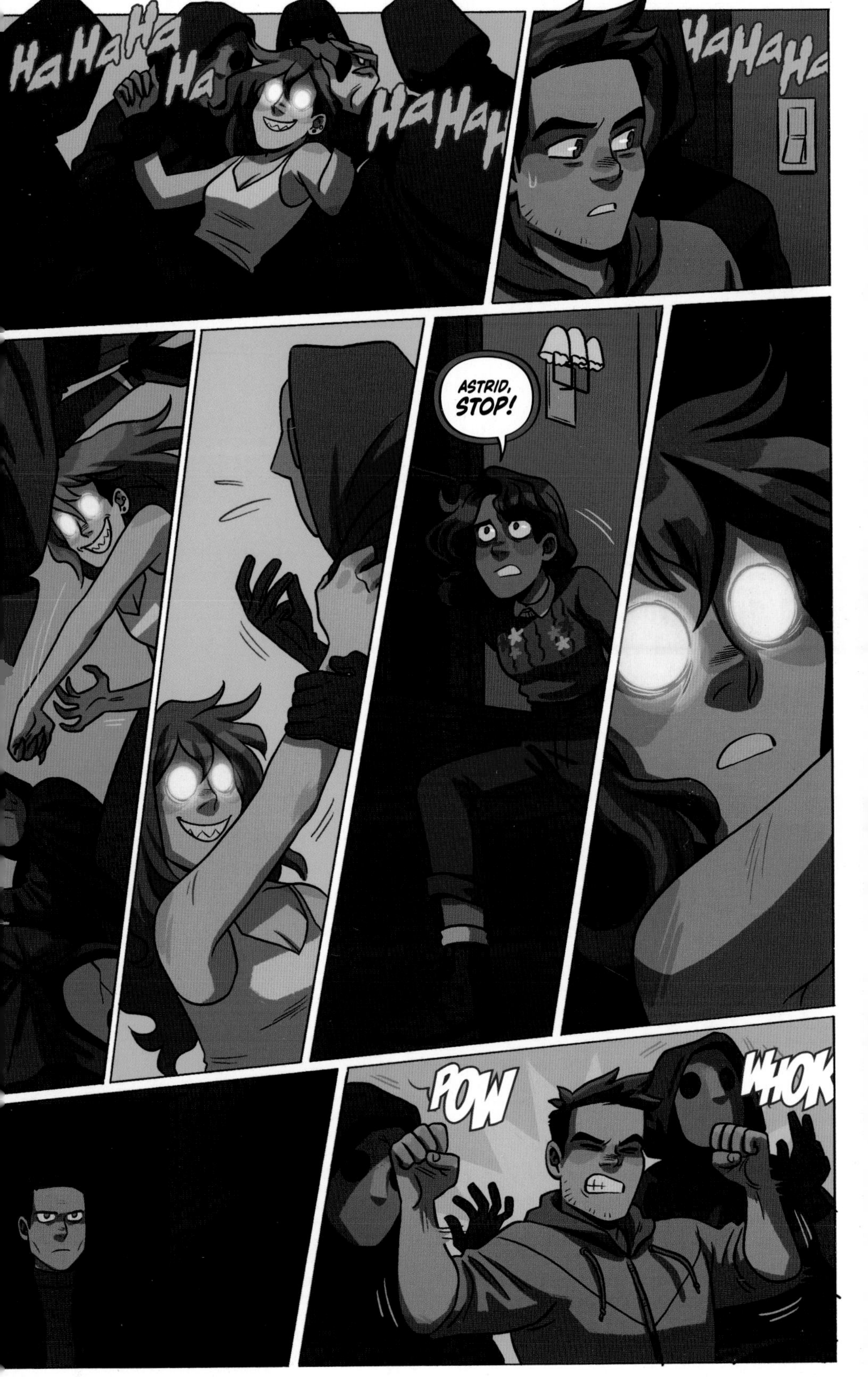
HaHaHa
Ha
HaHaHa
HaHaHa
ASTRID, STOP!
POW
WHOK

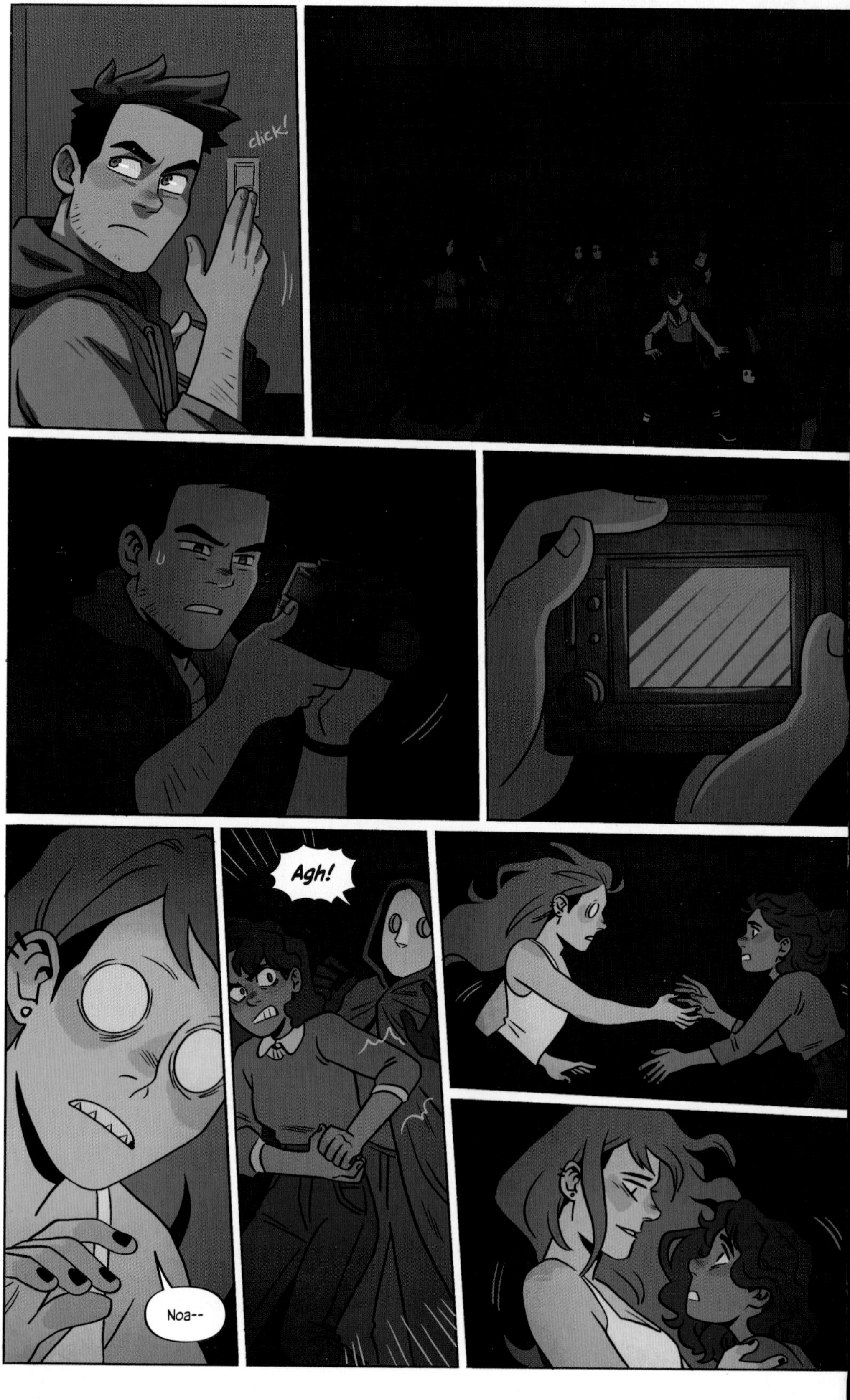
click!
Agh!
Noa--

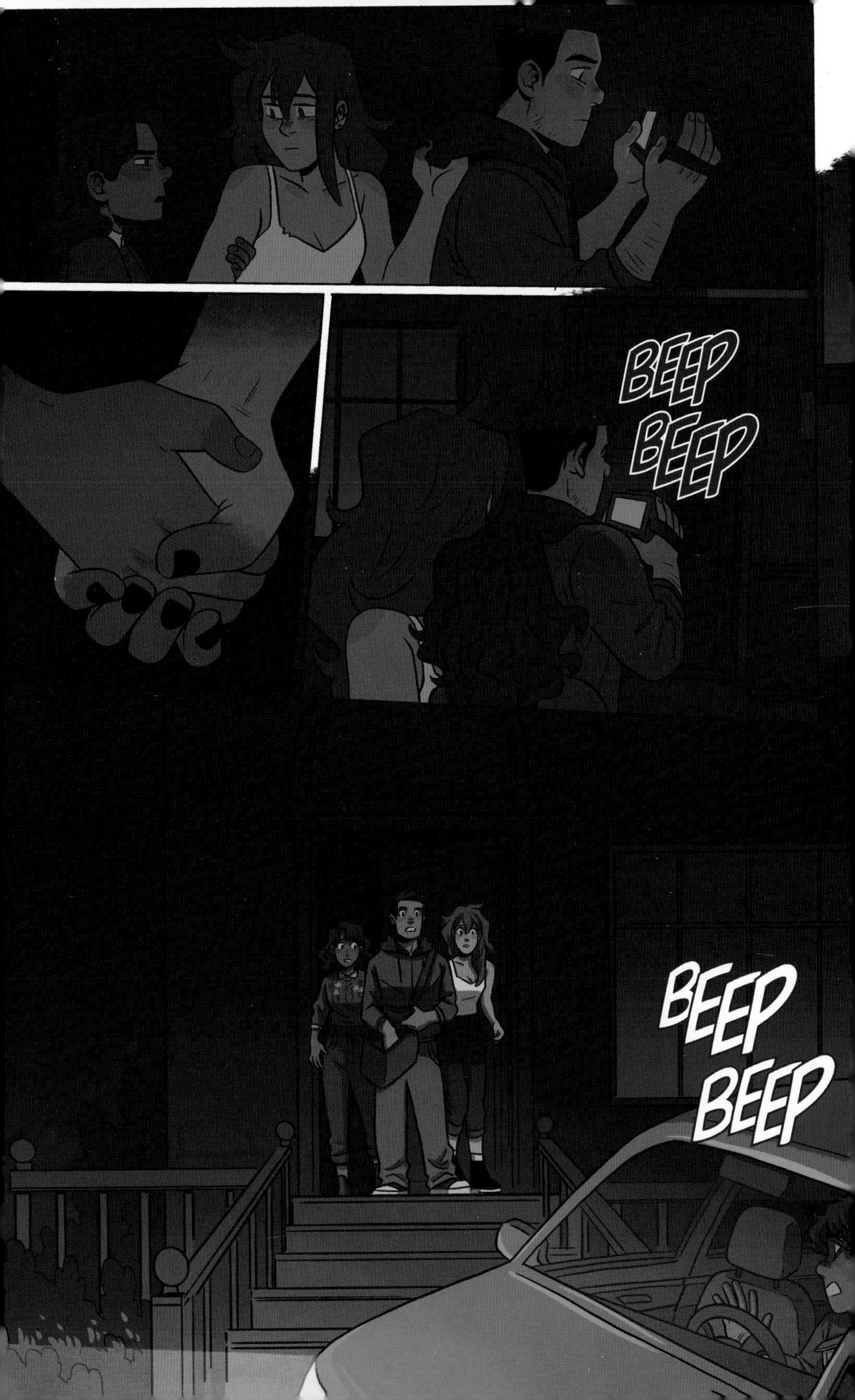

BEEP
BEEP
BEEP
BEEP

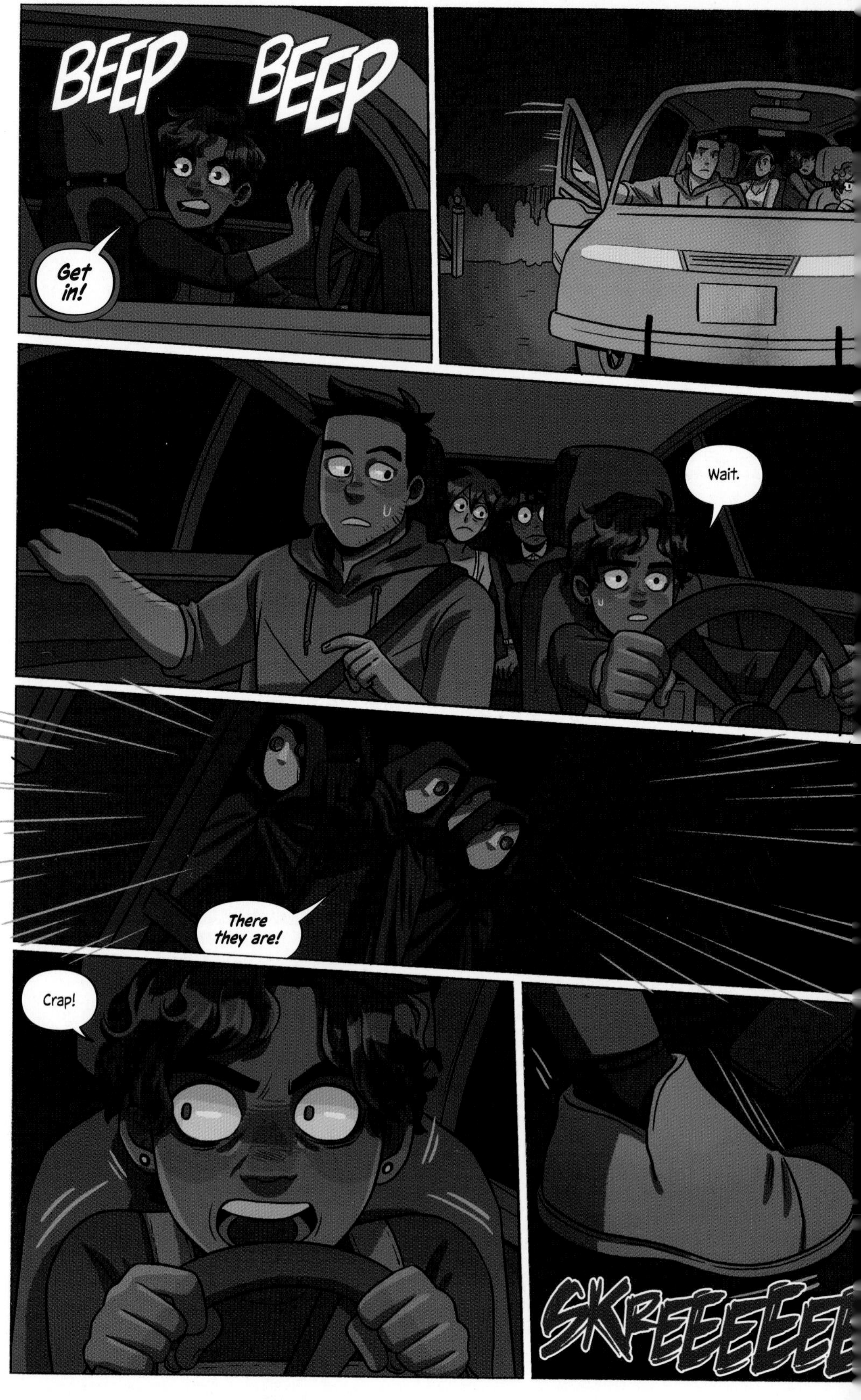
BEEP BEEP
Get in!
Wait.
There they are!
Crap!
SKREEEEEE

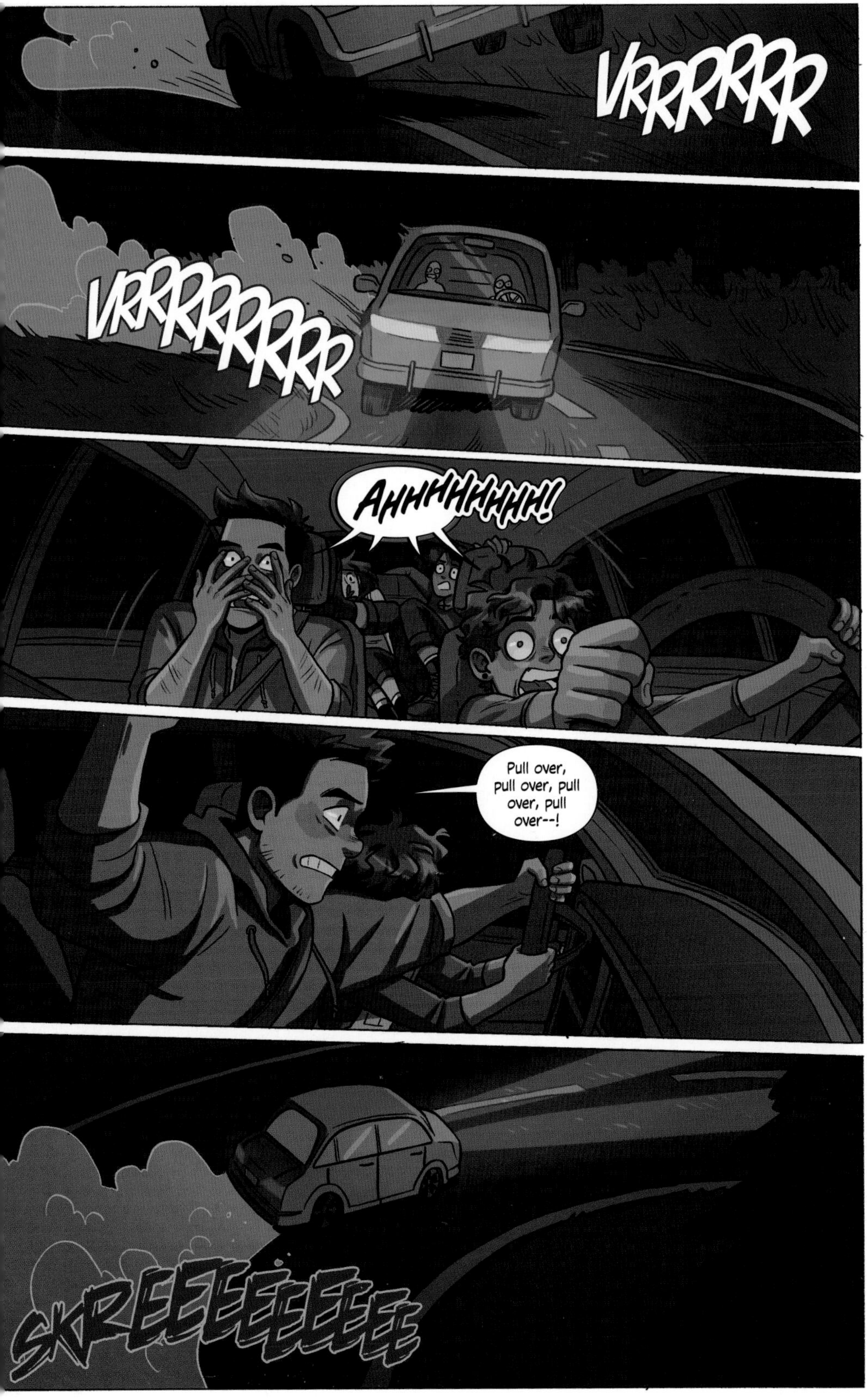

VRRRRRR
VRRRRRRRRR
AHHHHHHHH!
Pull over, pull over, pull over, pull over--!
SKREEEEEEEEE

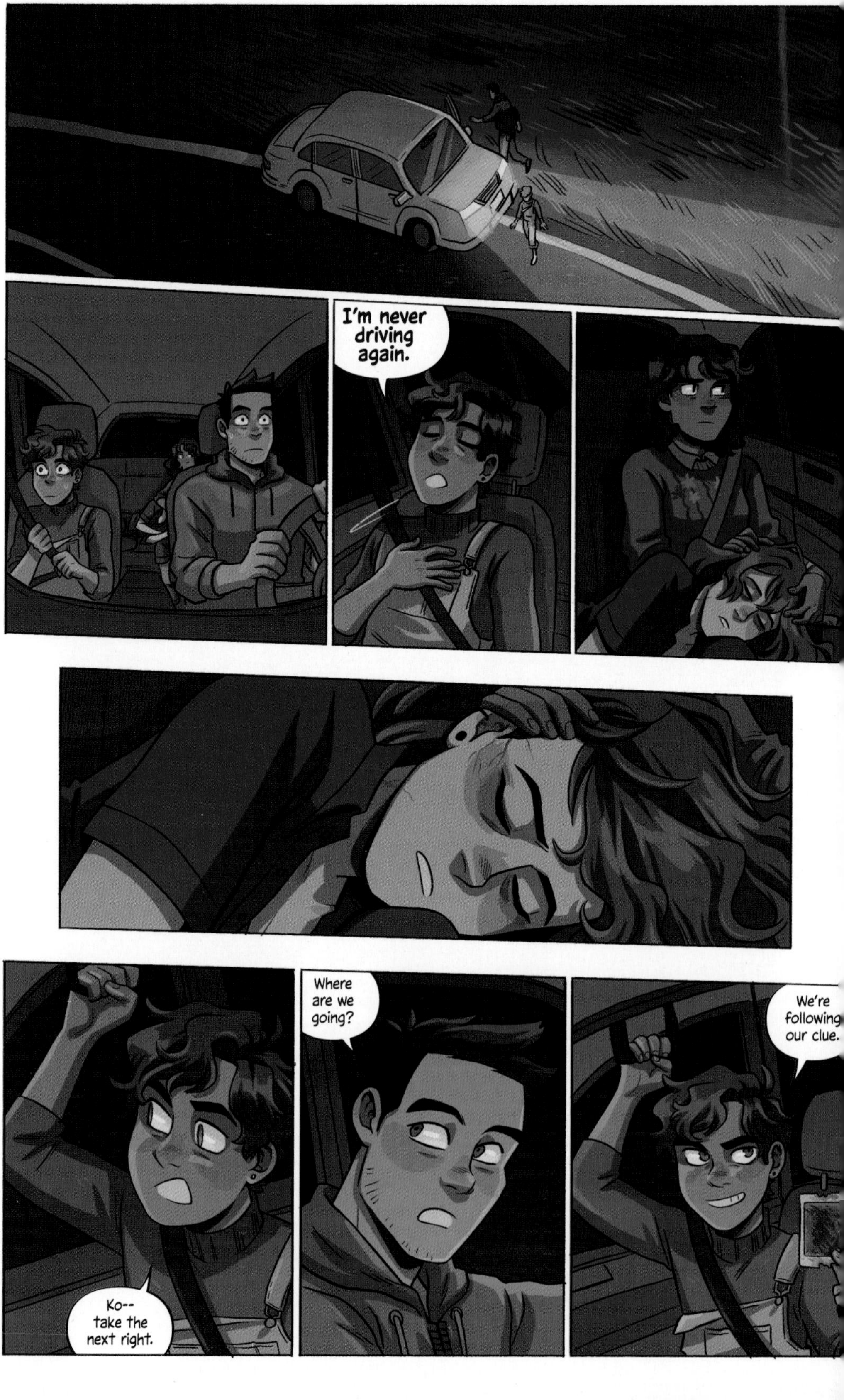
I'm never driving again.
Where are we going?
Ko-- take the next right.
We're following our clue.

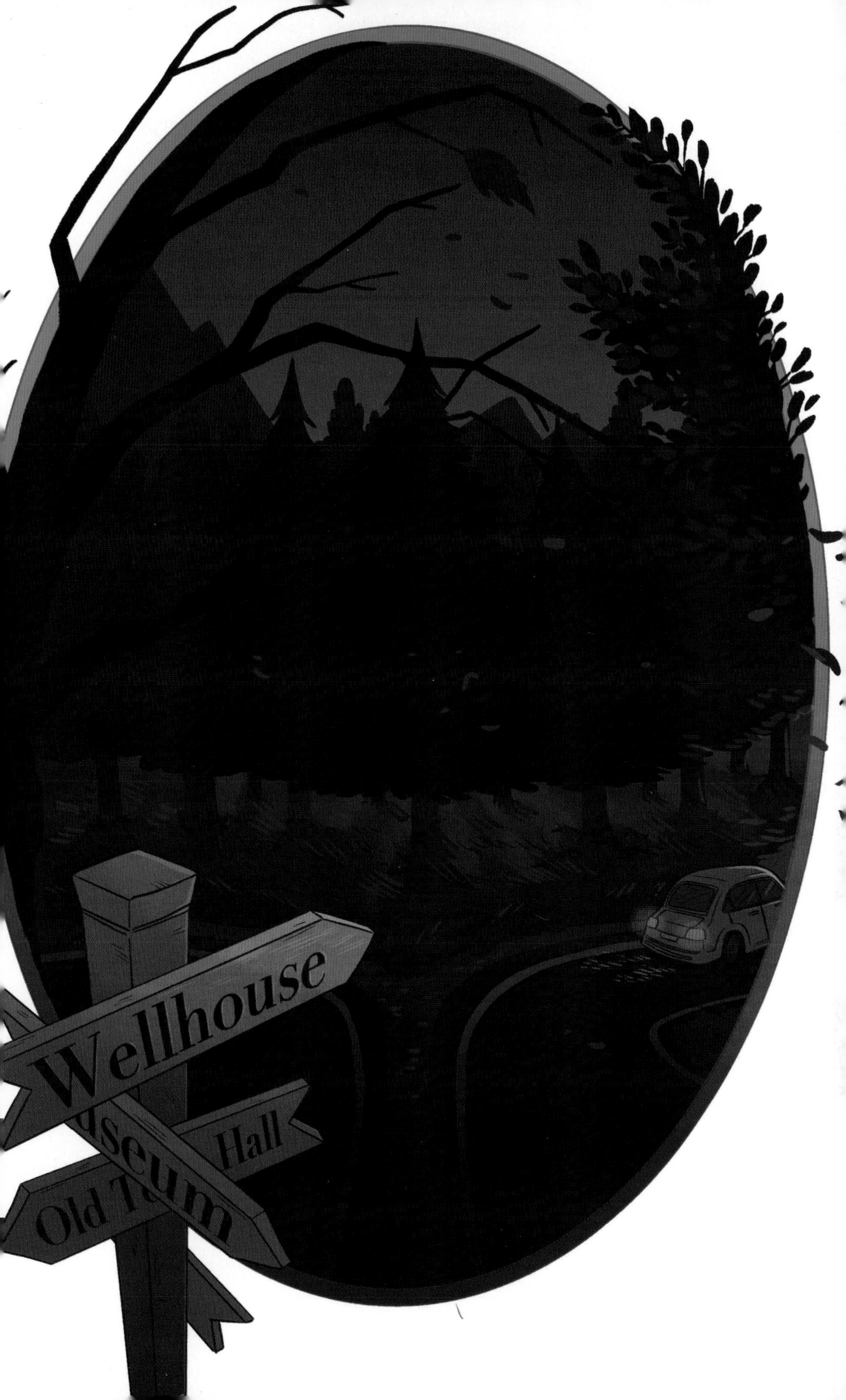
Wellhouse
Old
Hall

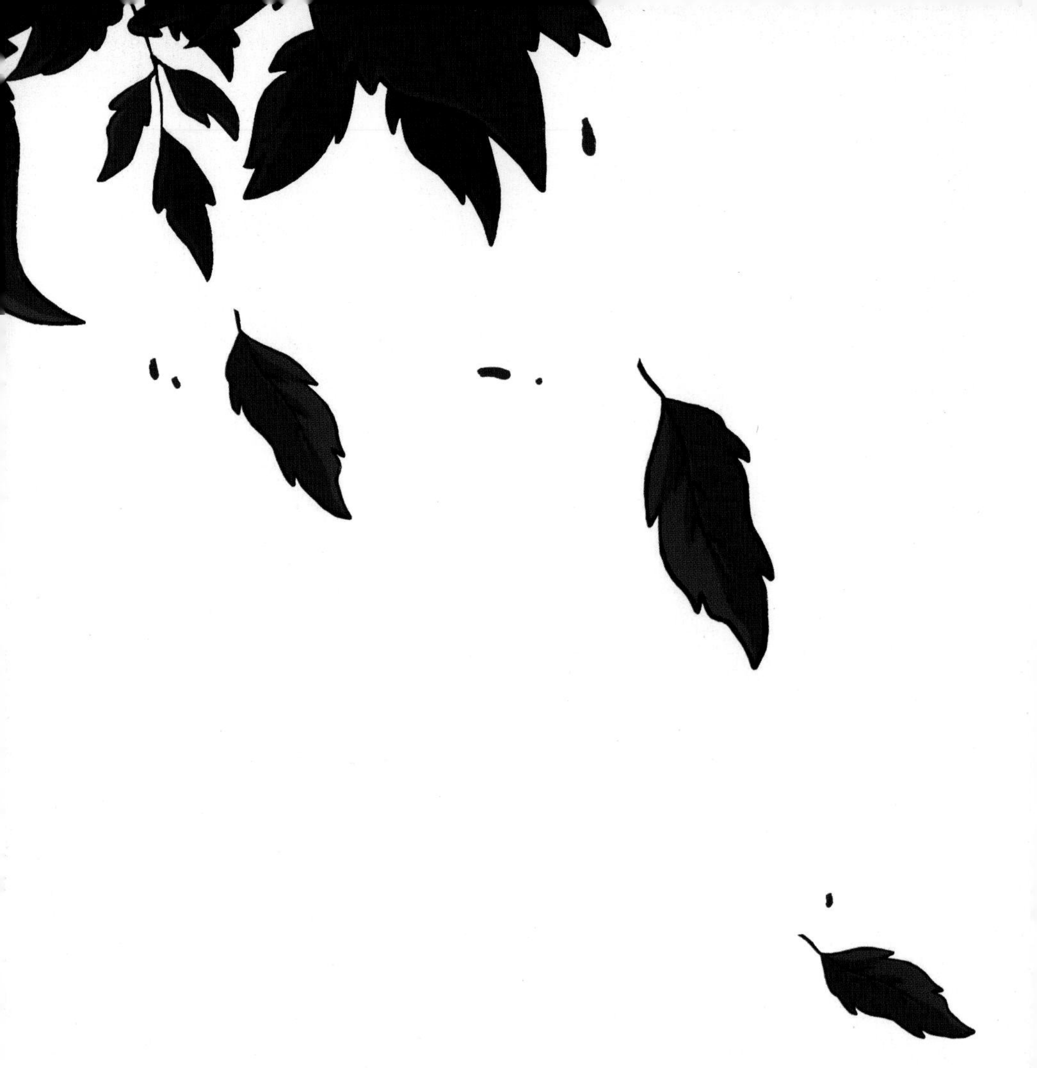

Episode Four
The Well

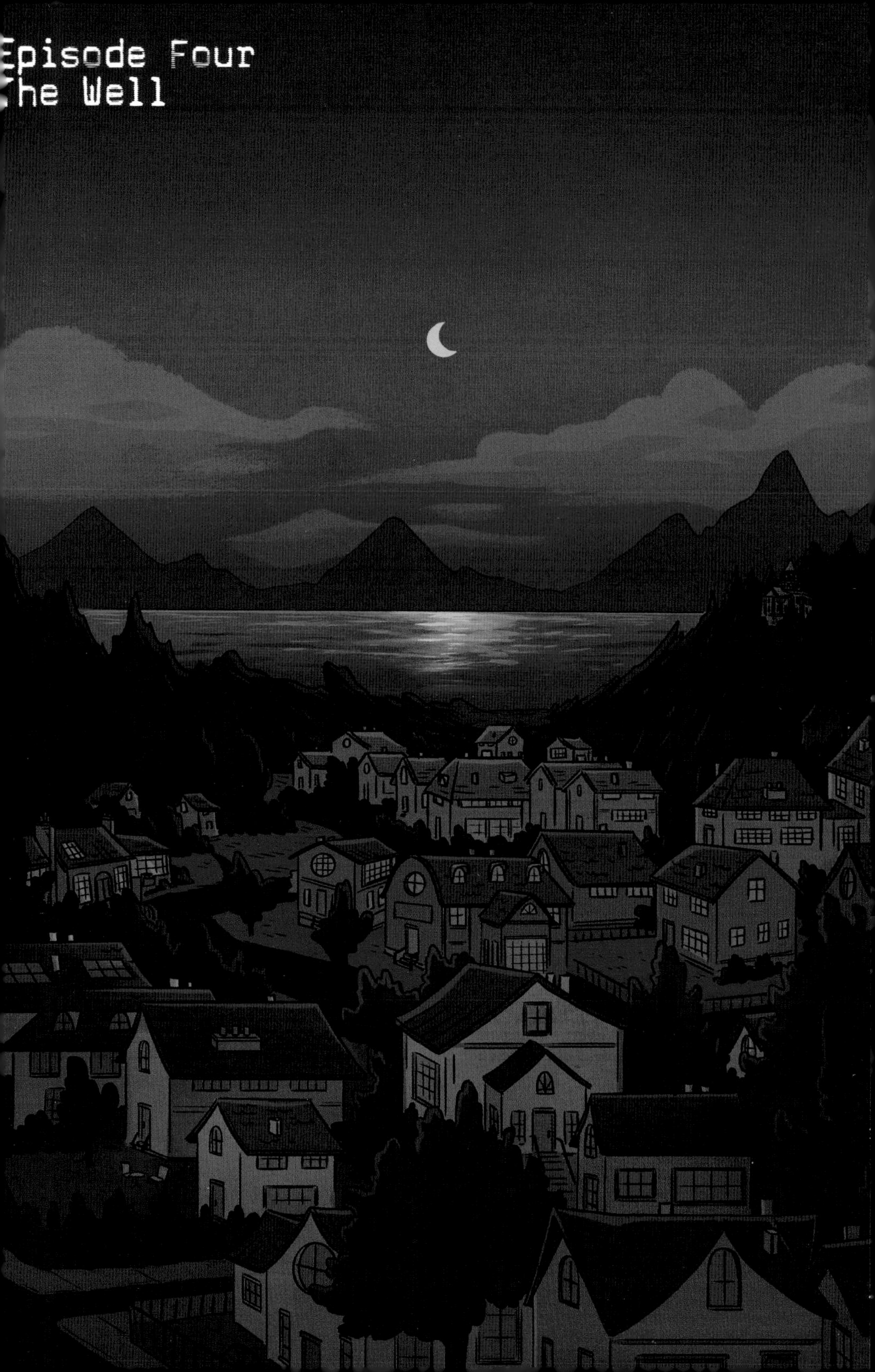

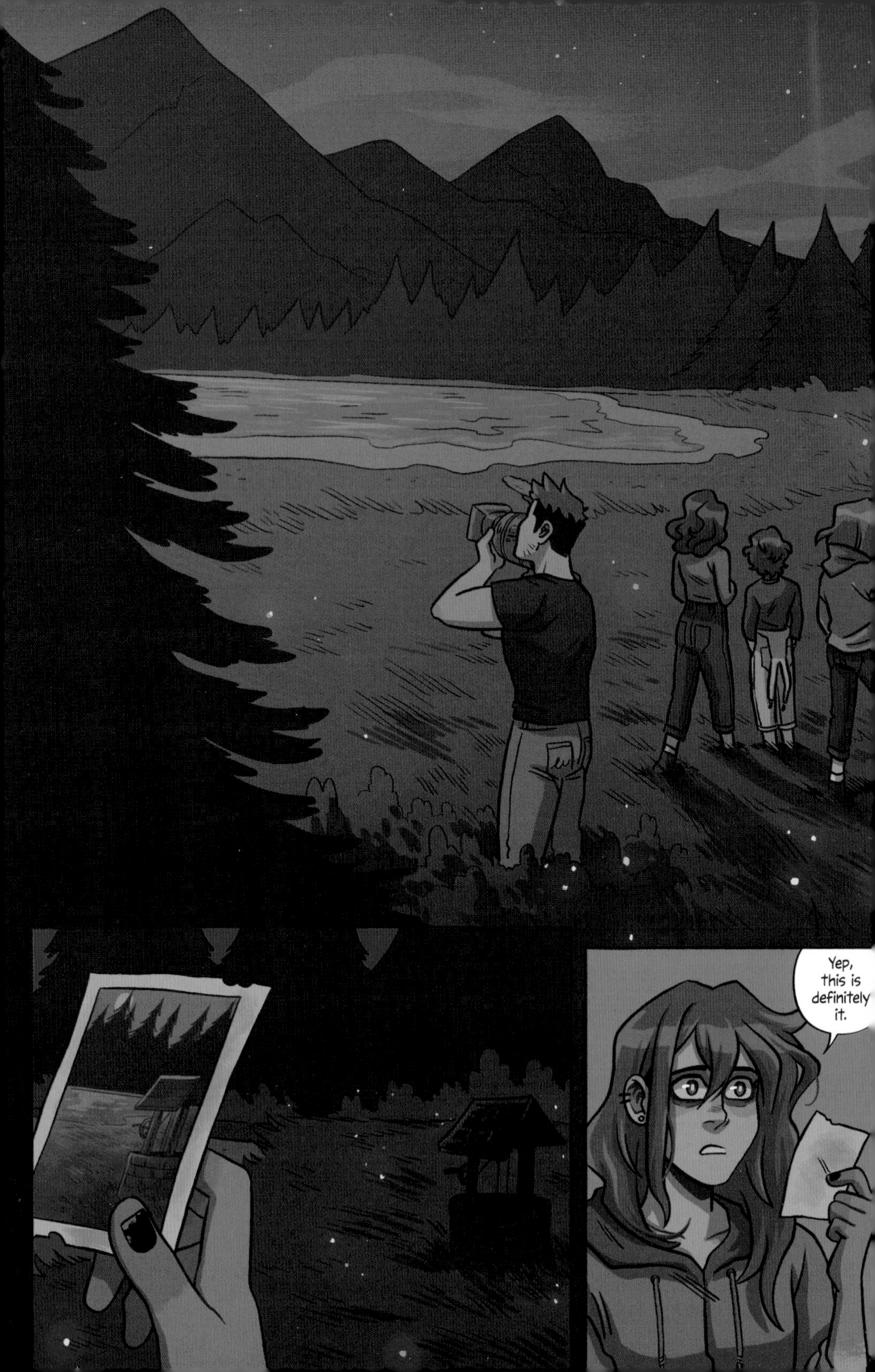
Yep, this is definitely it.

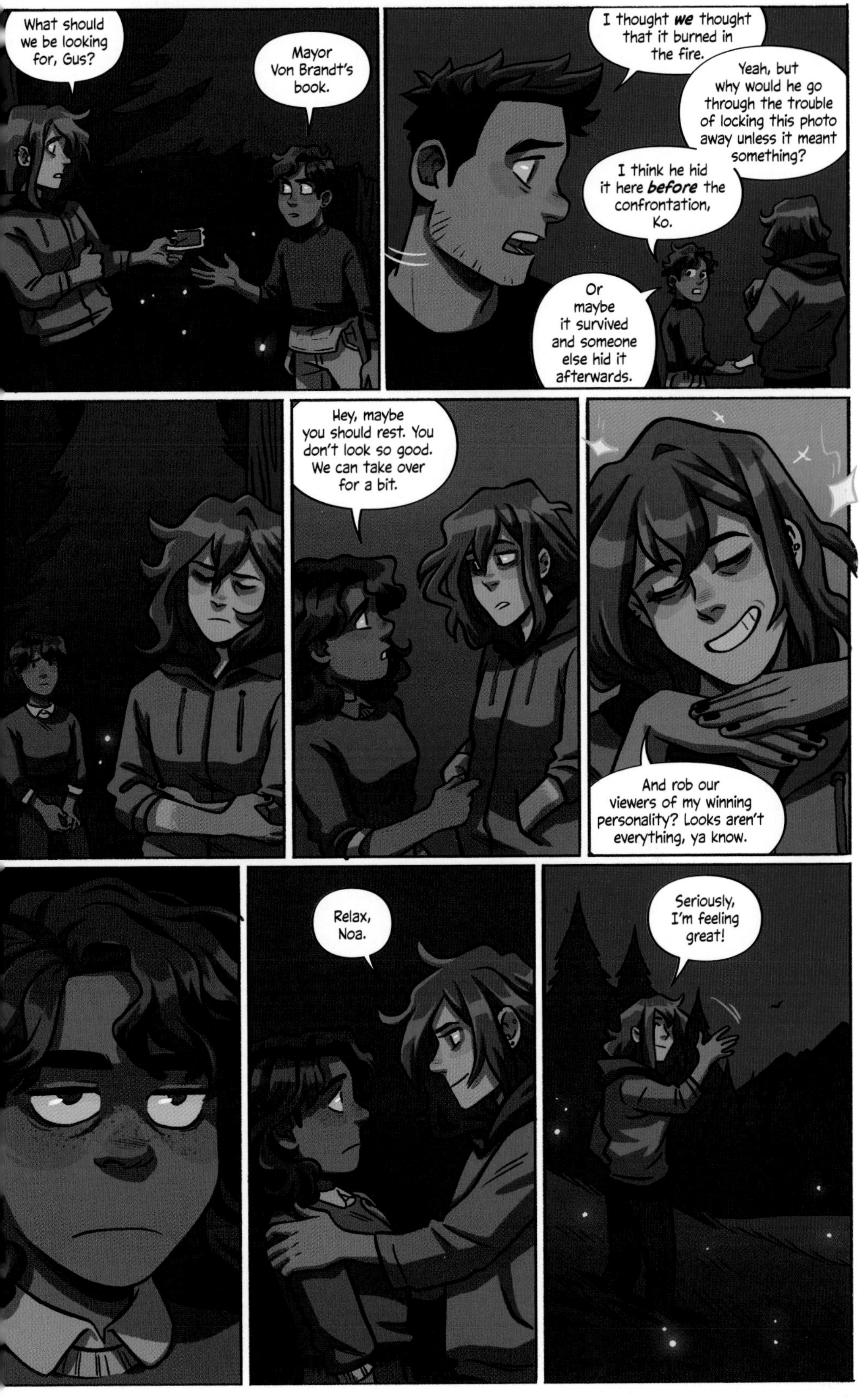
What should we be looking for, Gus?
Mayor Von Brandt's book.
I thought **we** thought that it burned in the fire.
Yeah, but why would he go through the trouble of locking this photo away unless it meant something?
I think he hid it here **before** the confrontation, Ko.
Or maybe it survived and someone else hid it afterwards.
Hey, maybe you should rest. You don't look so good. We can take over for a bit.
And rob our viewers of my winning personality? Looks aren't everything, ya know.
Relax, Noa.
Seriously, I'm feeling great!

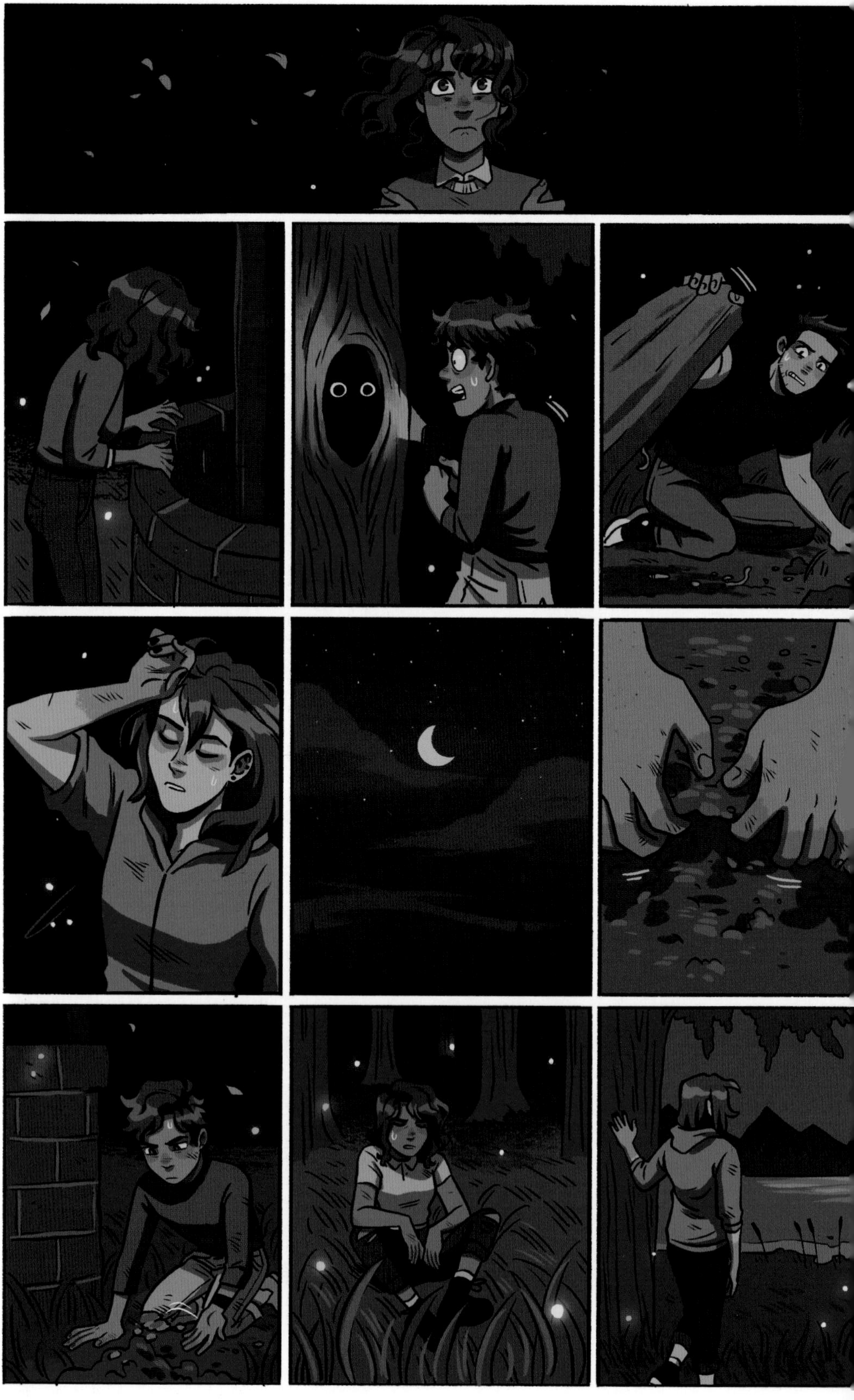

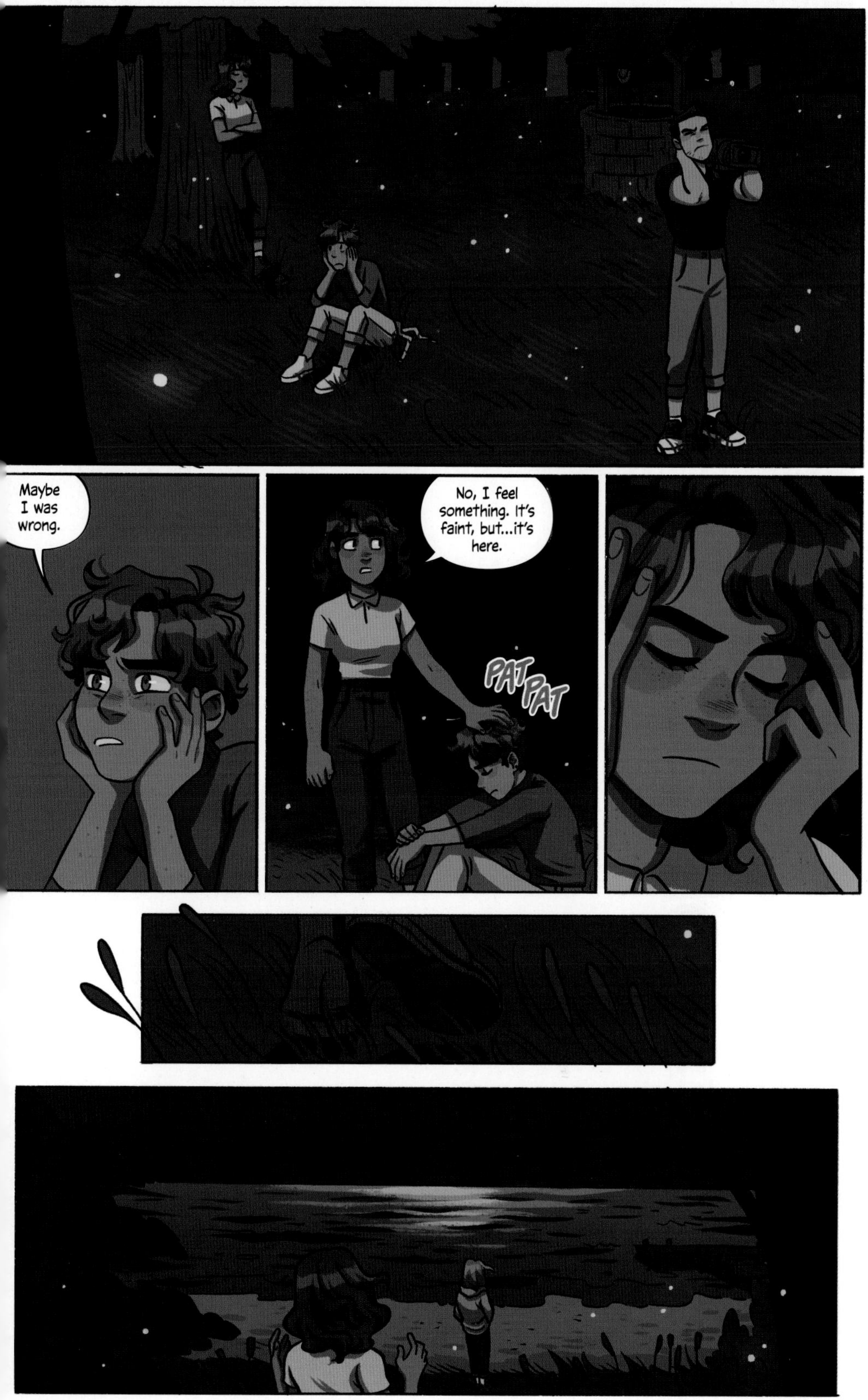
Maybe I was wrong.
No, I feel something. It's faint, but...it's here.
PAT PAT

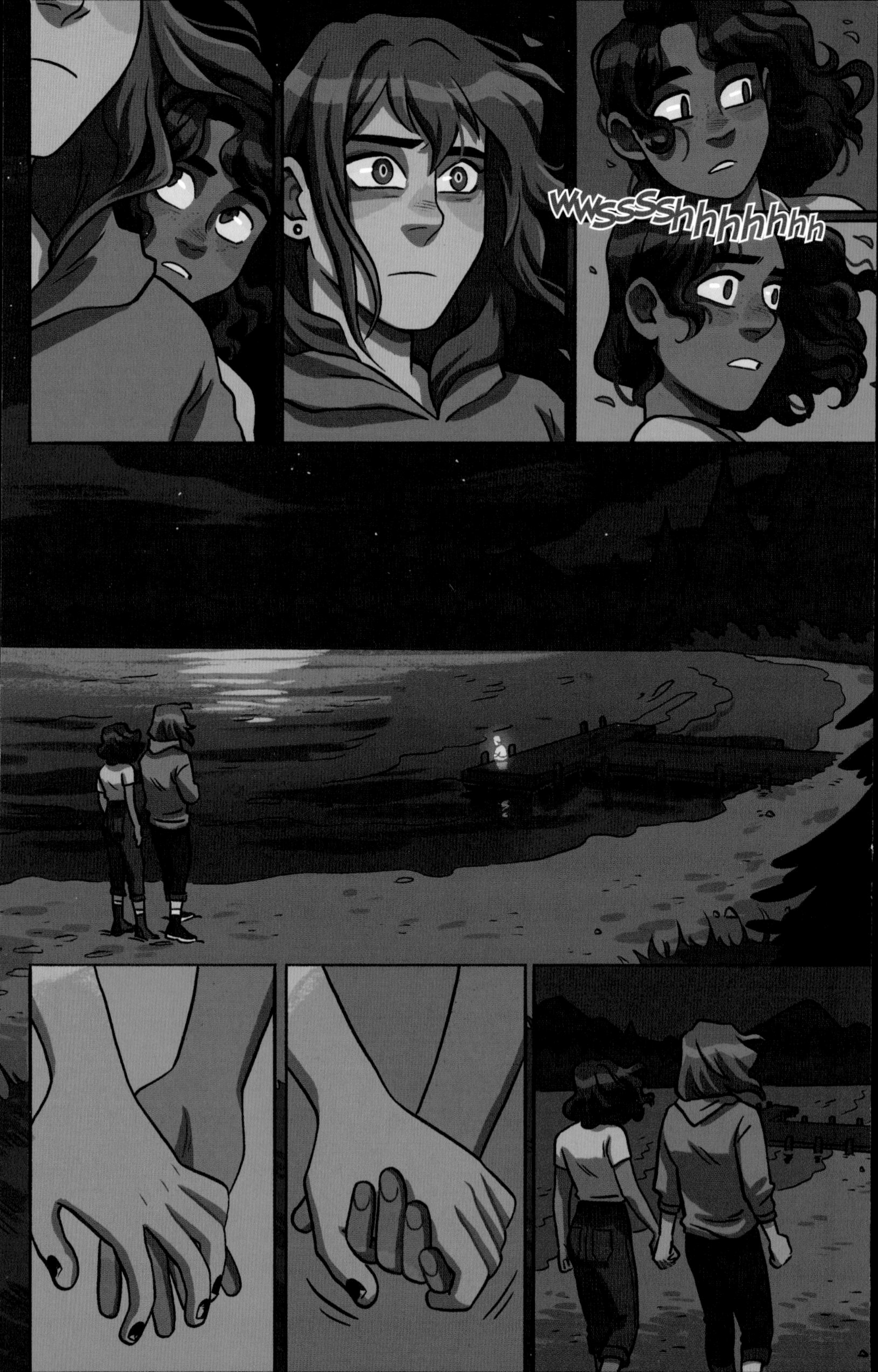
WWSSSShhhhhhh

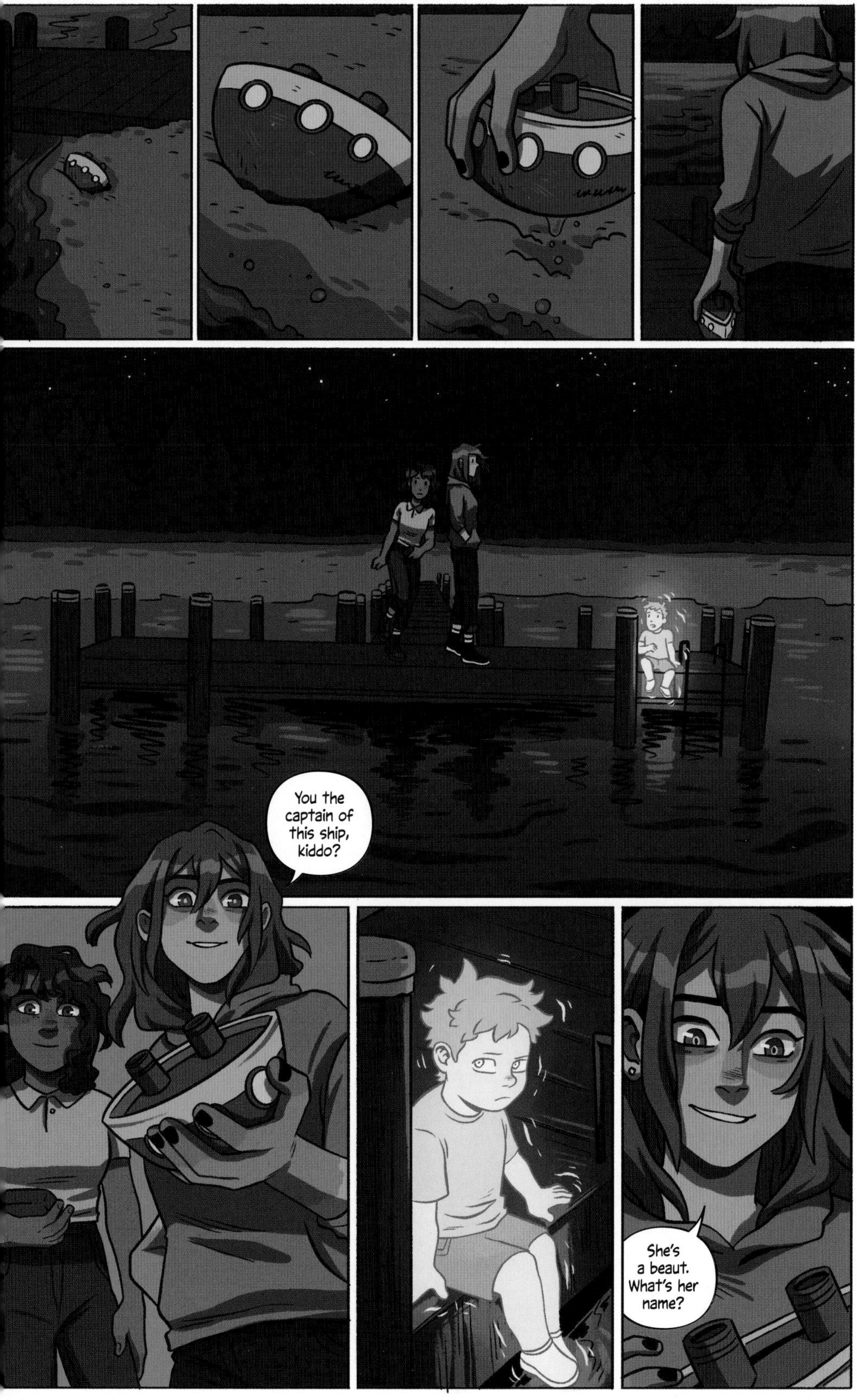

You the captain of this ship, kiddo?
She's a beaut. What's her name?

You talk funny.

That's quite a long name for a ship.

You're weird.

You don't know the half of it.

This is Astrid, and I'm Noa. What's your name?

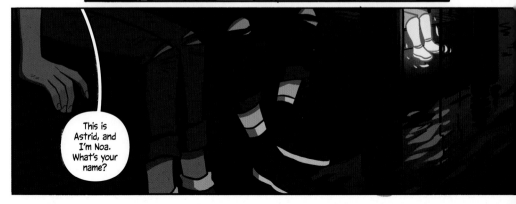

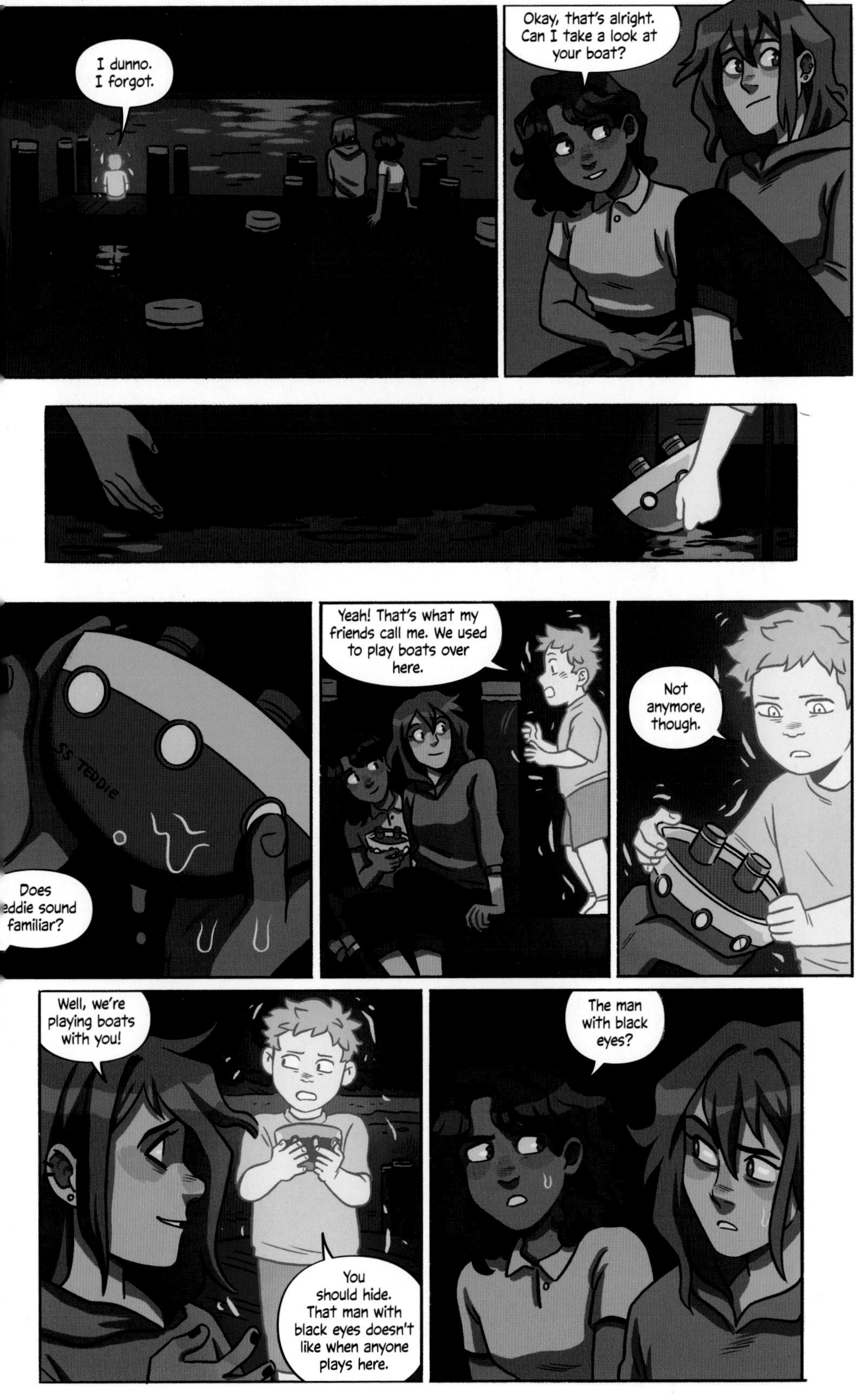
I dunno. I forgot.
Okay, that's alright. Can I take a look at your boat?
SS TEDDIE
Does eddie sound familiar?
Yeah! That's what my friends call me. We used to play boats over here.
Not anymore, though.
Well, we're playing boats with you!
You should hide. That man with black eyes doesn't like when anyone plays here.
The man with black eyes?

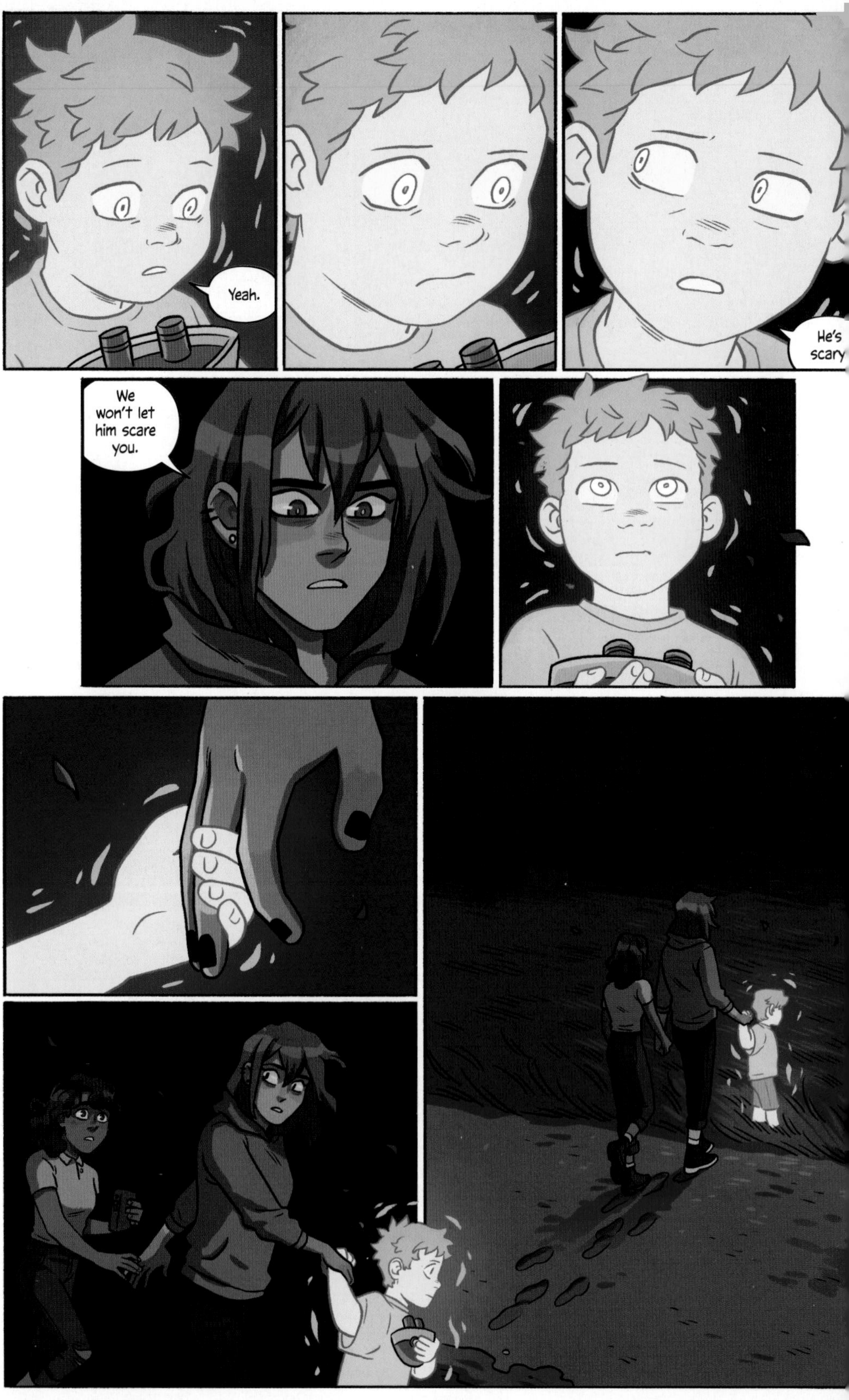
Yeah.
He's scary
We won't let him scare you.

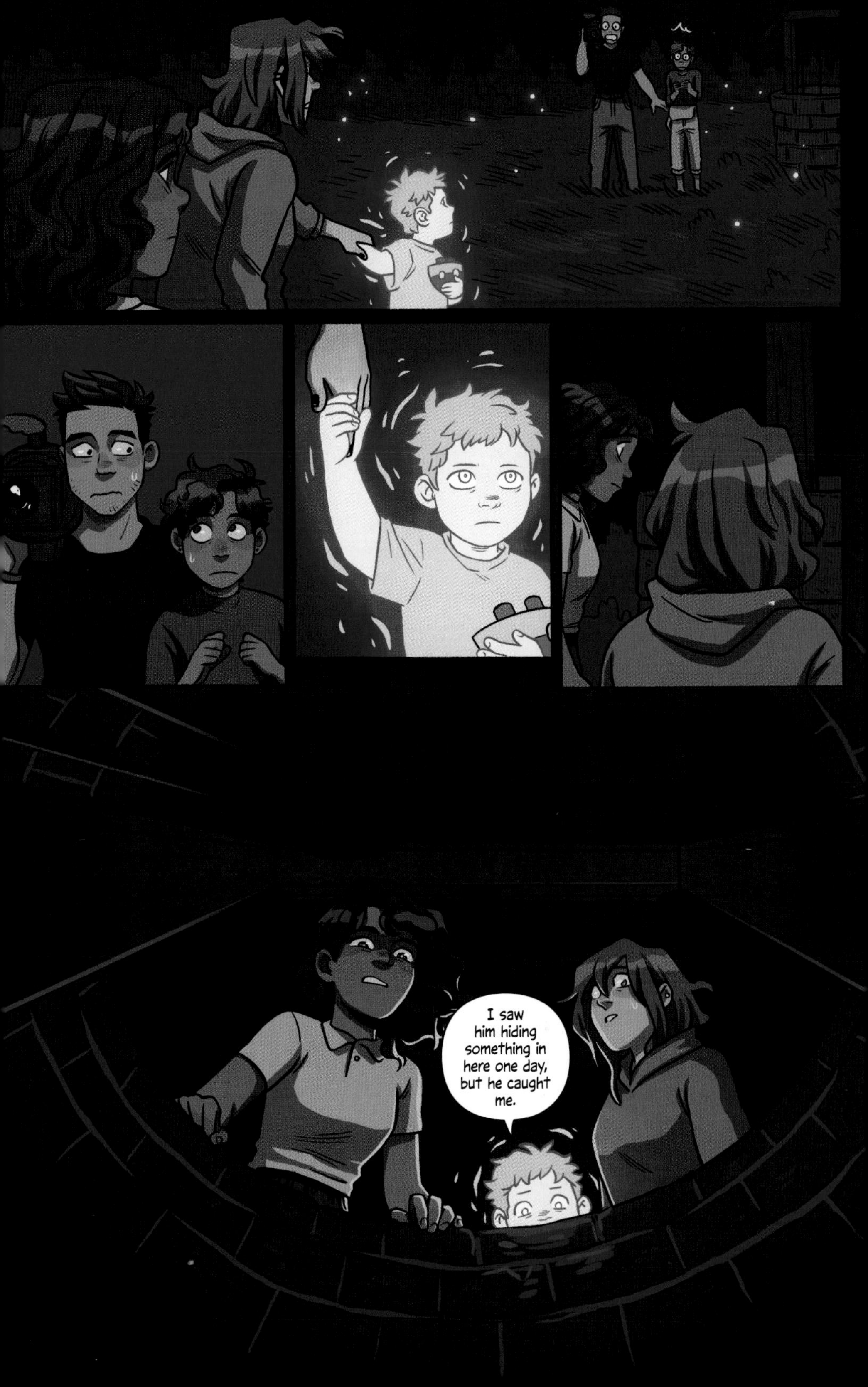
I saw him hiding something in here one day, but he caught me.

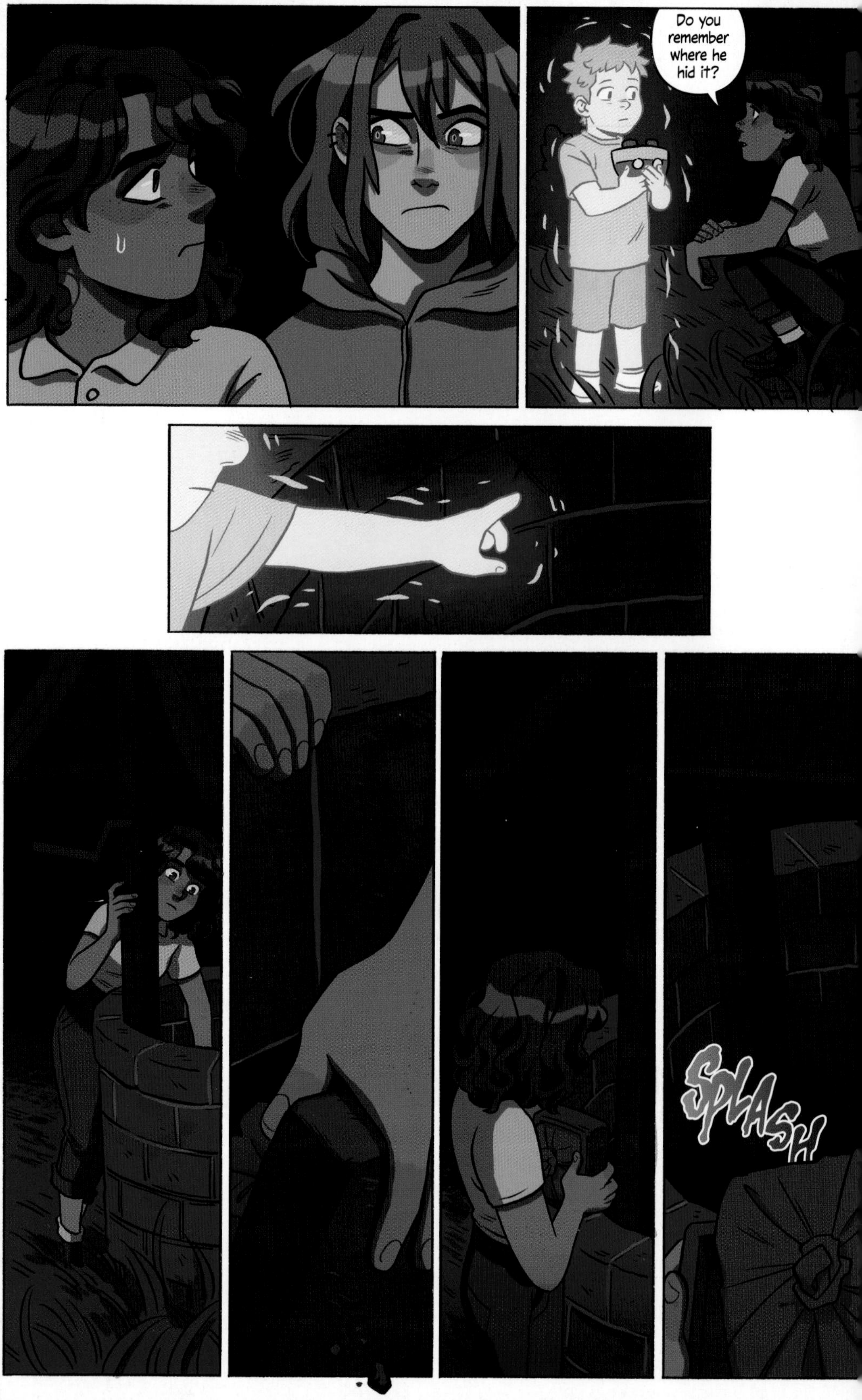
Do you remember where he hid it?
SPLASH

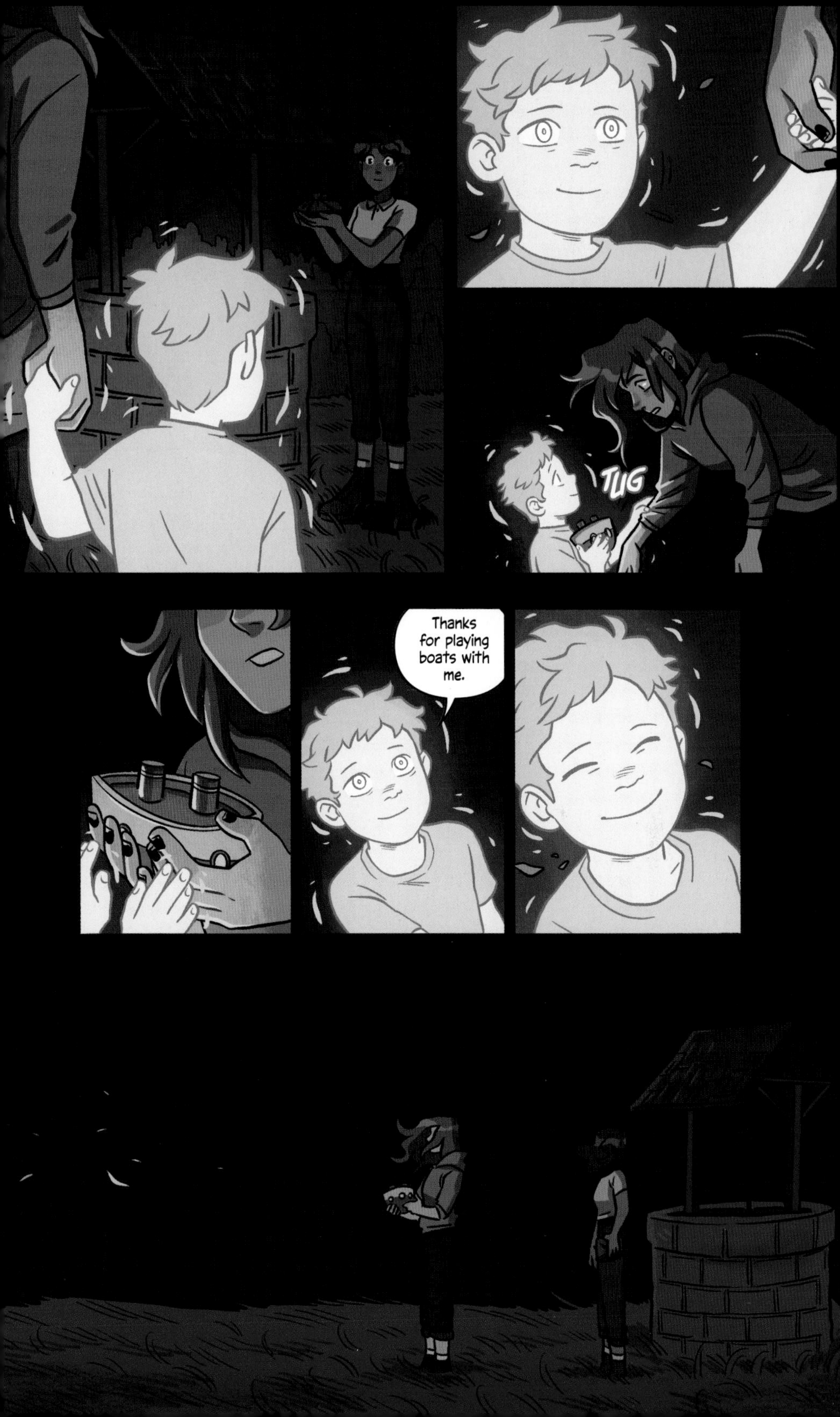
TUG
Thanks for playing boats with me.

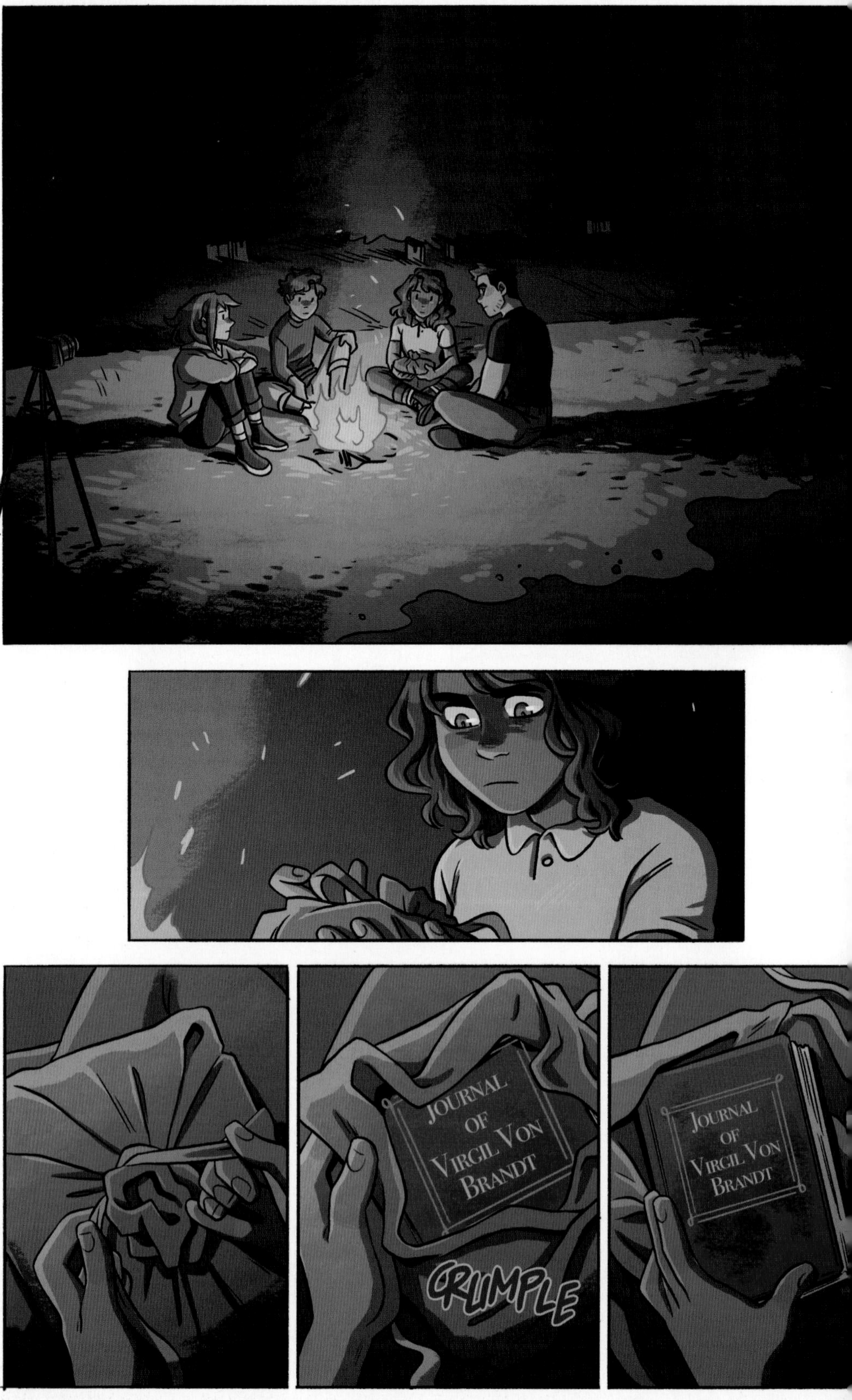
JOURNAL OF VIRGIL VON BRANDT
CRUMPLE
JOURNAL OF VIRGIL VON BRANDT

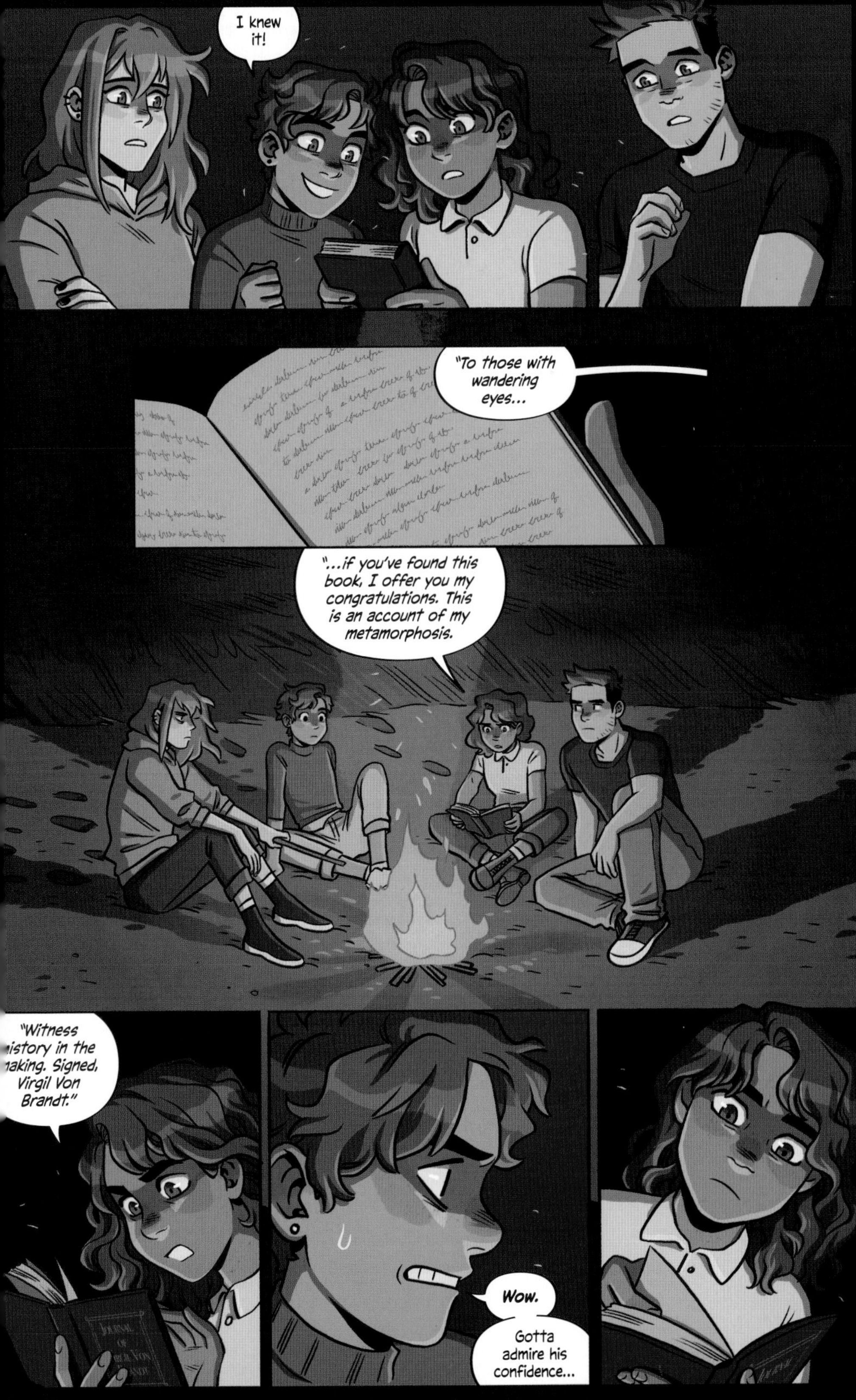
I knew it!
"To those with wandering eyes...
"...if you've found this book, I offer you my congratulations. This is an account of my metamorphosis.
"Witness history in the making. Signed, Virgil Von Brandt."
Wow.
Gotta admire his confidence...

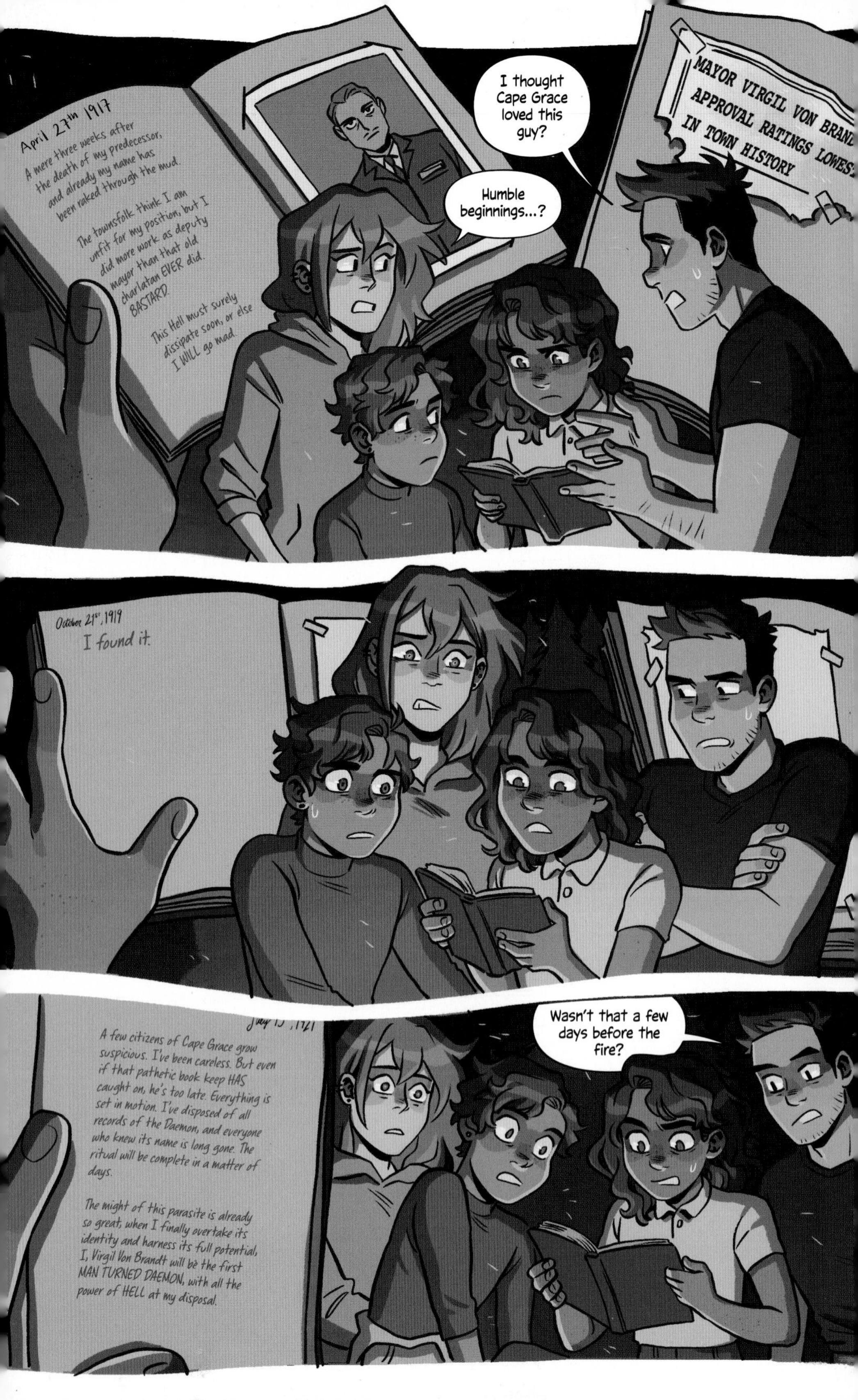
April 27th 1917
A mere three weeks after the death of my predecessor, and already my name has been raked through the mud.
The townsfolk think I am unfit for my position, but I did more work as deputy mayor than that old charlatan EVER did. BASTARD.
This Hell must surely dissipate soon, or else I WILL go mad.
MAYOR VIRGIL VON BRAND APPROVAL RATINGS LOWES IN TOWN HISTORY
I thought Cape Grace loved this guy?
Humble beginnings...?
October 21st, 1919
I found it.
A few citizens of Cape Grace grow suspicious. I've been careless. But even if that pathetic book keep HAS caught on, he's too late. Everything is set in motion. I've disposed of all records of the Daemon, and everyone who knew its name is long gone. The ritual will be complete in a matter of days.
The might of this parasite is already so great, when I finally overtake its identity and harness its full potential, I, Virgil Von Brandt will be the first MAN TURNED DAEMON, with all the power of HELL at my disposal.
Wasn't that a few days before the fire?

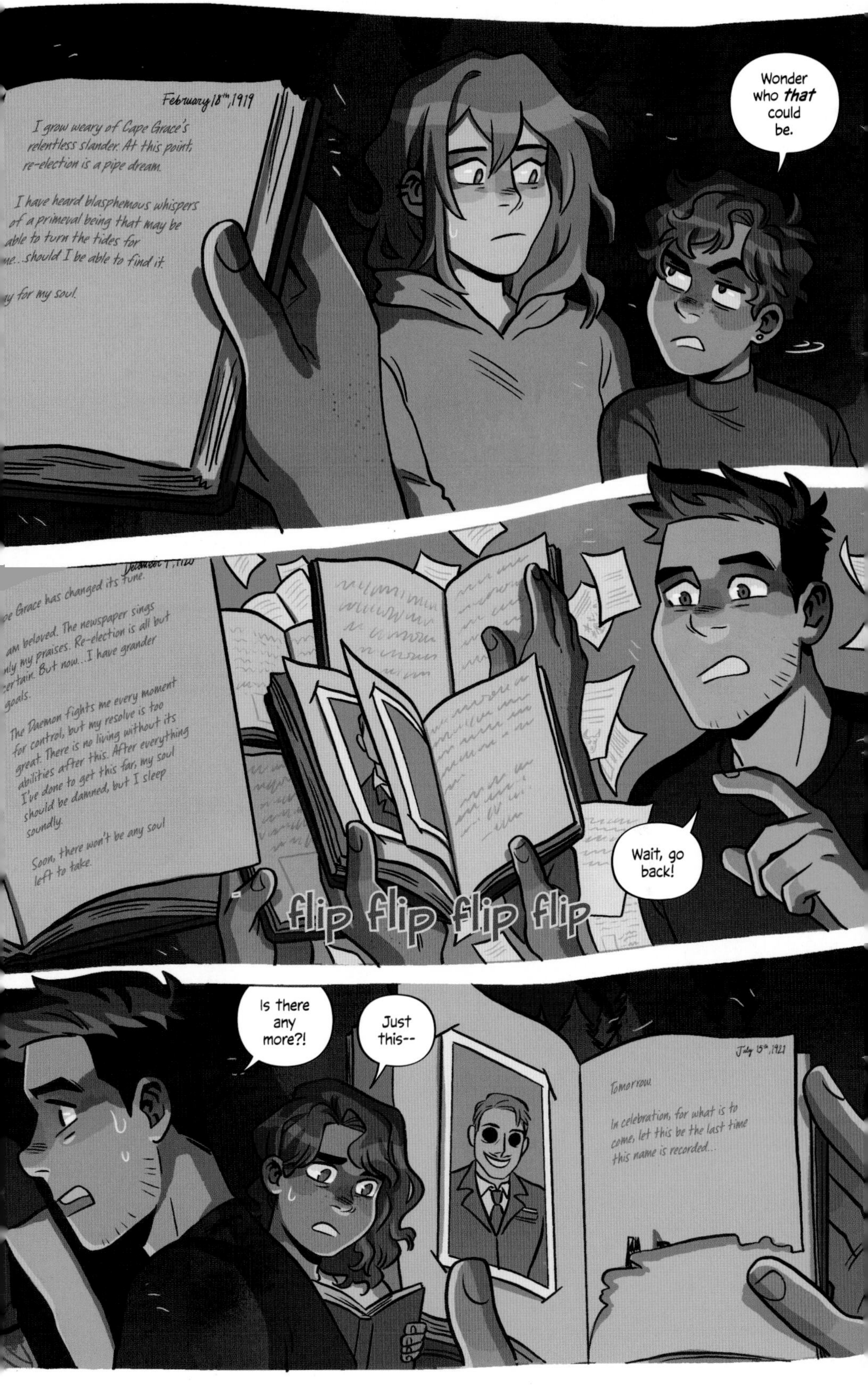
February 18th, 1919
I grow weary of Cape Grace's relentless slander. At this point, re-election is a pipe dream.
I have heard blasphemous whispers of a primeval being that may be able to turn the tides for me...should I be able to find it.
y for my soul.
Wonder who *that* could be.
pe Grace has changed its tune.
am beloved. The newspaper sings nly my praises. Re-election is all but ertain. But now... I have grander goals.
The Daemon fights me every moment for control, but my resolve is too great. There is no living without its abilities after this. After everything I've done to get this far, my soul should be damned, but I sleep soundly.
Soon, there won't be any soul left to take.
Wait, go back!
flip flip flip flip
Is there any more?!
Just this--
July 15th, 1921
Tomorrow.
In celebration, for what is to come, let this be the last time this name is recorded...

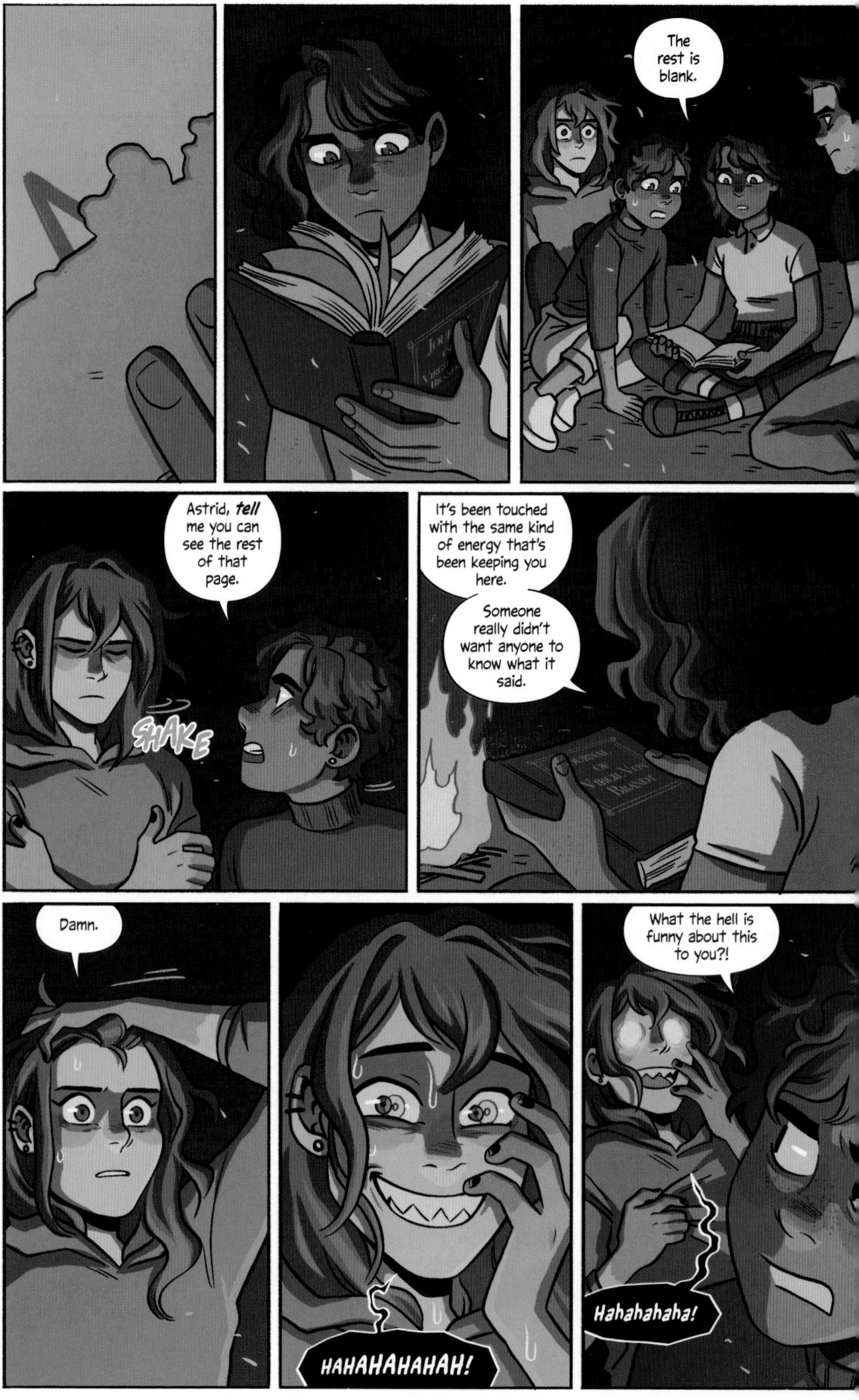
The rest is blank.
Astrid, **tell** me you can see the rest of that page.
SHAKE
It's been touched with the same kind of energy that's been keeping you here.
Someone really didn't want anyone to know what it said.
JOURNAL OF VIRGIL VON BRANDT
Damn.
HAHAHAHAHAH!
What the hell is funny about this to you?!
Hahahahaha!

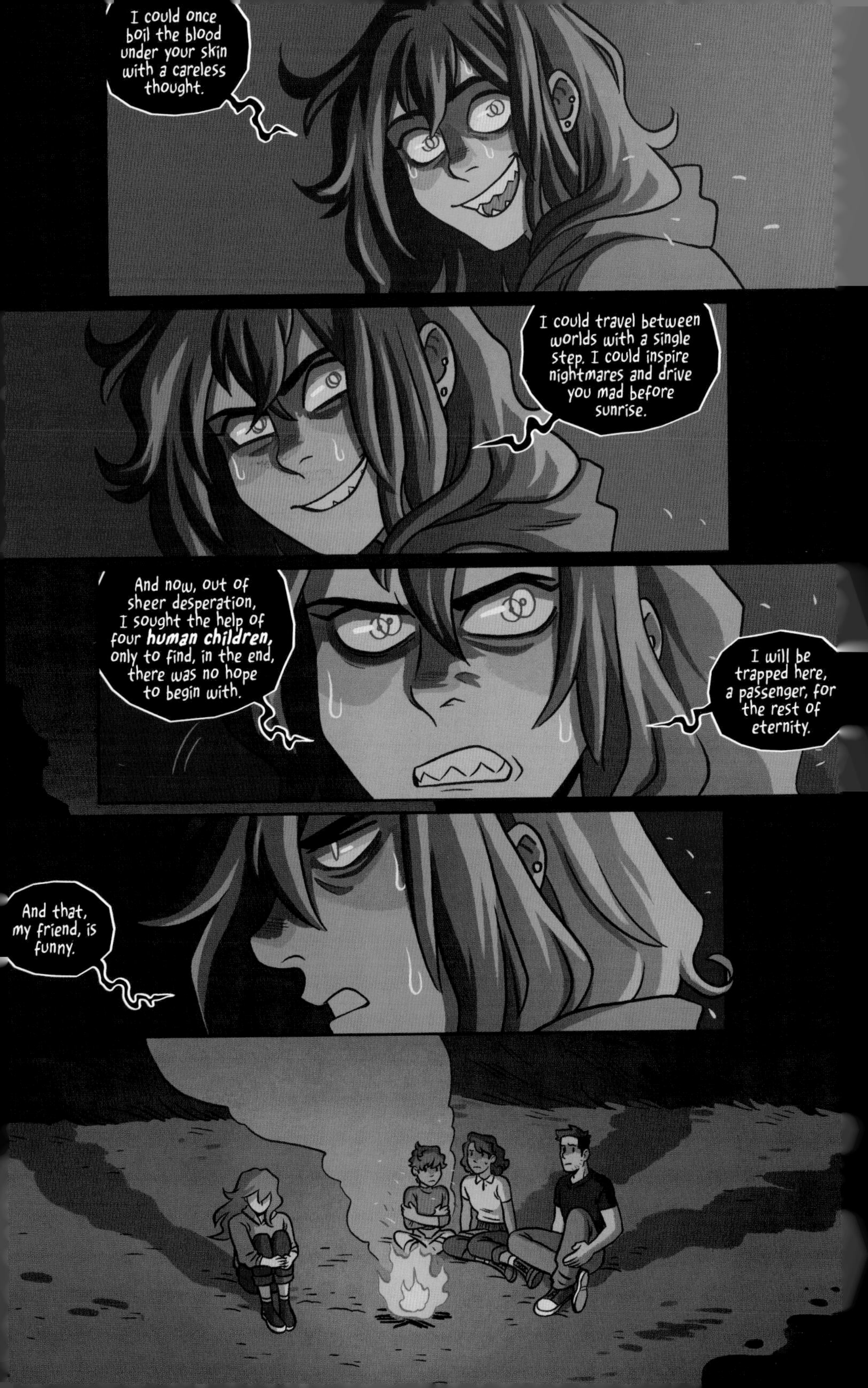
I could once boil the blood under your skin with a careless thought.
I could travel between worlds with a single step. I could inspire nightmares and drive you mad before sunrise.
And now, out of sheer desperation, I sought the help of four **human children,** only to find, in the end, there was no hope to begin with.
I will be trapped here, a passenger, for the rest of eternity.
And that, my friend, is funny.

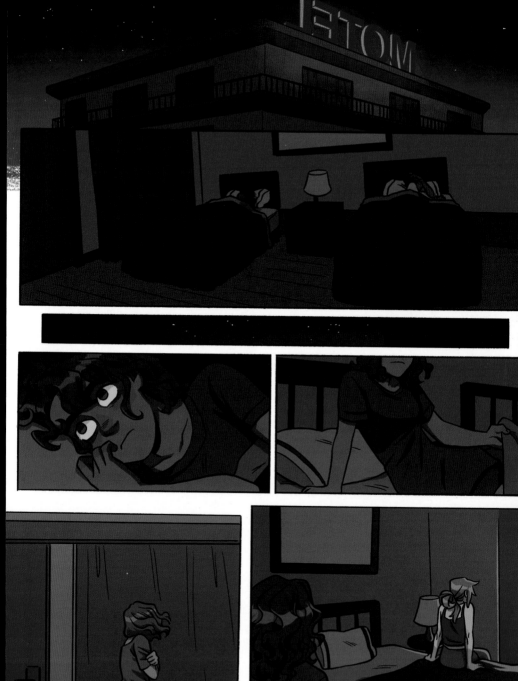

Hey.

I just--I wanted to say that what you did today was amazing.

You really helped that little boy. And... you really helped me, too.

I know that using these new abilities takes a lot out of you.

So it means a lot that you would do that for me.

I know that things seem a little lost right now, but we're all here for you. We care about you.

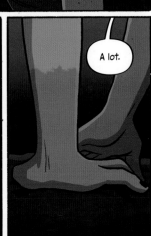

A lot.

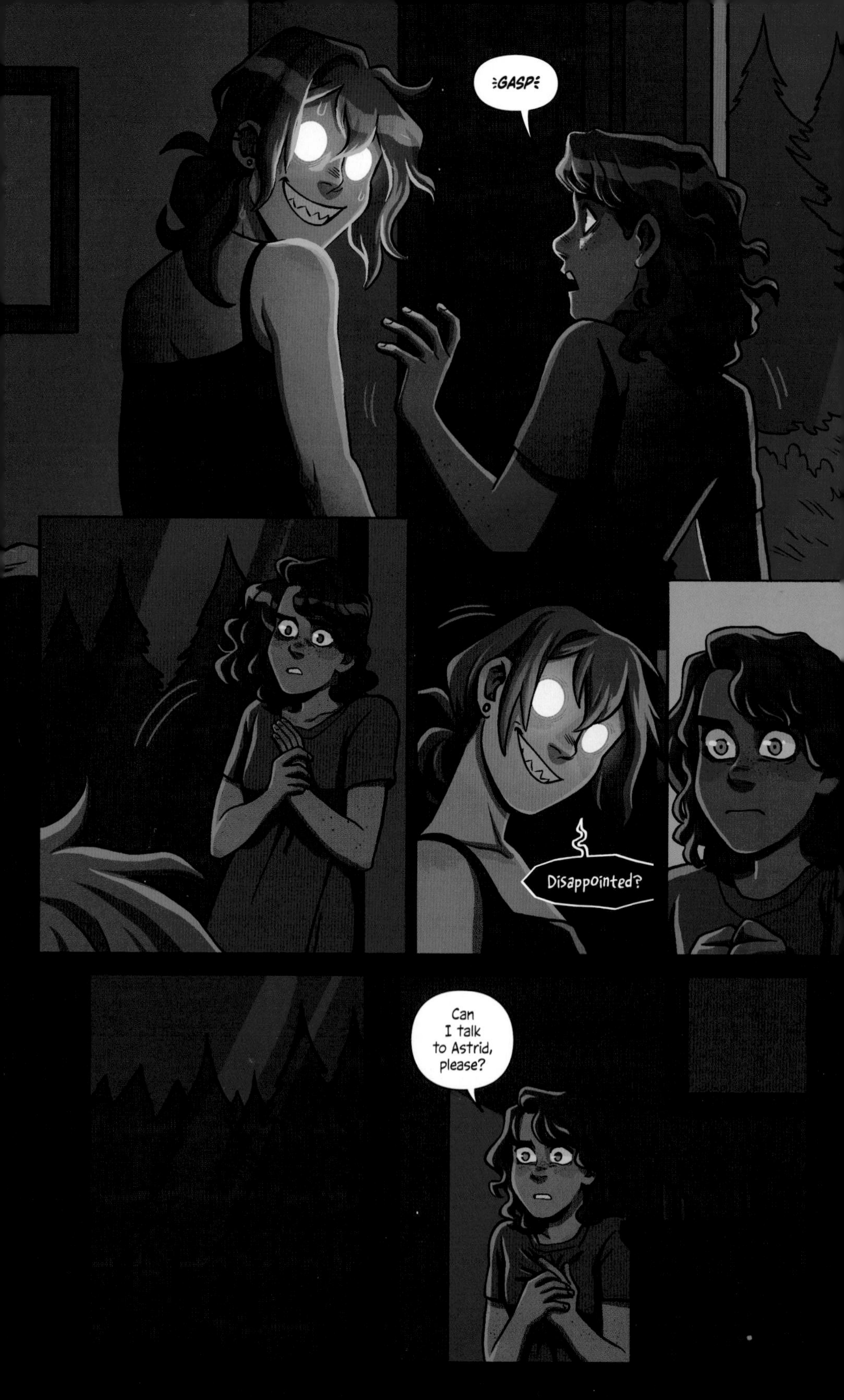
GASP
Disappointed?
Can I talk to Astrid, please?

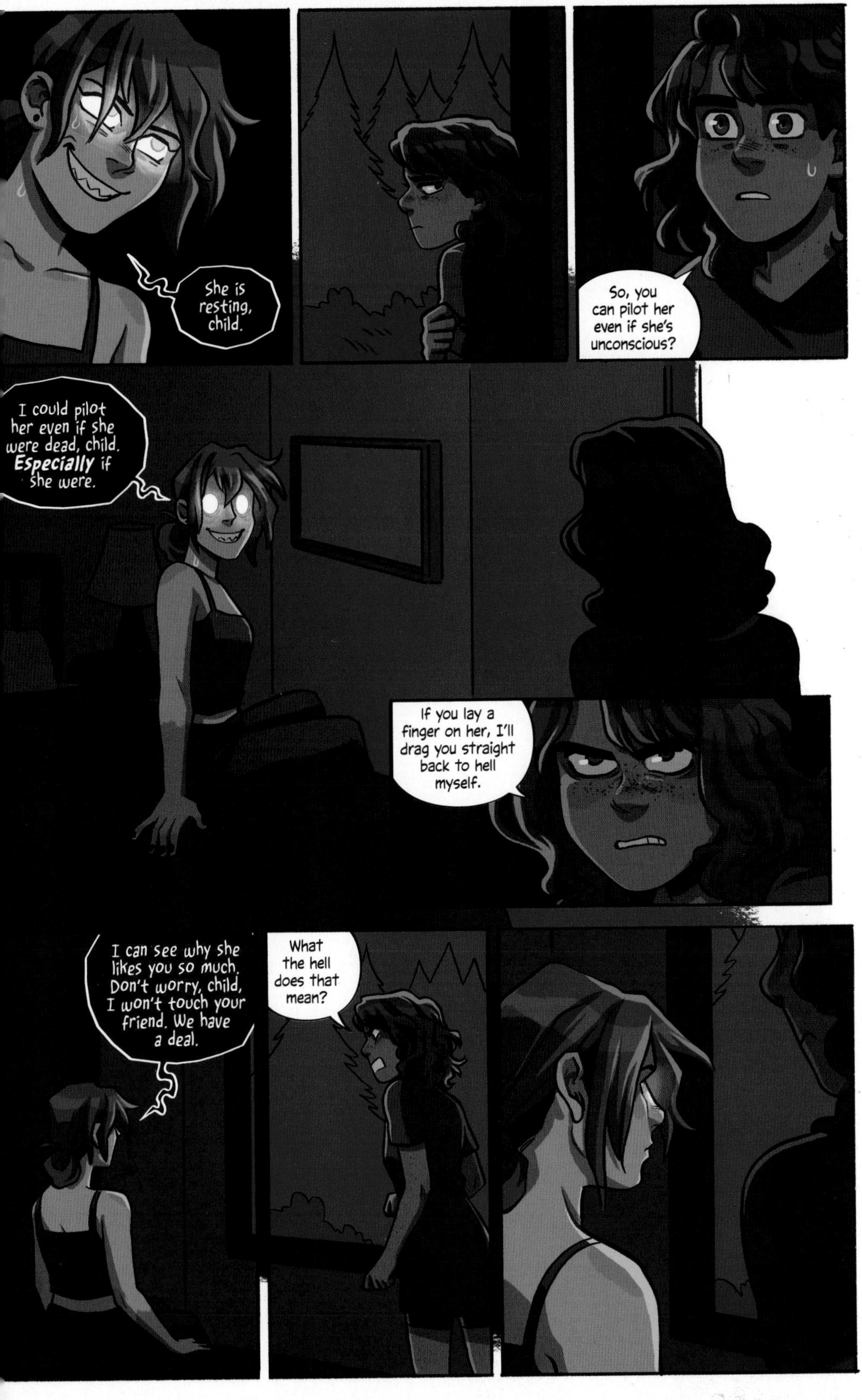
She is resting, child.
So, you can pilot her even if she's unconscious?
I could pilot her even if she were dead, child. **Especially** if she were.
If you lay a finger on her, I'll drag you straight back to hell myself.
I can see why she likes you so much. Don't worry, child, I won't touch your friend. We have a deal.
What the hell does that mean?

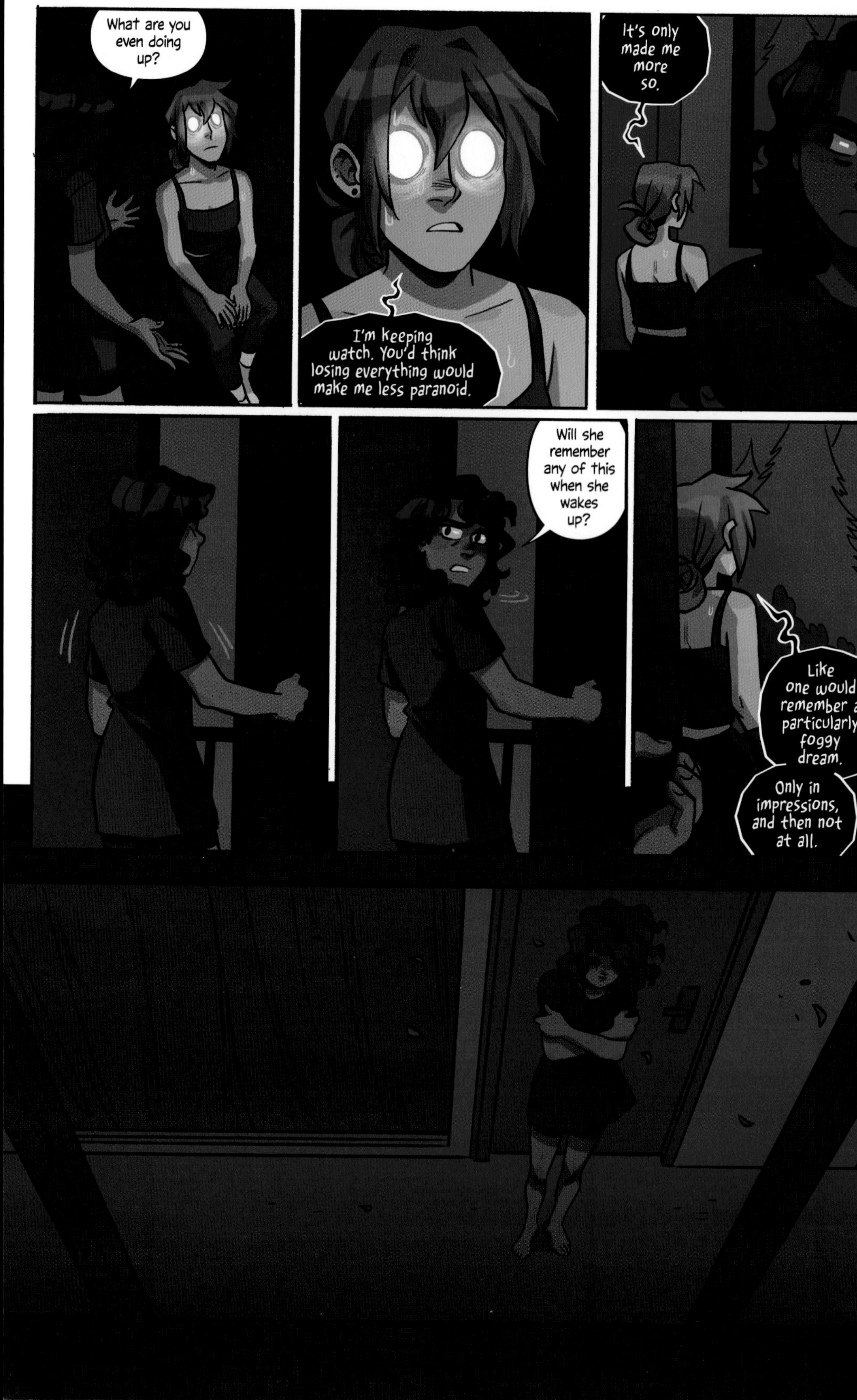
What are you even doing up?
I'm keeping watch. You'd think losing everything would make me less paranoid.
It's only made me more so.
Will she remember any of this when she wakes up?
Like one would remember a particularly foggy dream.
Only in impressions, and then not at all.

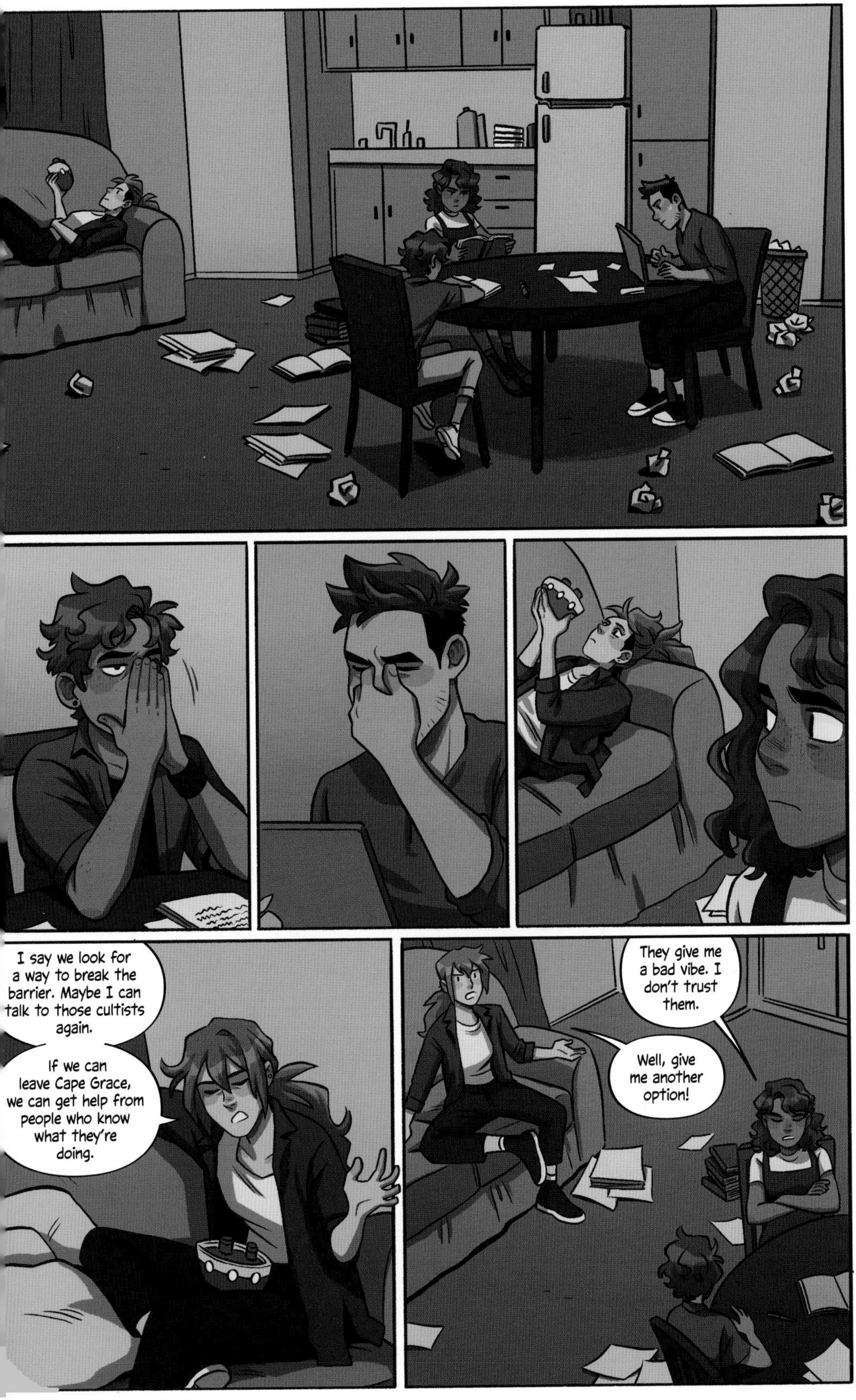
I say we look for a way to break the barrier. Maybe I can talk to those cultists again.
If we can leave Cape Grace, we can get help from people who know what they're doing.
They give me a bad vibe. I don't trust them.
Well, give me another option!

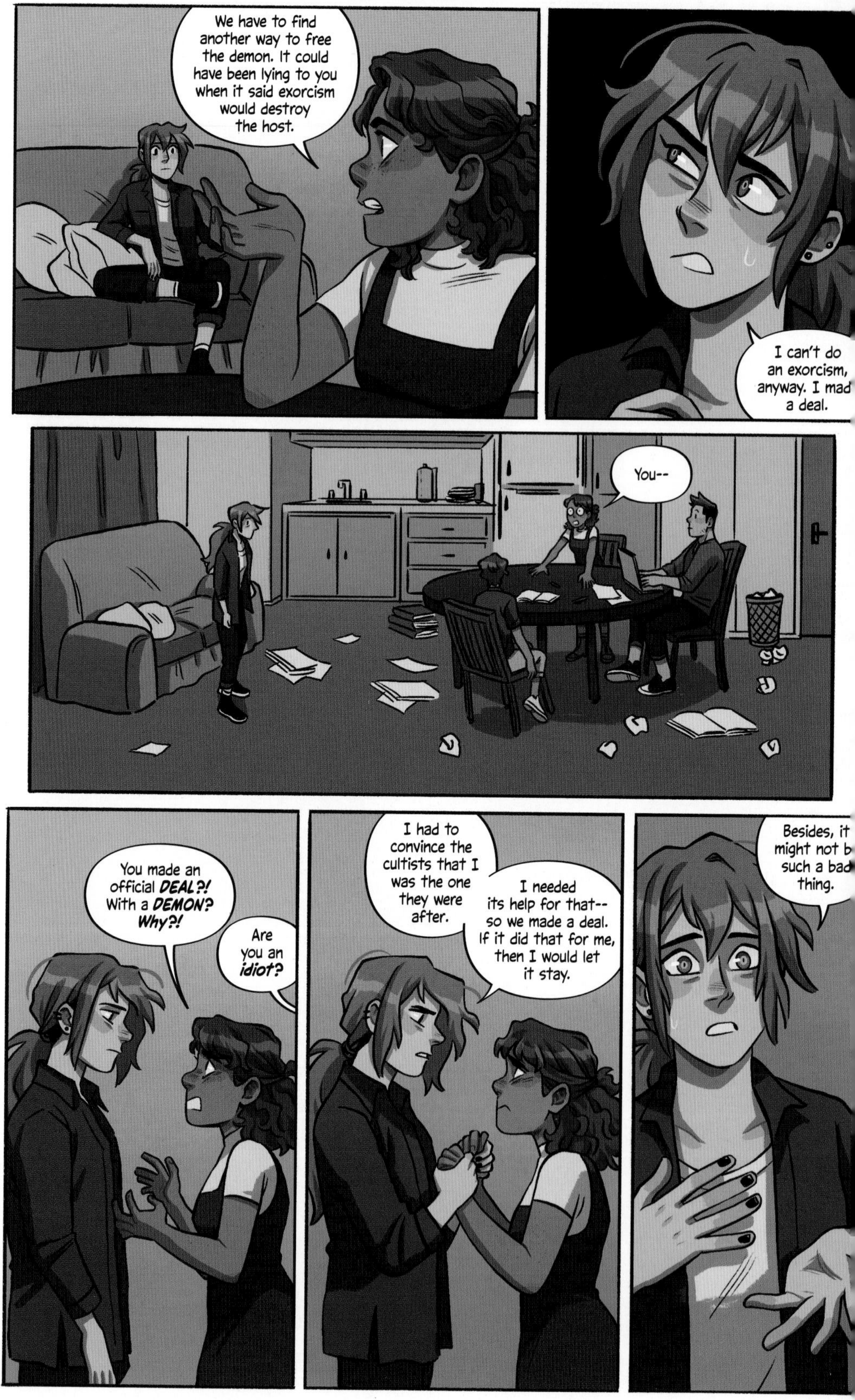

We have to find another way to free the demon. It could have been lying to you when it said exorcism would destroy the host.
I can't do an exorcism, anyway. I mad a deal.
You--
You made an official DEAL?! With a DEMON? Why?!
Are you an idiot?
I had to convince the cultists that I was the one they were after.
I needed its help for that-- so we made a deal. If it did that for me, then I would let it stay.
Besides, it might not b such a bad thing.

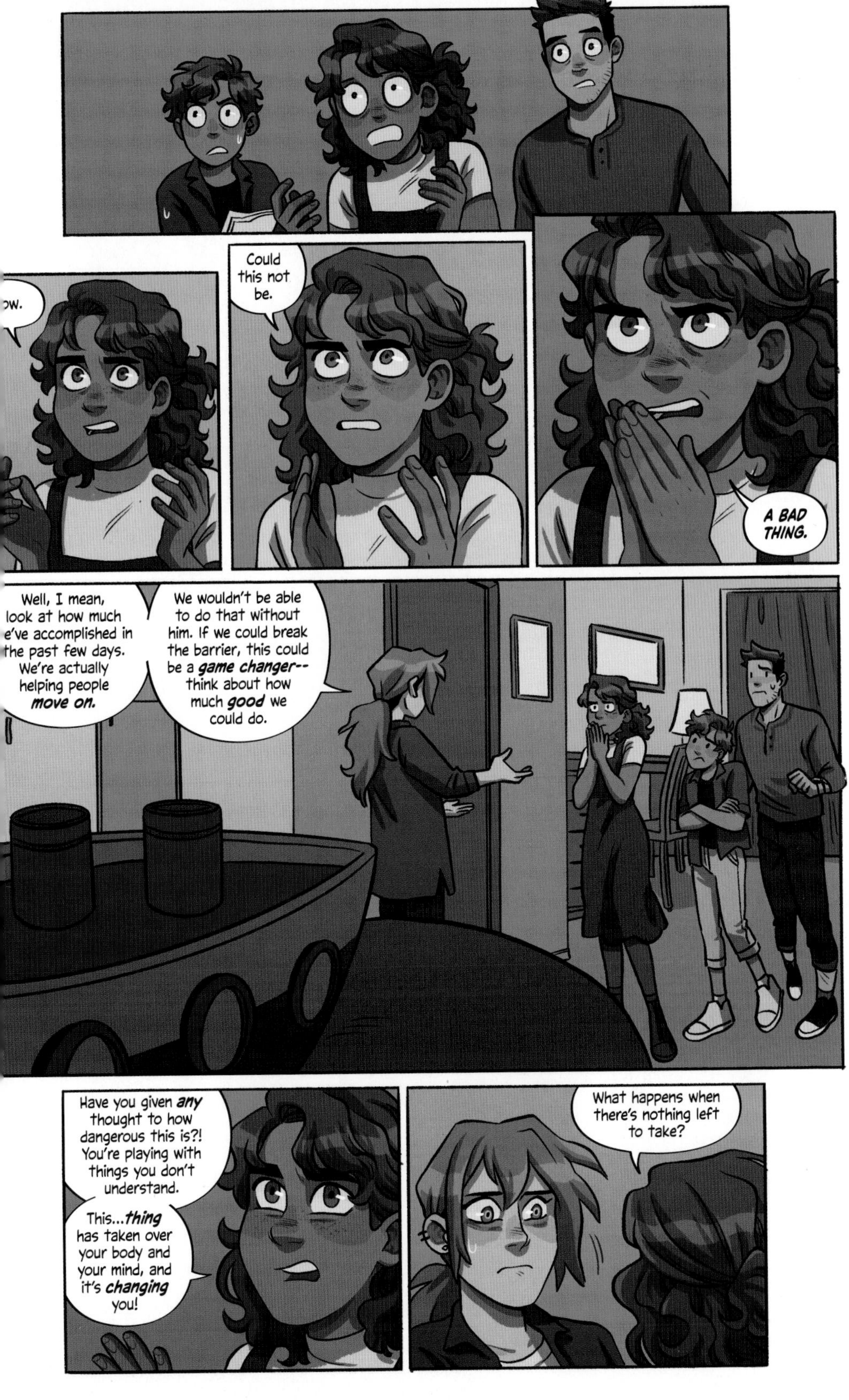

ow.
Could this not be.
A BAD THING.
Well, I mean, look at how much e've accomplished in the past few days. We're actually helping people *move on.*
We wouldn't be able to do that without him. If we could break the barrier, this could be a *game changer--* think about how much *good* we could do.
Have you given *any* thought to how dangerous this is?! You're playing with things you don't understand.
This...*thing* has taken over your body and your mind, and it's *changing* you!
What happens when there's nothing left to take?

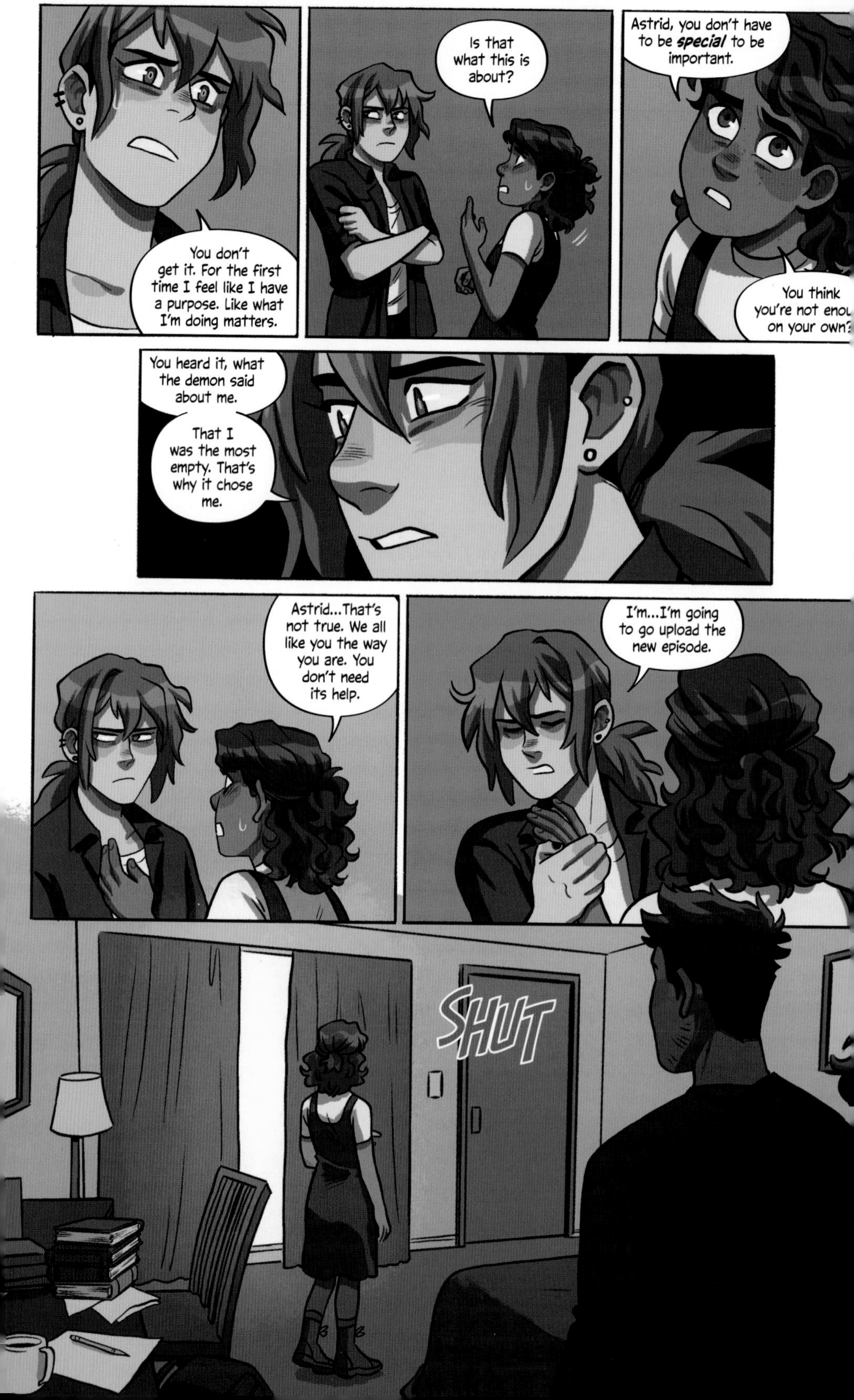
You don't get it. For the first time I feel like I have a purpose. Like what I'm doing matters.
Is that what this is about?
Astrid, you don't have to be ***special*** to be important.
You think you're not enou on your own?
You heard it, what the demon said about me.
That I was the most empty. That's why it chose me.
Astrid...That's not true. We all like you the way you are. You don't need its help.
I'm...I'm going to go upload the new episode.
SHUT

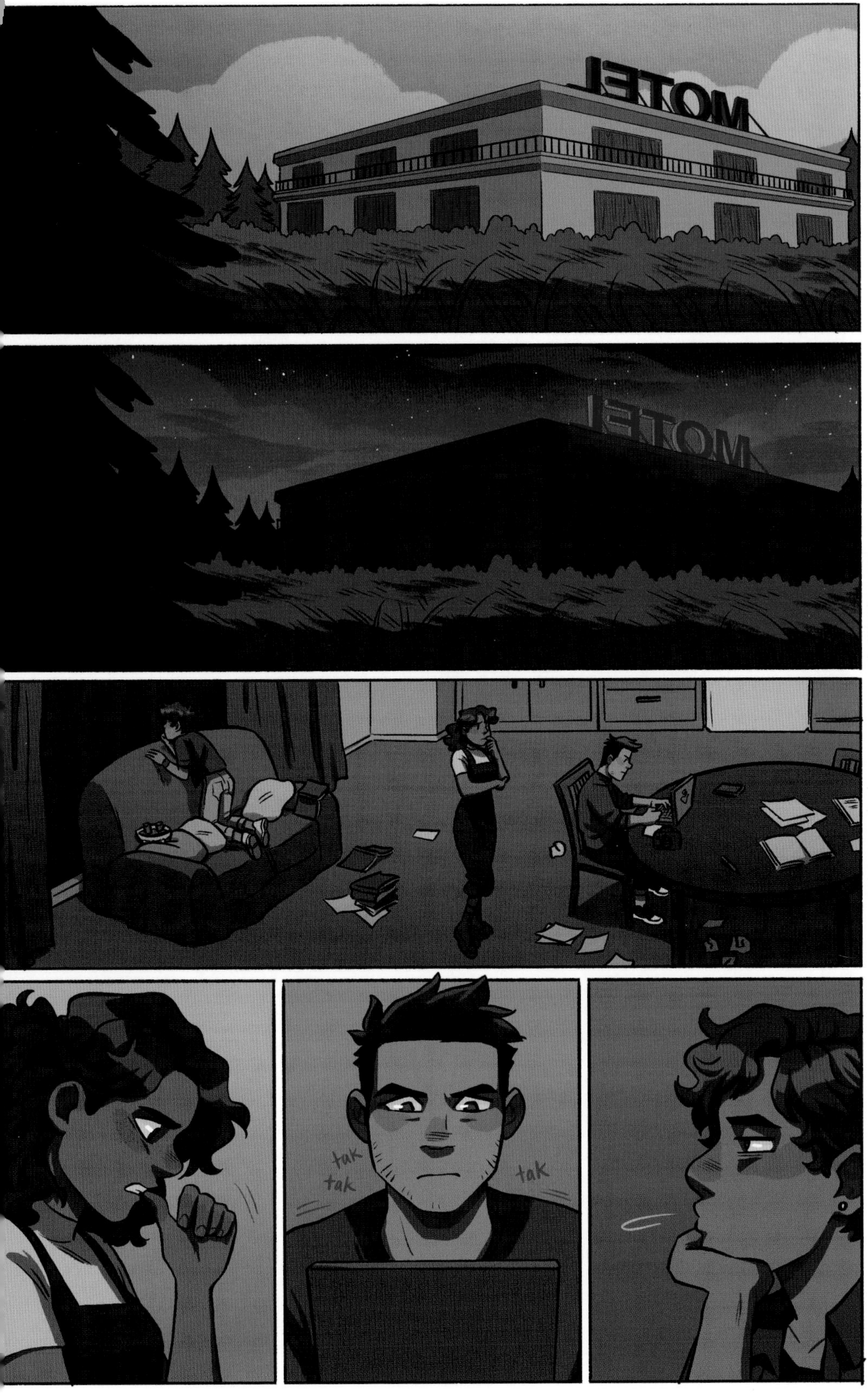
tak
tak
tak

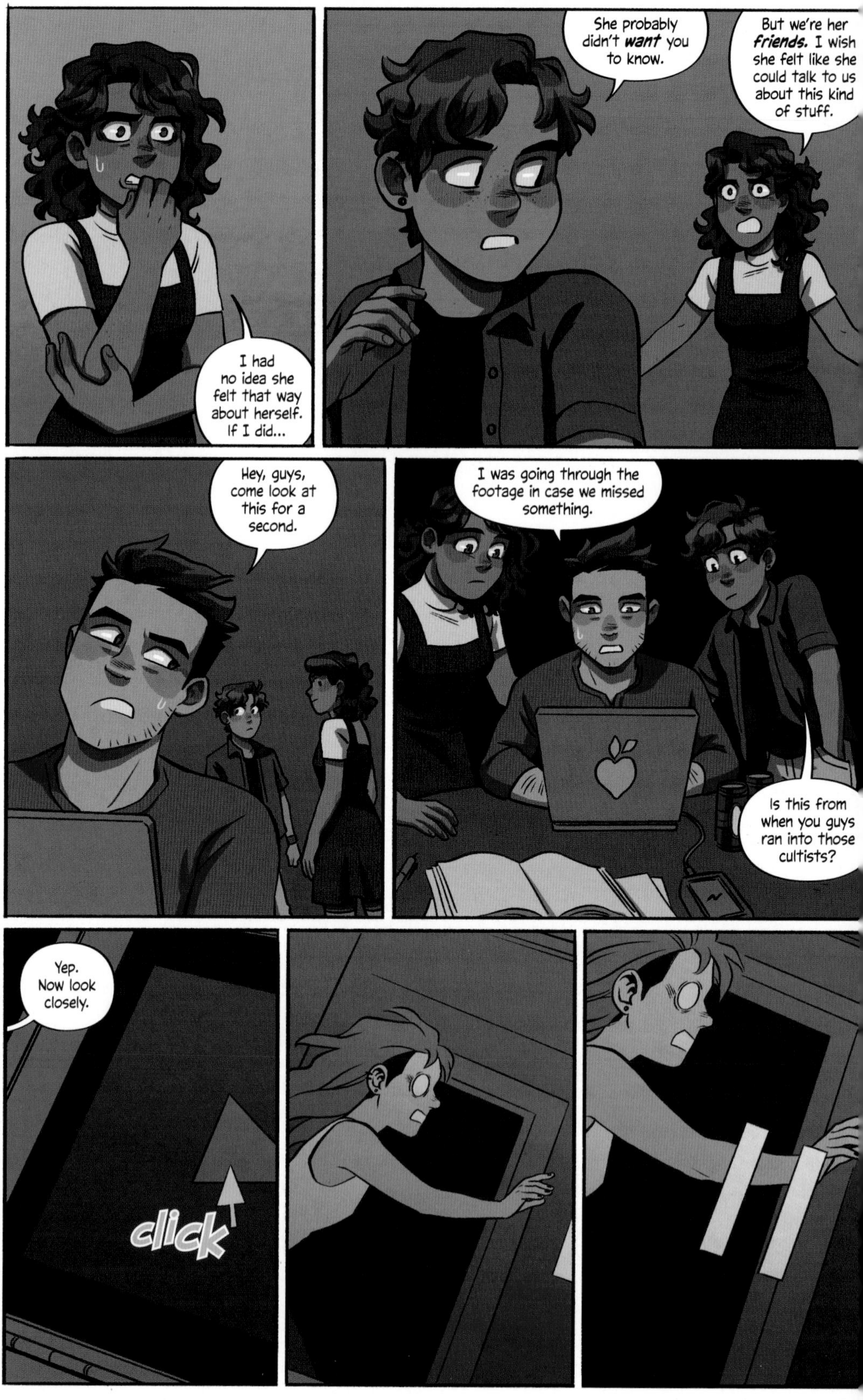
I had no idea she felt that way about herself. If I did...
She probably didn't *want* you to know.
But we're her *friends.* I wish she felt like she could talk to us about this kind of stuff.
Hey, guys, come look at this for a second.
I was going through the footage in case we missed something.
Is this from when you guys ran into those cultists?
Yep. Now look closely.
click

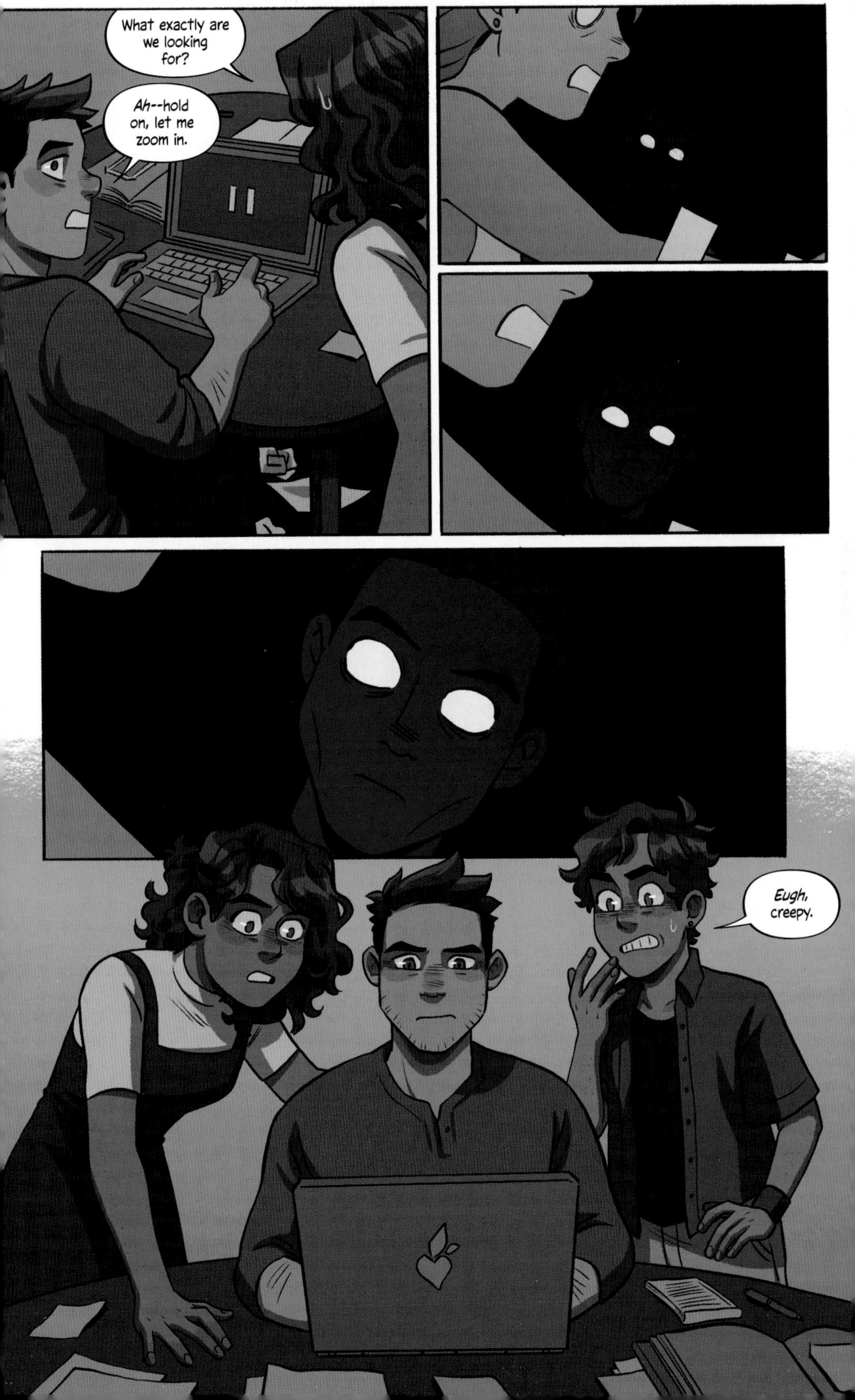
What exactly are we looking for?
Ah--hold on, let me zoom in.
Eugh, creepy.

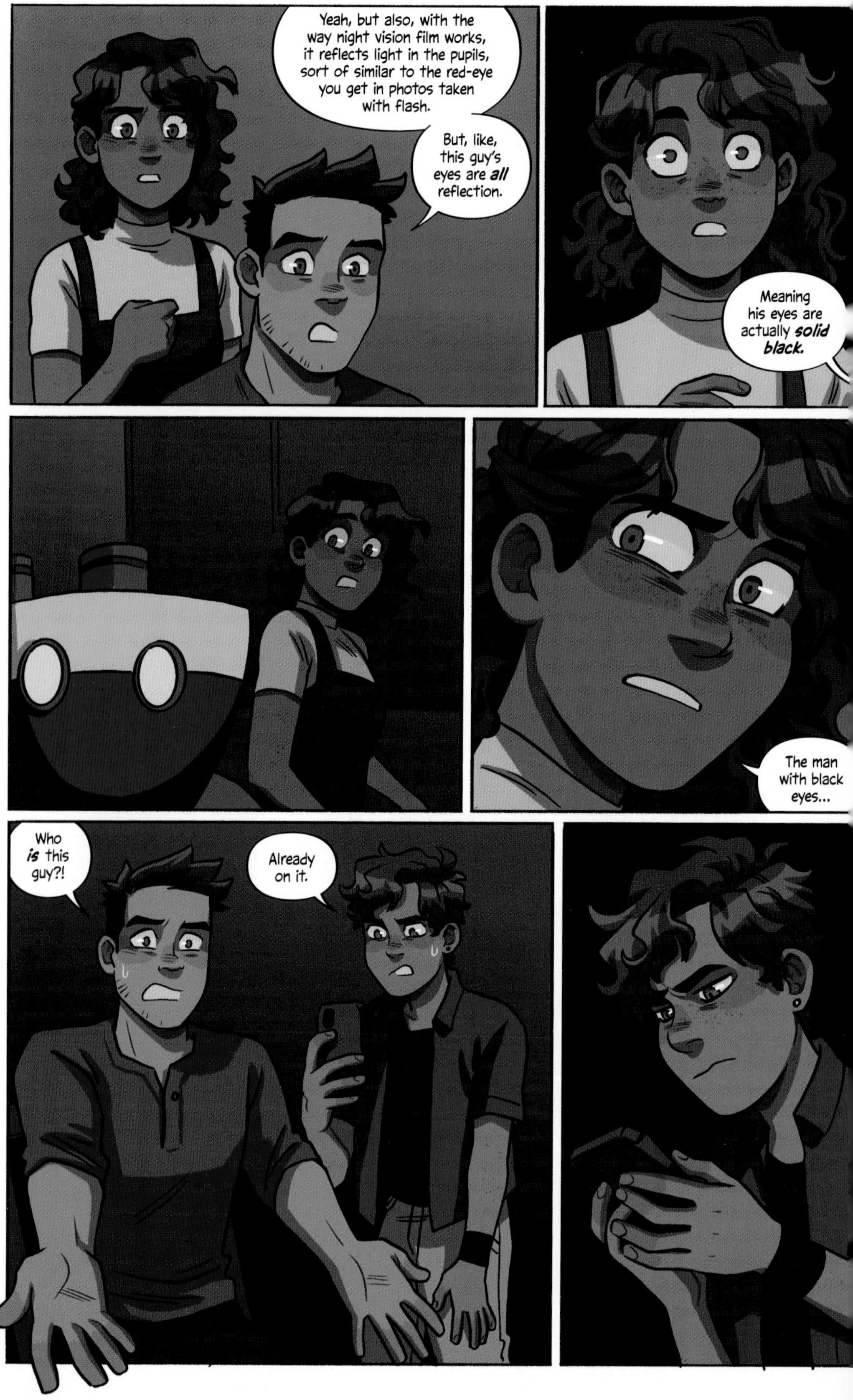
Yeah, but also, with the way night vision film works, it reflects light in the pupils, sort of similar to the red-eye you get in photos taken with flash.
But, like, this guy's eyes are *all* reflection.
Meaning his eyes are actually ***solid black.***
The man with black eyes...
Who *is* this guy?!
Already on it.

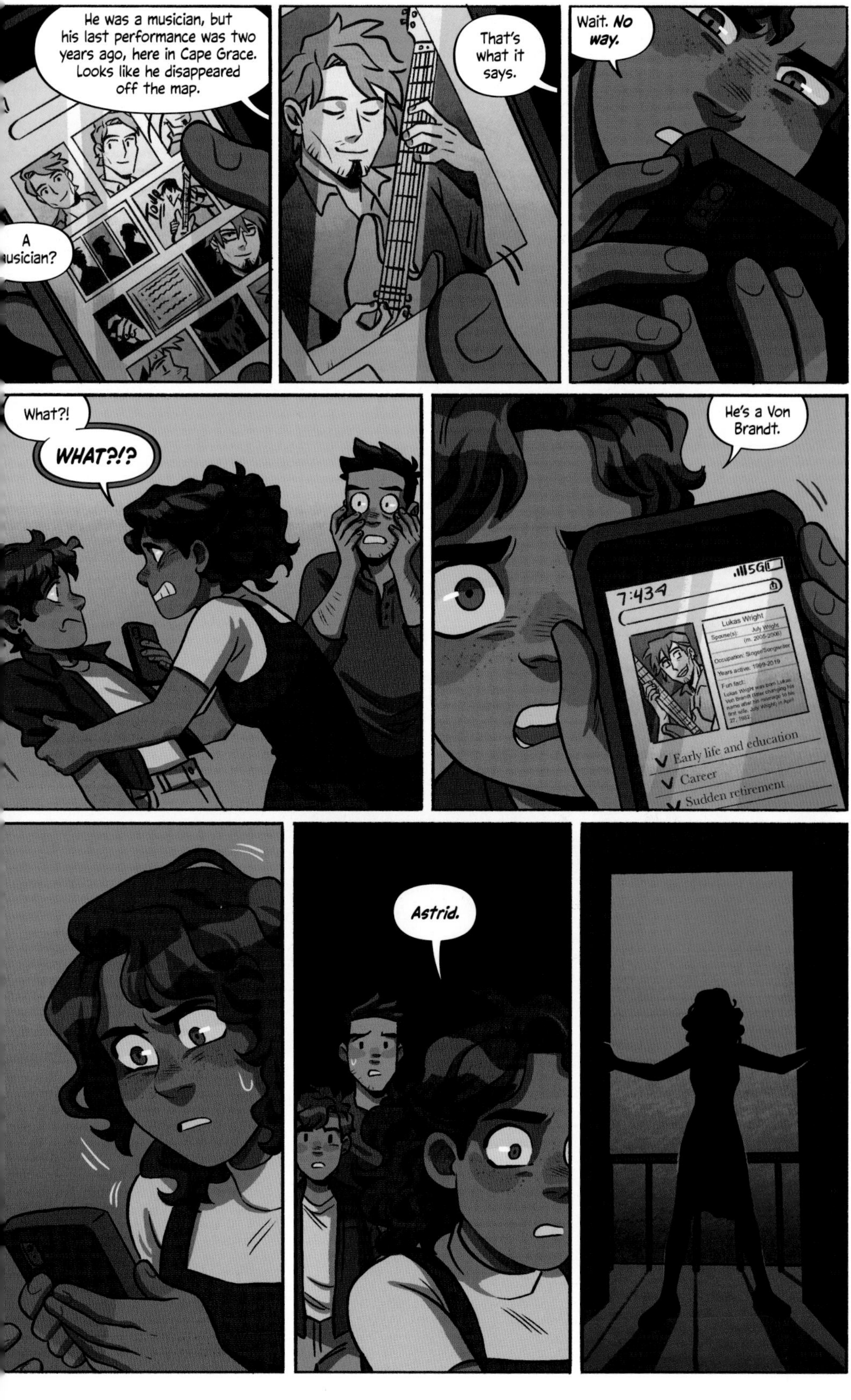
He was a musician, but his last performance was two years ago, here in Cape Grace. Looks like he disappeared off the map.
A usician?
That's what it says.
Wait. No way.
What?!
WHAT?!?
He's a Von Brandt.
7:434
5G
Lukas Wright
Spouse(s): July Wright (m. 2005-2006)
Occupation: Singer/Songwriter
Years active: 1999-2019
Fun fact:
Lukas Wright was born Lukas Von Brandt (later changing his name after his marriage to his first wife, July Wright) in April 27, 1982.
Early life and education
Career
Sudden retirement
Astrid.

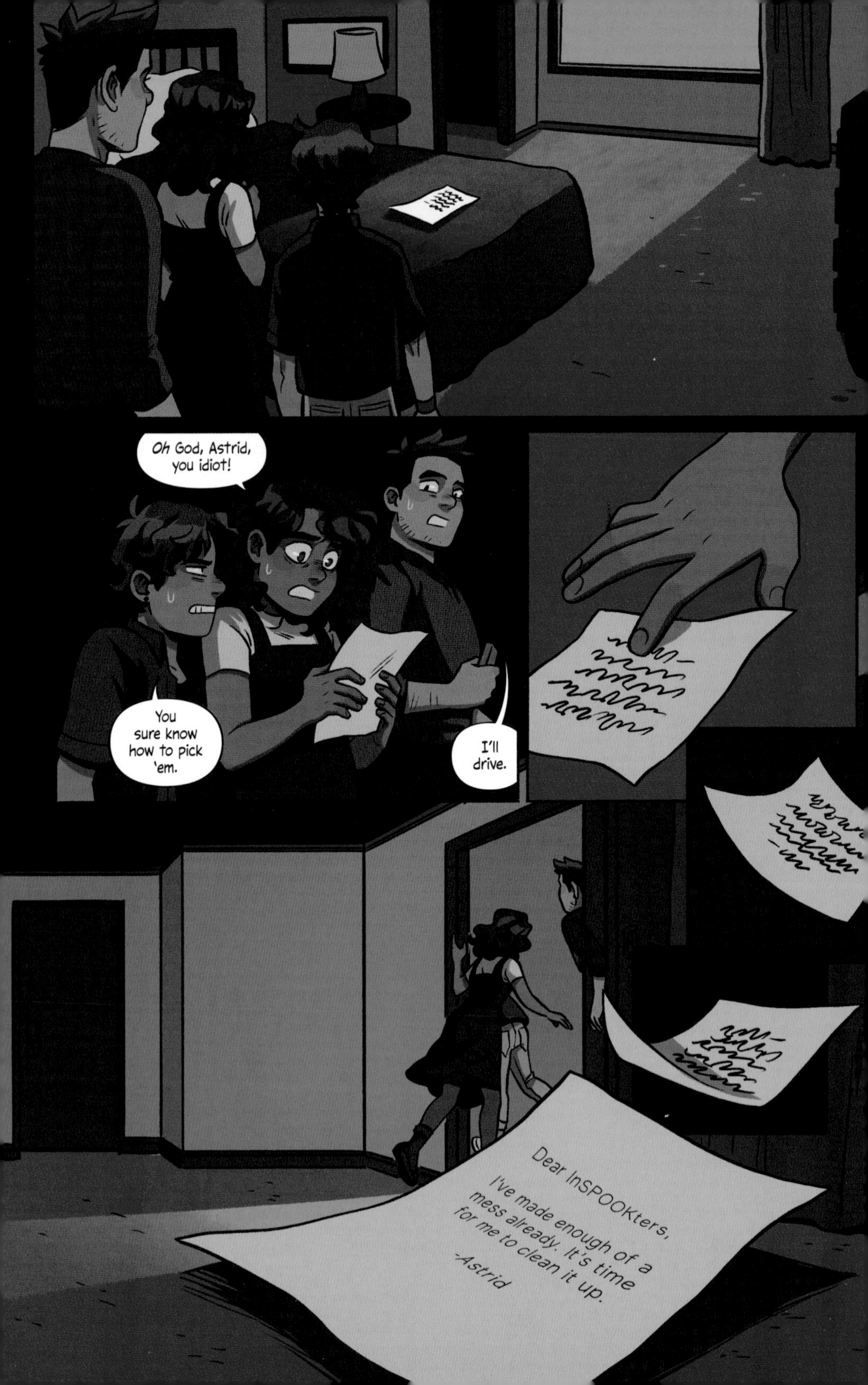

Oh God, Astrid, you idiot!
You sure know how to pick 'em.
I'll drive.
Dear InSPOOKters,
I've made enough of a mess already. It's time for me to clean it up.
-Astrid

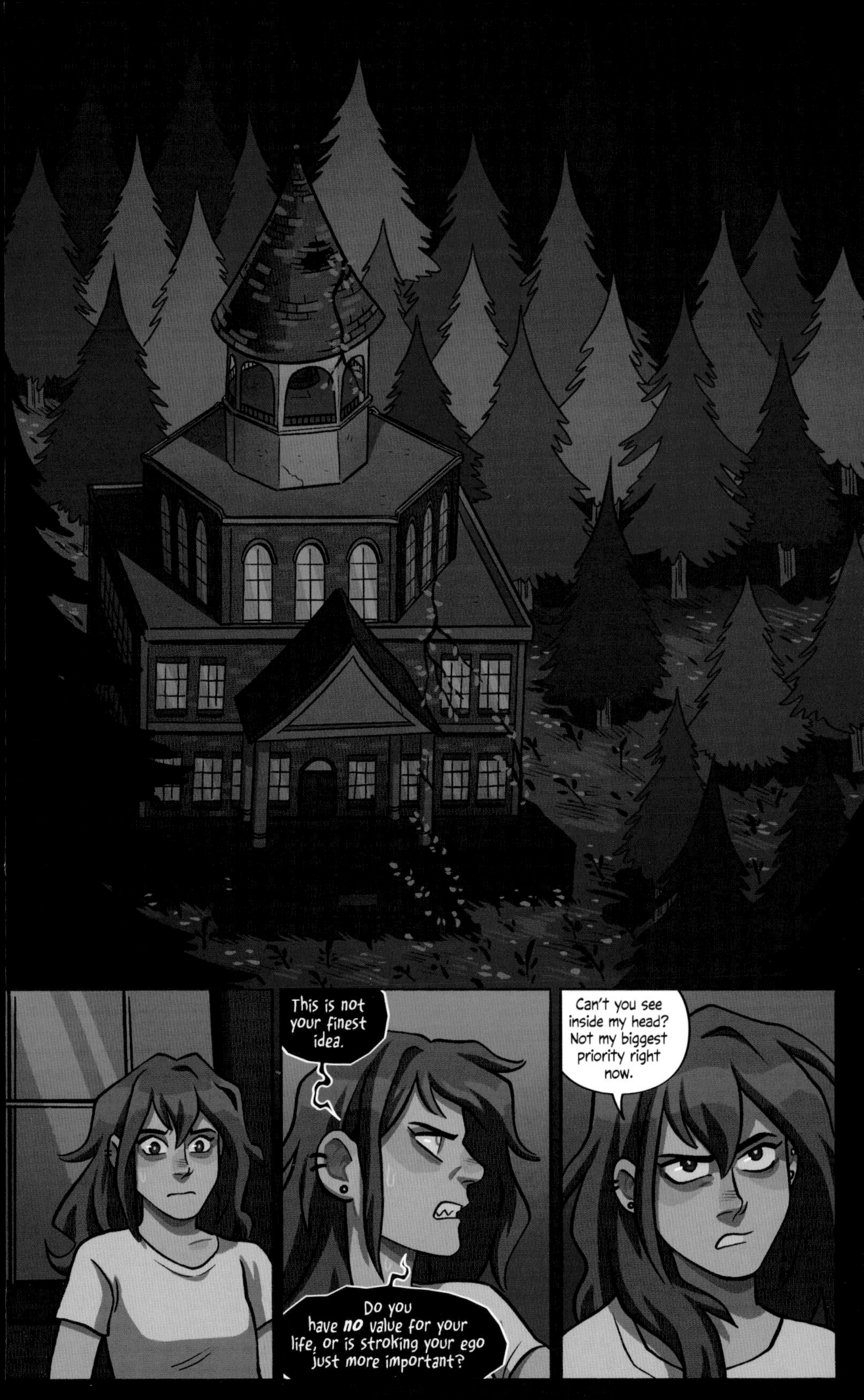
This is not your finest idea.
Do you have NO value for your life, or is stroking your ego just more important?
Can't you see inside my head? Not my biggest priority right now.

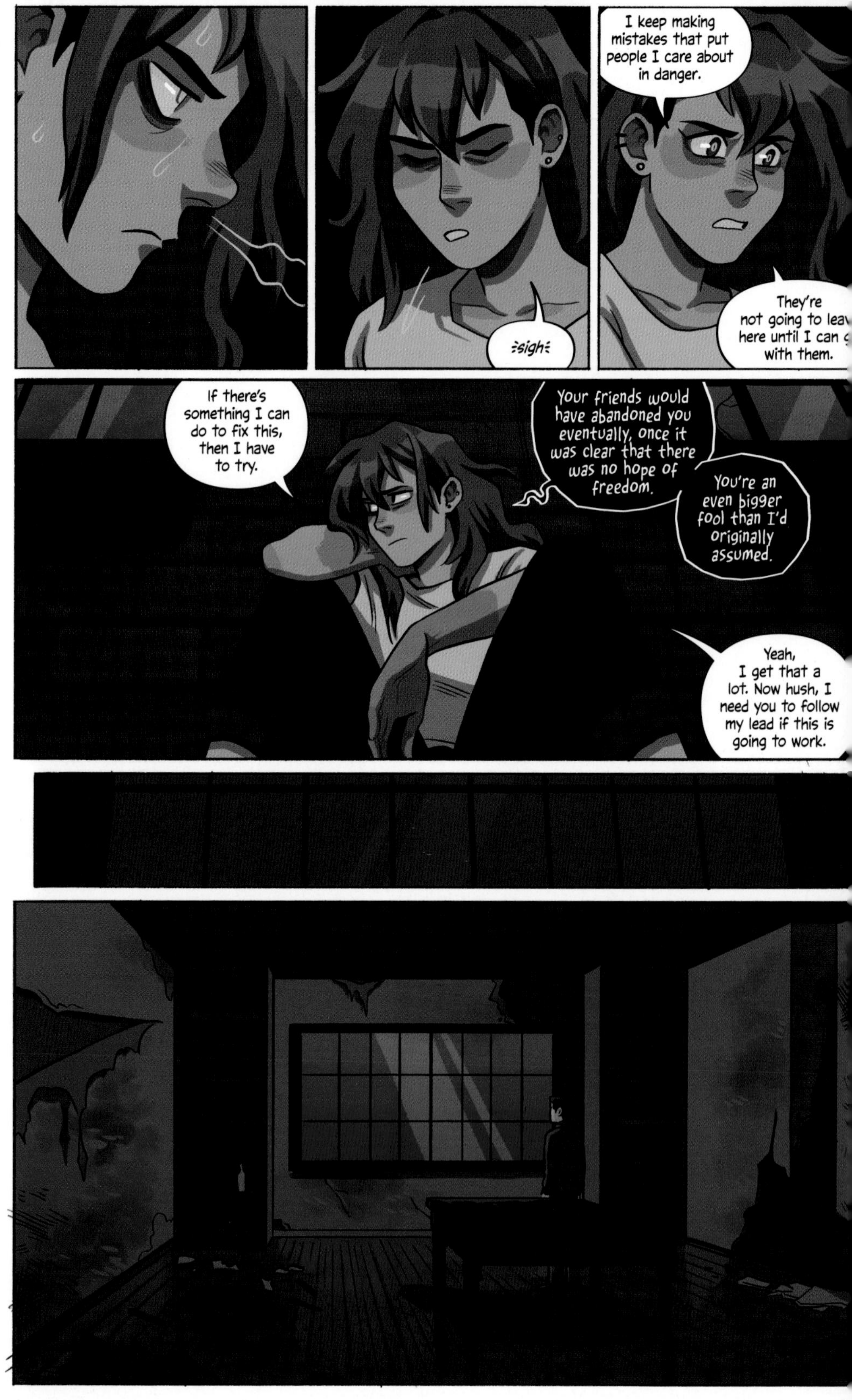
I keep making mistakes that put people I care about in danger.
sigh
They're not going to leav here until I can g with them.
If there's something I can do to fix this, then I have to try.
Your friends would have abandoned you eventually, once it was clear that there was no hope of freedom.
You're an even bigger fool than I'd originally assumed.
Yeah, I get that a lot. Now hush, I need you to follow my lead if this is going to work.

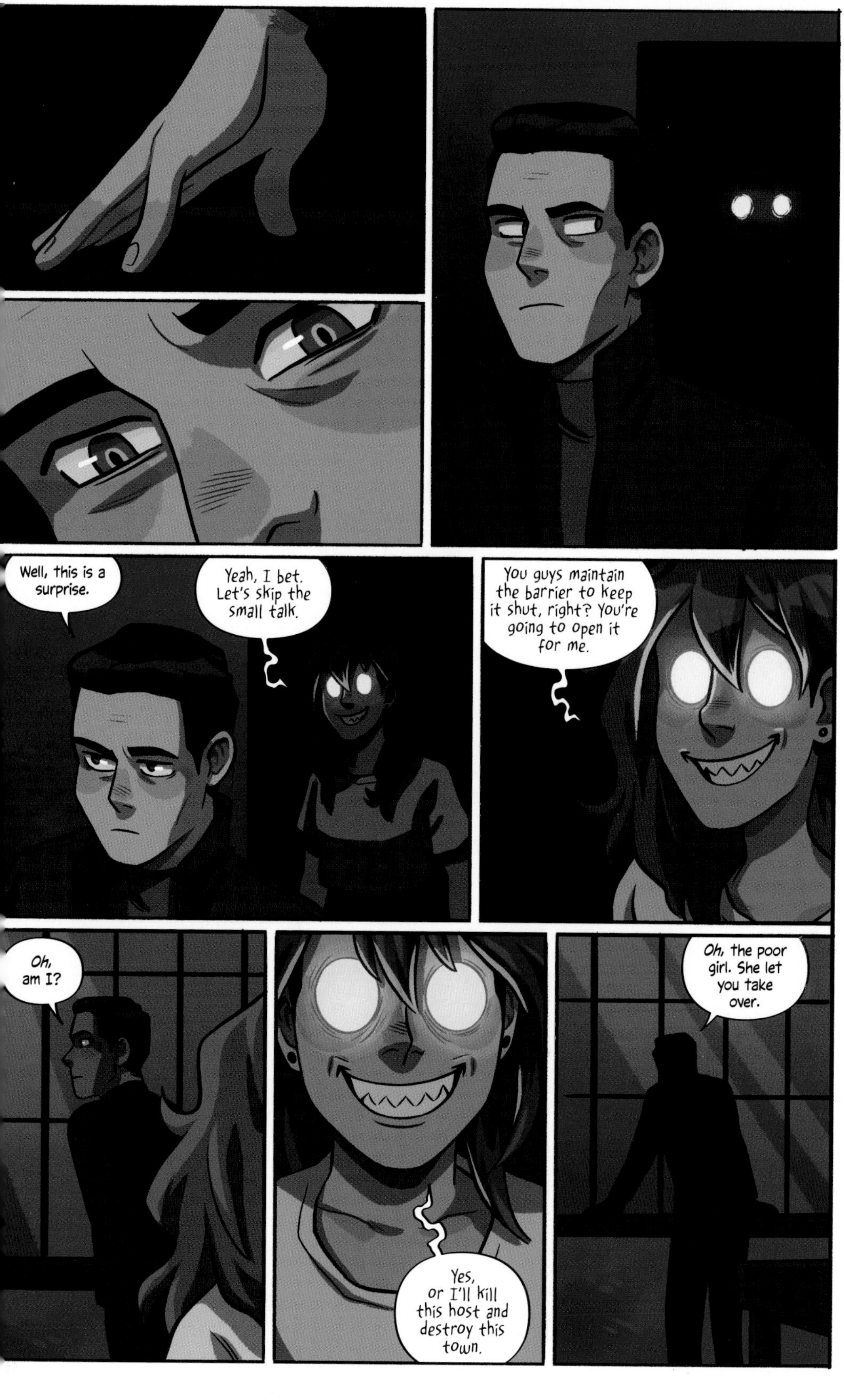
Well, this is a surprise.
Yeah, I bet. Let's skip the small talk.
You guys maintain the barrier to keep it shut, right? You're going to open it for me.
Oh, am I?
Yes, or I'll kill this host and destroy this town.
Oh, the poor girl. She let you take over.

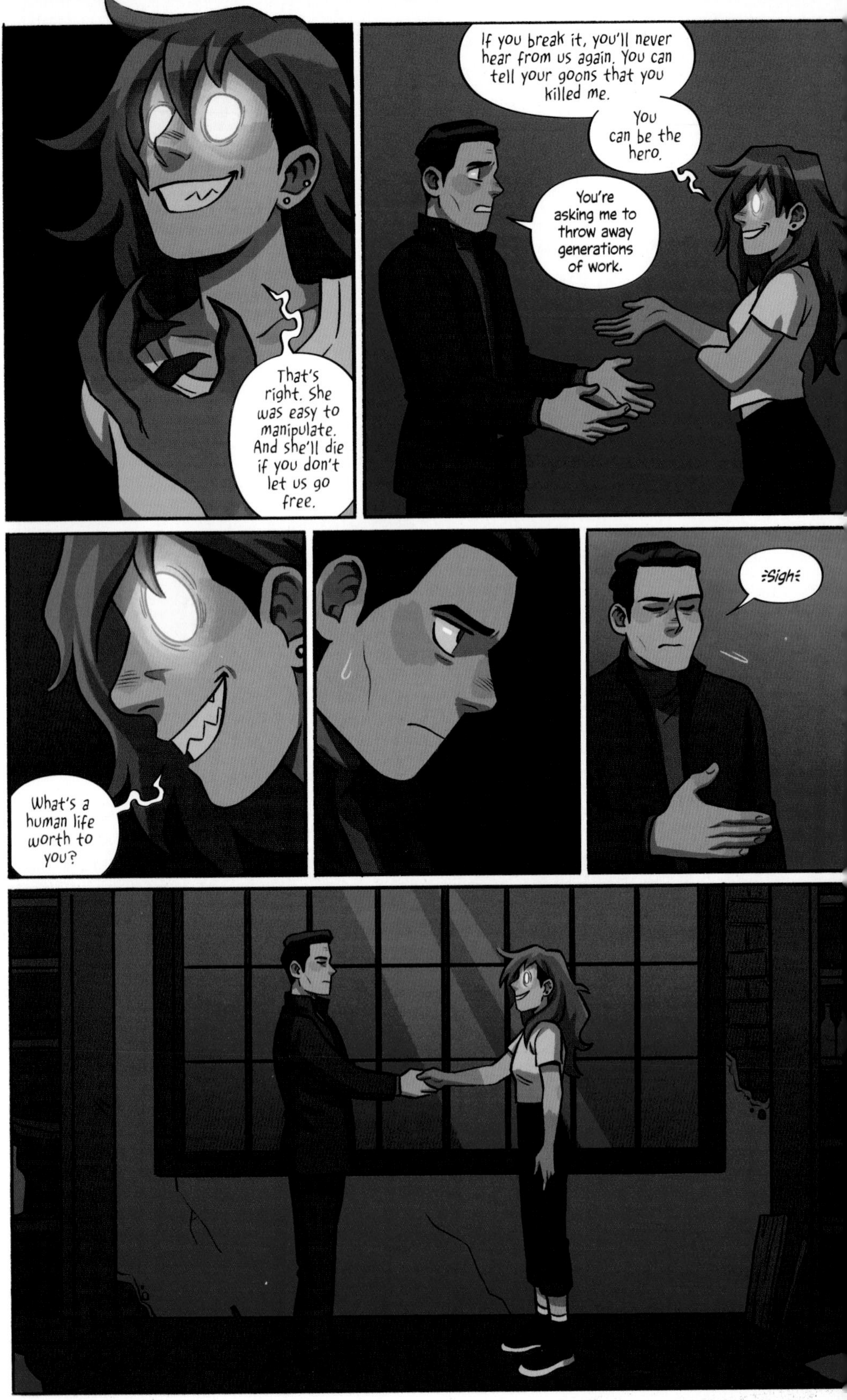
That's right. She was easy to manipulate. And she'll die if you don't let us go free.
If you break it, you'll never hear from us again. You can tell your goons that you killed me.
You can be the hero.
You're asking me to throw away generations of work.
What's a human life worth to you?
Sigh

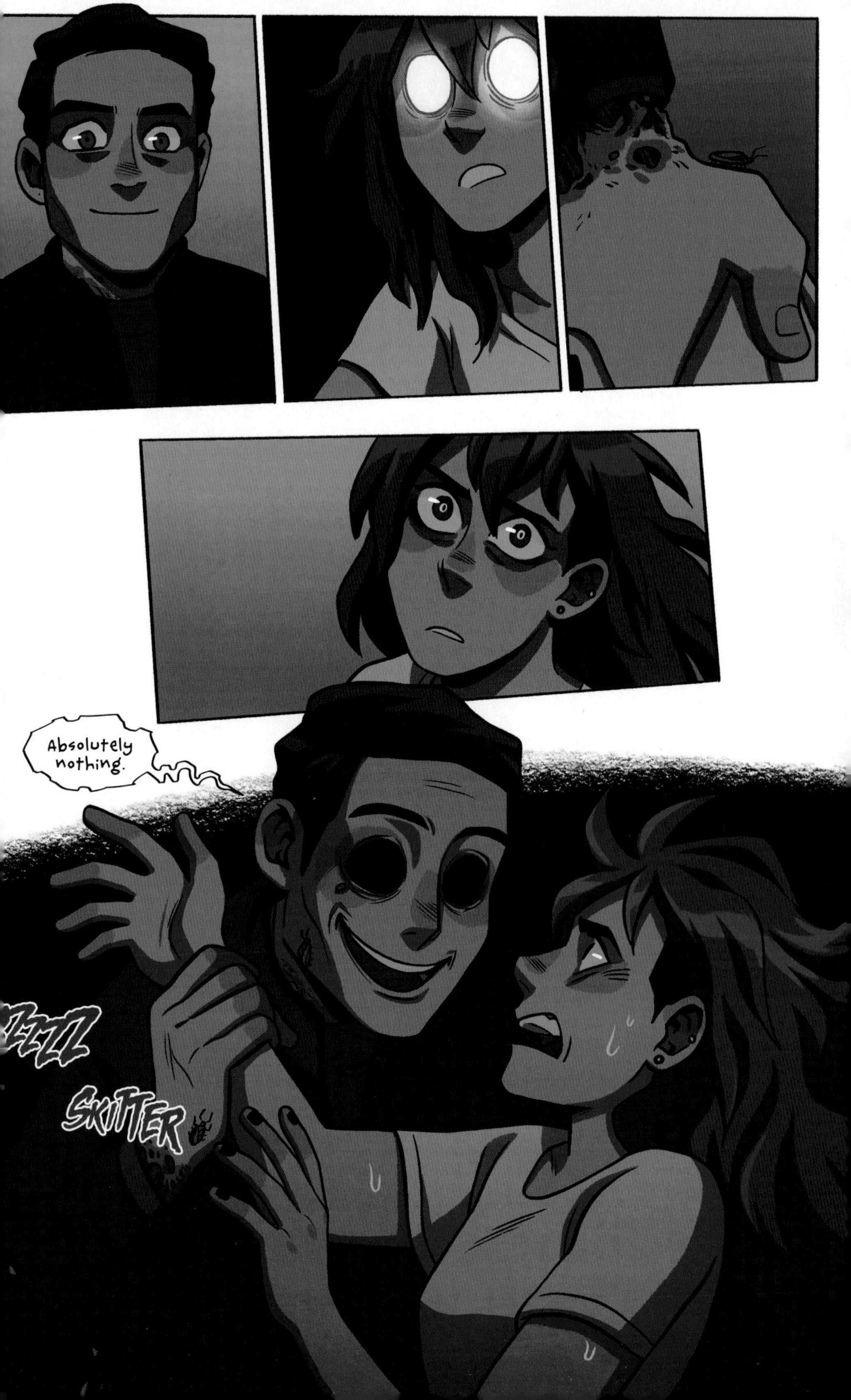
Absolutely nothing.
ZZZZZ
SKITTER

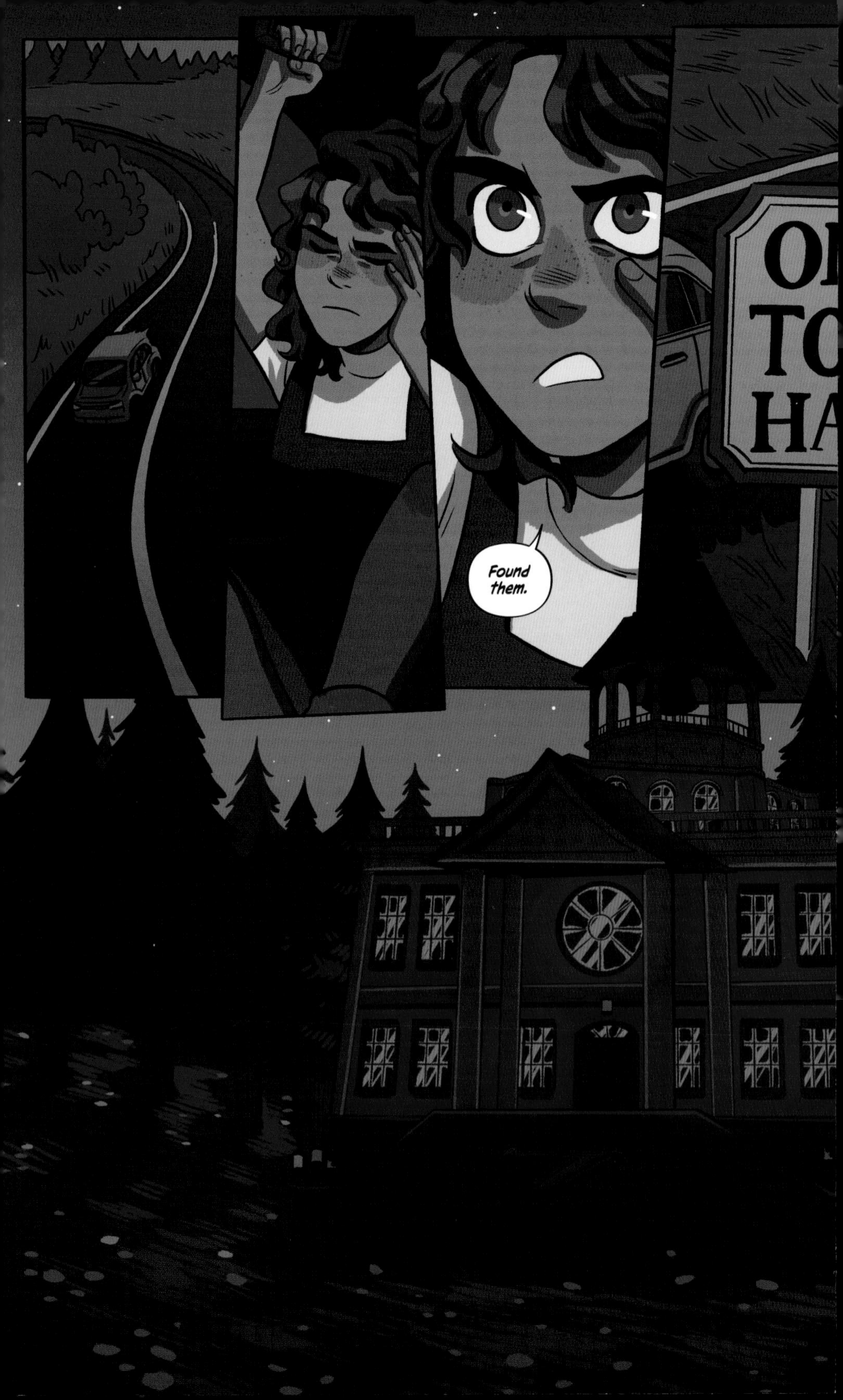
Found them.

Episode Five
The Ritual

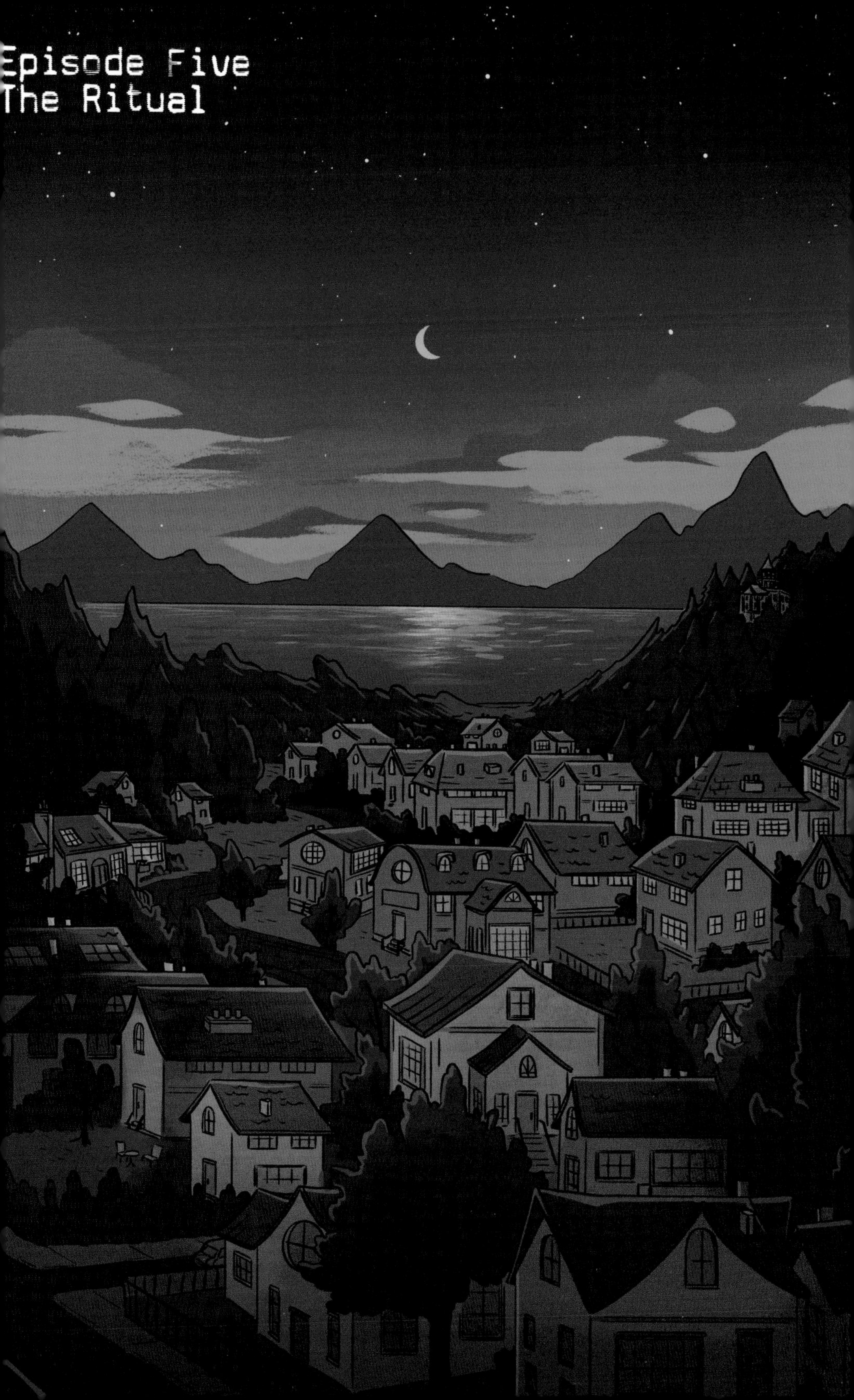

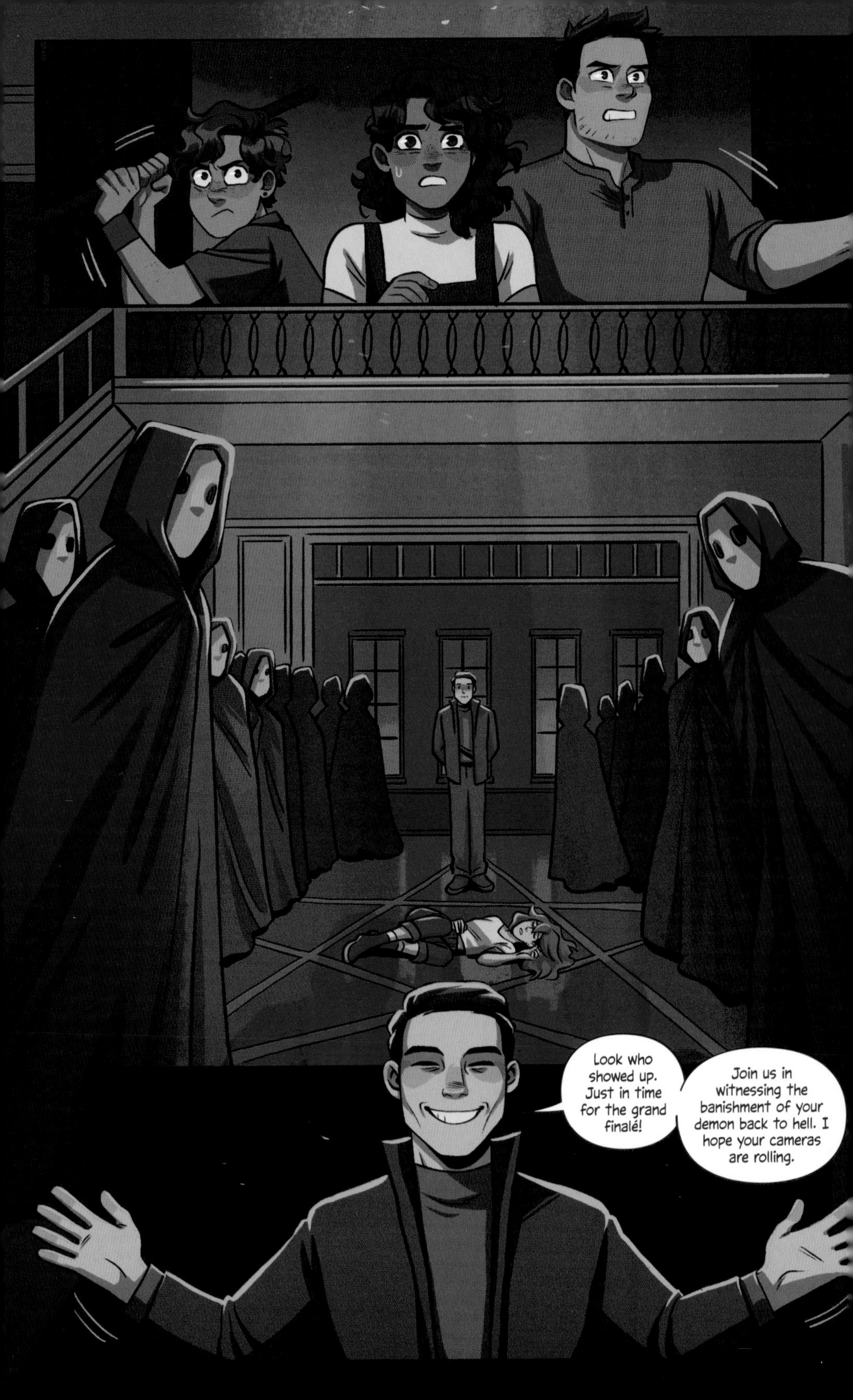
Look who showed up. Just in time for the grand finalé!
Join us in witnessing the banishment of your demon back to hell. I hope your cameras are rolling.

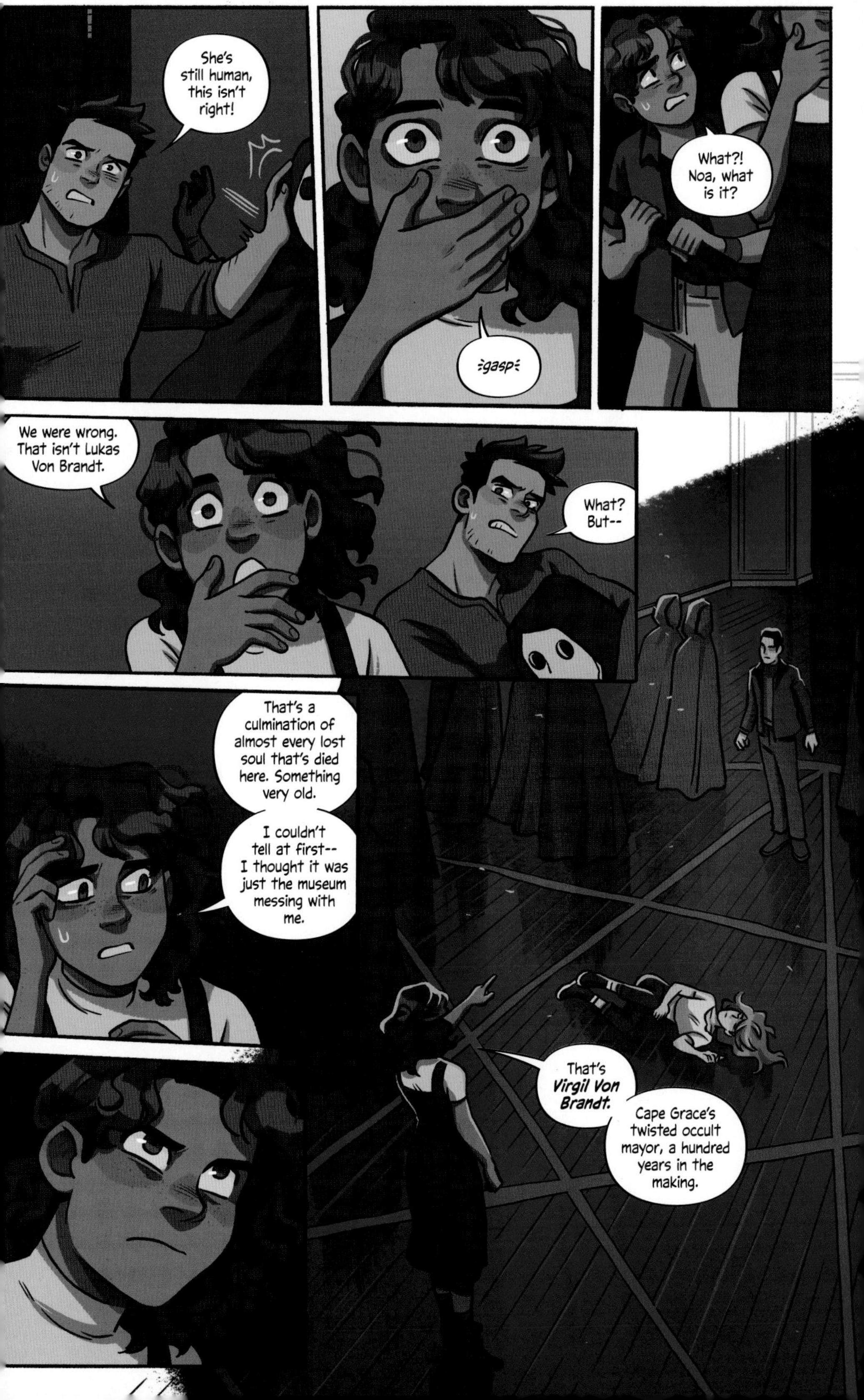
She's still human, this isn't right!
:gasp:
What?! Noa, what is it?
We were wrong. That isn't Lukas Von Brandt.
What? But--
That's a culmination of almost every lost soul that's died here. Something very old.
I couldn't tell at first-- I thought it was just the museum messing with me.
That's *Virgil Von Brandt.*
Cape Grace's twisted occult mayor, a hundred years in the making.

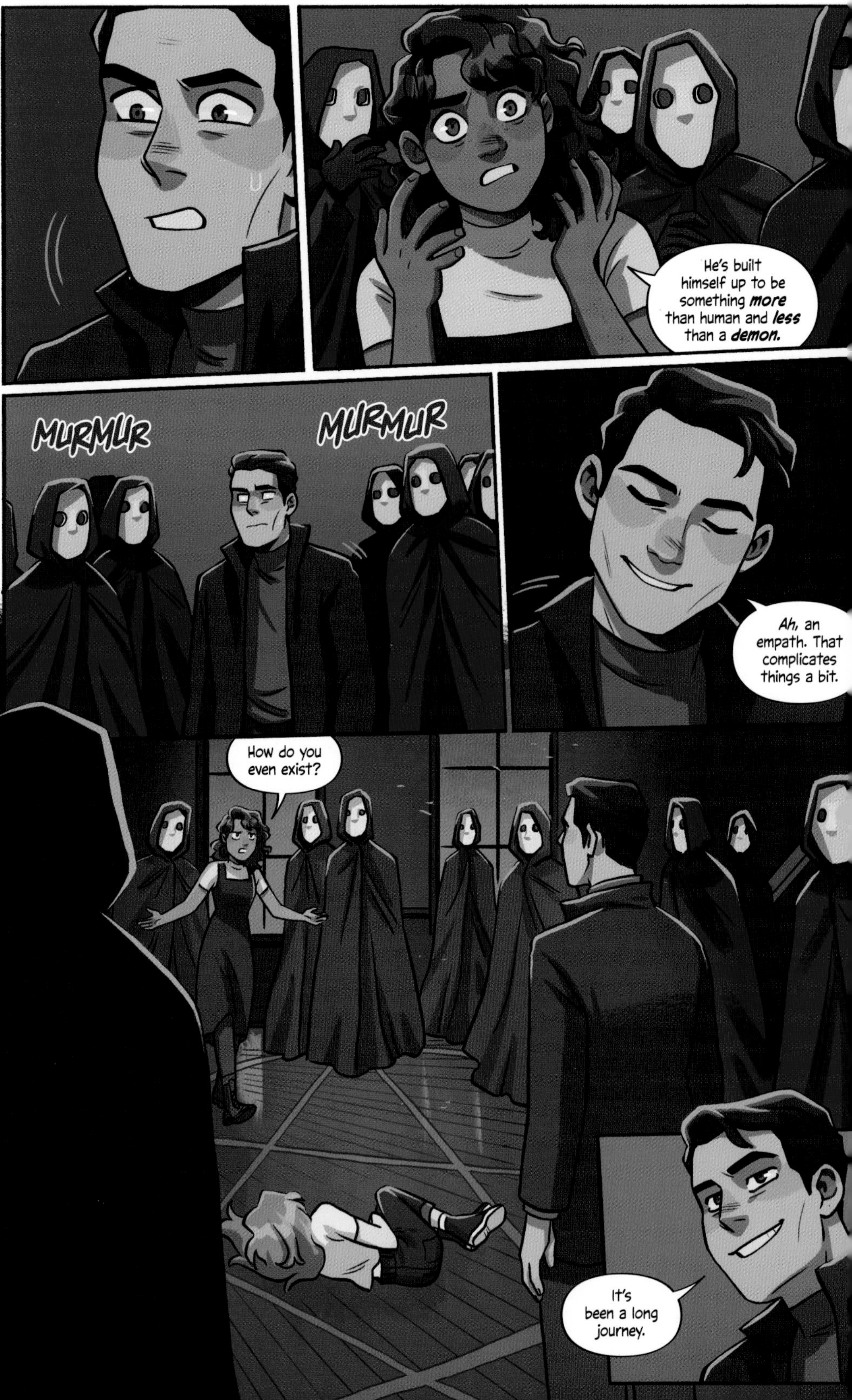
He's built himself up to be something *more* than human and *less* than a *demon.*
MURMUR
MURMUR
Ah, an empath. That complicates things a bit.
How do you even exist?
It's been a long journey.

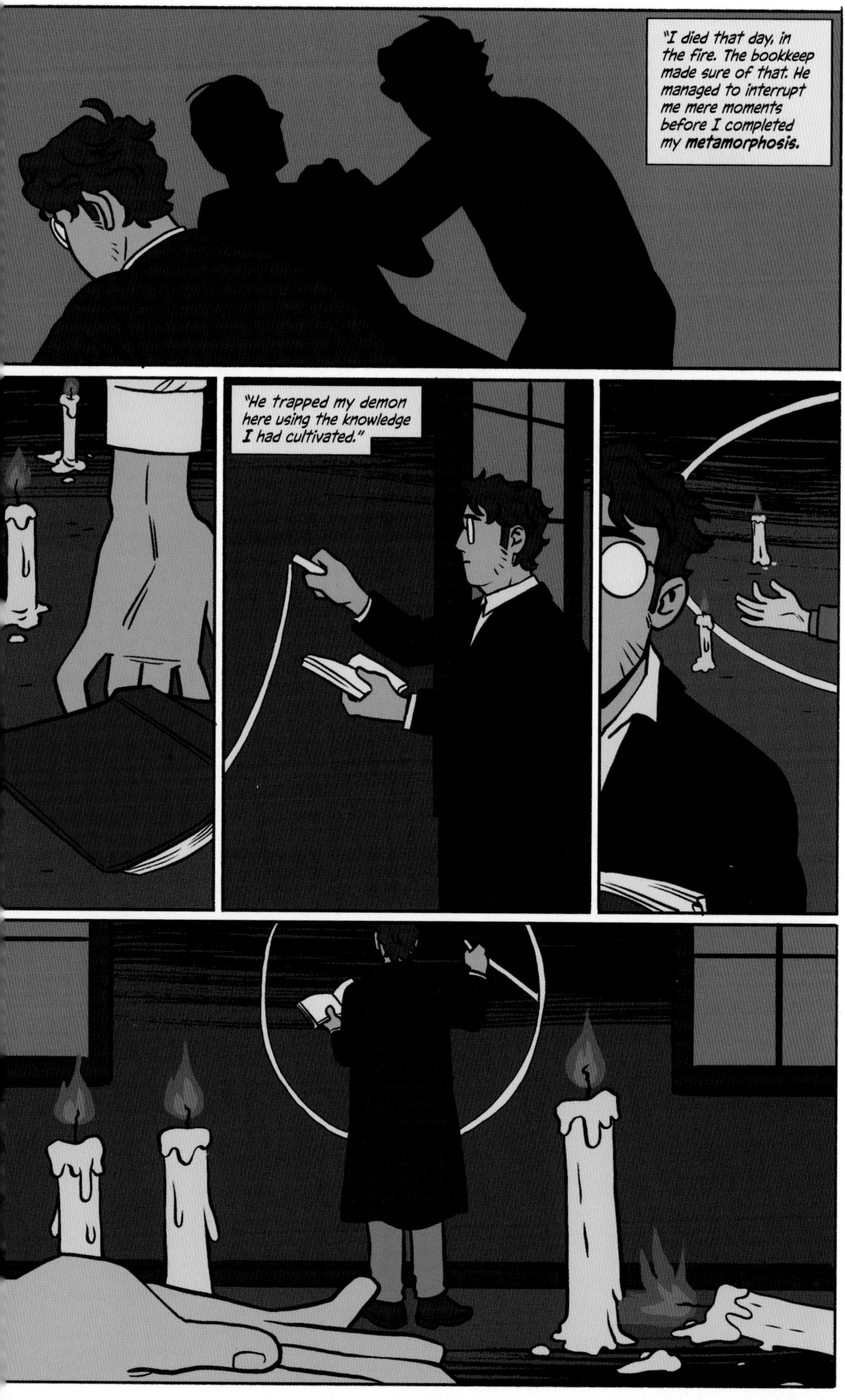
"I died that day, in the fire. The bookkeep made sure of that. He managed to interrupt me mere moments before I completed my **metamorphosis.**
"He trapped my demon here using the knowledge I had cultivated."

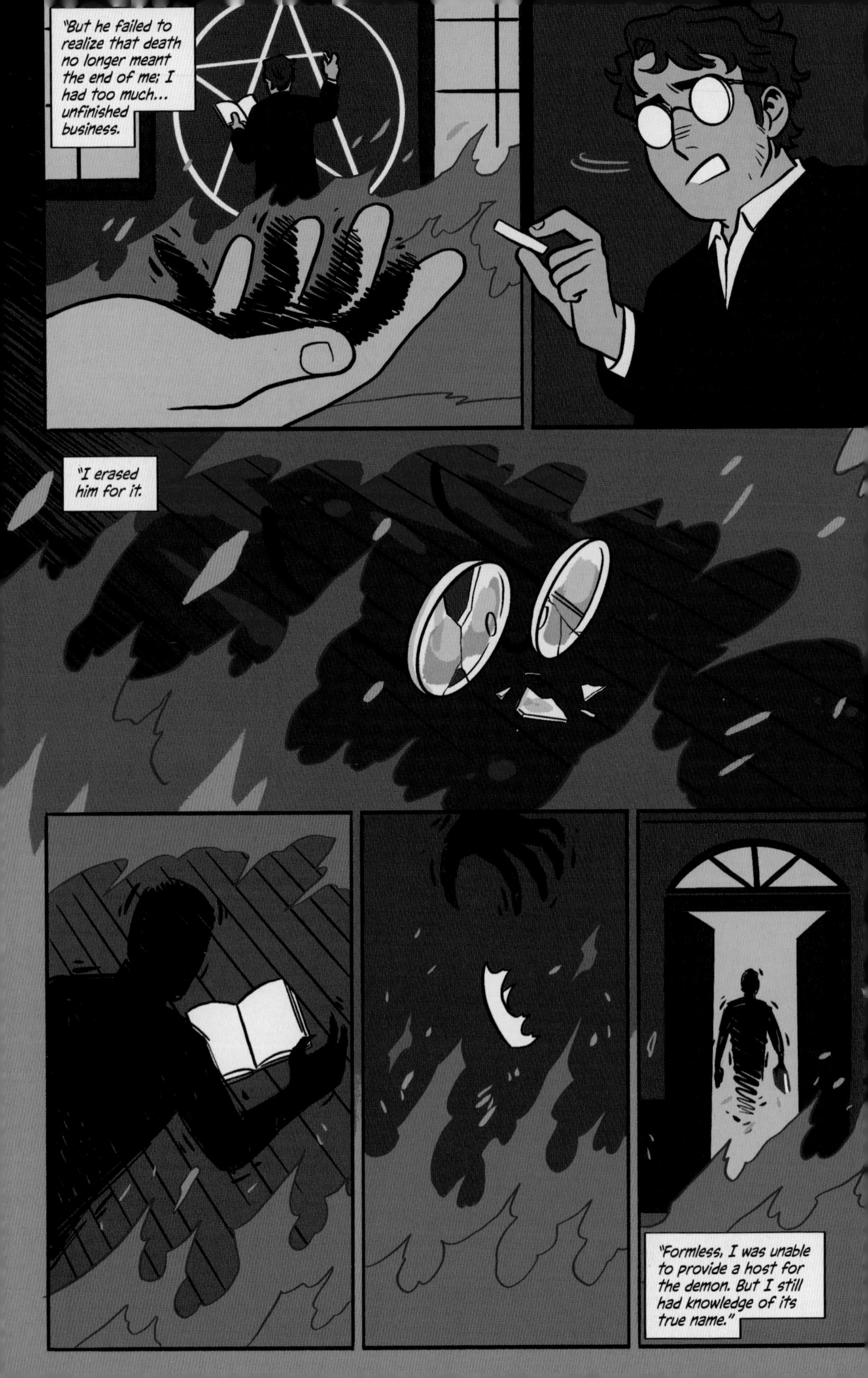
"But he failed to realize that death no longer meant the end of me; I had too much... unfinished business.
"I erased him for it.
"Formless, I was unable to provide a host for the demon. But I still had knowledge of its true name."

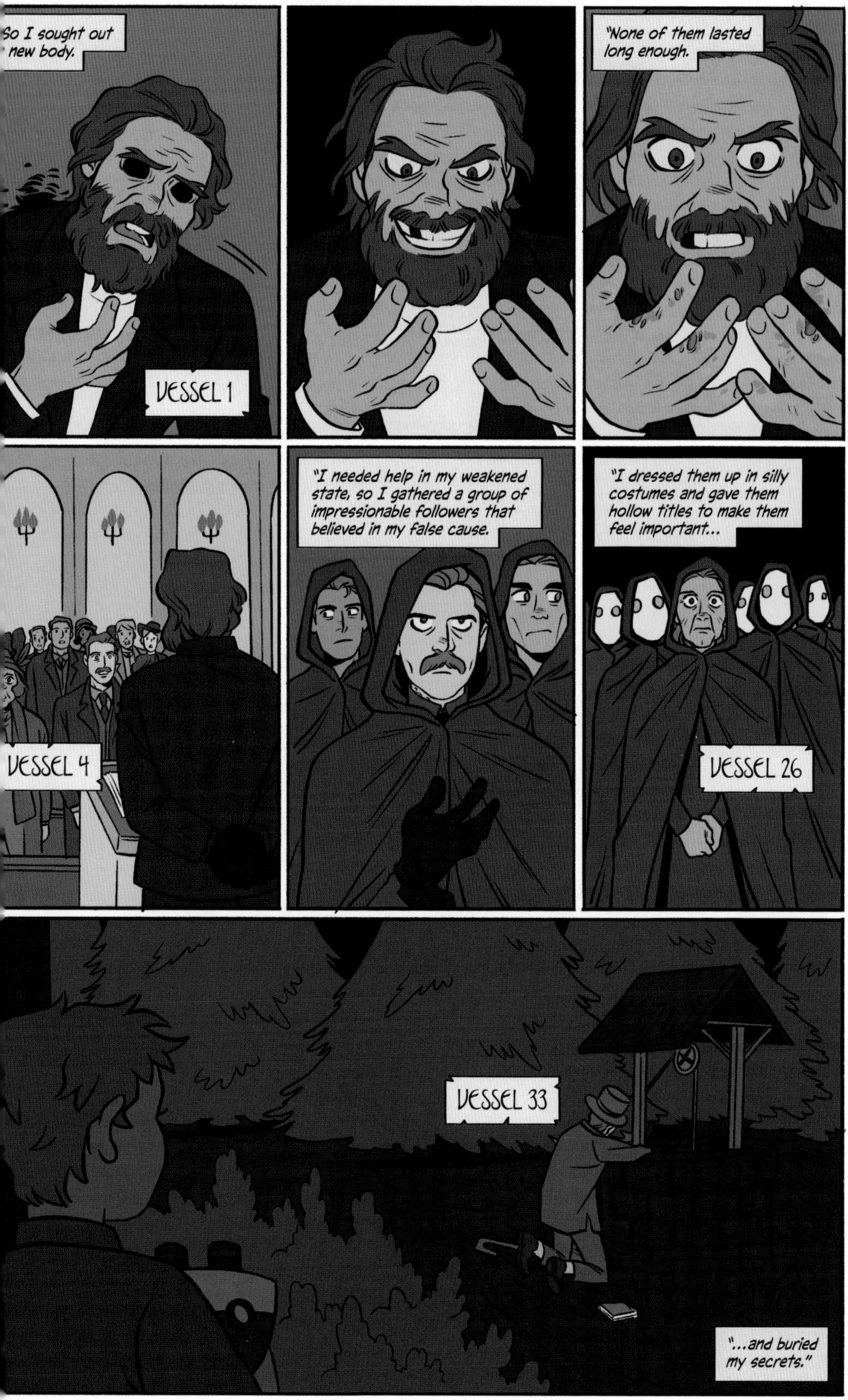

So I sought out
new body.
VESSEL 1
"None of them lasted
long enough.
VESSEL 4
"I needed help in my weakened state, so I gathered a group of impressionable followers that believed in my false cause.
"I dressed them up in silly costumes and gave them hollow titles to make them feel important...
VESSEL 26
VESSEL 33
"...and buried my secrets."

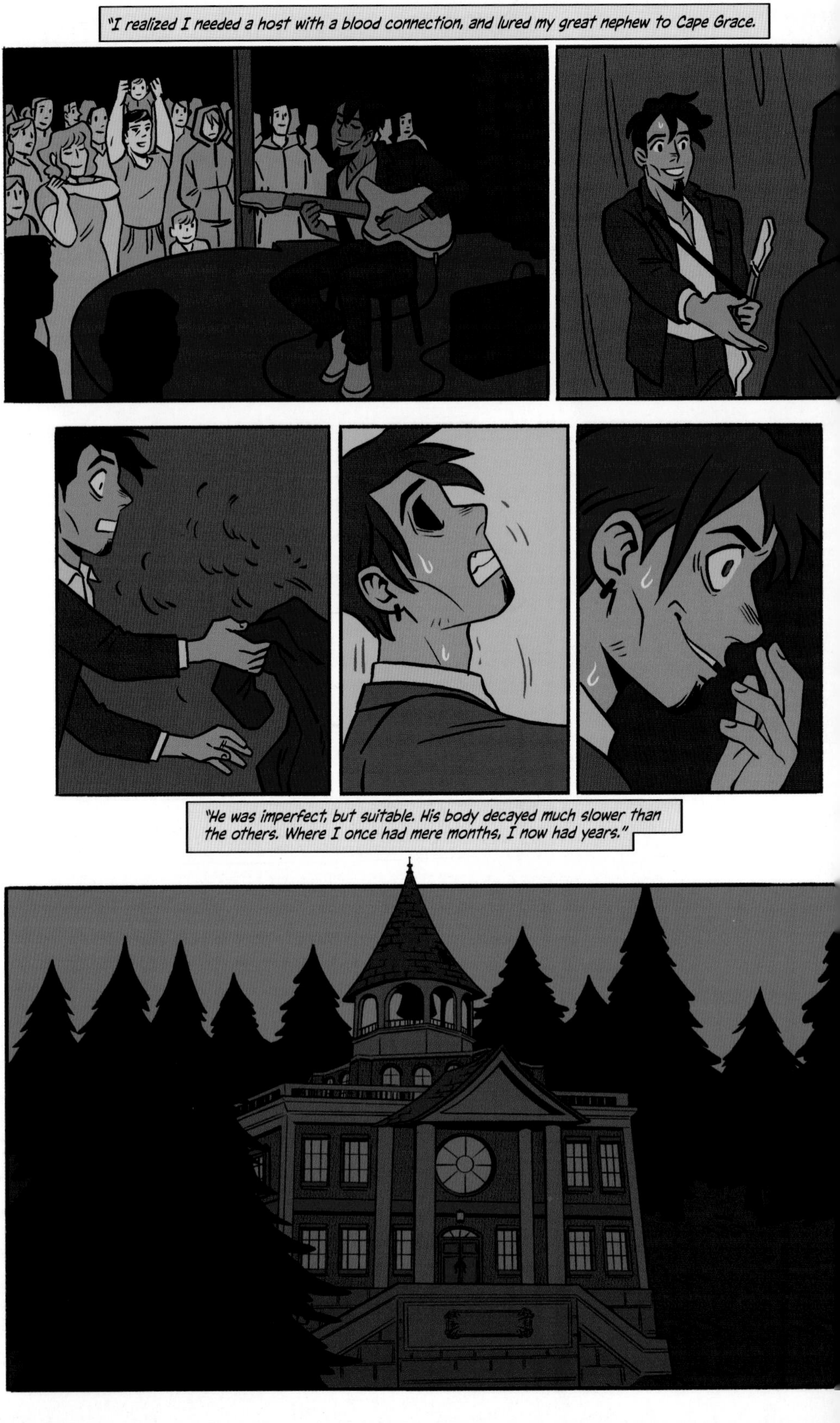
"I realized I needed a host with a blood connection, and lured my great nephew to Cape Grace.
"He was imperfect, but suitable. His body decayed much slower than the others. Where I once had mere months, I now had years."

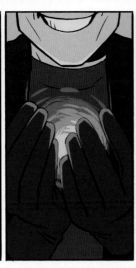

We had everything
place to complete
e ritual on the
nniversary of my
eath.

"And then you
showed up."

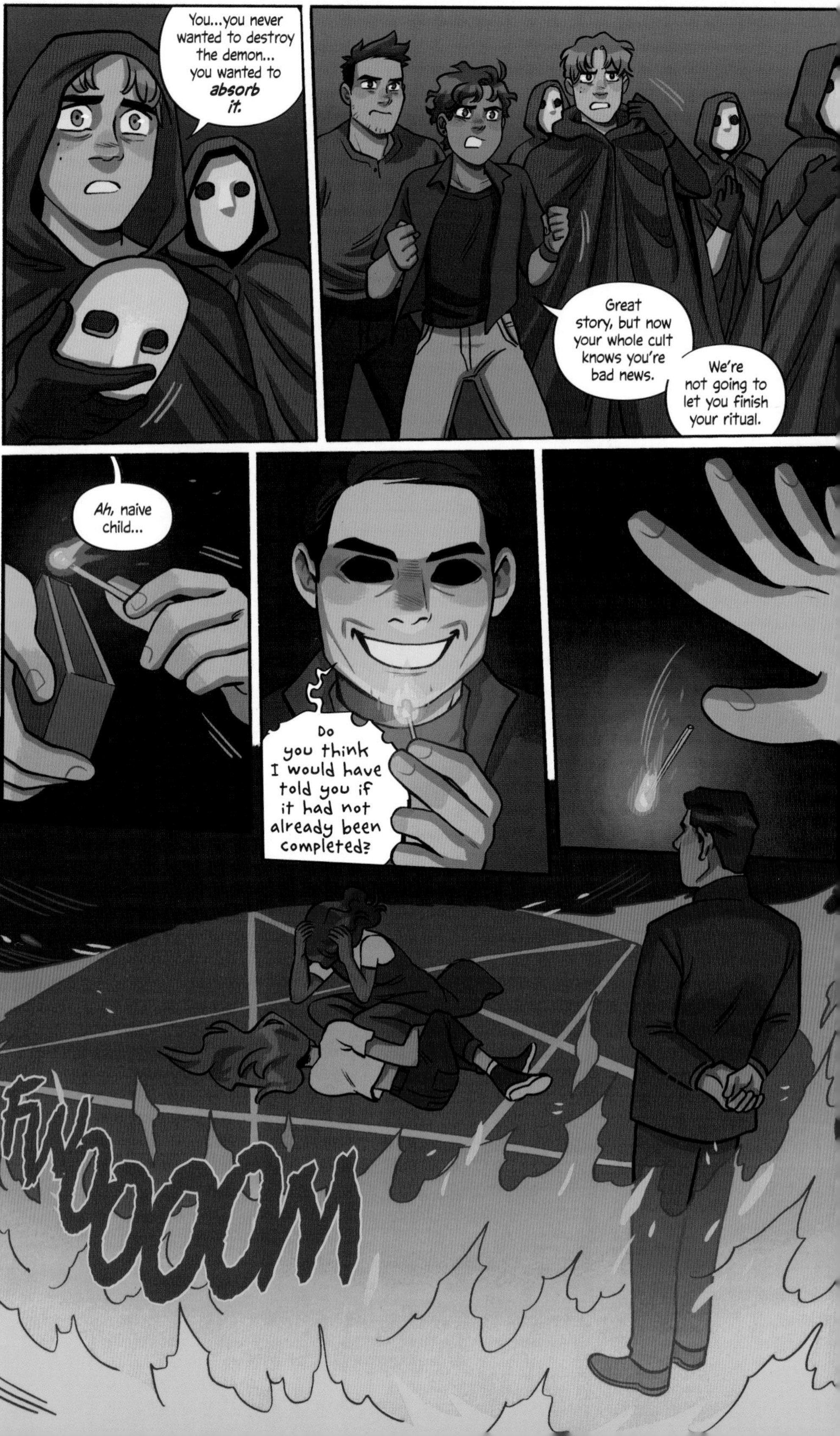

You...you never wanted to destroy the demon... you wanted to **absorb it.**
Great story, but now your whole cult knows you're bad news.
We're not going to let you finish your ritual.
Ah, naive child...
Do you think I would have told you if it had not already been completed?
FWOOOOOM

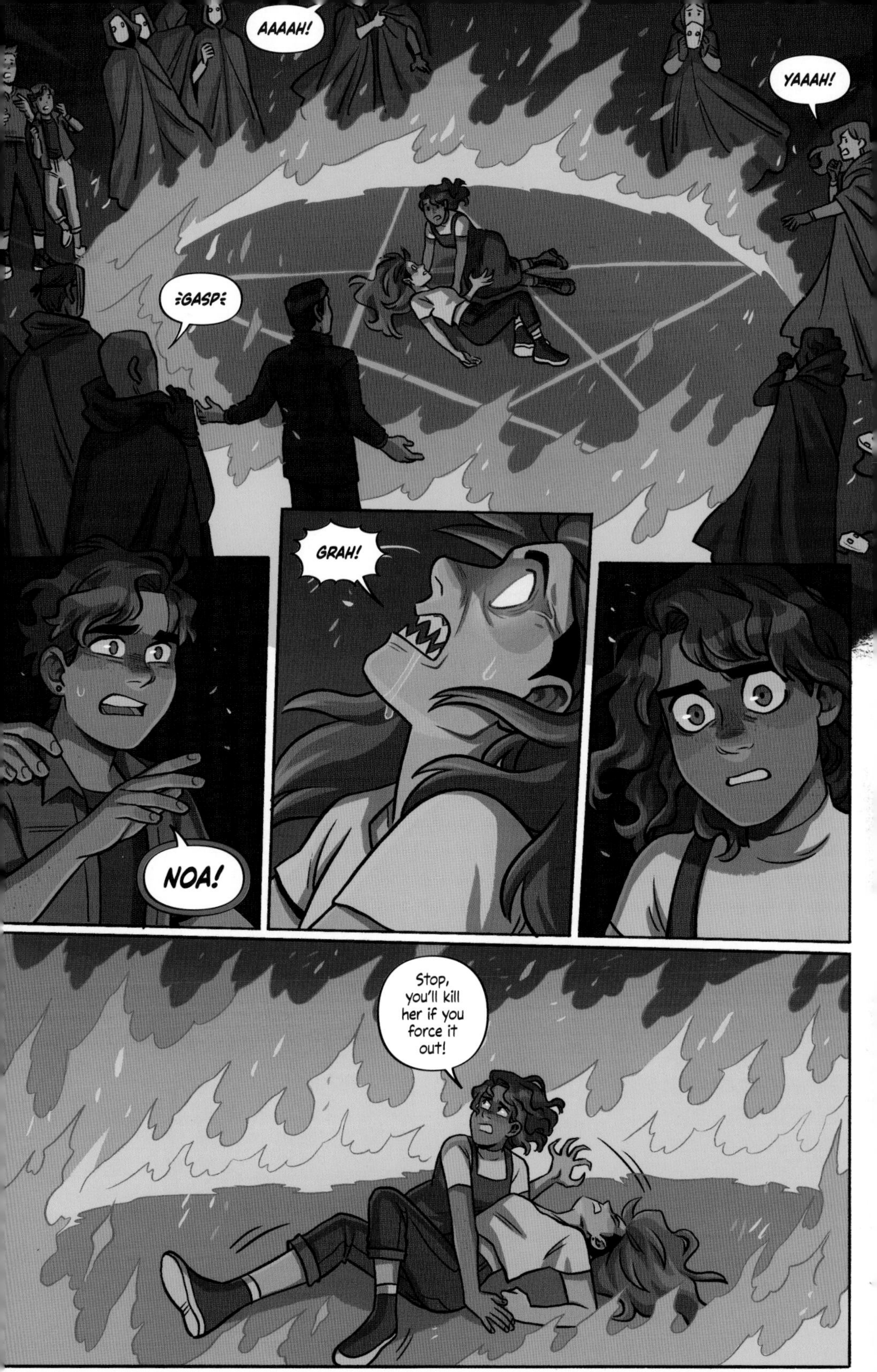
AAAAH!
YAAAH!
:GASP:
NOA!
GRAH!
Stop, you'll kill her if you force it out!

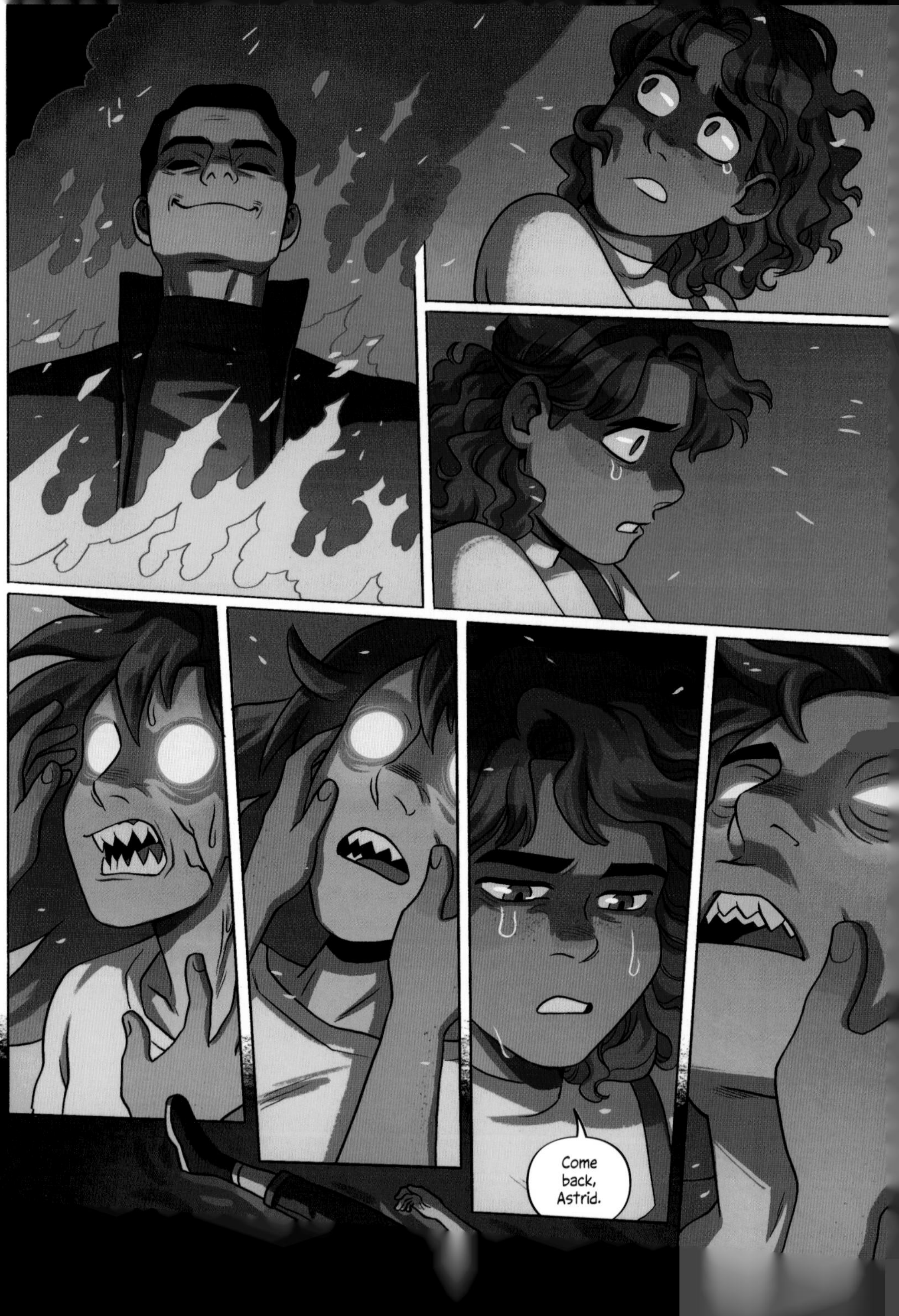
Come back, Astrid.

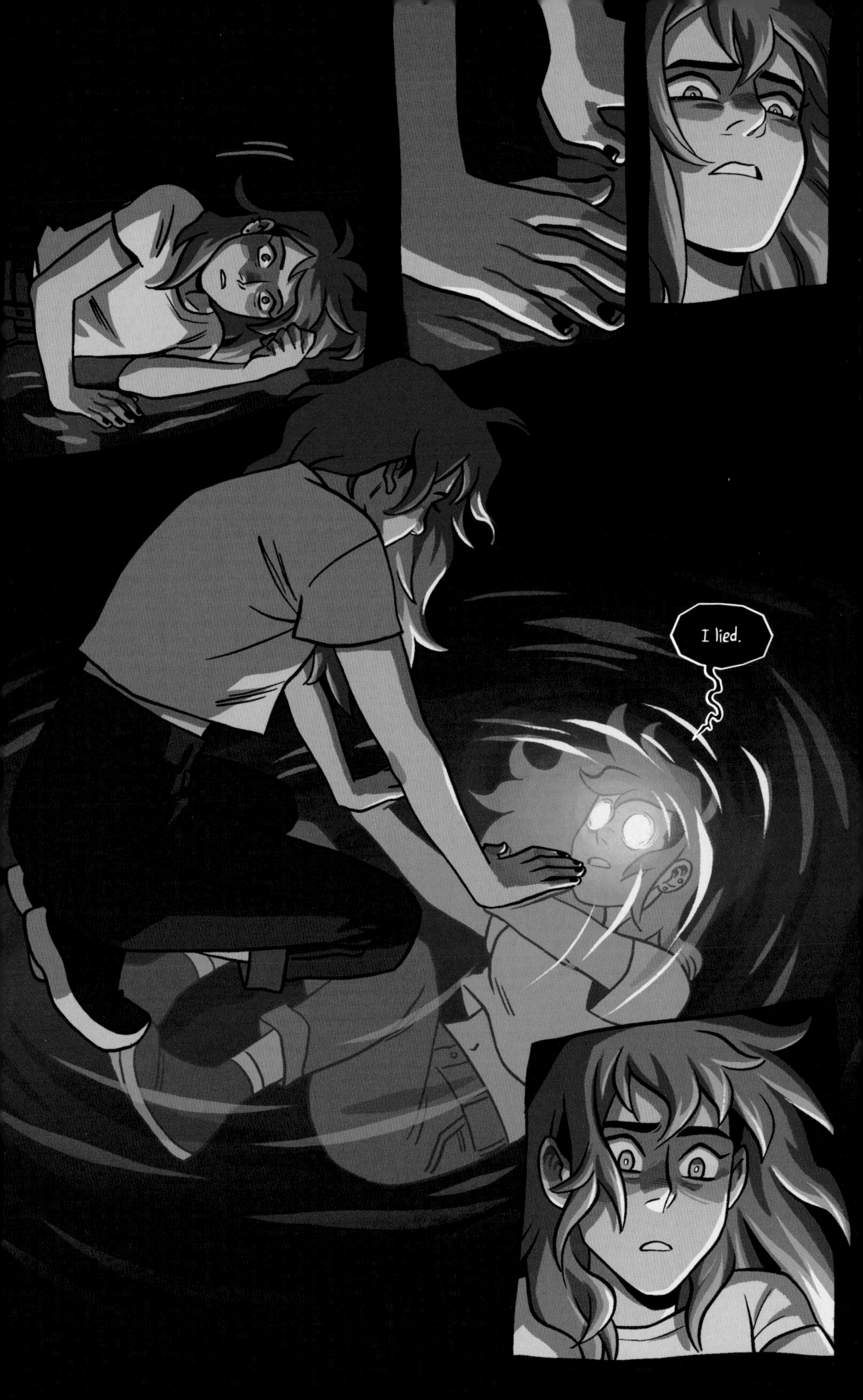
I lied.

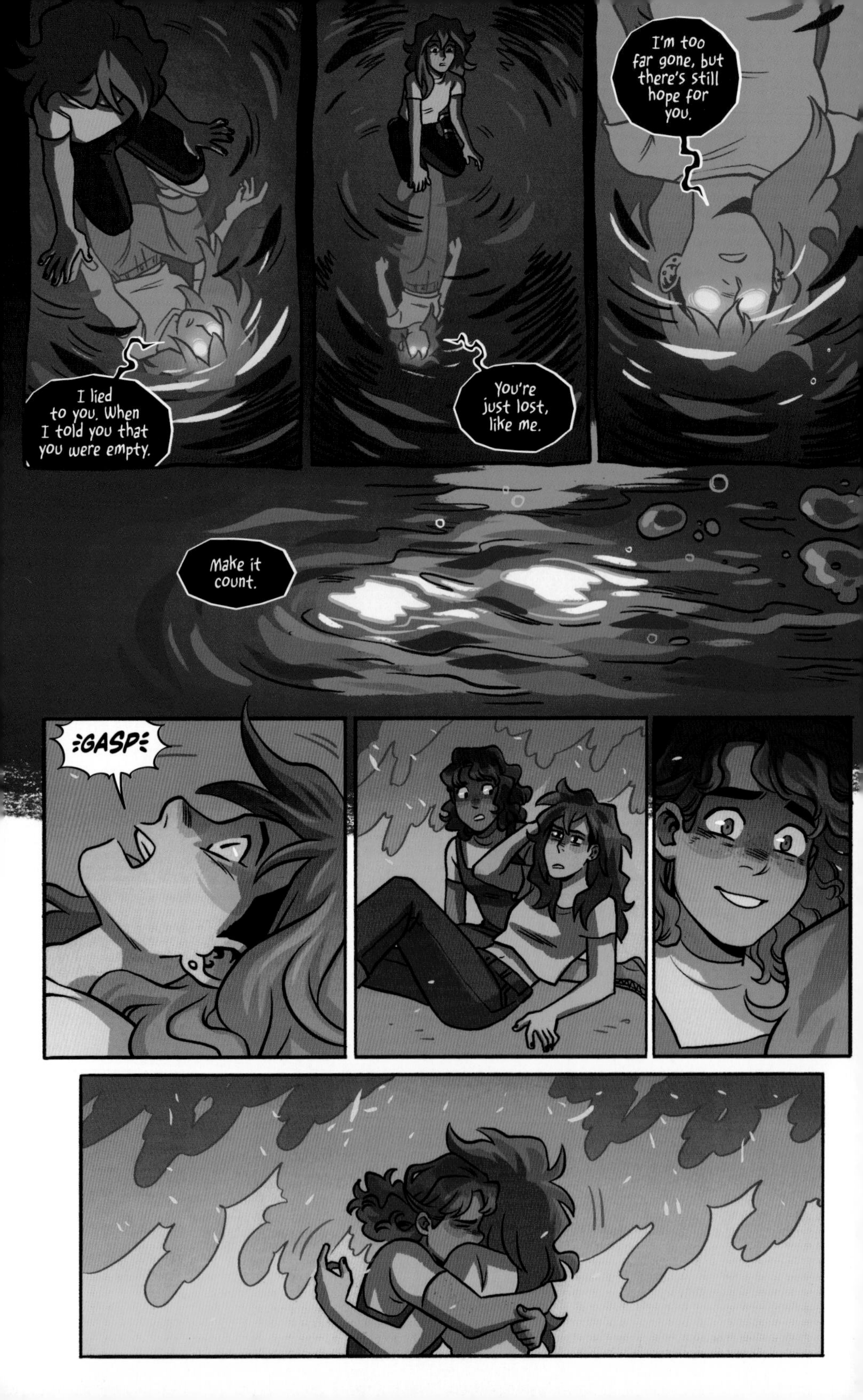

I lied to you. When I told you that you were empty.
You're just lost, like me.
I'm too far gone, but there's still hope for you.
Make it count.
GASP

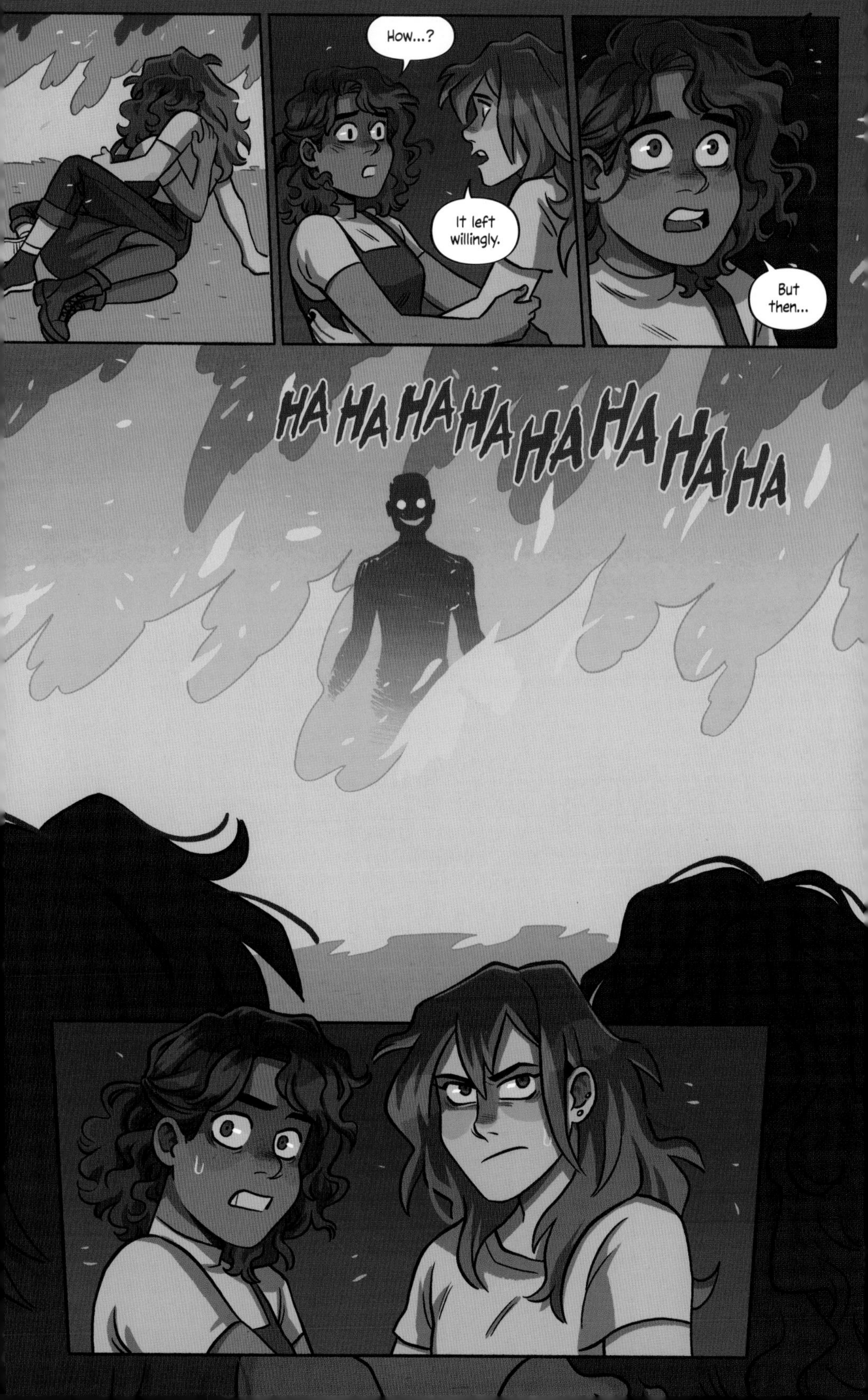
How...?
It left willingly.
But then...
HA HA HA HA HA HA HA HA HA HA

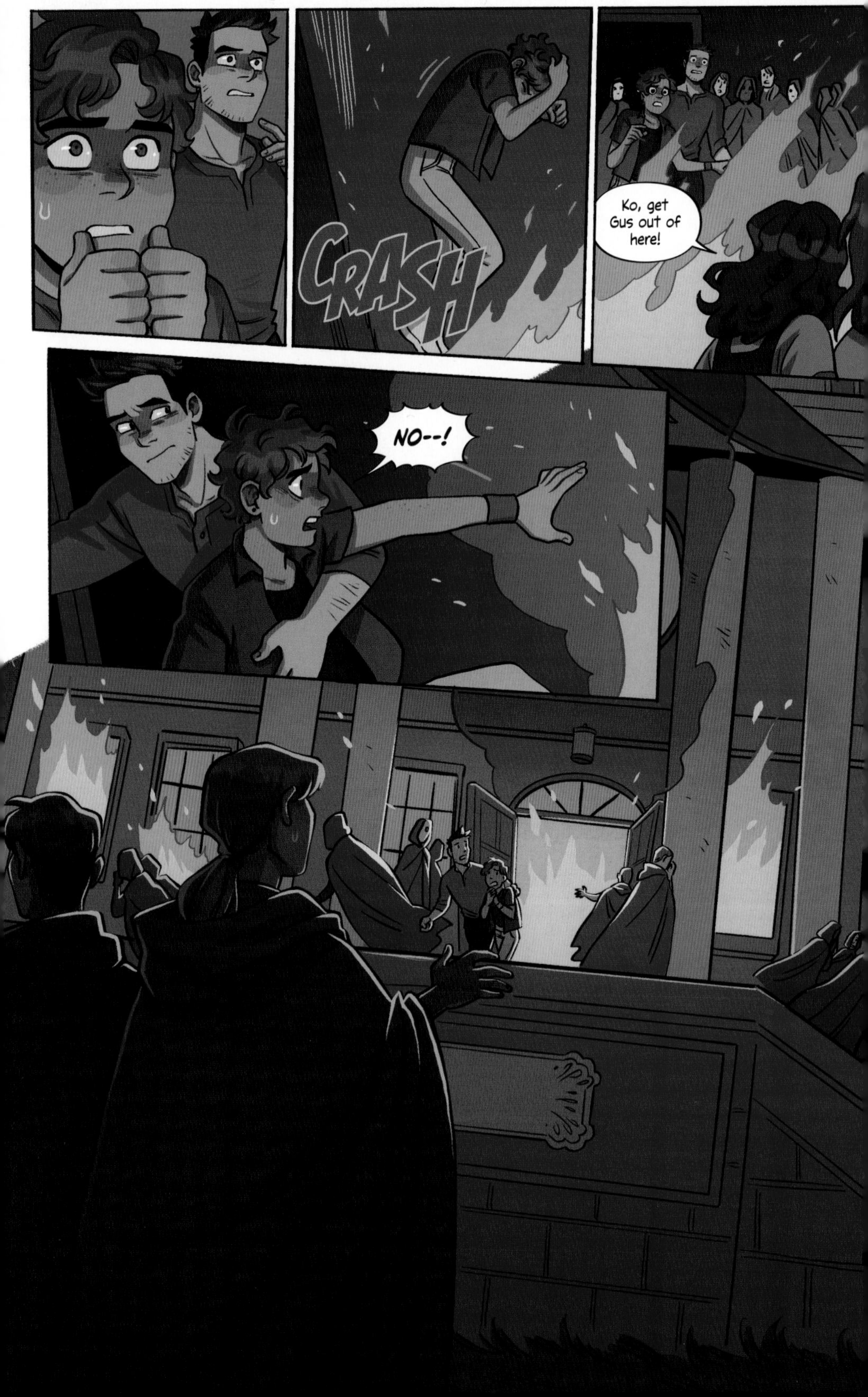
CRASH
Ko, get Gus out of here!
NO--!

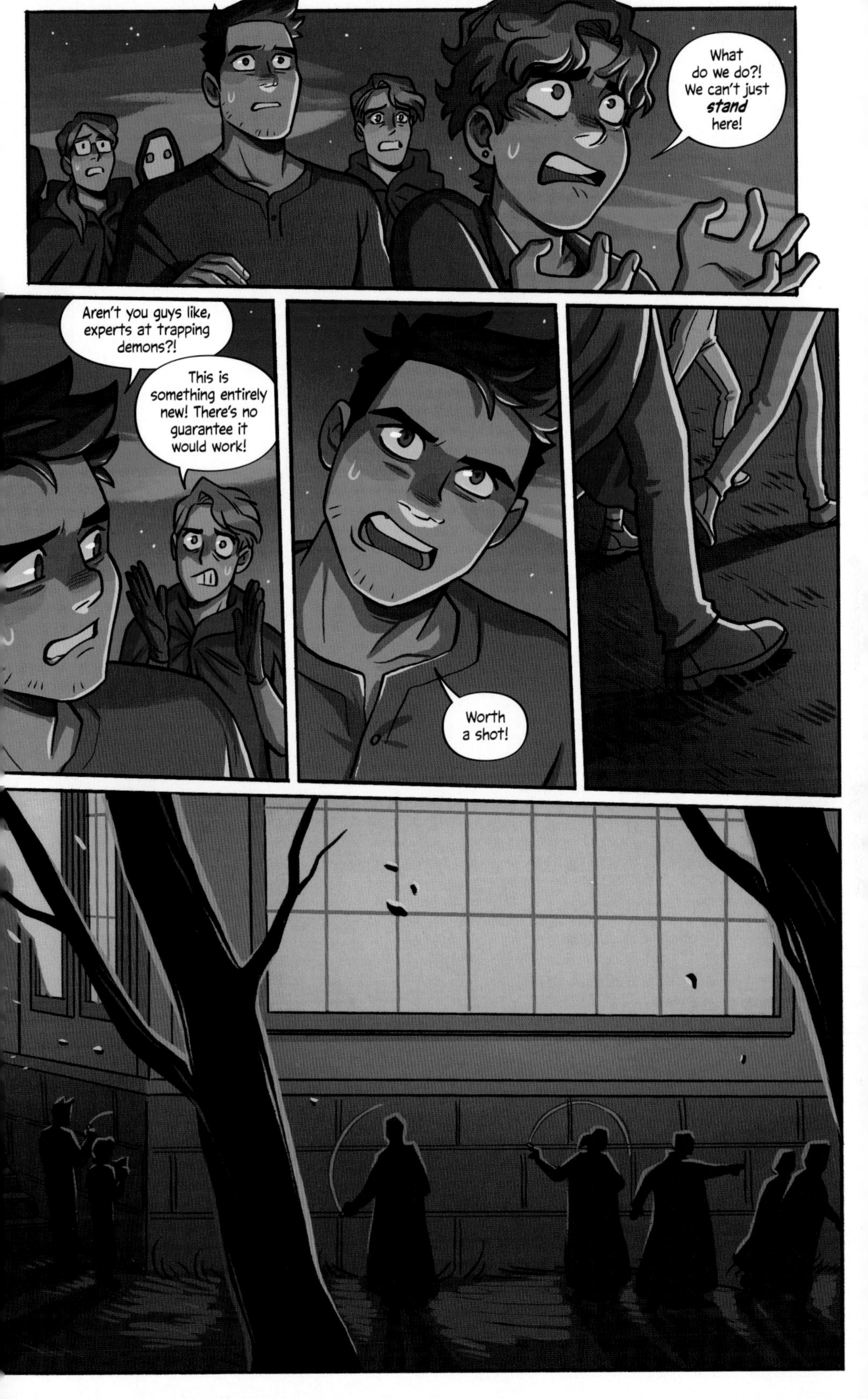
What do we do?! We can't just *stand* here!
Aren't you guys like, experts at trapping demons?!
This is something entirely new! There's no guarantee it would work!
Worth a shot!

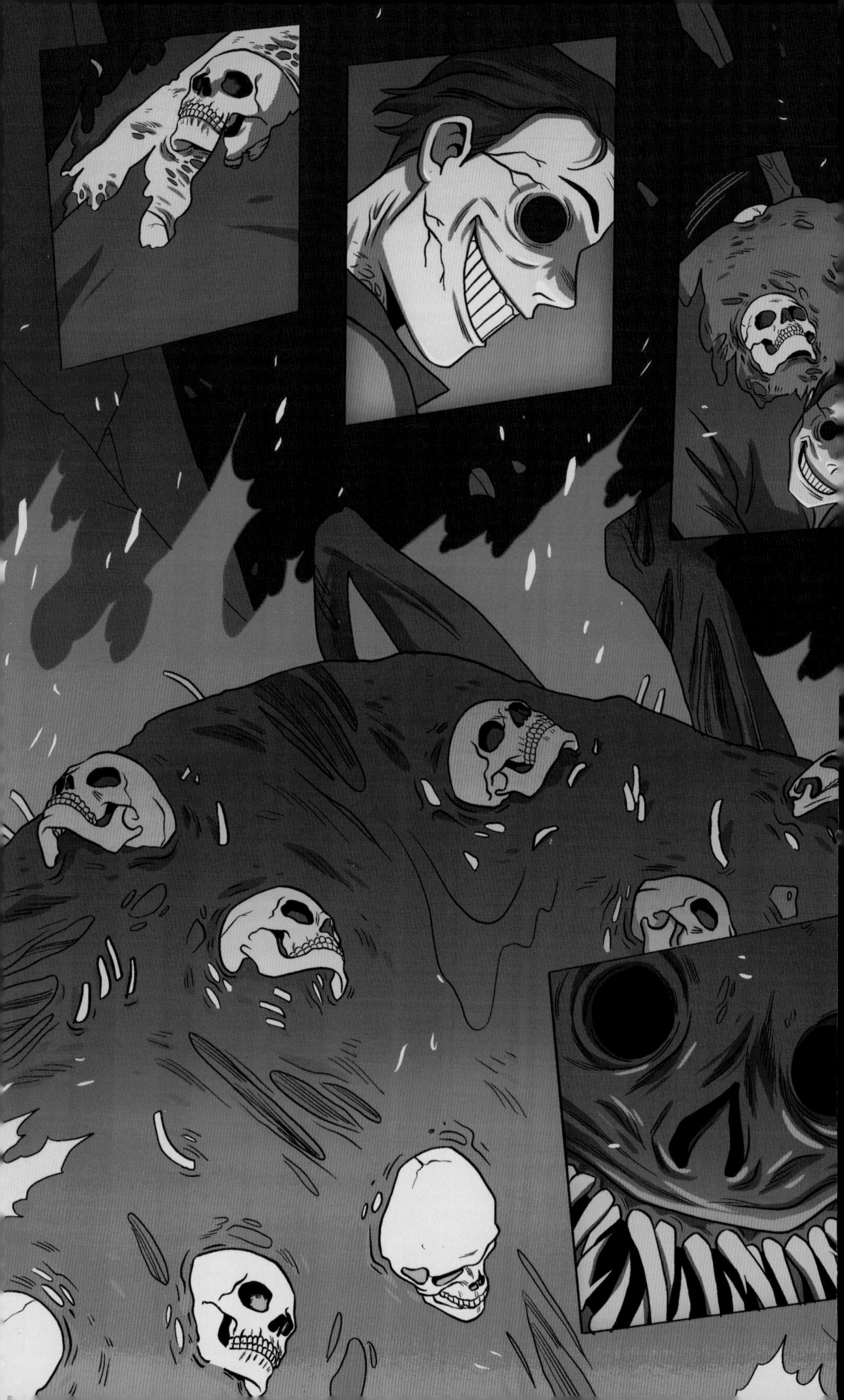

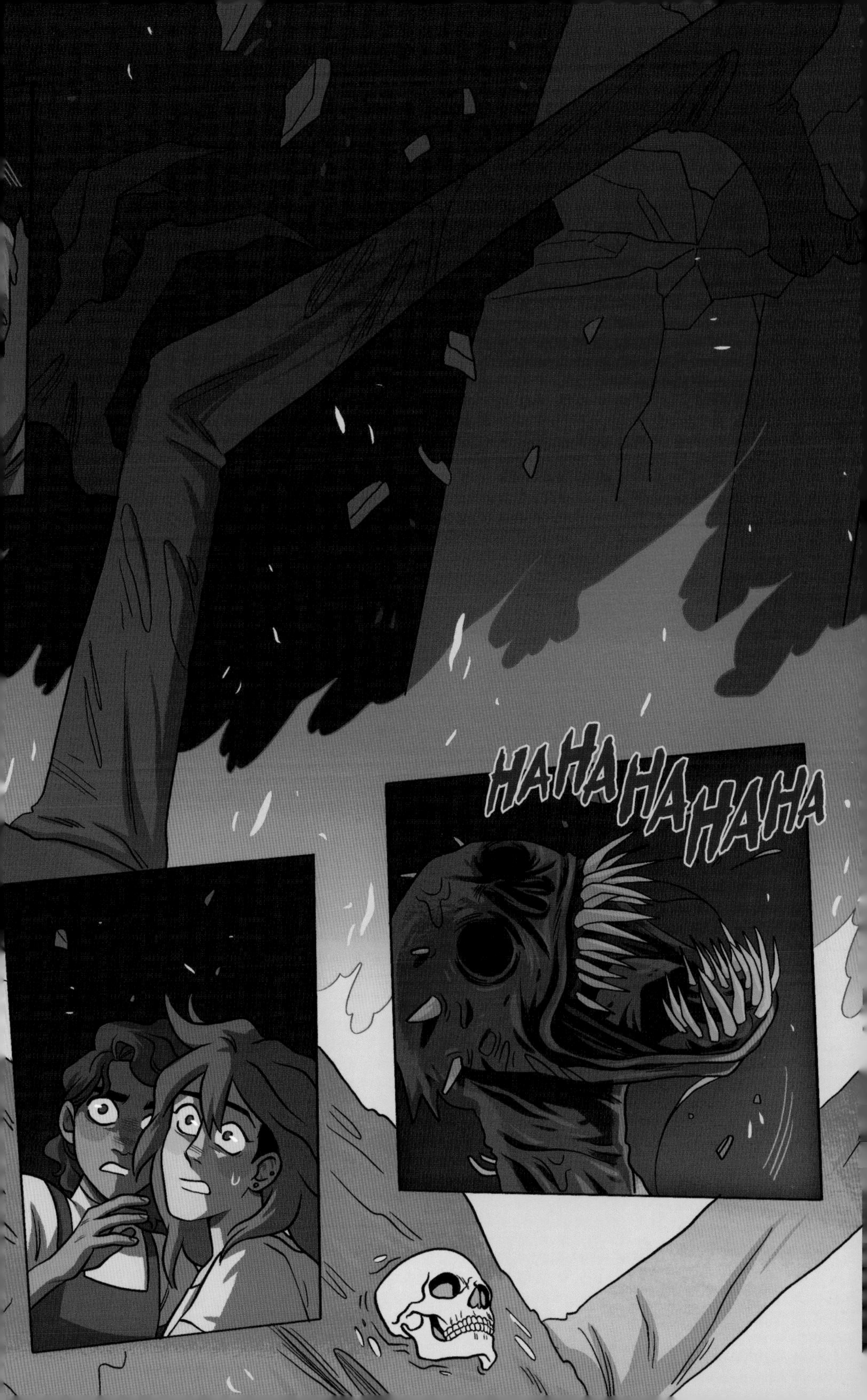
HAHAHAHAHAHA

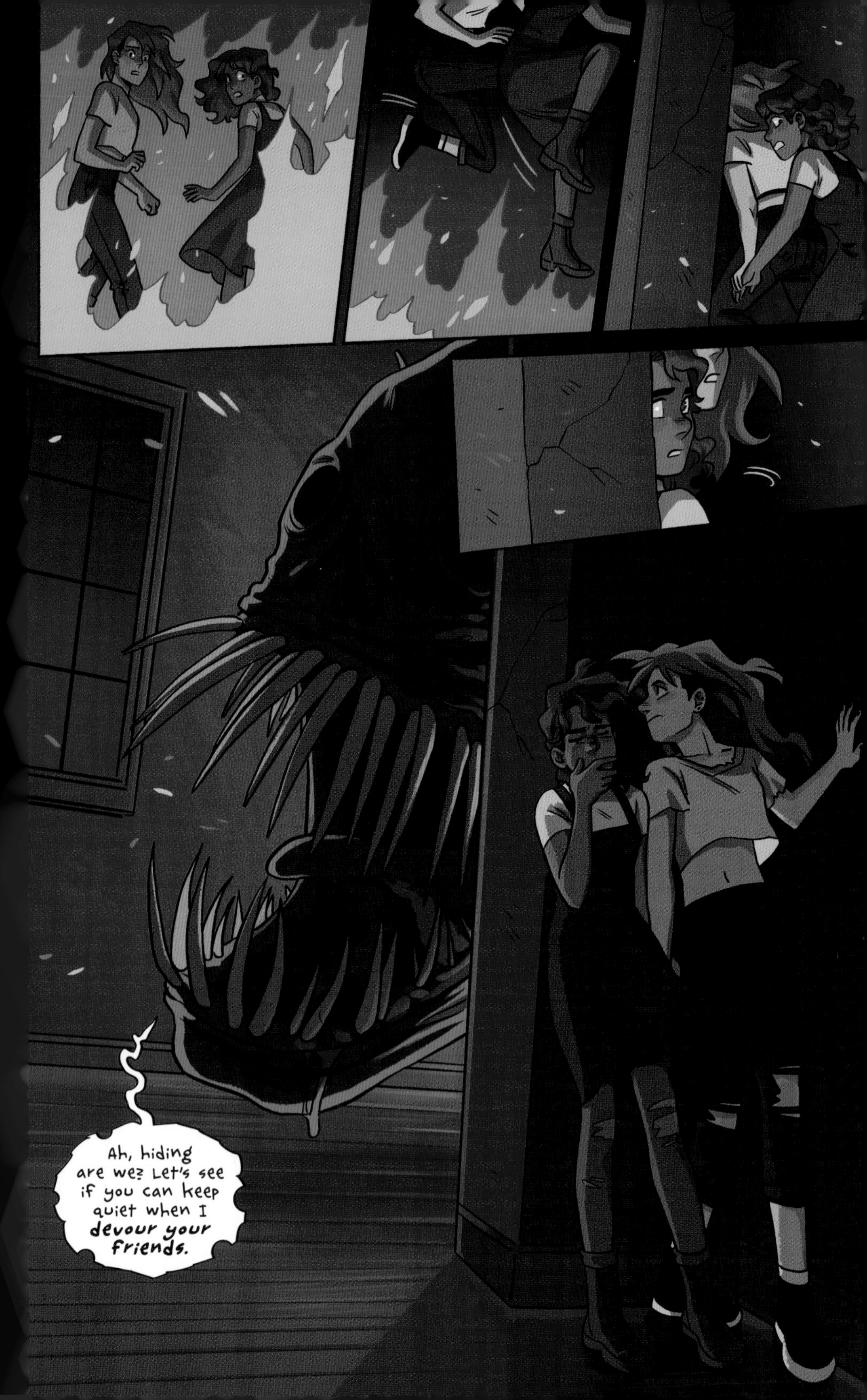
Ah, hiding are we? Let's see if you can keep quiet when I **devour your friends.**

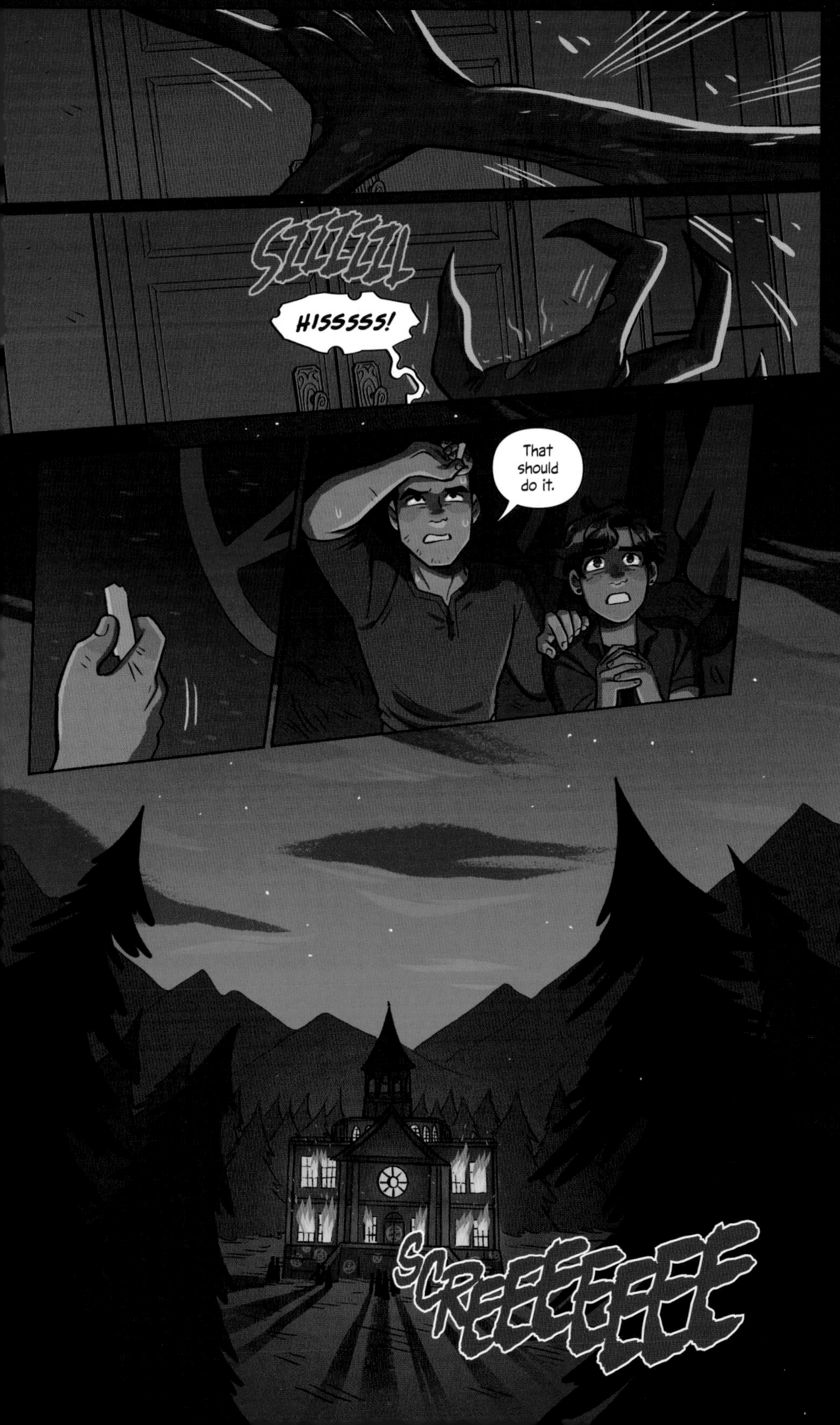
SIZZZZL
HISSSSS!
That should do it.
SCREEEEEEE

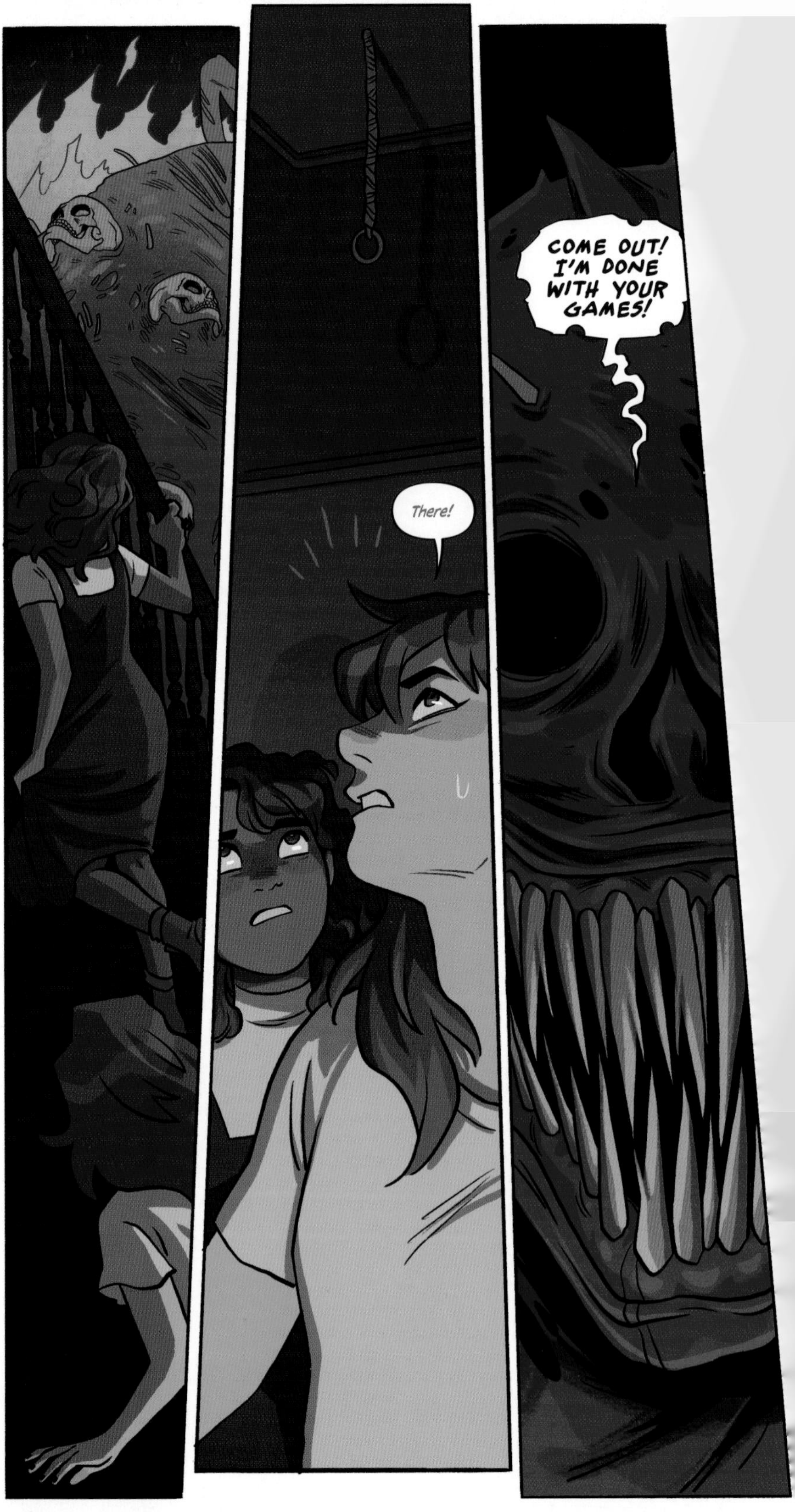
There!
COME OUT! I'M DONE WITH YOUR GAMES!

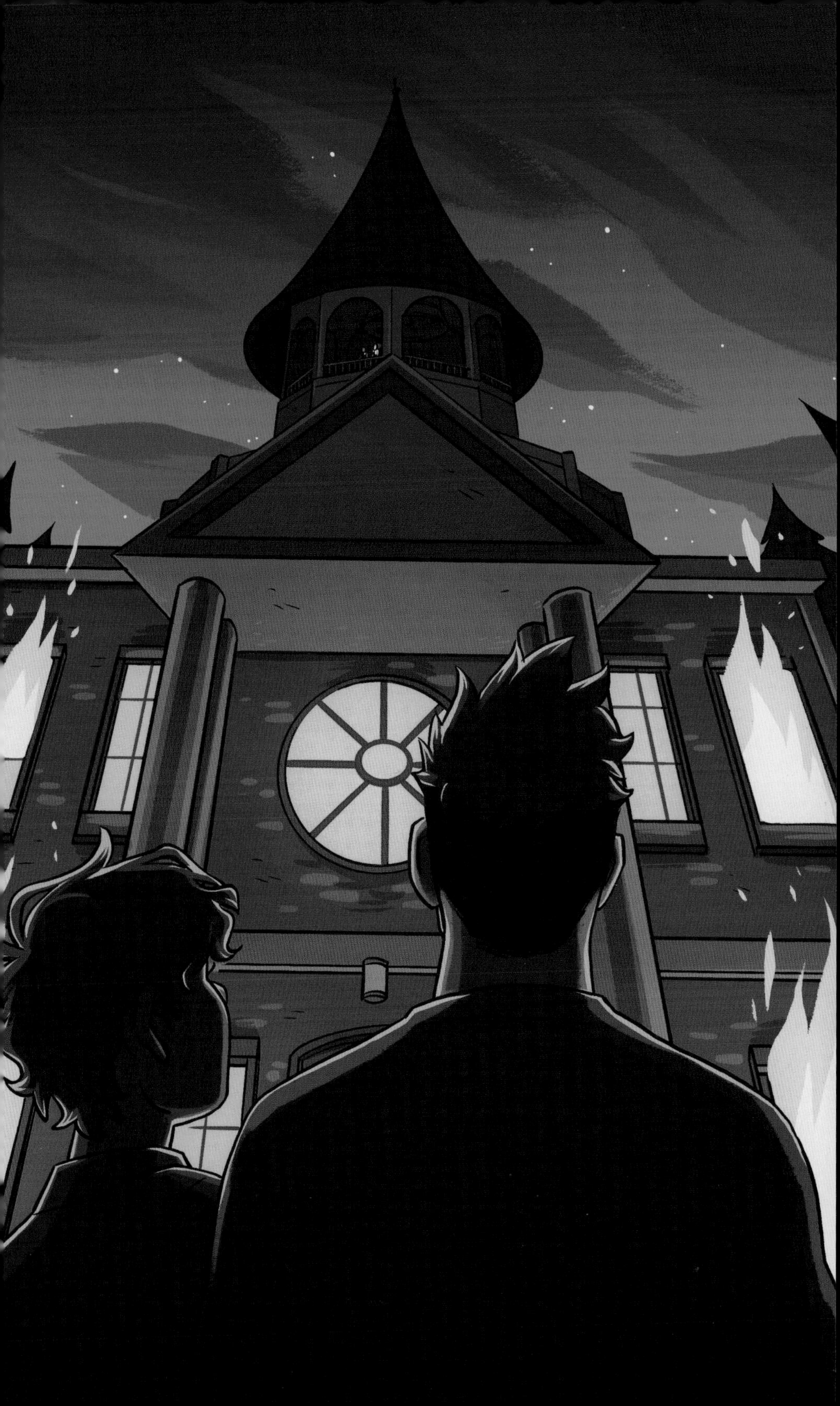

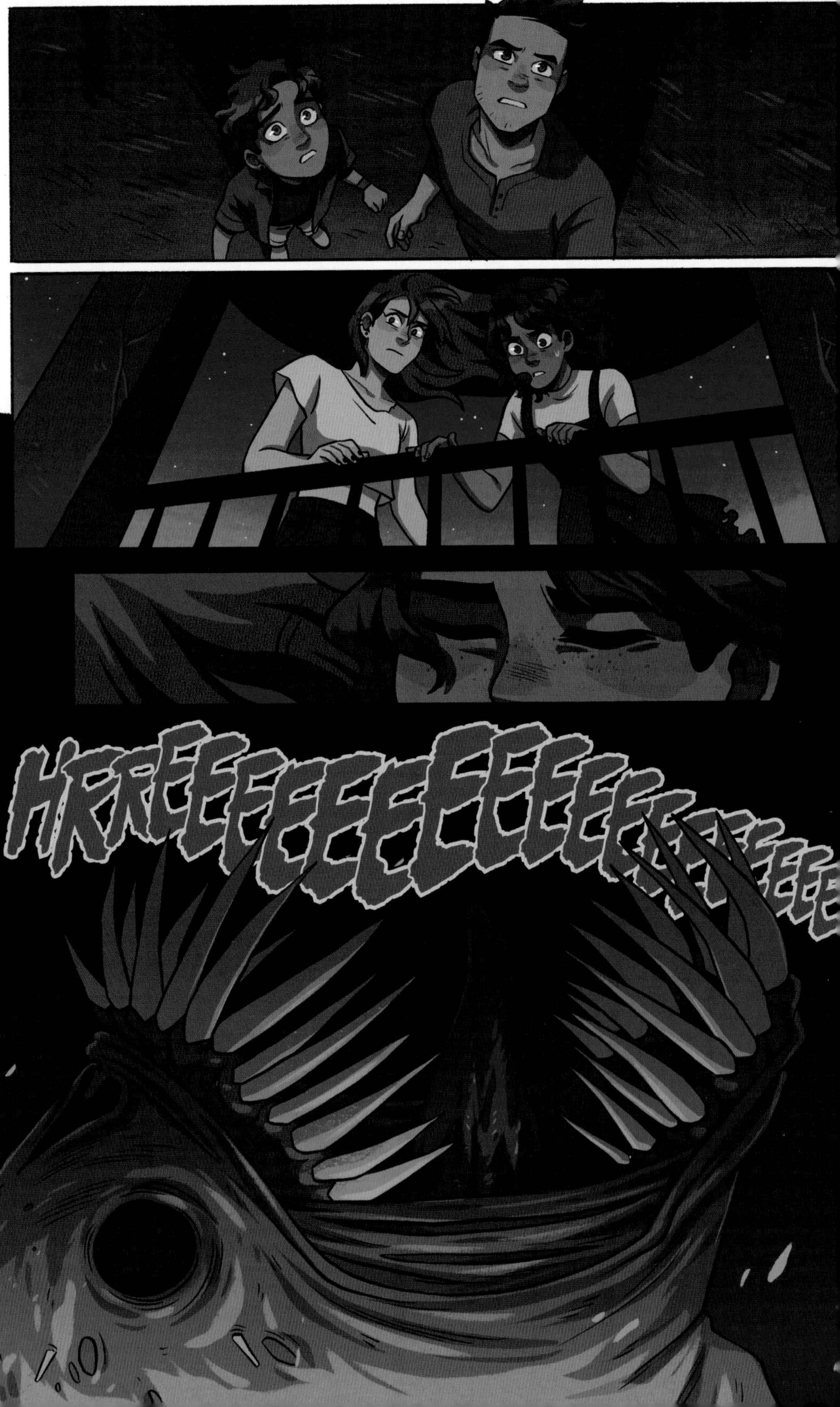
HRREEEEEEEEEEEEEEEEEEE

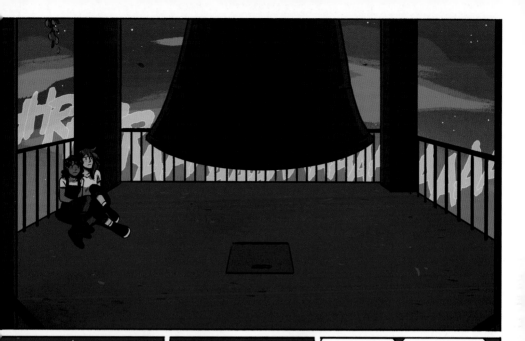

The funny part is, you were right Astrid.

If we'd faked the evidence like everyone else, we wouldn't be in this mess.

Are you kidding? This is *all* my fault. Everything about this is my fault.

Noa, I'm so sorry. *ESPECIALLY* for tampering with the evidence.

What? That doesn't matter anymore.

Of course it matters! It matters to you.

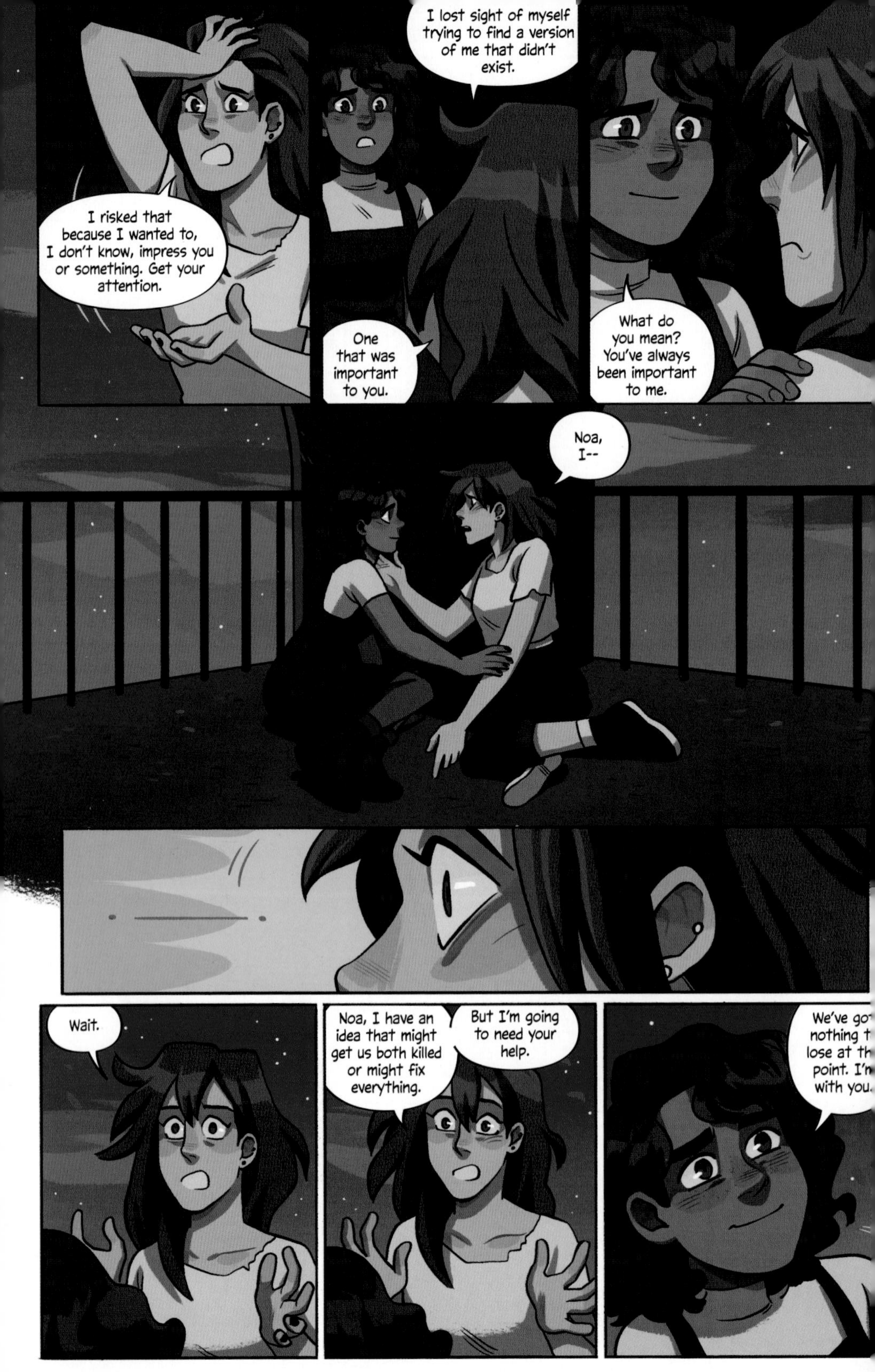
I risked that because I wanted to, I don't know, impress you or something. Get your attention.
I lost sight of myself trying to find a version of me that didn't exist.
One that was important to you.
What do you mean? You've always been important to me.
Noa, I--
. ——— .
Wait.
Noa, I have an idea that might get us both killed or might fix everything.
But I'm going to need your help.

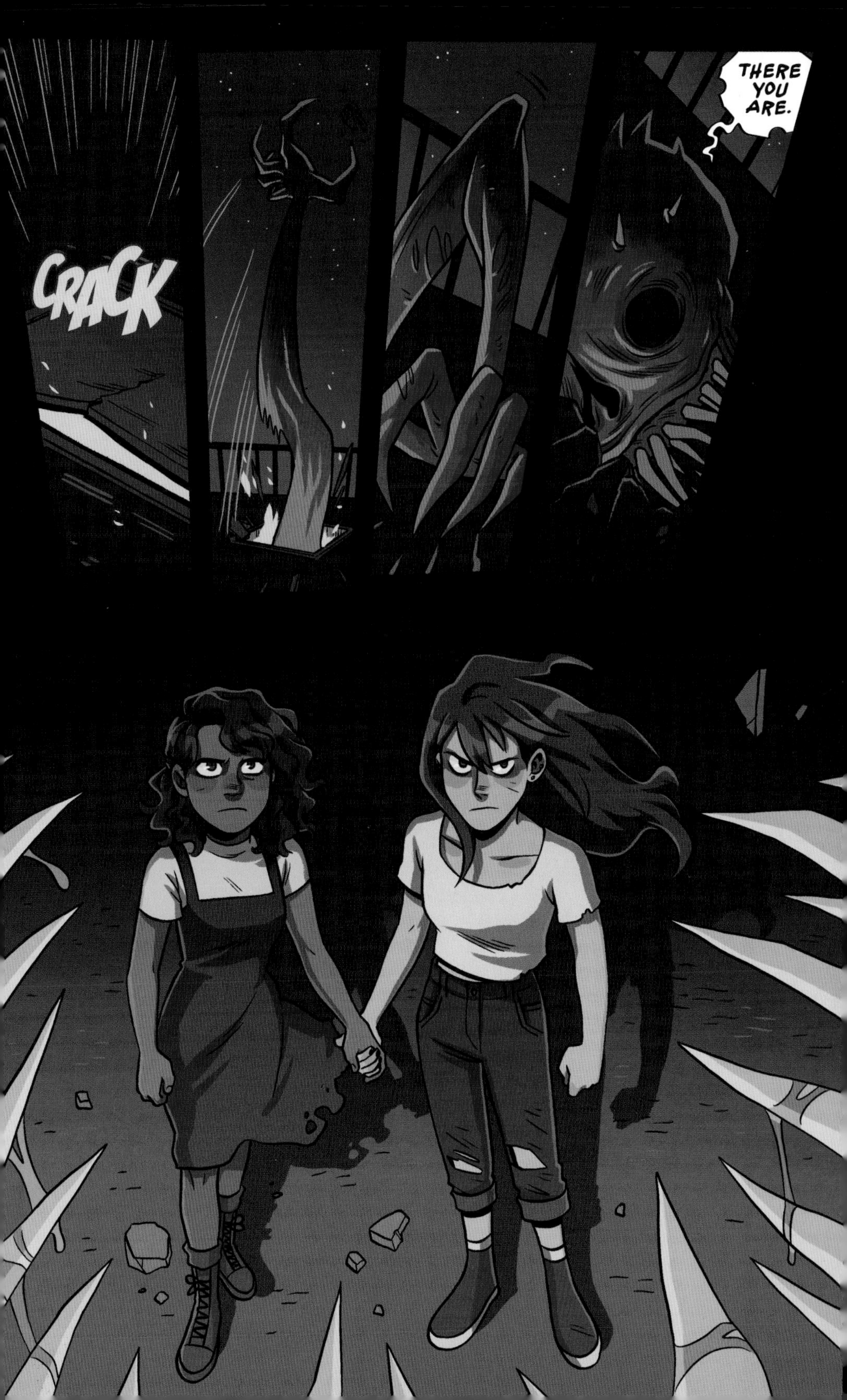
CRACK
THERE YOU ARE.

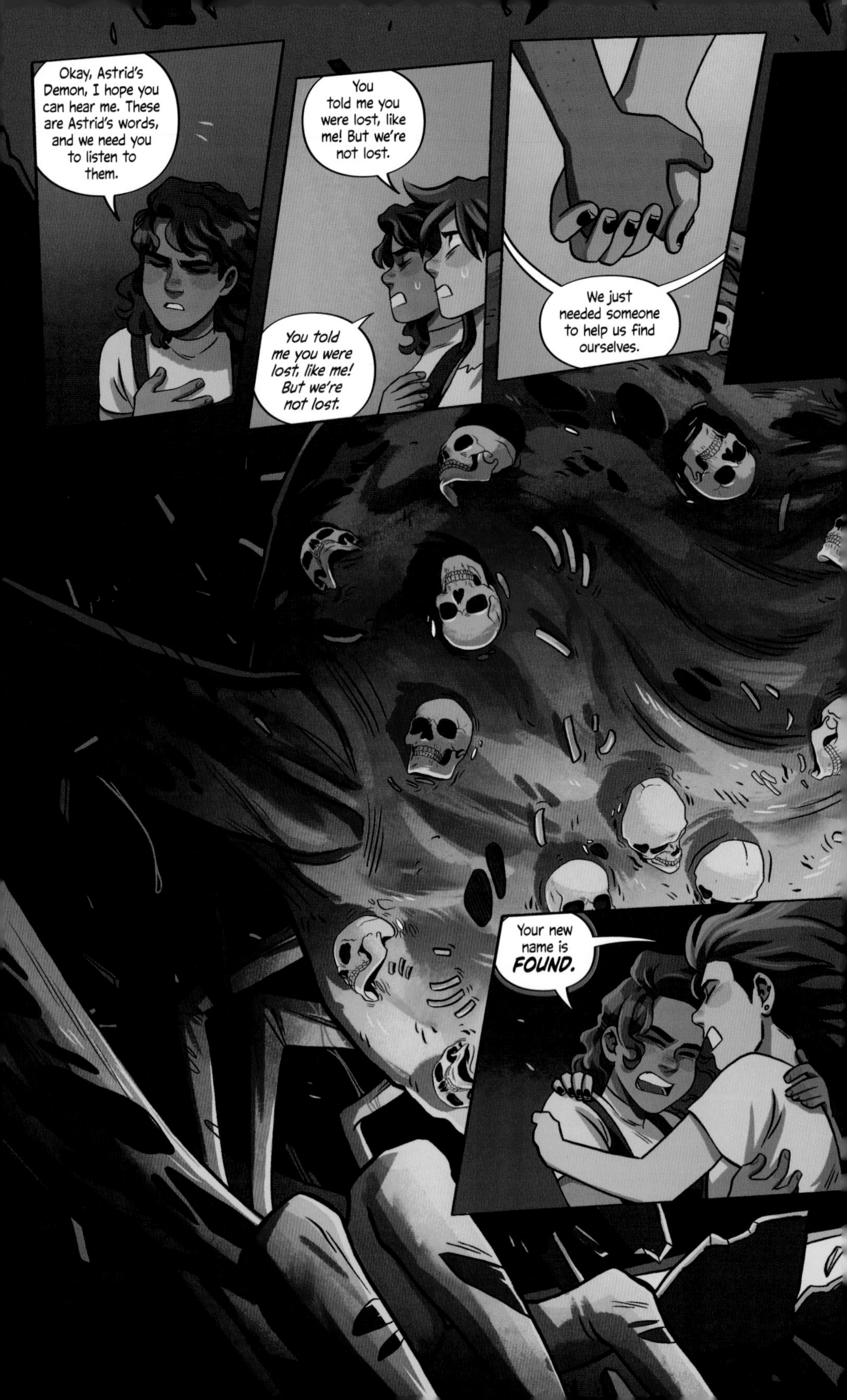
Okay, Astrid's Demon, I hope you can hear me. These are Astrid's words, and we need you to listen to them.
You told me you were lost, like me! But we're not lost.
You told me you were lost, like me! But we're not lost.
We just needed someone to help us find ourselves.
Your new name is ***FOUND.***

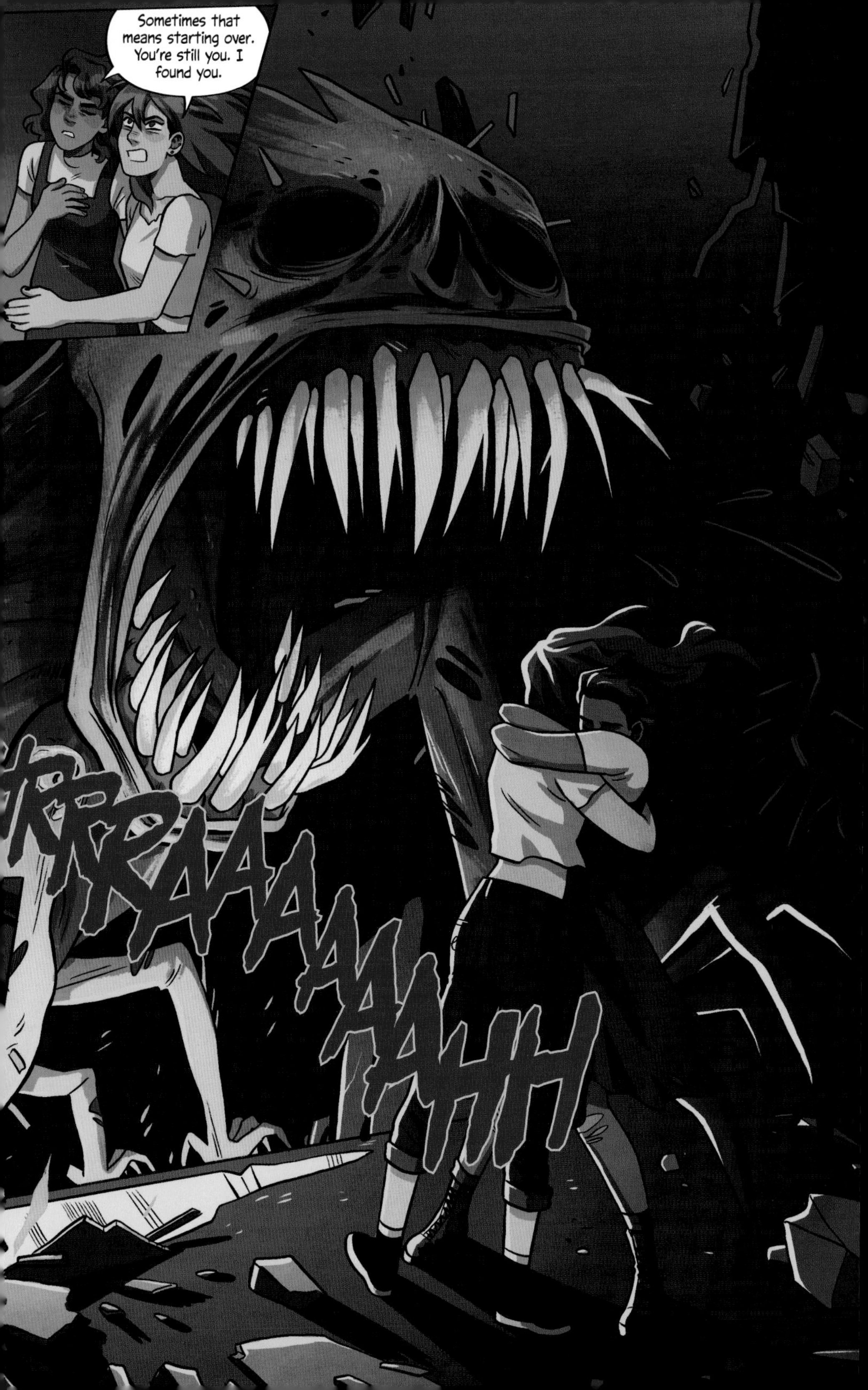
Sometimes that means starting over. You're still you. I found you.
RRAAAAAAHH

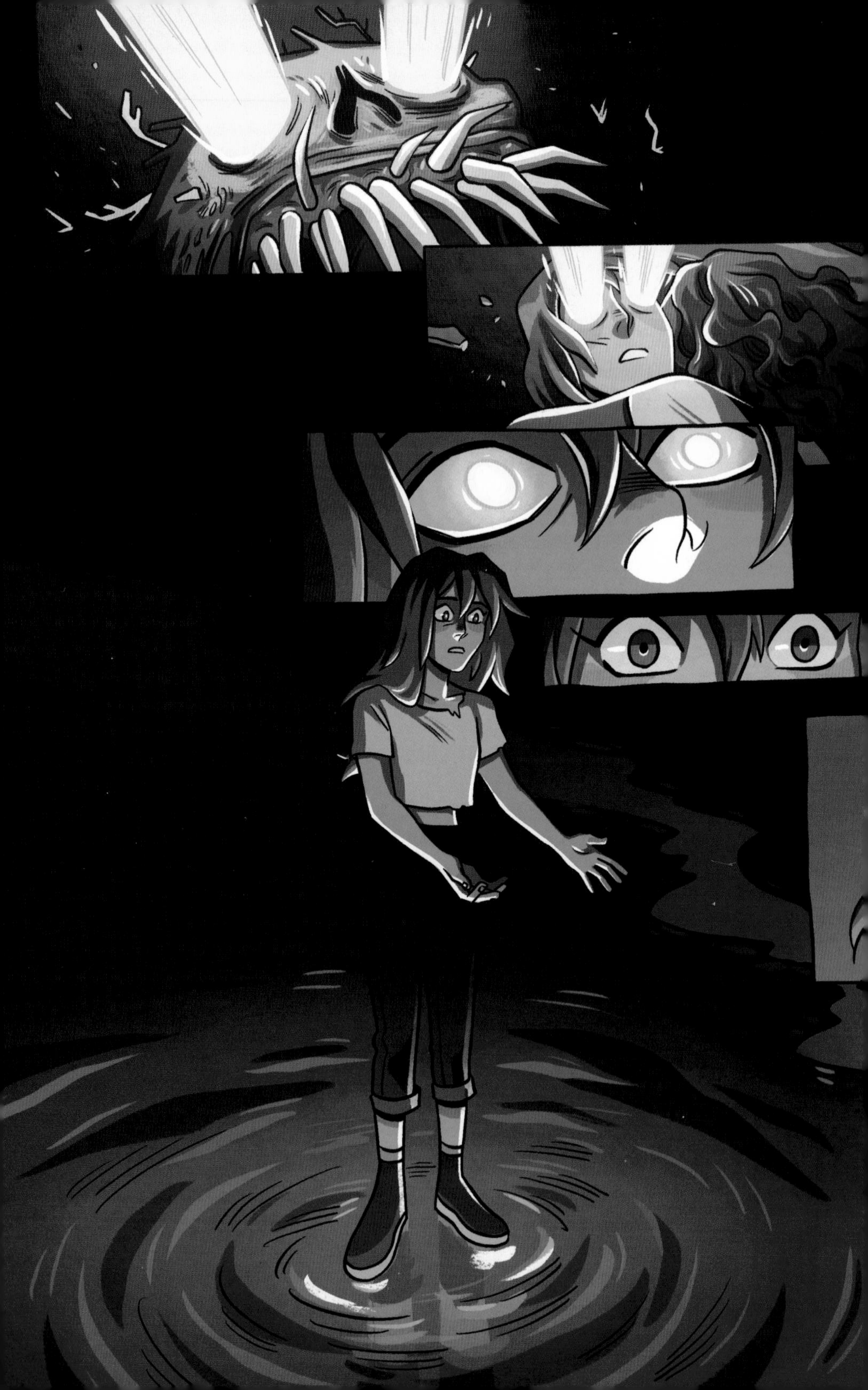

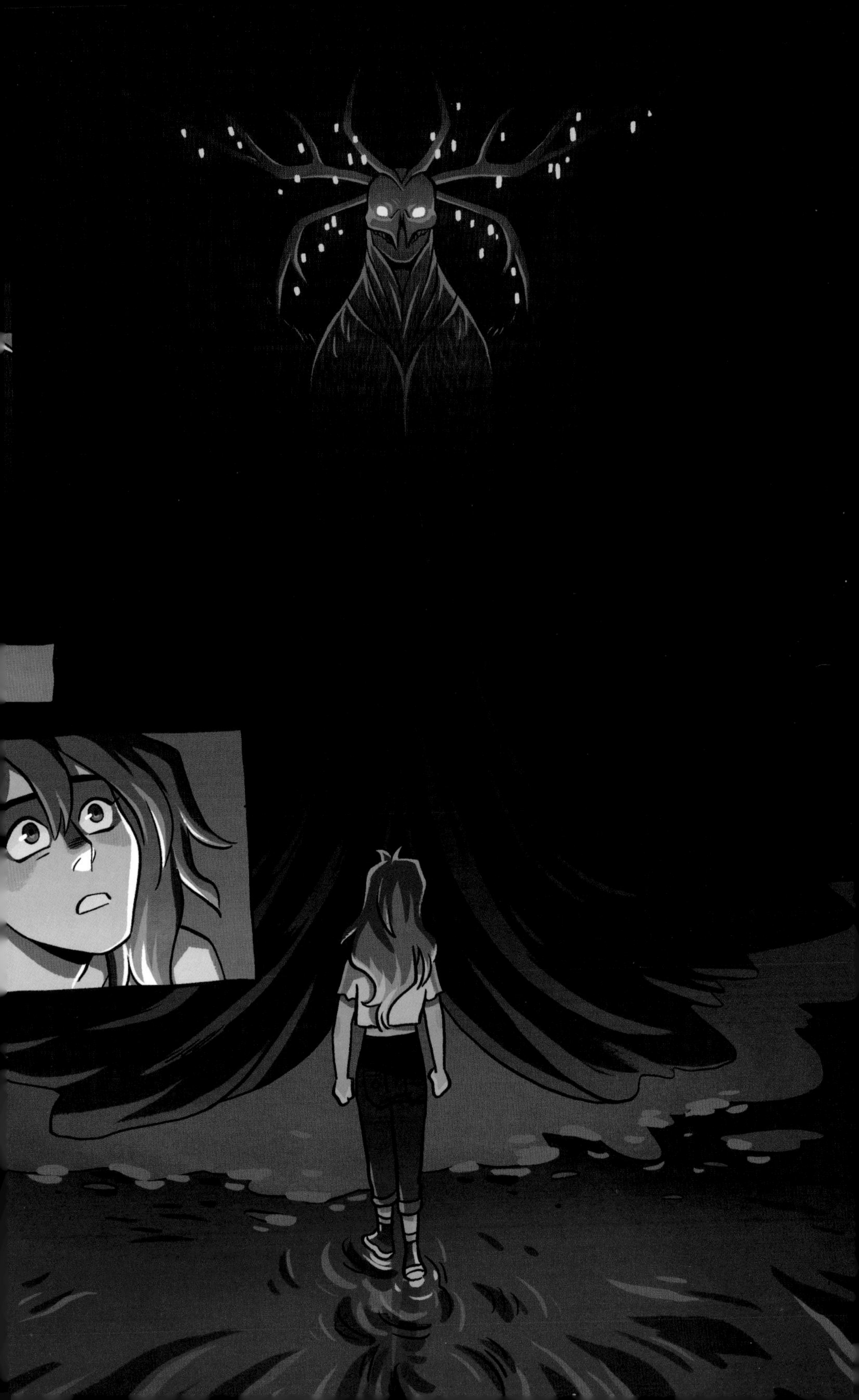

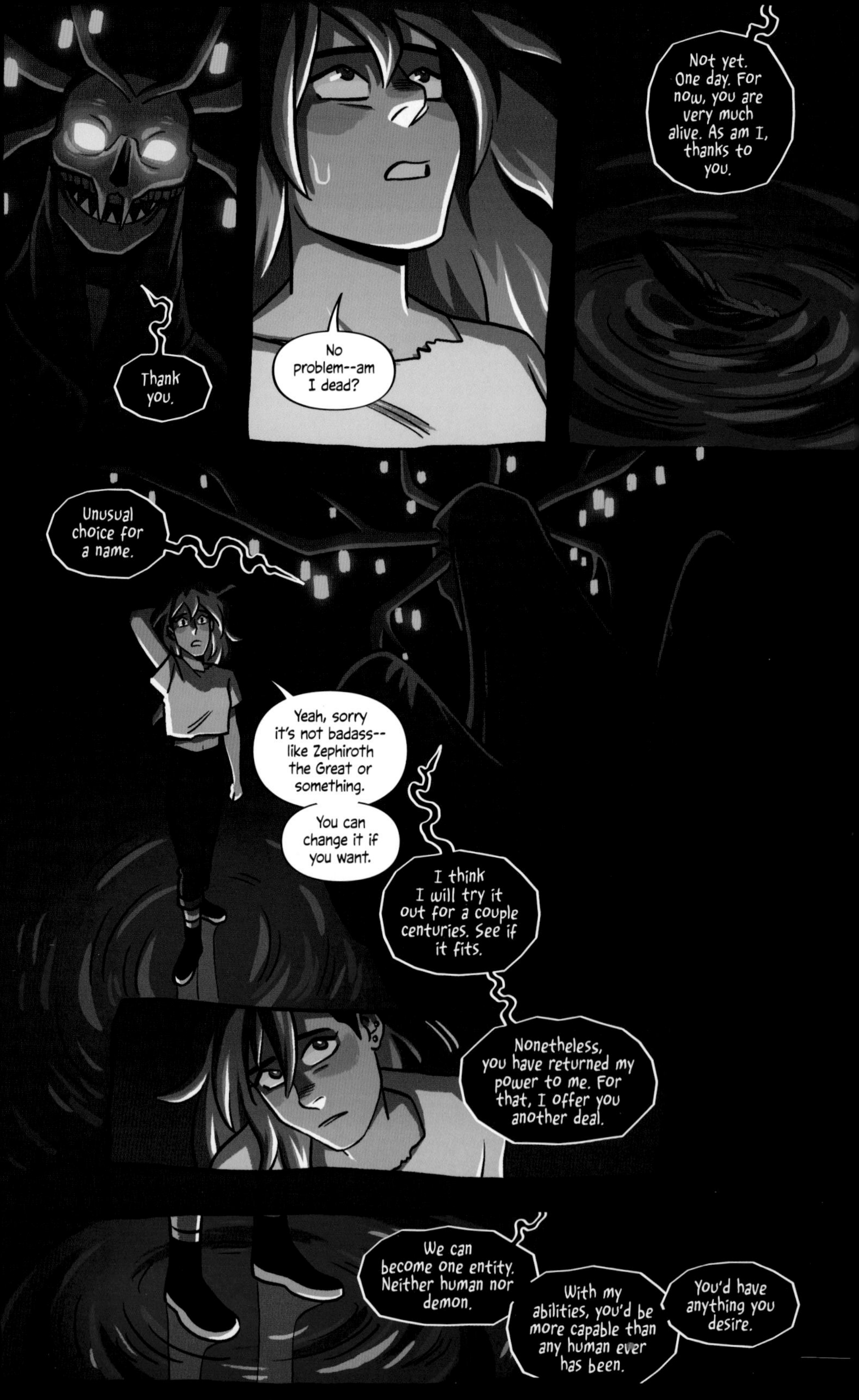
Thank you.
No problem--am I dead?
Not yet. One day. For now, you are very much alive. As am I, thanks to you.
Unusual choice for a name.
Yeah, sorry it's not badass--like Zephiroth the Great or something.
You can change it if you want.
I think I will try it out for a couple centuries. See if it fits.
Nonetheless, you have returned my power to me. For that, I offer you another deal.
We can become one entity. Neither human nor demon.
With my abilities, you'd be more capable than any human ever has been.
You'd have anything you desire.

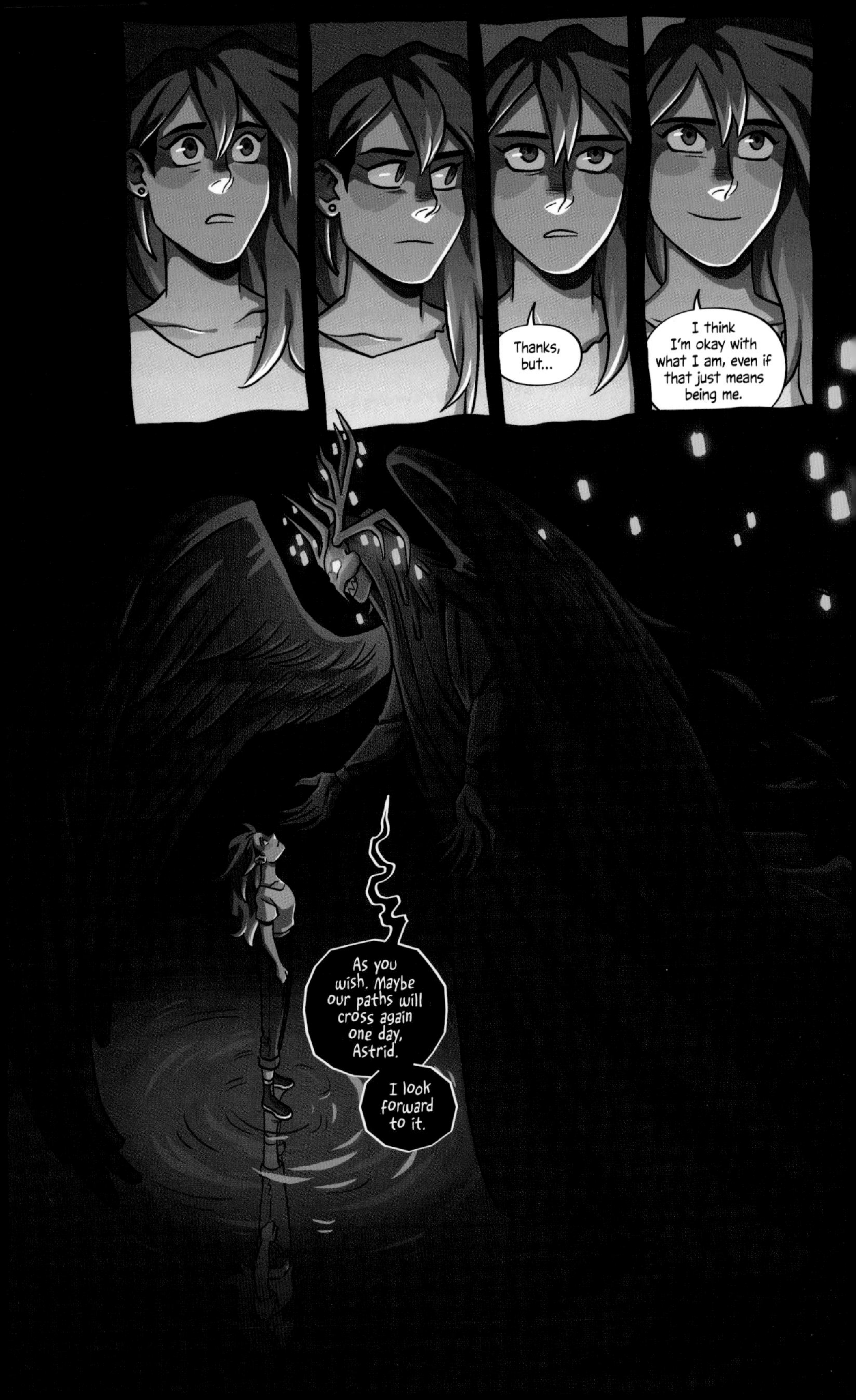
Thanks, but...
I think I'm okay with what I am, even if that just means being me.
As you wish. Maybe our paths will cross again one day, Astrid.
I look forward to it.

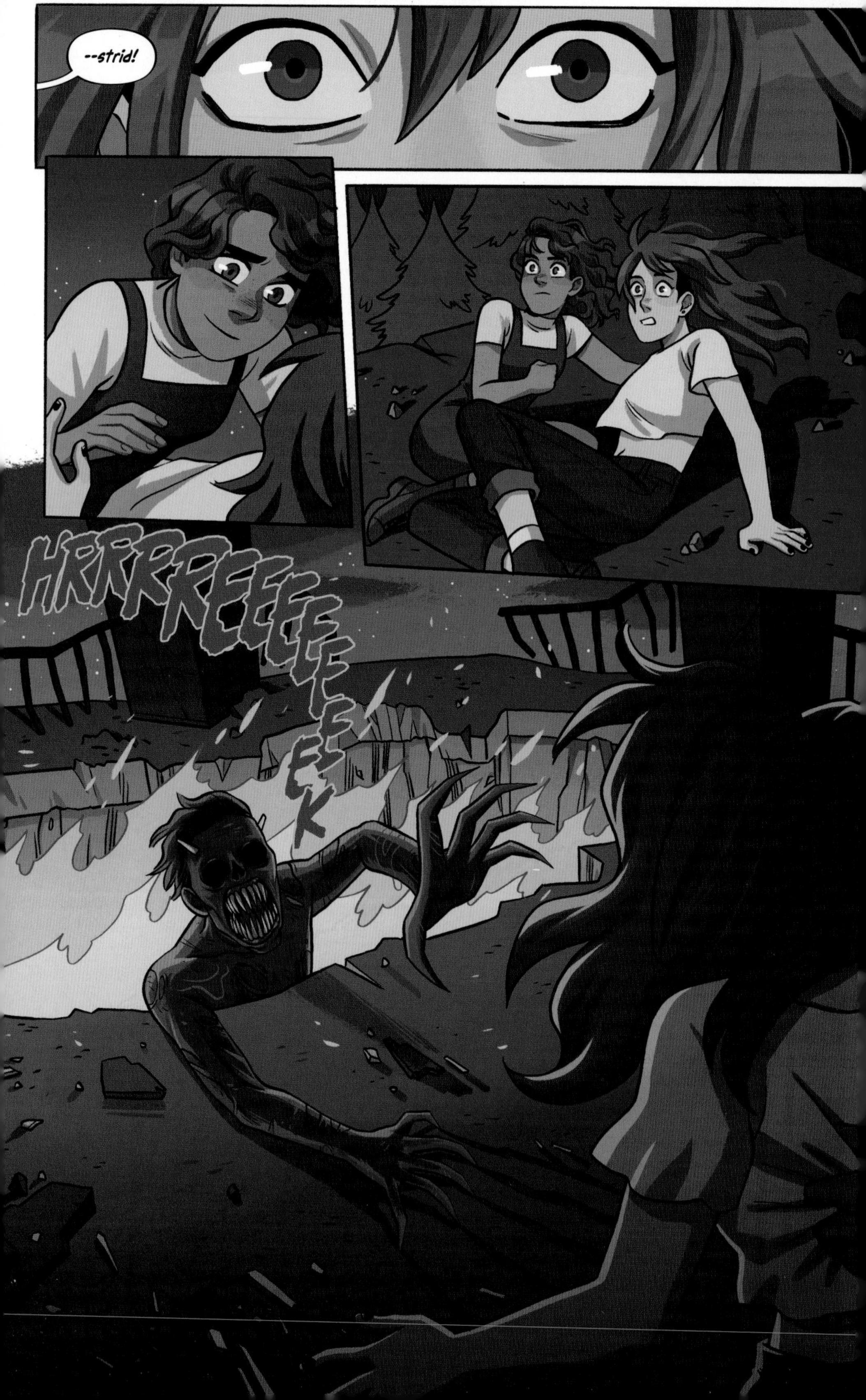
--strid!
HRRRREEEEEEEEEK

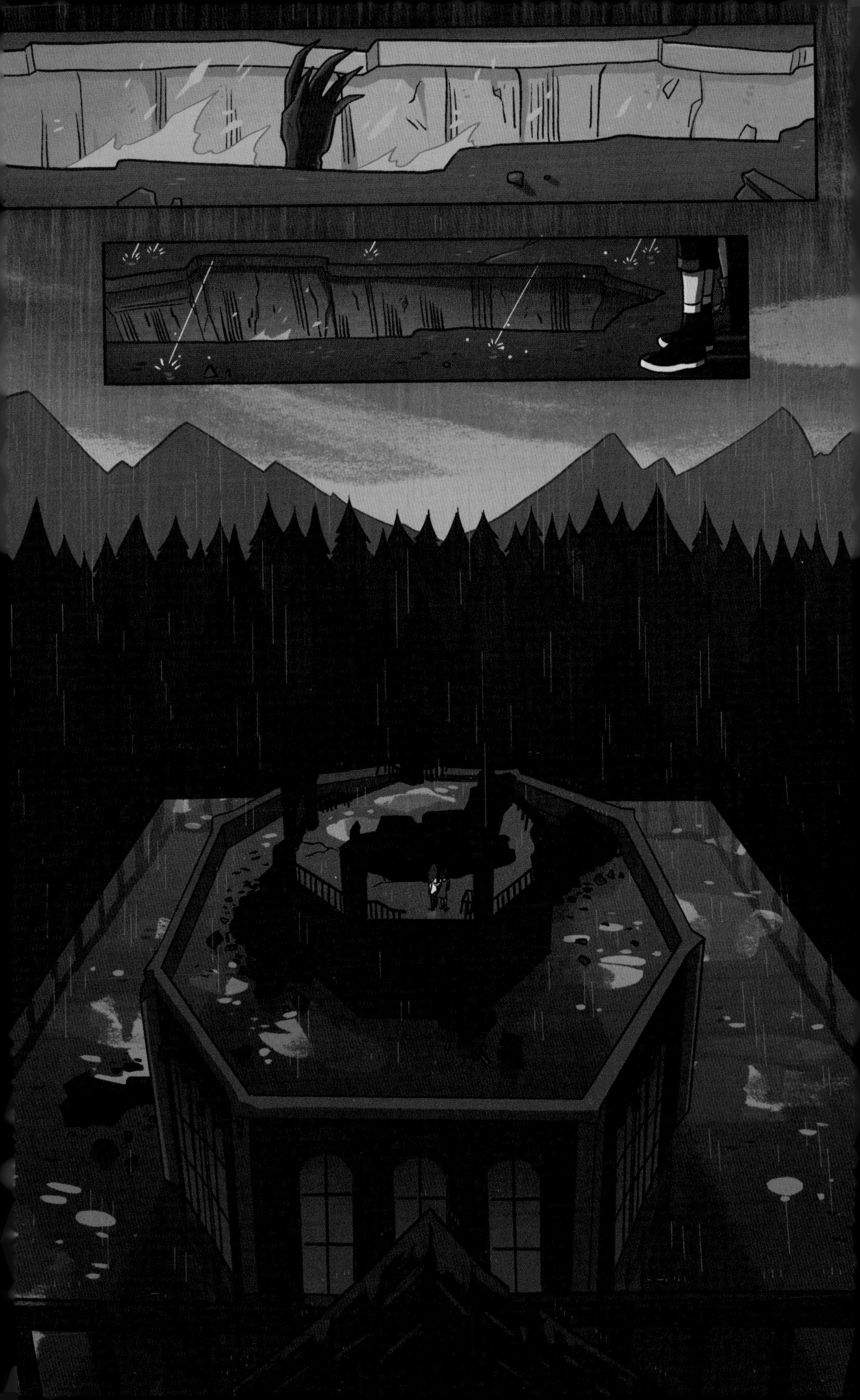

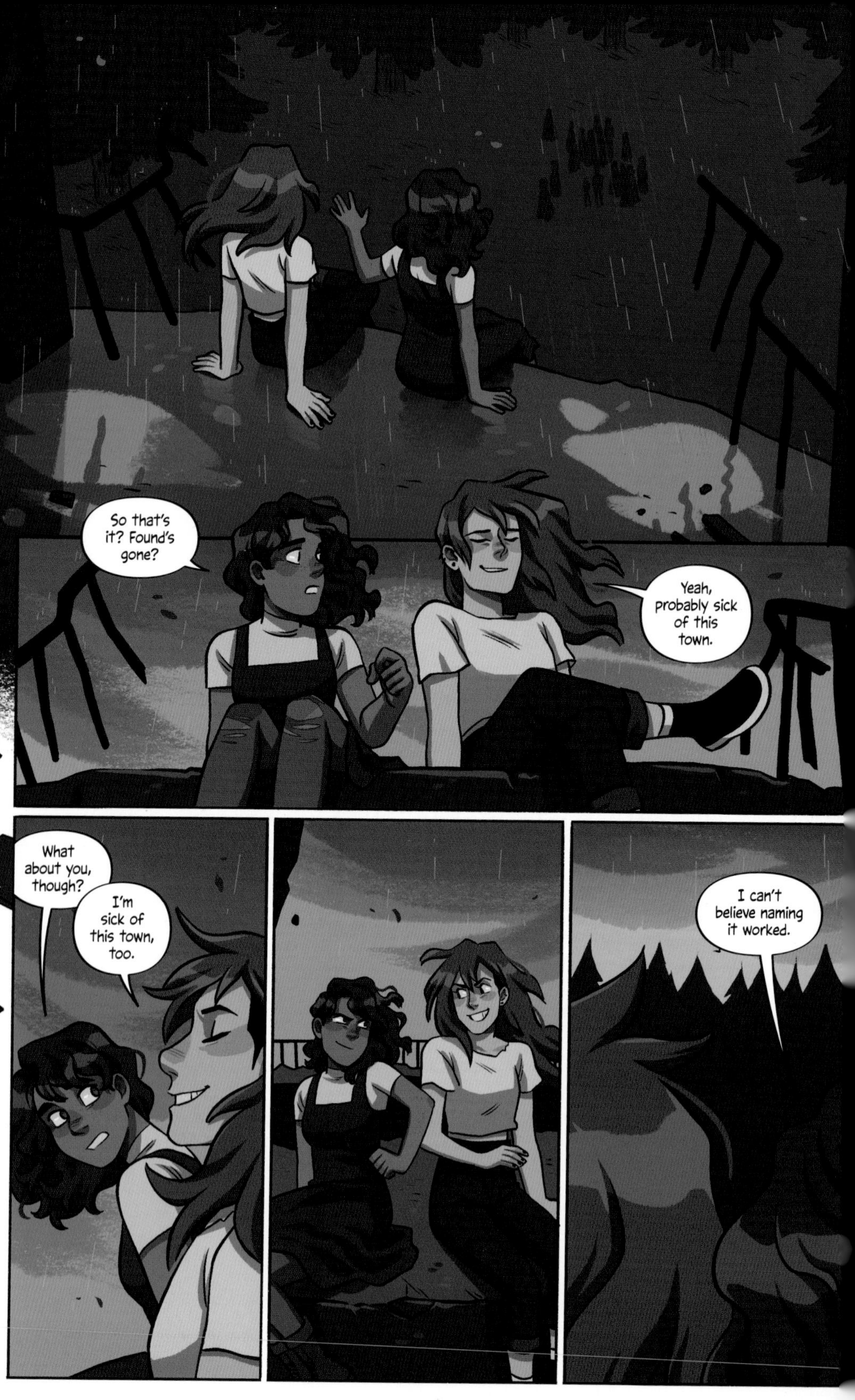
So that's it? Found's gone?
Yeah, probably sick of this town.
What about you, though?
I'm sick of this town, too.
I can't believe naming it worked.

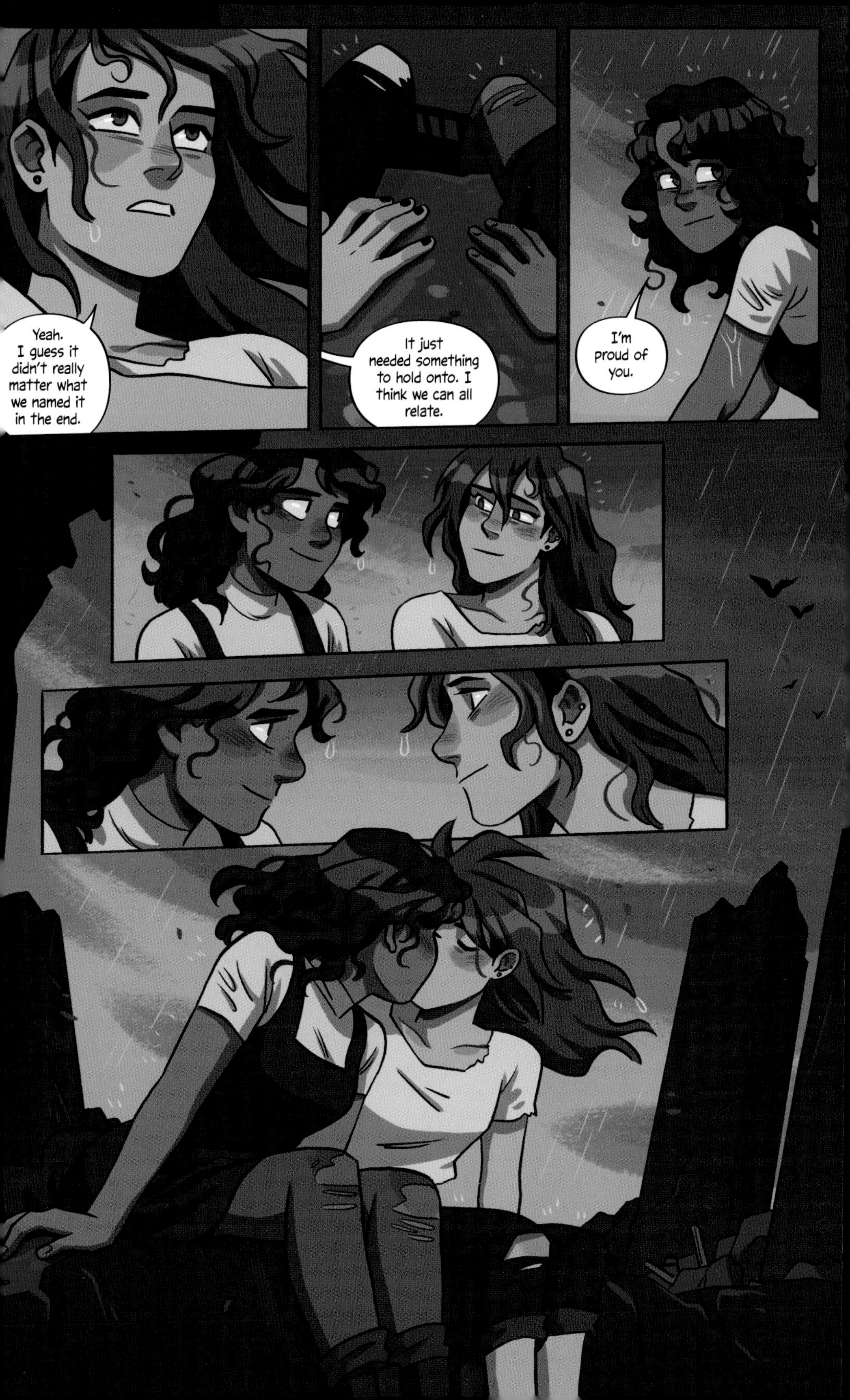
Yeah. I guess it didn't really matter what we named it in the end.
It just needed something to hold onto. I think we can all relate.
I'm proud of you.

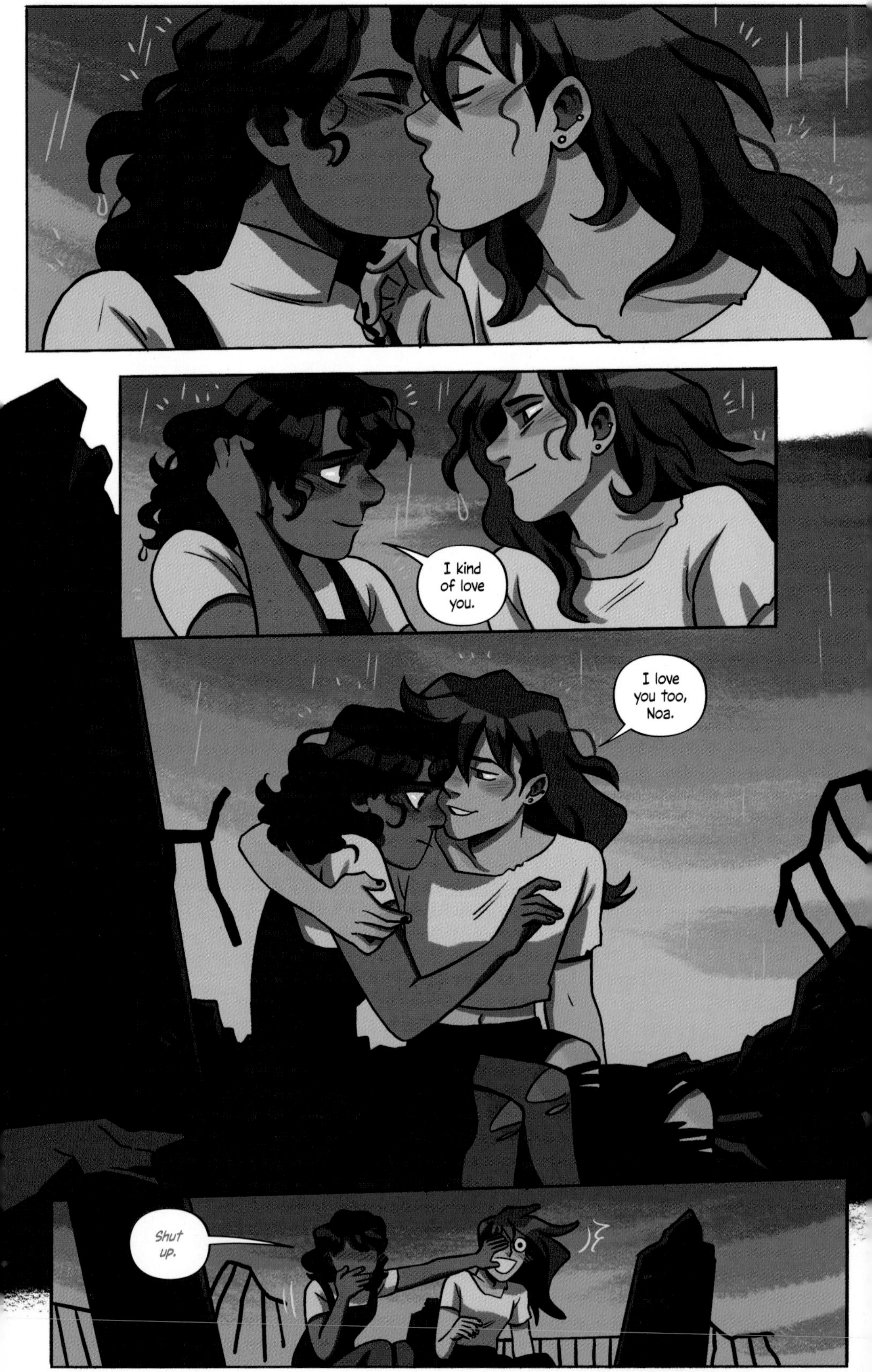
I kind of love you.
I love you too, Noa.
Shut up.

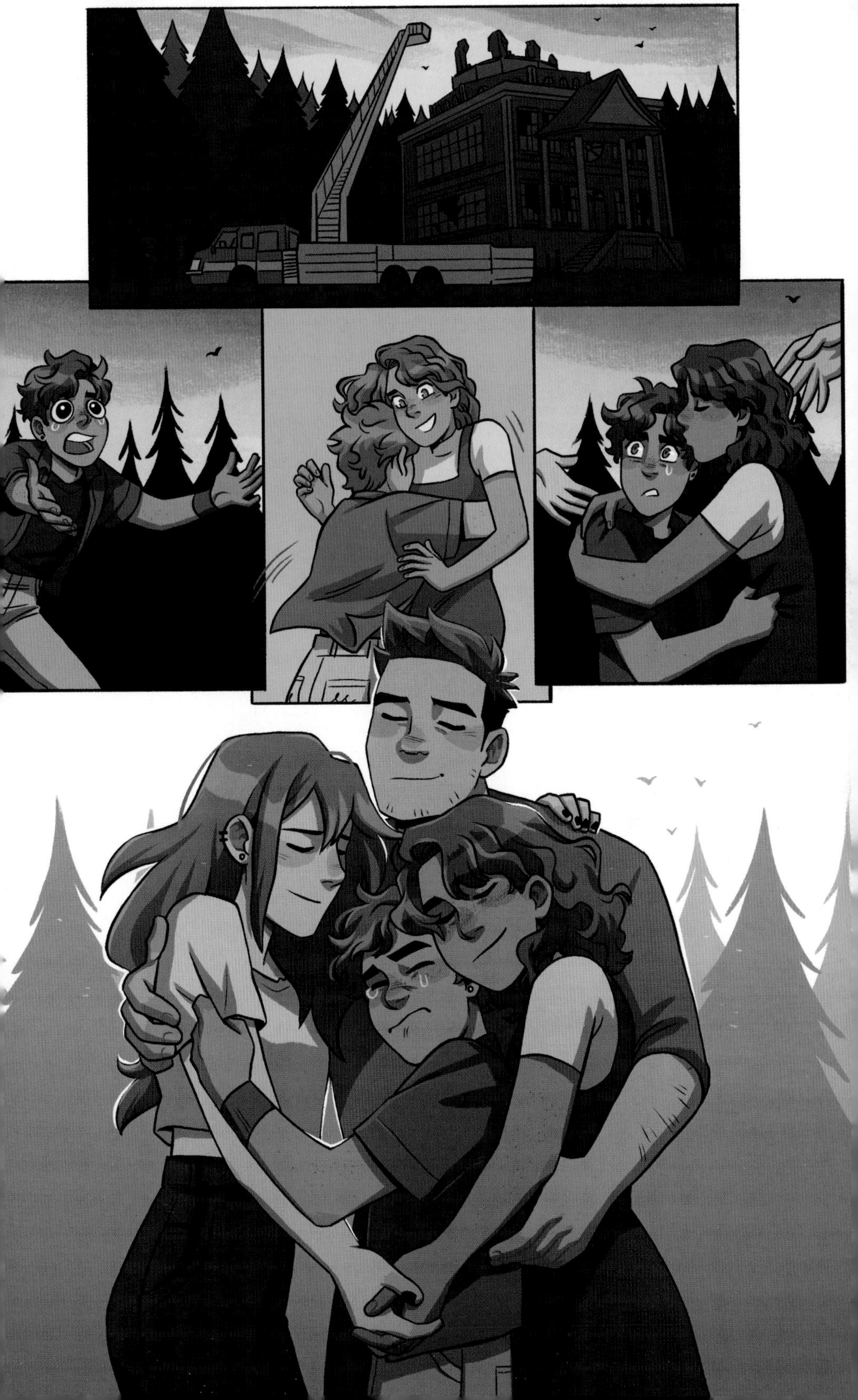

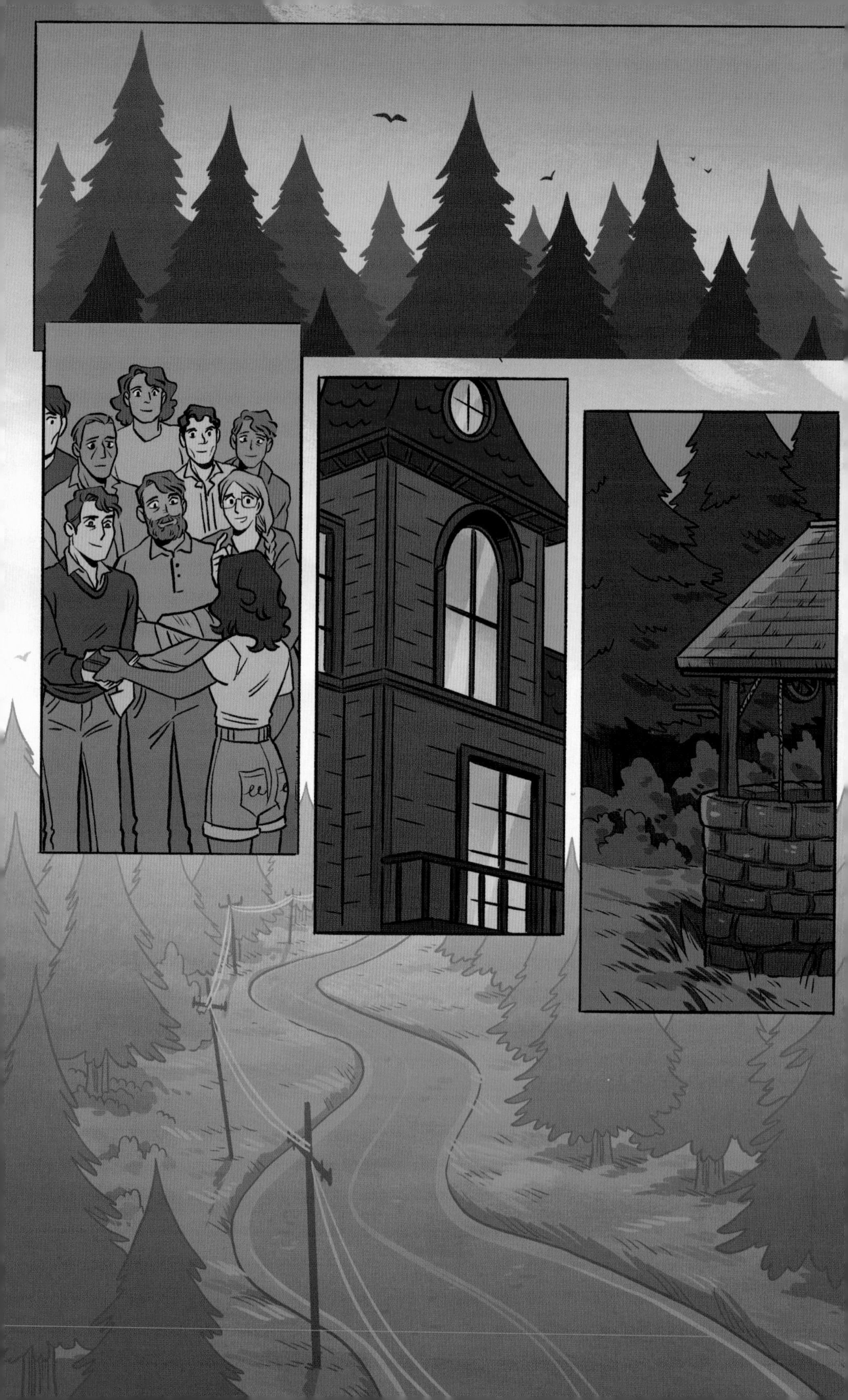

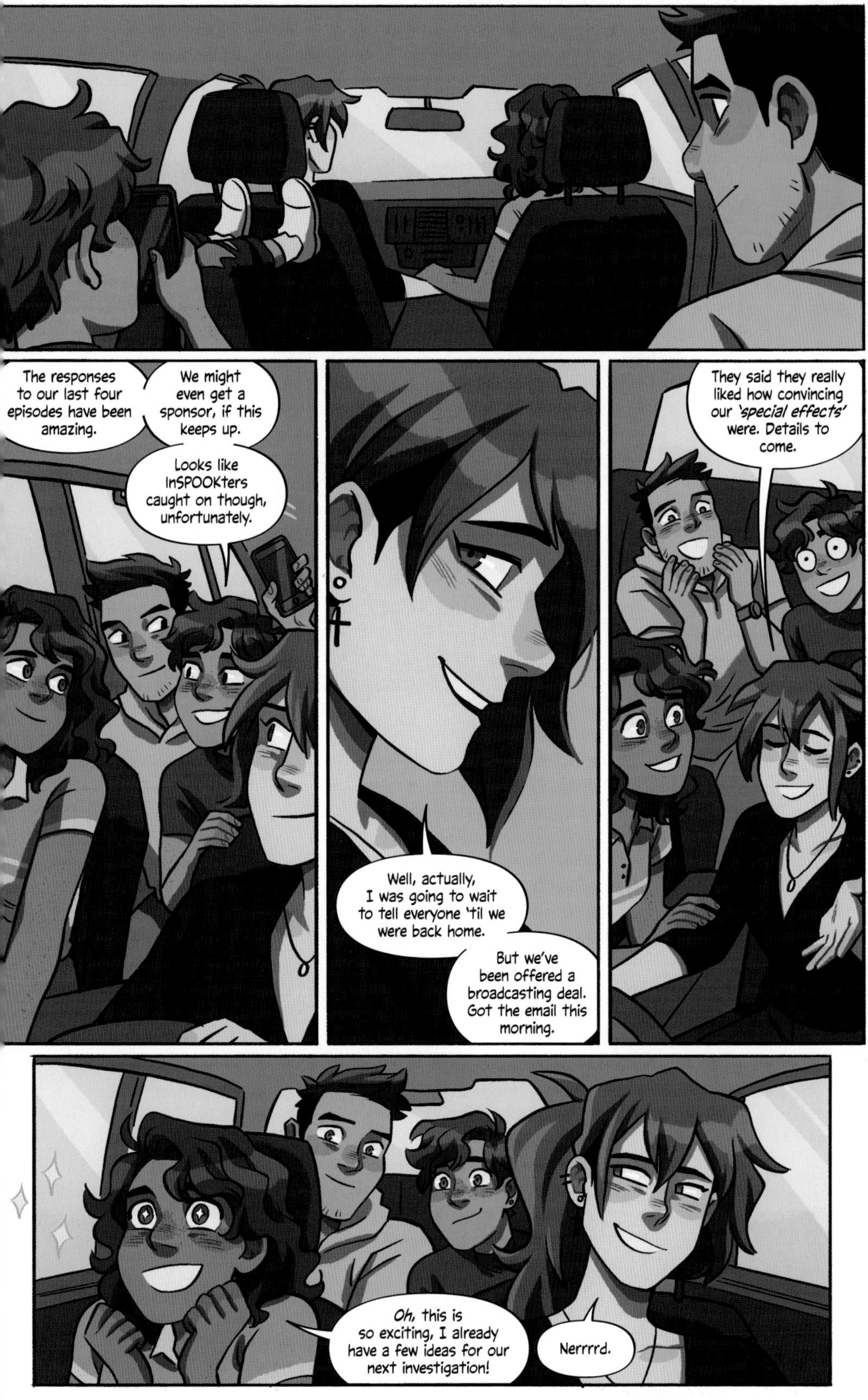
The responses to our last four episodes have been amazing.
We might even get a sponsor, if this keeps up.
Looks like InSPOOKters caught on though, unfortunately.
Well, actually, I was going to wait to tell everyone 'til we were back home.
But we've been offered a broadcasting deal. Got the email this morning.
They said they really liked how convincing our *'special effects'* were. Details to come.
Oh, this is so exciting, I already have a few ideas for our next investigation!
Nerrrrd.

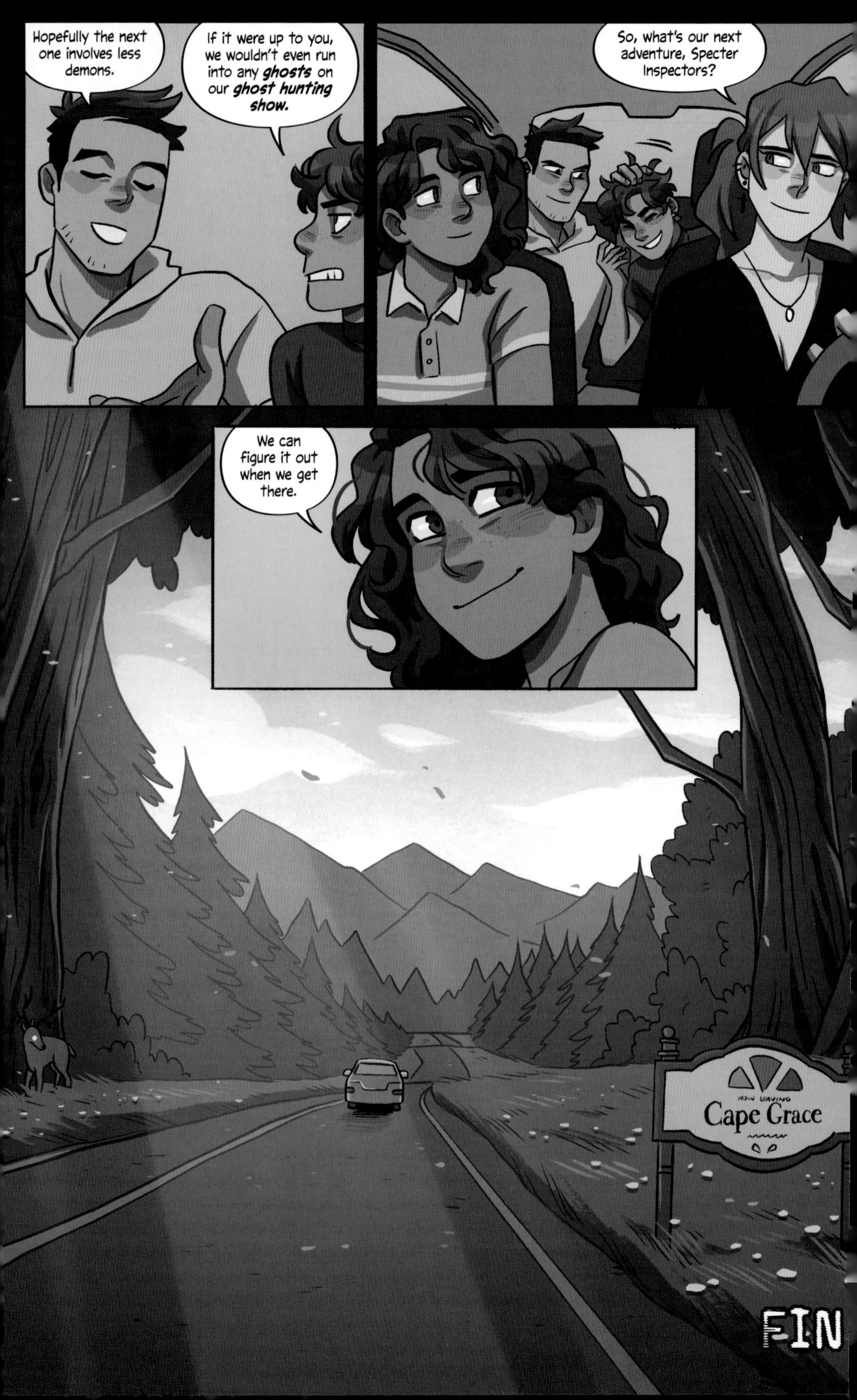
Hopefully the next one involves less demons.
If it were up to you, we wouldn't even run into any ***ghosts*** on our ***ghost hunting show.***
So, what's our next adventure, Specter Inspectors?
We can figure it out when we get there.
NOW LEAVING
Cape Grace
FIN

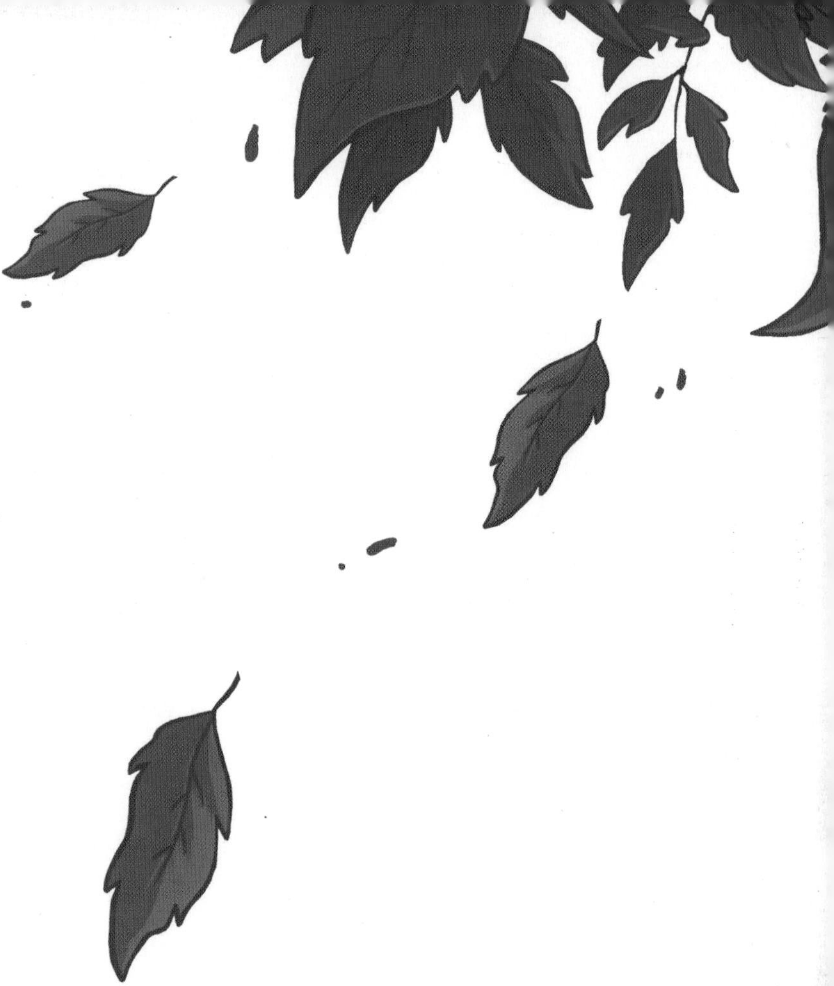

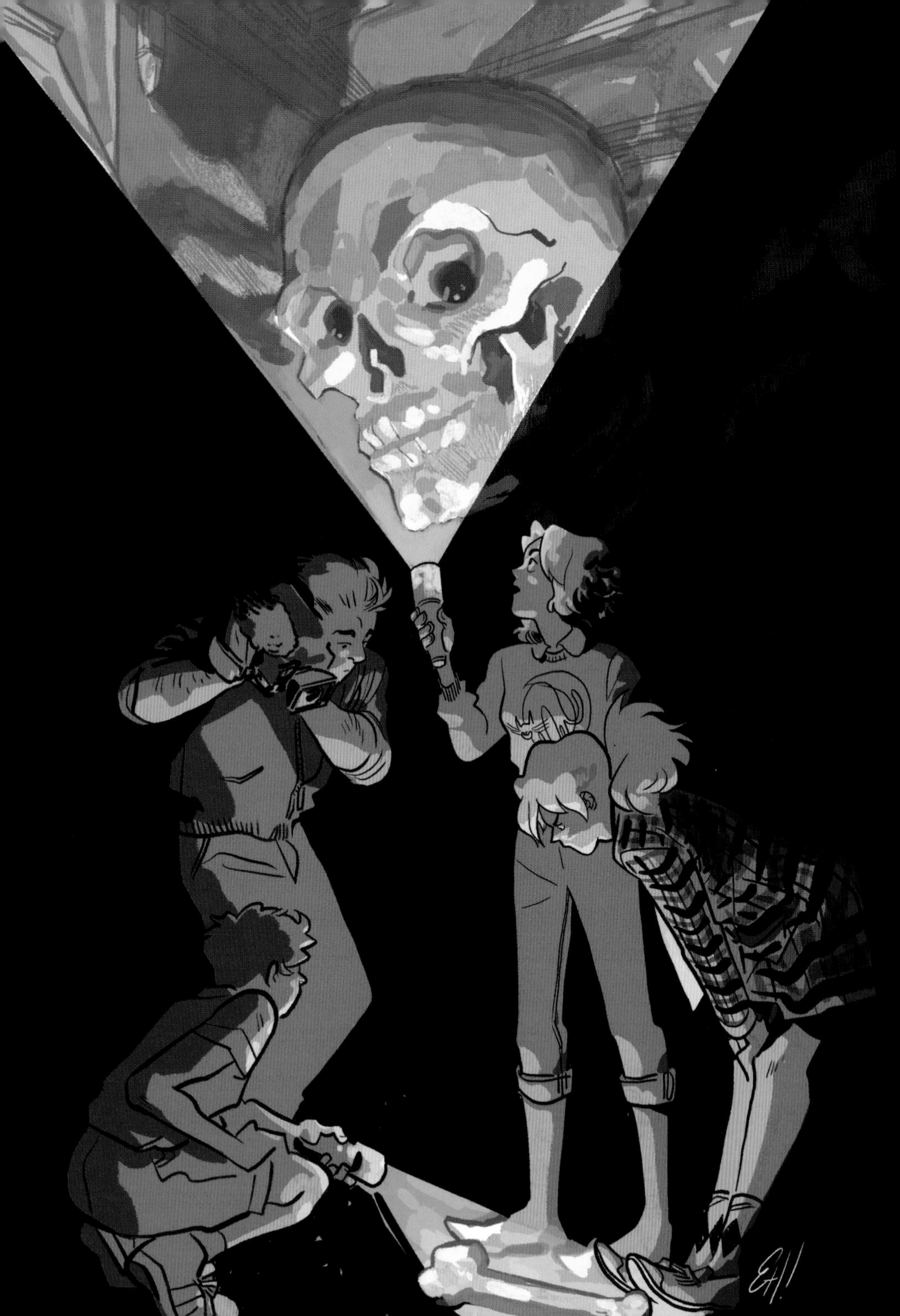

Issue One Pocket Book Variant Cover by Erica Henderson

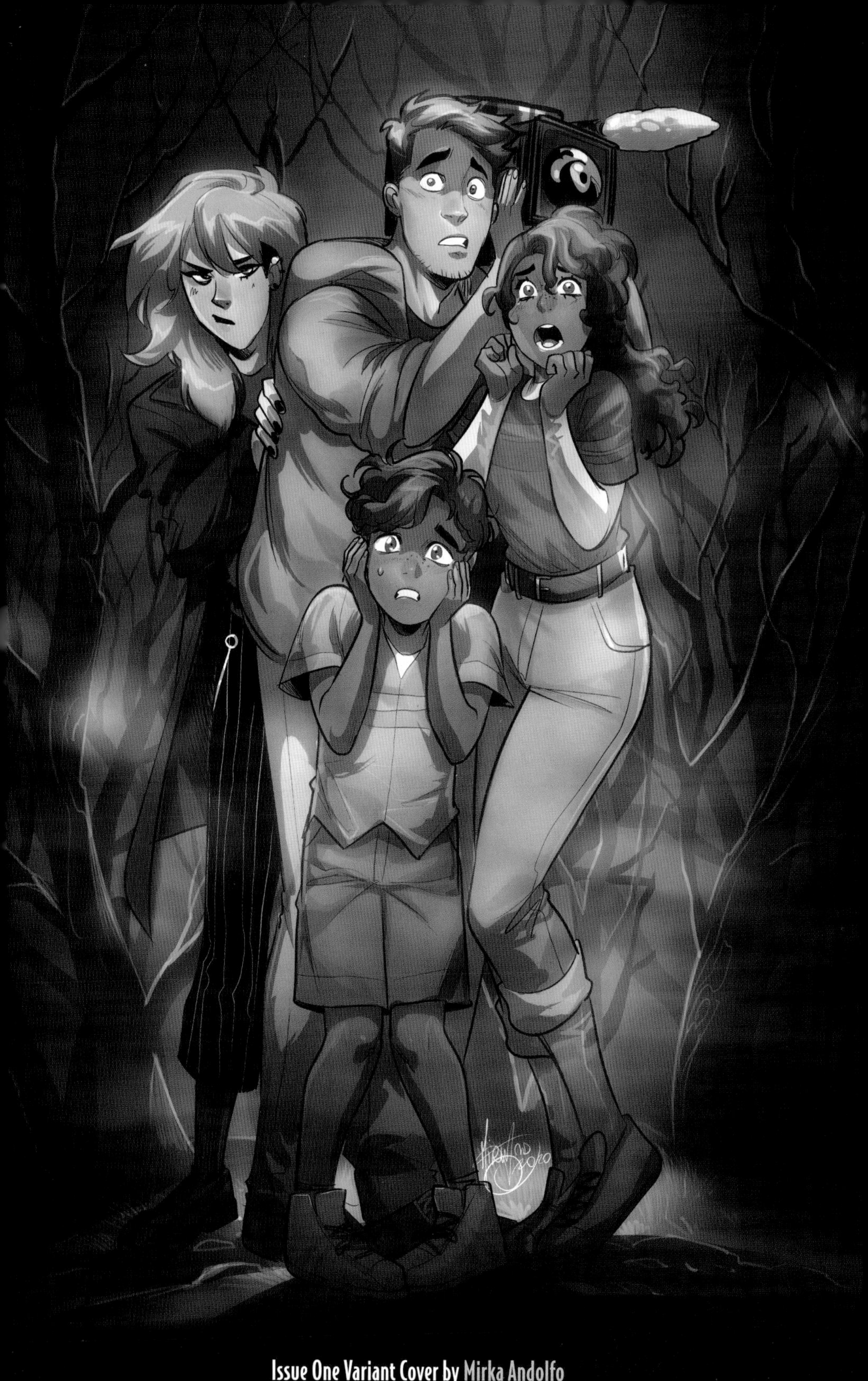

Issue One Variant Cover by Mirka Andolfo

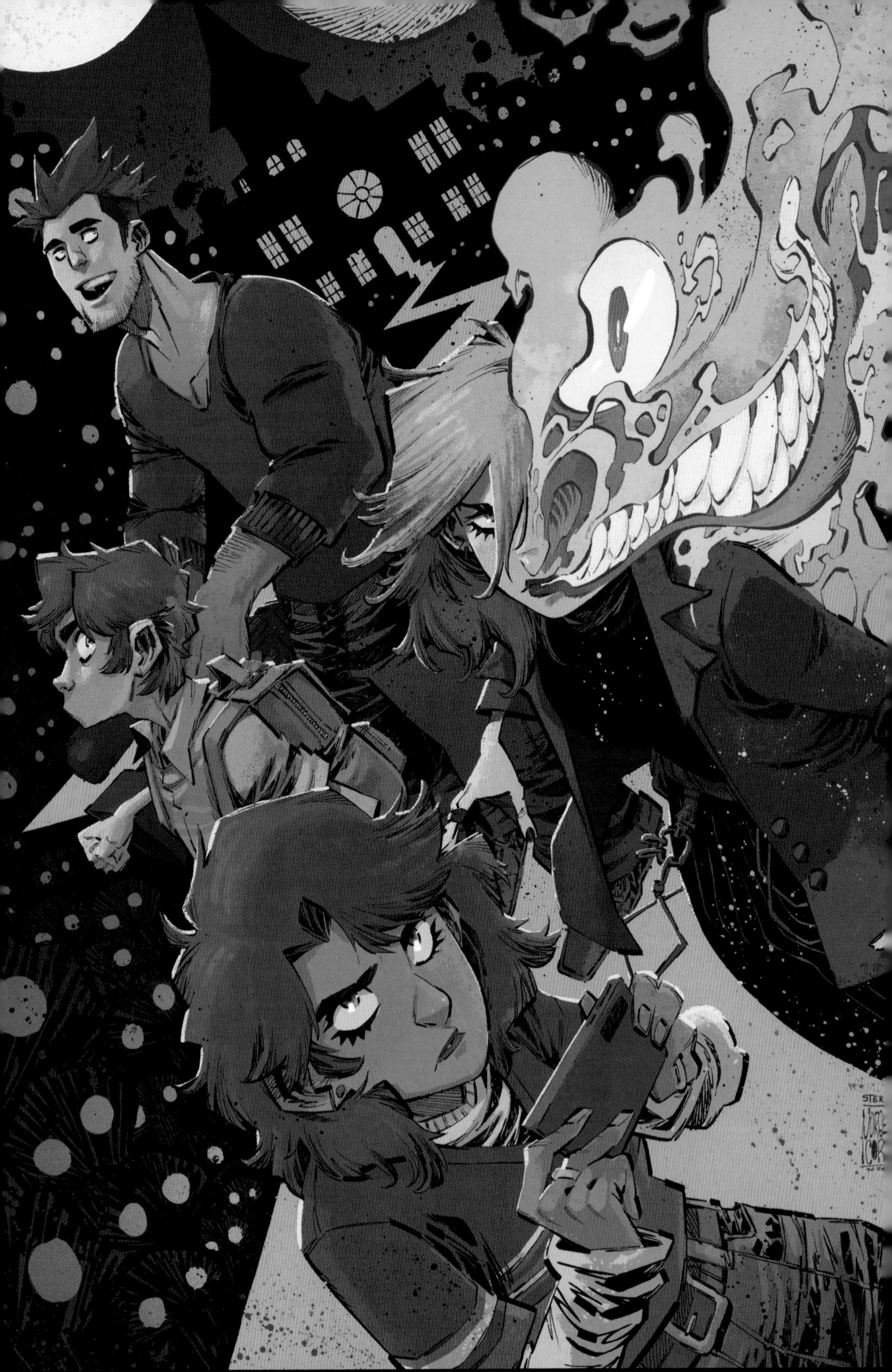

Issue One Cover Alpha Exclusive Variant Cover by Jorge Corona with colors by Sarah Stern

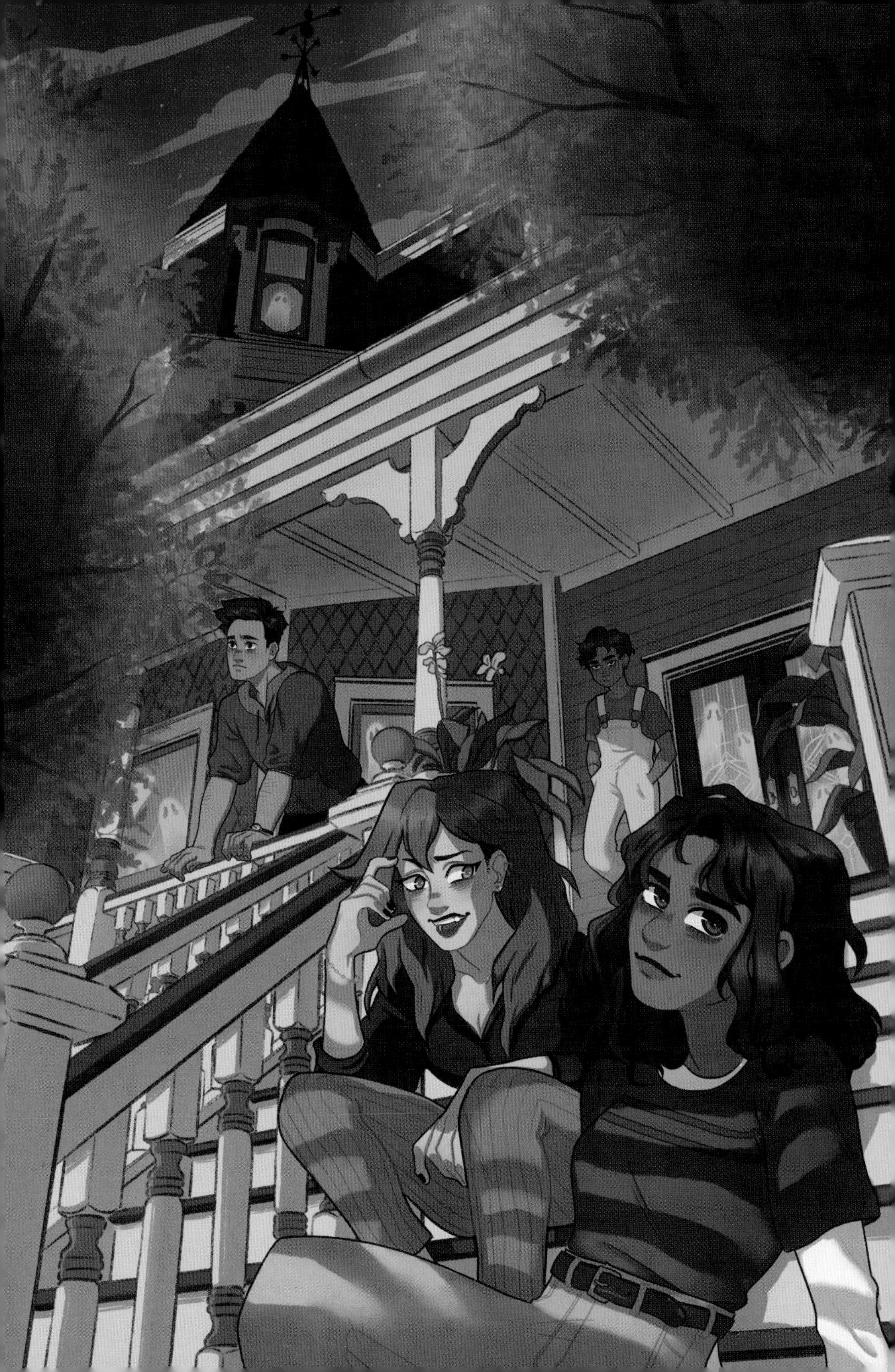

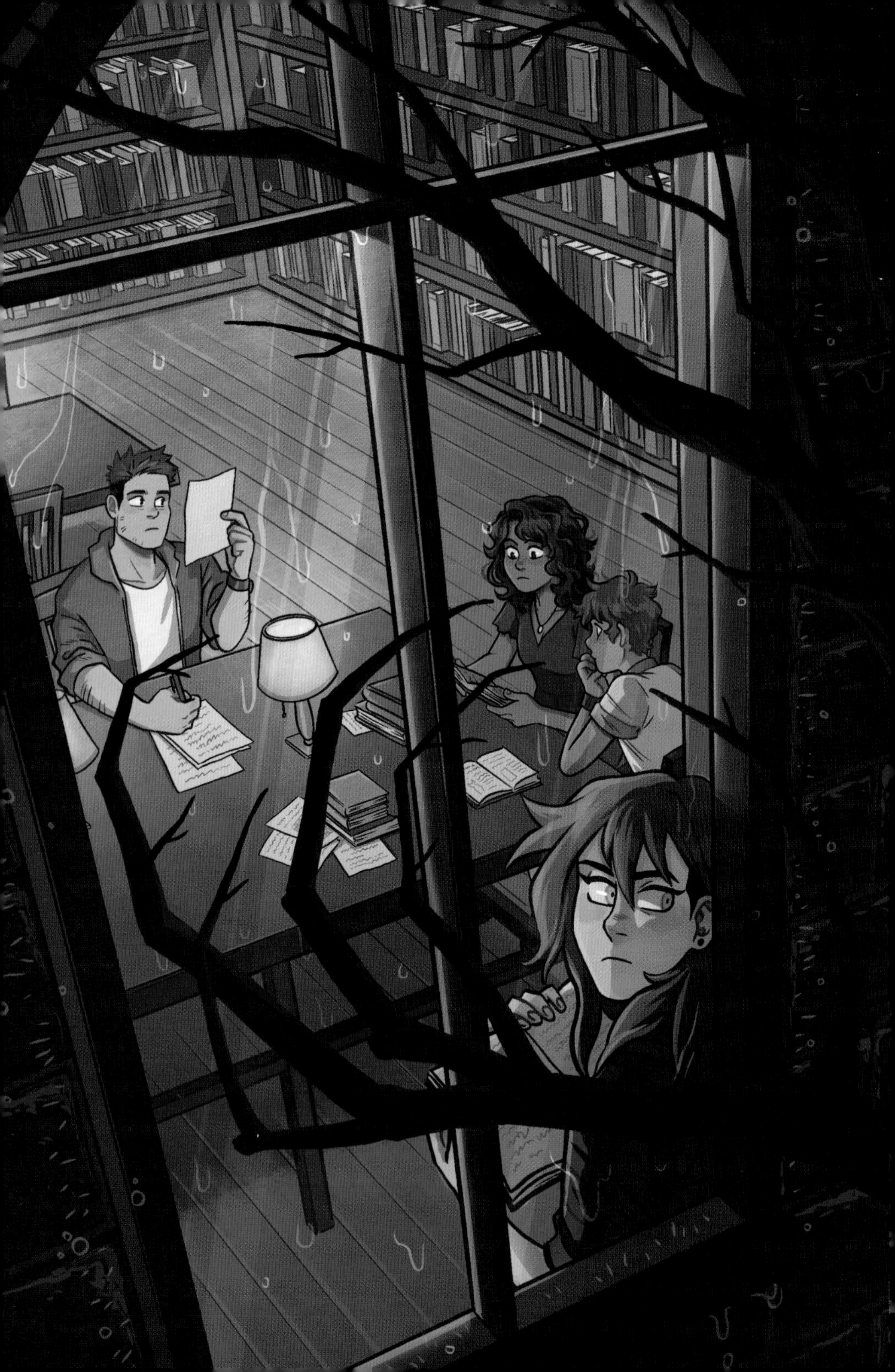

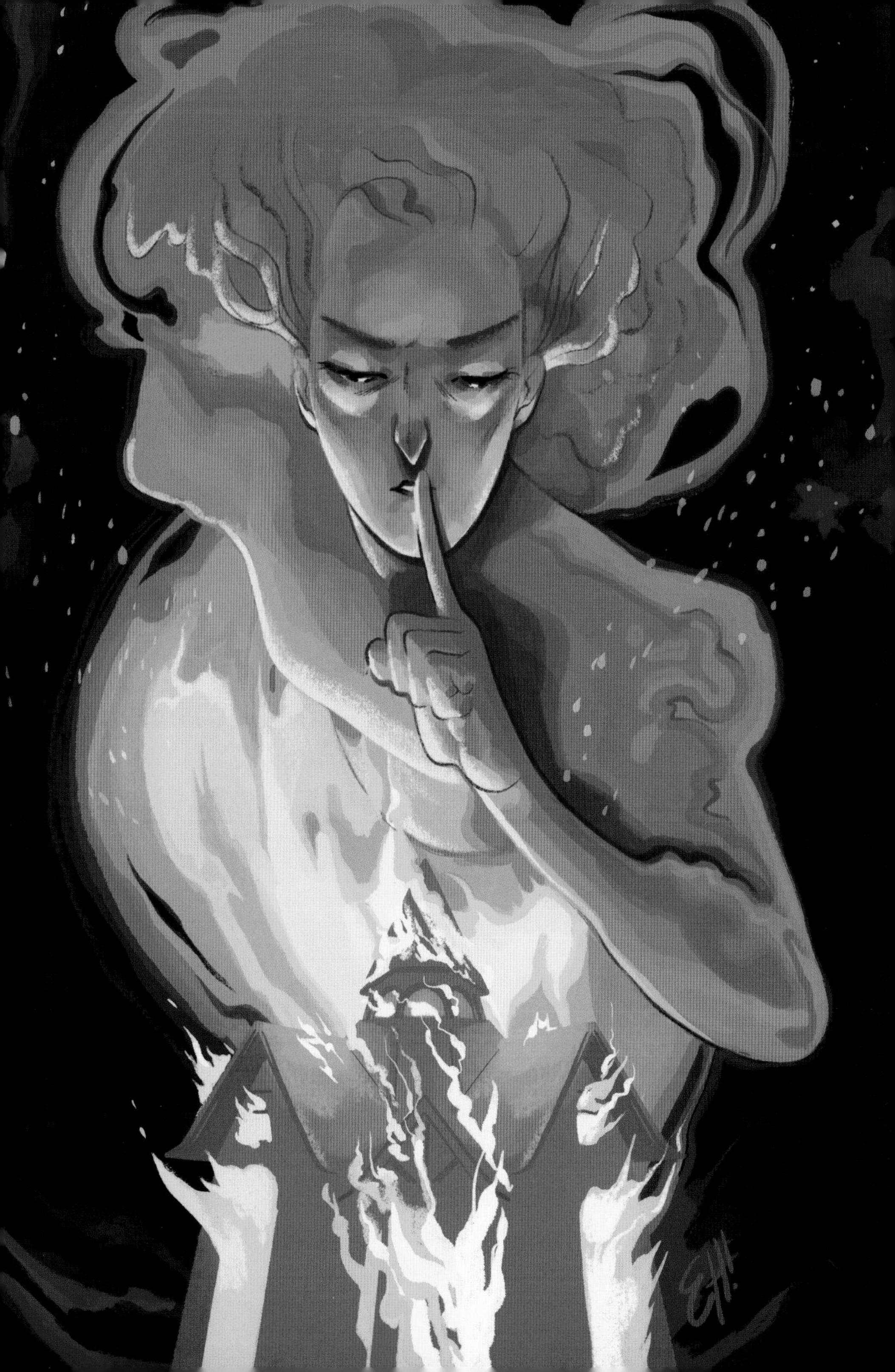

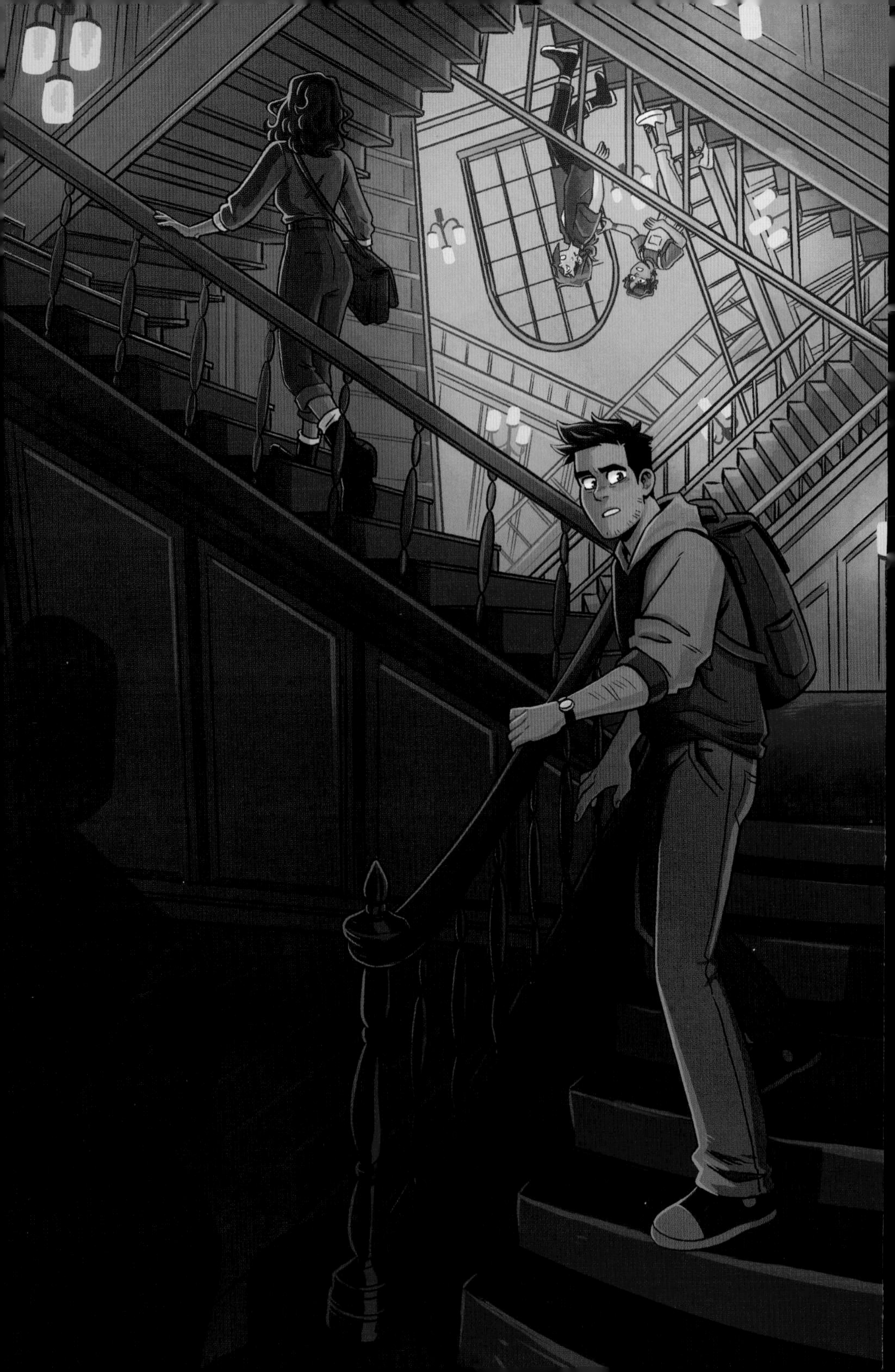

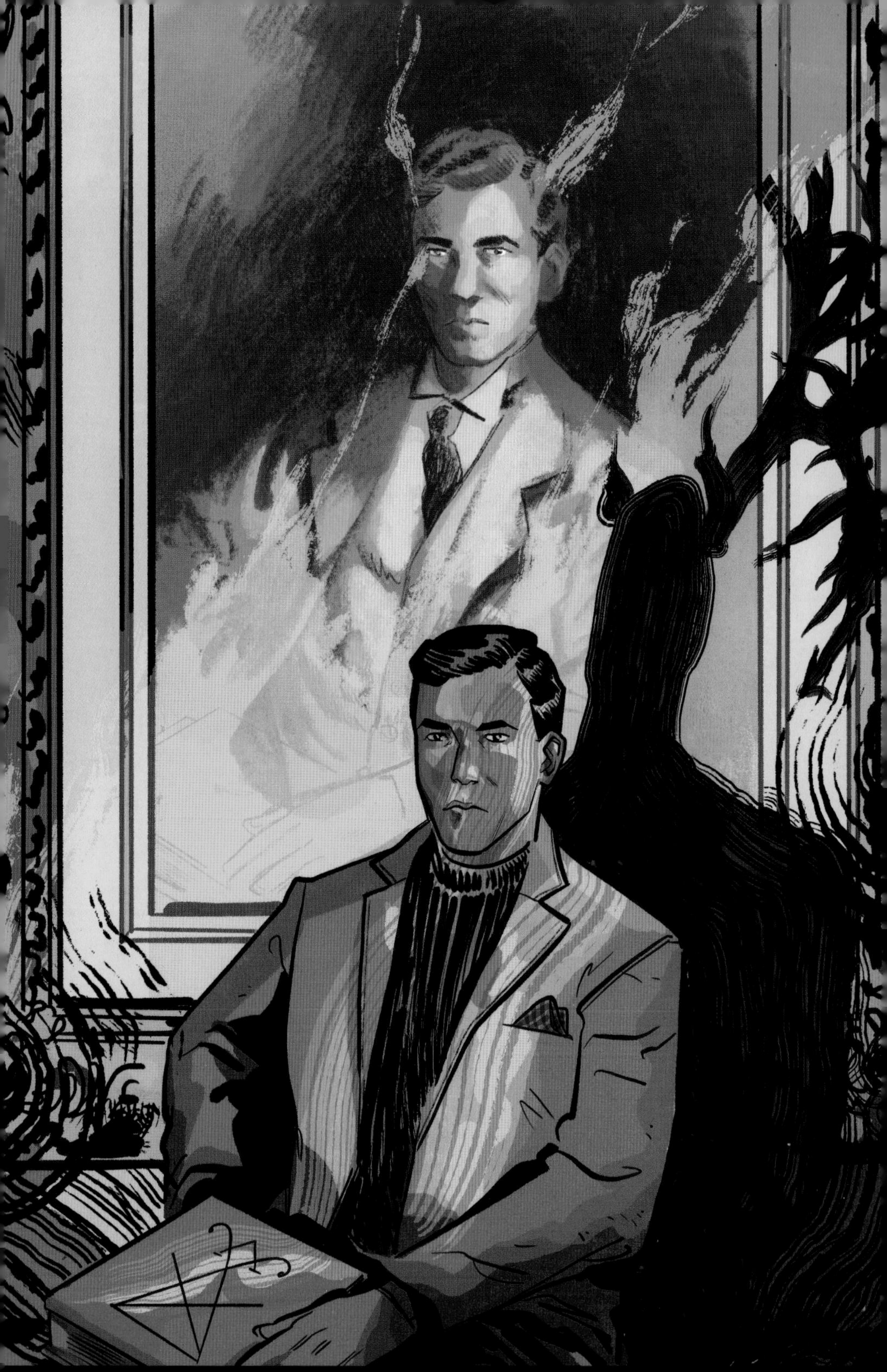

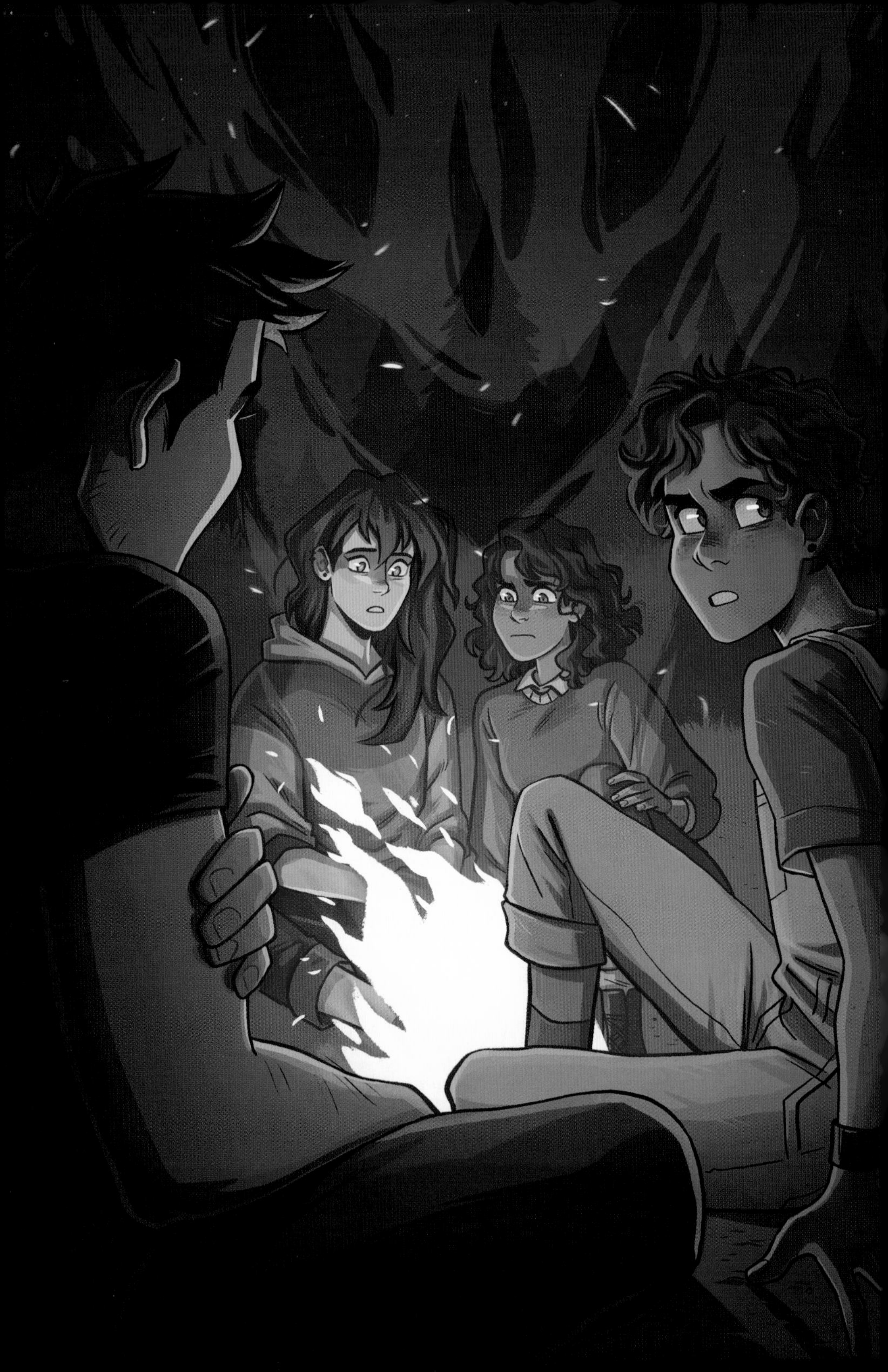

Issue Four Main Cover by Bowen McCurdy

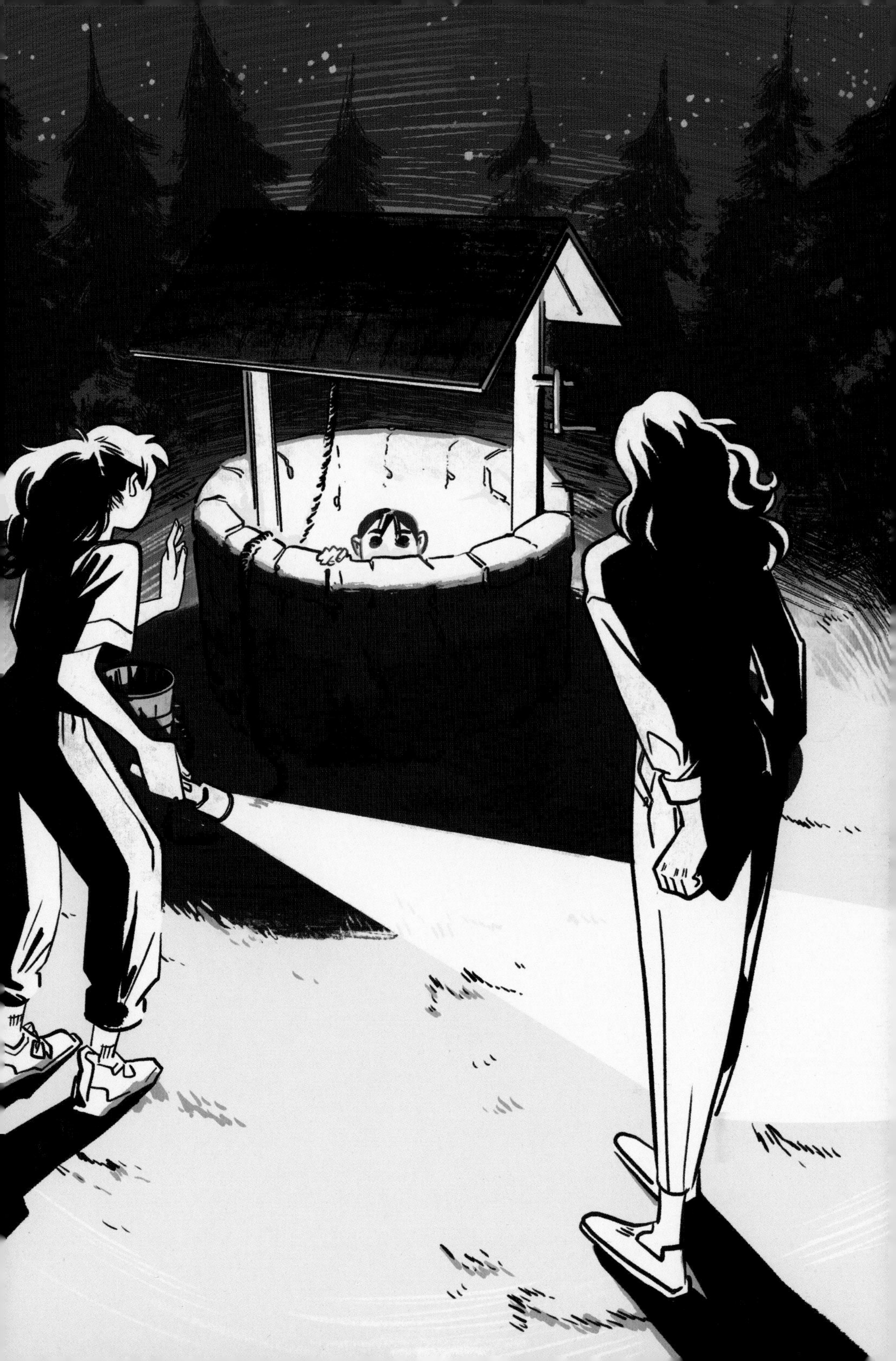

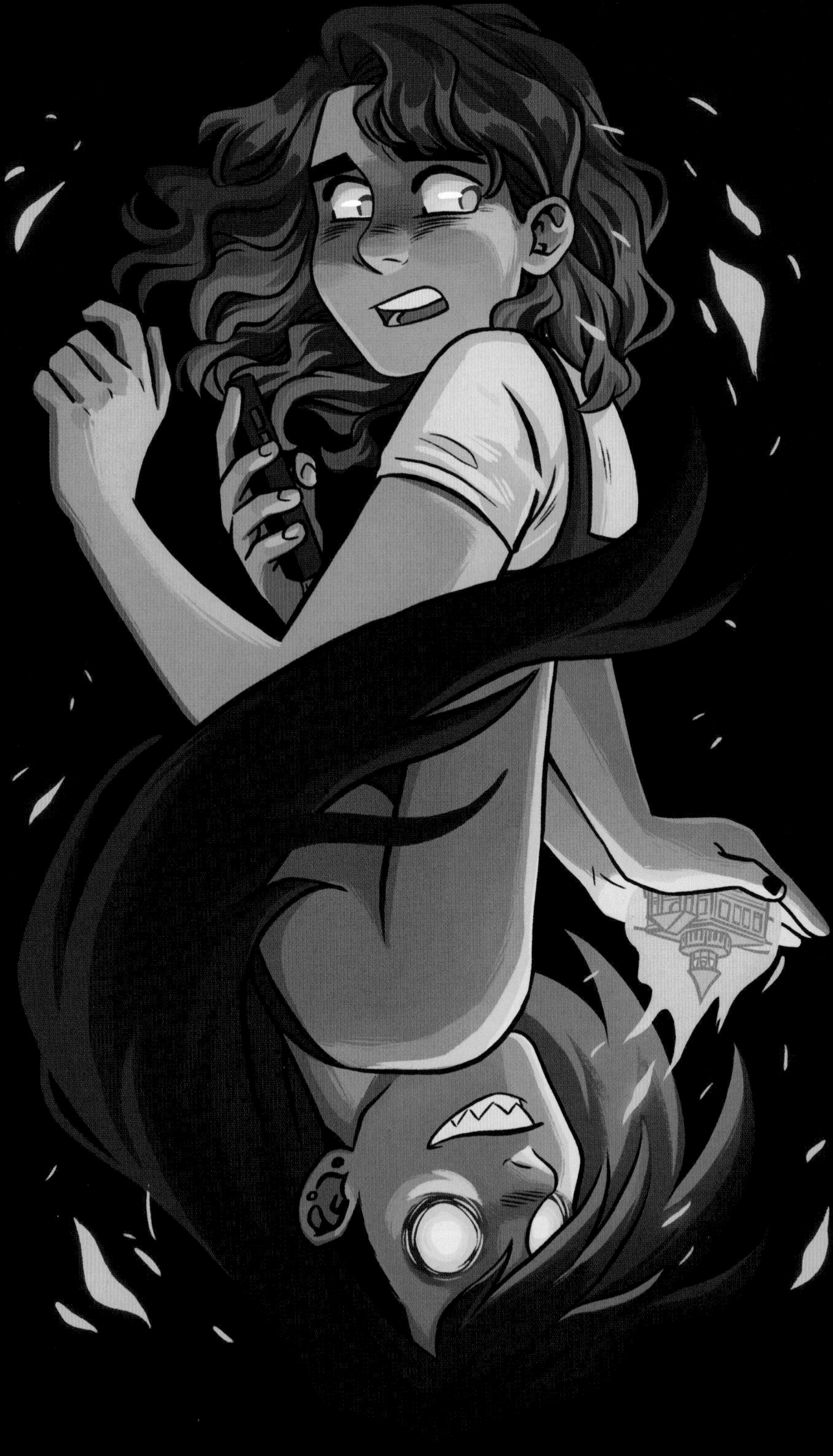

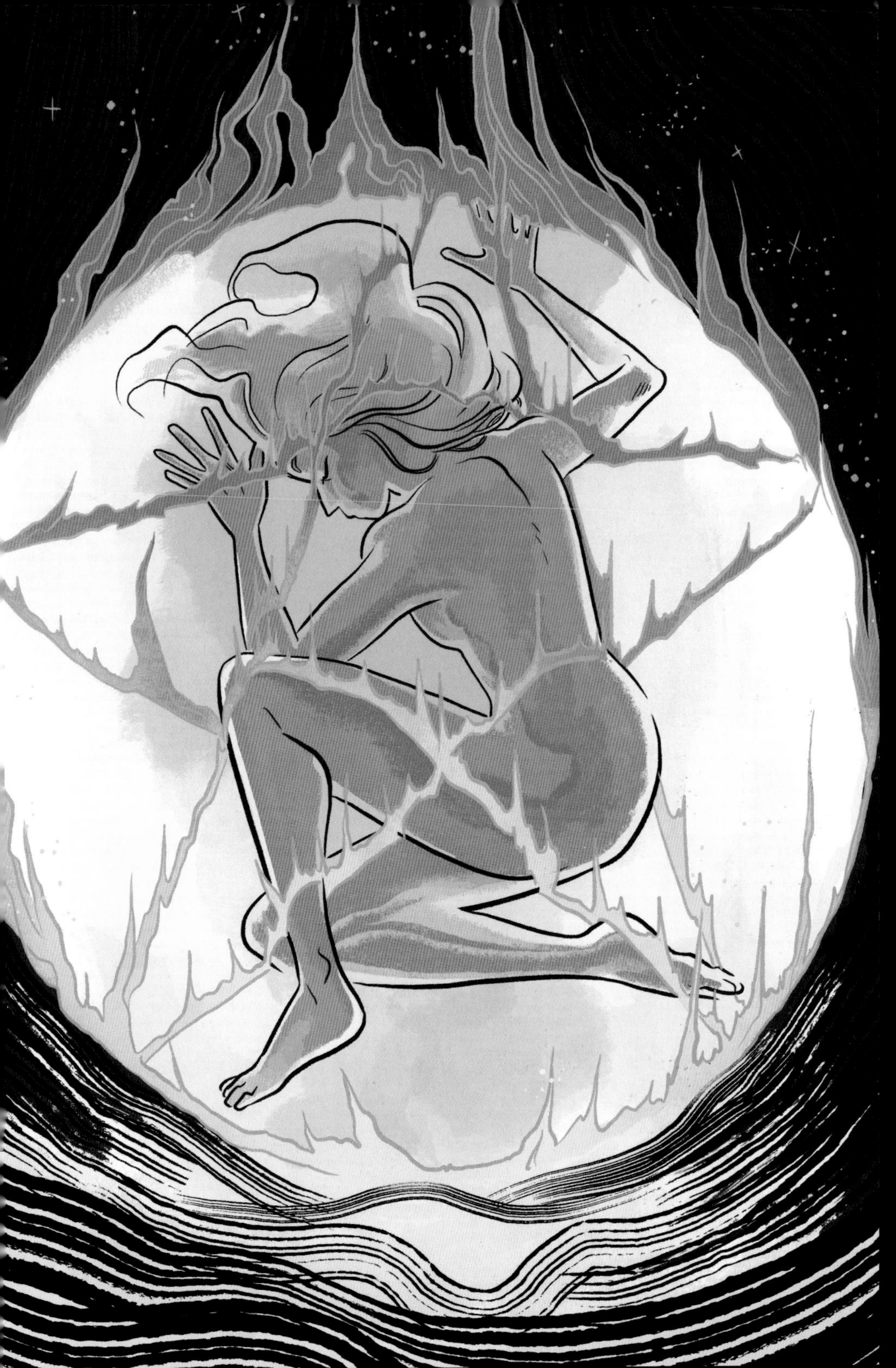

Issue Five Pocket Book Variant Cover by Erica Henderson

DISCOVER
ALL THE HITS

STEVENSON • ELLIS • WATTERS • ALLEN
LUMBERJANES
BEWARE THE KITTEN HOLY
NEW YORK TIMES BESTSELLING SERIES

Allison + Treiman + Cogar
GIANT DAYS
VOLUME ONE

RIBON • FISH • PEER
SLAM!
VOLUME ONE

Hope Larson • Brittney Williams • Sarah Stern
GOLDIE VANCE
"Scoot over Nancy Drew..."
—Los Angeles Times
Volume One

THE BACKSTAGERS

TYSON HESSE'S
DIESEL
IGNITION

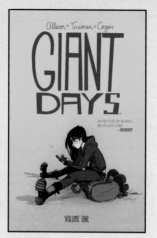

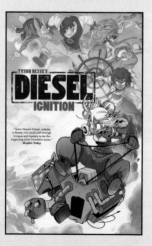

Lumberjanes
ND Stevenson, Shannon Watters, Grace Ellis, Gus Allen, and Others
Volume 1: Beware the Kitten Holy
ISBN: 978-1-60886-687-8 | $14.99 US
Volume 2: Friendship to the Max
ISBN: 978-1-60886-737-0 | $14.99 US
Volume 3: A Terrible Plan
ISBN: 978-1-60886-803-2 | $14.99 US
Volume 4: Out of Time
ISBN: 978-1-60886-860-5 | $14.99 US
Volume 5: Band Together
ISBN: 978-1-60886-919-0 | $14.99 US

Giant Days
John Allison, Lissa Treiman, Max Sarin
Volume 1
ISBN: 978-1-60886-789-9 | $9.99 US
Volume 2
ISBN: 978-1-60886-804-9 | $14.99 US
Volume 3
ISBN: 978-1-60886-851-3 | $14.99 US

Jonesy
Sam Humphries, Caitlin Rose Boyle
Volume 1
ISBN: 978-1-60886-883-4 | $9.99 US
Volume 2
ISBN: 978-1-60886-999-2 | $14.99 US

Slam!
Pamela Ribon, Veronica Fish, Brittany Peer
Volume 1
ISBN: 978-1-68415-004-5 | $14.99 US

Goldie Vance
Hope Larson, Brittney Williams
Volume 1
ISBN: 978-1-60886-898-8 | $9.99 US
Volume 2
ISBN: 978-1-60886-974-9 | $14.99 US

The Backstagers
James Tynion IV, Rian Sygh
Volume 1
ISBN: 978-1-60886-993-0 | $14.99 US

Tyson Hesse's Diesel: Ignition
Tyson Hesse
ISBN: 978-1-60886-907-7 | $14.99 US

Coady & The Creepies
Liz Prince, Amanda Kirk, Hannah Fisher
ISBN: 978-1-68415-029-8 | $14.99 US

BOOM! BOX™

AVAILABLE AT YOUR LOCAL COMICS SHOP AND BOOKSTORE
To find a comics shop in your area, visit www.comicshoplocator.com
WWW.**BOOM-STUDIOS**.COM